ARK OF WAR

The Solomon Secret
Book I

Charles E. Feldmann

To order additional copies of this book, contact:
Xlibris
1-888-795-4274
www.Xlibris.com
Orders@Xlibris.com
597772

Dedication

To the Cities of Jerusalem, Zurich, Tel Aviv, Frankfurt, Tokyo, New York City, Kuwait City and all of the other many wonderful locations who inspired this book.

And to Solomon Goldman and Eteye Azeb. I have so enjoyed your companionship over the eight years this book brought us together. Safe travels and Godspeed.

Third Edition

In memory of my Grandfathers
Charles Howard Feldmann and John DeLone Ellis.
Thank you for making my childhood unforgettable.

When the Ark of God came into the camp, all Israel raised such a great shout that the ground shook . . . the Philistines were afraid. "A god has come into the camp," the Philistines said. "Oh no! Nothing like this has happened before . . . So the Philistines fought, and the Israelites were defeated . . . The slaughter was very great, and . . . The Ark of God was captured, . . . "The Glory has departed from Israel, for the Ark of God has been captured."

After the Philistines had captured the Ark of God, they took it to Ashdod. Then they carried the Ark into Dagon's temple and set it beside Dagon . . . But the following morning when they rose, there was Dagon, fallen on his face on the ground before the Ark! His head and hands had been broken off and were lying on the threshold; only his body remained . . .

The LORD's hand was heavy on the people of Ashdod; he brought devastation on them and afflicted them with tumors . . . When the people of Ashdod saw what was happening, they said, "The Ark must not stay here with us, because his hand is heavy on us and on Dagon our god." . . . But after they had moved it, the LORD's hand was against that city, throwing it into a great panic.

He afflicted the people of the city, both young and old, with an outbreak of tumors . . . So they called together all the rulers of the Philistines and said, "Send the Ark away; let it go back to its own place, or it will kill us and our people." For death had filled the city with panic; God's hand was very heavy on it.

Those who did not die were afflicted with tumors, and the outcry of the city went up to heaven.

I Samuel 4:5 – 6:19

Prologue

1300 B.C.
Capital City of the Egyptian Empire

The plague devoured its way through the Egyptian capital city, like a ravenous beast after a lengthy winter of starvation. More people were dead than alive in the Capital City of Gold and Light. A somber resignation to doom had replaced the recent mass hysteria amongst the surviving Egyptians inhabiting the banks of the Nile River. The capital city was confused and angered: their pharaoh's God had not saved them from the plague's ravenous appetite.

A decade ago, Amenhotep IV had become pharaoh over the two kingdoms of the Egyptian empire – one empire to the north and one to the south. After his religious awakening, he had changed his name to Akhenaten and built his new capital in the desert, along the Nile River, between Thebes and Alexandria. The City of the Horizon was its official Egyptian name, but ever since the Treasure of Egypt had arrived from Giza, the new capital had been called the City of Gold and Light. But now it lay dying from the plague, and the stirrings of a revolt brewed among the former High Priests in Thebes and Memphis.

Pharaoh Akhenaten had prohibited the worship of all the ancient gods of Egypt long ago, but now his people had begun to wonder if their old, forbidden gods were punishing them for their abandonment.

"Why did your God take my daughters from me?" Nefertiti sobbed, weeping over the frail, lifeless bodies of her two young girls. The royal heirs were last night's most-recent victims to the plague. She attempted to regain her composure as she spoke to the man that was both her husband and king, Pharaoh Akhenaten. "The people don't know the One True God like you do. When you banished the ancient gods, you took away centuries of their faith. You took away their freedom. Now they have no gods to save them from this plague. They have no one to pray to . . ." Her voice quivered as she continued. "How many more of your daughters must perish? What if your son, the throne's heir, is next?"

"The One True God is not just the supreme God, but the only God!" the bald, divine ruler of Egypt answered, her words awakening him from his grieving trance.

"You closed all of the temples except *your* God's. You transformed the High Priests into commoners when you smashed the statues of their so-called *'false idols.'* Did you really have to destroy the images of their deities?" Nefertiti cried out. "What have you done to us? What have you done to your kingdom?"

"There can be no graven images of the false gods. That is what the One True God told me."

The long-faced pharaoh walked out to the bedroom balcony of his palace. He gazed upon the city he had built – a city dedicated to the One True God. Doubt entered his mind. *She couldn't be right, could she? This Angel of Death, this plague, this black cloud of pestilence that had descended on his city and murdered his own children in the night—surely that was not punishment from the false gods. It could not be true!*

Despite his queen's words, the pharaoh believed with the entirety of his heart that the One True God was not just an Egyptian god, but rather a god that shone upon every living thing – the Supreme Ruler over all of mankind, the Creator of All!

The pharaoh's whispers were interrupted by the royal guards at the bedroom's door as they introduced the chief vizier. Vizier Ay entered, immediately bowing his head to the royal couple. He looked at the two dead girls and the poised Nefertiti sitting over them. She had remnants of tears on her cheeks.

"Divine Being, have you called for the royal embalmers yet?" Vizier Ay asked.

"Not yet," the pharaoh whispered.

"I will have them summoned at once. But we must discuss the uprisings that are occurring all over Egypt. Both the armies in the northern and the southern kingdoms are on the move, and they have sedition in their hearts. They are even saying that the god Amon has unleashed his chief Angel of Death against the royal family to punish you for banishing Egypt's gods."

Ay walked to where the two young girls lay, pale and lifeless. Their heads had been shaven, with the exception of a single, long lock of hair that protruded from the side of each of their heads – the only remnants of their once-thick, flowing black locks.

"Once word spreads that two of the royal children have been taken by this Angel of Death, I fear open revolt will break out against you and the One True God," he said. "The people will see the death of the royal children as an omen."

He looked up from the diminutive corpses as he addressed the pharaoh. "If your son, Tutankaton, falls victim to the plague, there will be no stopping them."

"This city once flowed with milk and honey. It was everything I had ever dreamed it could be. Why has He let all of this happen?" the Pharaoh asked, turning to Nefertiti.

"Your announcement that the Aten was to be the One and Only God of Egypt created severe division. Telling them that everything they and their ancestors had worshiped since the foundation of civilization was false—that they could only worship this One True God—was an unorthodox and controversial political decision."

"I am the supreme ruler of the two kingdoms," Pharaoh said, standing rigidly in an attempt to behave like the most powerful ruler in the civilized world. "I tell my subjects who is God. They do not tell me!"

Ay turned to Queen Nefertiti. Her grief had rendered her numb, and she did not acknowledge his stare.

"General Horemheb, Commander of Ten Thousands, is reported to have left Thebes with his army, and I am told that he plans to march against you and the One True God of Egypt. I fear he desires the throne," Ay said. The statement caught the attention of the pharaoh, who had sat down on a solid-gold chair next to the royal bed.

"You have come here for a purpose. What do you wish to tell me?" he asked.

Unbeknownst to the pharaoh, Ay had already prepared the queen for the shocking advice he was about to give his ruler.

"You must use the Treasure of Egypt against General Horemheb and his armies."

"Use the divine treasure as a weapon of war against my own people?!" the pharaoh shouted, incredulity emanating from his voice.

"It has been used for that purpose before," Ay said.

"That was a long time ago, before there even *was* an Egypt. I will *never* use our holiest treasure against my own people," the pharaoh said. He looked at Nefertiti, his eyes seeking her thoughts on the matter.

"You have no other choice, my king," his wife said, emotionlessly. "If you do not use the Treasure of Egypt against General Horemheb, he will take it for himself. And he will not hesitate to use it against you."

"There must be another way," the pharaoh said, walking away, back to the balcony, to clear his thoughts.

"You must be brave and think for all of us," Nefertiti said. She stood and joined her husband, wrapping her delicate, brown arms around him from behind.

"I simply *cannot* use the Treasure of Egypt against General Horemheb!" he repeated. He refused to look at Ay as he spoke.

"You *must* use the treasure as a weapon. Your own general marches here to take the throne for himself as we speak," Nefertiti said.

The pharaoh began to pace as he tried to come to terms with the advice from the two people closest to him. "I cannot let the Treasure of Egypt fall into the hands of General Horemheb. He will enslave the world with it."

"I agree," Vizier Ay said from across the room. "He would use it against you or anyone else that got in his way."

The pharaoh remained silent for several minutes, wrestling with the future of his family and his kingdom.

"I must seek direction from the One True God. Please leave me now," he said.

Vizier Ay and Queen Nefertiti left the royal bedroom without a word.

The pharaoh remained in his bedroom for three days. He did not once speak, eat, or bathe. Two more of his daughters fell prey to the ravages of the plague before he received a vision from the One True God.

Finally, on the third day, he summoned Ay and Queen Nefertiti. When they arrived at the bedroom, neither spoke.

"The One True God has given me a vision," the pharaoh said. "He has told me how to deliver His people from the oppression we now face."

Ay and Nefertiti anxiously awaited his decision. Time was of the essence, and General Horemheb and his armies drew closer to the capital with each passing moment.

"I shall lead my people to the desert, across the Nile, and into the land from which my mother's people came," he said. "We must build a new empire, away from this land, in the land of my mother's ancestors – a new nation that will only know and worship the One True God and not the many false gods of our past."

"How can you move an entire city?" Nefertiti asked.

"It can be done, but we must move quickly," Ay responded. He had heard the finality in the pharaoh's tone: his decision had been made.

"I will not use the Treasure of Egypt against my people. Instead, we will let it lead us to the Promised Land."

"You must hurry. The armies draw closer every day. I will begin organizing the masses for the exodus from the city," Ay said, his mind already consumed with the thousands of orders and details that needed to be put in place to accomplish such a massive evacuation in such a short period of time. "There is great wisdom in your vision. I am proud to begin anew with you in the lands of my ancestors. With the Treasure of Egypt gone, and with the exodus of the Pharaoh and his One True God, the revolt will smolder out quickly. It is truly a divine vision, my king."

Two weeks later, before General Horemheb's army arrived at the City of Gold and Light, Pharaoh Akhenaten led its inhabitants into the eastern Egyptian desert. The merchants had removed everything of value from the city – they would need it to begin their new life in the land to the east. The pharaoh's faithful army led the enormous evacuation, the Treasure of Egypt proudly displayed at the front of their massive caravan. They left the ghost town of the desolate metropolis behind.

Clouds of smoke, ash, and whirling flame rose into the hot desert sky like a well-behaved tornado. The cloud of fire emanating from the Treasure of Egypt reached so far into the air that even the very last citizen in the traveling column could follow it like a beacon. The people's fear of the plague slowly diminished with each step as they marched to the unknown territory that Pharaoh's One True God called *The Promised Land*.

Part I

1

May 16th
Annapolis, Maryland

A naked woman's body landed forcefully on the shadowy, vacant parking lot's concrete. One hundred yards away, Sergeant O'Kelly's wide eyes watched in shock as the passenger door of a black Chevy truck swung closed after dumping out the body. He stood straight as his grip on the cup of hot coffee in his hand tensed, adrenaline pumping through his blood stream. Although Sergeant O'Kelly, a thirteen-year police veteran with two army combat tours, could not actually hear the woman's white skin strike the hard parking lot blacktop from his position, his mind substituted its audio nonetheless.

"Oh, shit," he muttered.

O'Kelly's partner of eight years immediately reacted to his alarm.

"Fuck me," he said as they watched the naked woman's body roll several times before finally stopping, facedown.

The short-bed Chevy Silverado quickly sped forward while the passenger's door swung open and closed. The older-model truck began to accelerate as it fled the dimly-lit and deserted parking lot.

Dumbfounded, the two officers stared across the street at the empty lot of the vacant Blockbuster. It was surrounded by yellow overhead lights, which flickered on and off intermittently. The stark-white, nude female body contrasted sharply with the black, dirty surface of the lot.

Way too fucking early in my shift for a homicide crime scene, O'Kelly thought to himself.

The two veteran police officers stood outside the front doors of the local twenty-four-hour convenience store, their black-and-white police cruiser parked directly in front of them. His partner called in the description of the truck from his mobile radio and sprinted to their squad car.

The woman's body had remained motionless after rolling. Her face was turned away from them, and her naked back, legs, and butt appeared to be covered in dirt or soot. *Something* made her white skin appear unusual beneath the overhead lights. O'Kelly never took his eyes off her – hoping to see movement, hoping to see some part of her body react to the cold black top – but she never moved.

His partner jumped in the driver's seat of the police cruiser.

"Get in!" he yelled at O'Kelly, who was already sprinting to the passenger side of the car. His partner quickly put the cruiser in drive and started to chase after the truck that had fled the parking lot. Both police officers knew the interstate highway was only a few blocks away.

"I can't read the plate," his partner said.

"Fuck the plate! Get to the girl!" O'Kelly snapped pointing at the immobile body.

His partner had never even considered the woman that now lay directly in front of them. His entire focus had been in catching, cutting off, or smashing into the truck that was attempting to flee the murder scene. He now realized that O'Kelly was absolutely right. They needed to get to her first and radio in the fleeing truck.

It took a few seconds to drive over the two curbs in front of them and reach the corpse, which glowed faintly yellow under the vacant store's street lamp. O'Kelly nearly gasped aloud as he jumped from the patrol car and ran to the victim.

Suddenly, she sat up and looked directly at him, her face dazed and vacant. Her body was covered, head-to-toe, in words written with a black permanent marker. He had never seen such a thing. Words covered her face, her buttocks, inside her legs, and her stomach. As he got closer to the woman, he began to make them out:

BITCH. SLUT. WHORE.

"What the . . . " was all O'Kelly could say as he watched the dead woman, now alive, cover her face with both her hands and sob hysterically.

2

November 8th
United States Naval Academy

The prosecution's case ended before it even had a chance to begin.

The two female military prosecutors sitting at the government's table looked and acted the part of hard-nosed attorneys from beginning to end of the court-martial. The lead prosecutor was petite and athletic, but she was too boring for the military tribunal she was in charge of handling.

Her opening statement explained to the all-male jury that the accused, an Annapolis cadet who sat at the defense table, had abducted and brutally raped the wife of a local state senator, although he had not known who she was when he had kidnapped her. The cadet's barbaric acts included marking the victim from head-to-toe in black permanent marker with demeaning words. The prosecutor described in a tedious monotone manner that, after gang raping the victim on the United States Naval Academy campus, the cadet and another midshipman had then drugged her, dumped her desecrated body in a deserted parking lot in town, and fled the scene. Two local police officers had observed his truck at the scene and had witnessed the victim's body being dumped out of his truck. The all-male jury looked at the midshipman sitting at the defense table and gave him and his two attorneys hard, stern looks as they listened.

After a short pause to clear the air after the government's opening statement, Solo Goldman, the lead civilian defense counsel for the accused, stood from the defense table and stared at the jury. He could tell they were waiting for him to make his opening statement, for him to somehow offer a sane explanation for the horrific acts that had just been described to them by the dull military prosecutor. Solo walked to the middle of the courtroom and intentionally delayed beginning. He stood tall, with his arms hanging comfortably at his sides. His six-foot, athletic stature commanded the military tribunal, and his dark Hickey Freeman suit completed his wordless monologue. He and his female co-counsel were the only civilians in the courtroom, as he had been privately hired by the family of the accused.

Solo did not move or say a word. He simply stood in the middle of the small military courtroom and looked intently at the jury. To them, his silence seemed to last forever, but Solo knew that simple moments of quiet inside a courtroom were pure, persuasive power. He had learned this trial lawyers' trick early in his career, and – instead of talking incessantly, like most nervous attorneys did – he used silence as the most-persuasive tool in his litigator's tool belt.

Solo turned and looked back at his young client behind him, who was dressed in his dark Navy midshipman's uniform. The uniform resembled the military's version of a business suit, except it was covered with patches and ribbons, like a Boy Scout uniform. The young man's blue eyes were narrowly opened, and his white skin contrasted against the tan and elegant woman sitting next to him.

Solo's co-counsel, Ella Franks, was a magnificent beauty, with long legs and big, dark eyes. She was a top-of-her-class Harvard graduate, and she was as ruthless as she was stunningly seductive. For effect, Ella quietly and slowly leaned across the defense table and handed Solo, in a well-practiced and fluid motion, the brown file folder sitting on the table in front of her. Solo slowly turned back to the jury and theatrically opened the brown folder. The jury, as if by cue, leaned forward to see what was inside. Solo suppressed his smile at his artificial creation of drama.

He pulled out two 8x10 color photographs and set the folder on the defense table. He then held up both photographs in front of the jury. The photo in his left hand showed a white woman in her forties with long, brown, curly hair, on her hands and knees, like a dog. She was naked. In the photograph, a man stood and looked directly at the camera, a beer in one hand, the other on the back of the woman's head as she performed oral sex on him. The man in the photograph was the accused.

The photograph in Solo's right hand was of the same woman. Again, she was naked. This time, she had a beer in one hand and a black magic marker in the other. No one else was in the photograph. The image showed her laughing as she wrote, with her own hand, the word "SLUT" in large, black letters on her surgically-augmented left breast.

The senior prosecutor, who was all of five feet tall and wore a tight bun in her Catholic-black hair, jumped to her feet and screamed a rambling objection the second she saw the two photos. Solo took a step closer to the jury.

"He has never disclosed those photographs to the government, Your Honor!" she blurted out.

Solo did not look at the prosecutor. He continued his slow march toward the jury, holding the photos at chest-level in each hand. The men on the jury were riveted by the pornographic photographs displayed before them, and they unabashedly tried to digest the details of the large, color glossies as fast as they could. Somehow they knew they had to gobble up the gory sexual details before the judge ripped the photos from their sight.

"Judge! Defense counsel is still showing them to the jury! Please, Your Honor!" the prosecutor begged.

Solo thought to himself, *Almost there . . . just another second or two, and this trial will be over.*

The military judge sat up straight in his chair. He wore the rank of a full-bird Colonel, or a Captain, as the Navy called that particular high-level rank. He had short, cropped, dark-gray hair, and a set of glasses rested halfway down his nose. The glasses seemed to be there more for effect than for any actual medical purpose.

"Mr. Goldman, have the photographs you are so generously showing to the jury been previously shared with the government or admitted by this Court in a prior session?"

Solo did not turn toward the judge. Instead, he continued to stand firmly in front of the jury box with the two photographs of the naked woman engaged in consensual sex with his client and simply said, "No, Your Honor."

"Then I would ask you to immediately refrain from publishing those photographs to the jury until I have directed you to do so!" the judge ordered.

Solo Goldman now shifted slightly, and, instead of addressing the military judge, he began to speak directly to the prosecutor, who had stomped from behind her table to within an arm's length of him.

"Your Honor, the government has accused this young midshipman from the United States Naval Academy of forced sexual assault. Based solely on the word of their *alleged* victim, they have dragged my client into this courtroom and placed him on trial for his life. Never once did the prosecution in this case investigate the background of their accuser. They did nothing more than write down her statement and then *haul* this young man into this courtroom.

"I offer two photographs for your consideration – the first of many that clearly show that this so called '*victim*' in fact engaged in consensual and bizarre sexual activities with my client, marked on herself with a magic marker, and then – as the night progressed – became so agitated and dangerously bizarre that my client dumped her in a parking lot in an act of panic. Conduct unbecoming of a gentleman and an officer? Maybe. But *rape*? Not even close. Had the government attempted to investigate this case beyond the headlines they were hoping for—"

The judge interrupted him.

"I did not ask you for your opening statement, Mr. Goldman!"

"Actually, you did, Your Honor. And this is my opening statement," Solo shot back. "This victim has been in and out of mental hospitals since she was twelve. She may be the wife of a state senator, but she certainly was not raped by my client – and these pictures prove that beyond *any* doubt.

"In fact, I request that the government investigate the history of the senator and his wife to see what other outrageous conduct they have attempted to cover up by accusing innocent people. It is clear that the victim's husband – a senator, who has sworn to uphold the Constitution – has allowed this injustice to protect his political ambitions."

The prosecutor and the judge looked at each other, then at the jury. Solo could tell that they both thought the same thing: you cannot un-ring a bell, and Solo Goldman had just rung a loud and obnoxious one in front of the jury.

The judge regained control and addressed the jurors.

"Gentlemen, it is obvious that these lawyers and I have some matters to discuss outside of your presence. I am going to excuse you, so we can discuss these matters privately. Bailiff, please escort the jury members out of the courtroom."

"All rise!" the pudgy Navy seaman that had been assigned bailiff duties yelled. Everyone in the courtroom stood, and the members, still shaking their heads, started filing out from behind the jury box and into the deliberation room. The heavyset bailiff followed them out the door.

Solo walked to his table and pulled out the remaining eight photographs. He already knew they'd result in the dismissal of all charges. He dropped them casually on the prosecutor's table.

"You are a son of a bitch," she muttered, picking up the photos and looking through them with disdain. "I'll have you brought up on ethical charges for not disclosing these prior to trial." She looked to the judge, seeking his support for her threat against the defense attorney.

Solo remained quiet. He had learned long ago to keep his mouth shut when things were going his way. *Sometimes, the more you argue, the less convincing you are – and now was the time to let the evidence do the talking*, he thought. He ran his fingers through his jet-black hair, sprinkled with gray, as he waited for the judge's reaction.

The crisp, stern prosecutor shifted to her emotional appeal.

"Your Honor, this is a clear breach of the military rules for courts-martial, along with every single ethical rule I can think of. Defense counsel had these photographs from the beginning and never disclosed them to the government, as he is required to do. Instead, he waited until the jury had been selected and then ambushed us in front of them at trial – a clear violation of every rule known to these proceedings."

The judge rose from his bench and gathered his books and manuals. He seemed to not have listened to the objections of the prosecutor. Solo watched the judge intently – he knew the prosecutor was right. He had committed numerous violations by not disclosing the photographs at the beginning of the case, or at least whenever they had come into his possession.

Having seen just two of the photographs – not to mention the others that were currently in the hands of the outraged prosecutor – it was obvious that the judge had made his decision. Solo watched in silence as the judge packed his trial manuals and left the bench, declining to listen further to the prosecutor's protests. He knew what the judge had just decided, what the jury had decided, and what the prosecutor was slowly beginning to realize:

This case was over.

3

November 8th
Annapolis, Maryland

The media had set up camp outside the front gate of the Naval Academy. It was not very often that the son of a high-ranking Navy admiral was accused of a horrific sexual assault. Solo Goldman headed straight into the beehive of swarming reporters and cameras.

"Is it true the government just dismissed all charges against your client?" a *New York Times* reporter blurted out before anyone could get the jump on her.

"Please," Solo stated. "I have a statement to read. Then I will try to answer all your questions." He paused before reading from the script that his co-counsel, Ella, had just handed to him.

"Today, the United States government dismissed all charges against Midshipman Flores," he began. Reporters flashed photos in rapid-fire sequence as he continued. "My client is anxious to put these false and terrible accusations behind him. It is our hope that the government's alleged victim gets the mental health treatment she desperately needs. My client and his family feel extraordinary relief at his exoneration here today."

"Why were the charges dismissed after opening statements?" a tall, blonde FOX News reporter in a short, red dress interrupted.

"Mr. Goldman, the Commandant of the Naval Academy, Rear Admiral Flores, hired you himself to represent his son. Can you comment on the Commandant's involvement in this case?" another reporter asked over the heads of the group.

The Public Affairs Officer for the Naval Academy walked over to Solo and interrupted the conversation. With a monotone voice, he began describing the legal events that had just unfolded inside the courtroom.

Generally, Ella Franks seldom left Solo's side, and she stood just behind him now. The other partners in the law firm called her Solo's Sergeant Major, although never to her face. The two of them spent considerable time together, and she ran Solo's personal and professional life like a Tourbillion wristwatch.

Solo's cell phone vibrated, and she answered it before handing it to him.

"It's the Commandant," she said.

Solo took the phone and began wandering away from the noisy crowd to speak with his client's father. Ella momentarily watched him out of the corner of her eye, but her attention remained on the press conference occurring in front of her. She needed to write Solomon's formal press release before the evening news aired.

"Sir, Goldman here," Solo said.

"Mr. Goldman, you have my eternal gratitude for clearing my son and my family's name in this matter. I know I questioned your tactics throughout the trial preparations, but, in the end, you were absolutely right," Commandant Flores said, his gratitude radiating from his voice.

"Sir, your son is a great kid, and I'm glad he'll be back at school," Solo said. "I have no doubt you will help him make better choices in the future. I am proud I've gotten to know your family so well.

Please tell your wife I'll miss her great cooking – especially that pound cake. I'll miss our meetings at your beautiful home."

"I owe you everything I have, Mr. Goldman. If you need anything – and I mean *anything* – you know where to find me."

The line went dead.

At that moment, the lead prosecutor in the failed court-martial emerged from the building, directly behind the gathered group of media professionals. She walked briskly up to the group of reporters while holding a prepared statement that she very obviously wanted to deliver. Mixed emotions of defeat and anger shadowed her face.

"I, too, would like to read a statement," she began.

Ella tapped notes from the prosecutor's statement into her iPad. She would use the prosecutor's comments against her in Solo's press release later that evening. She didn't notice Solo's unintentional ambling further away from the group as he spoke to the Commandant.

When Solo ended his conversation, he found himself standing before a black town car, which idled alongside the parking lot. Amongst the flurry of the T.V. and studio vans and people moving around the crowded parking lot, the vehicle had not drawn any special attention.

Its door opened. A woman emerged, and she reached out, gently taking Solo's hand in hers. A sudden, brief pinprick on his neck turned his attention away from her as he noticed for the first time a man with a shaved head in a dark suit directly behind him.

As Solo's attention turned back to the woman, he felt her warm, gentle hand for a moment before feeling dizzy. The next thing he knew, he was sitting in the back seat of the town car, and his consciousness was fading. In the haze of his mind, he realized that he had just been drugged. The woman sat next to him.

"Mr. Goldman, I'm not going to hurt you," she said. "I've been looking for you for a very long time. My apologies that we had to approach you this way. However, we need you, and your brother needs you even more. When you wake up, I'll answer all your questions. But, for now, just relax and sleep."

Her voice sounded kind and familiar, and it had the slightest hint of an accent. As his eyelids grew heavy, he did just as she had instructed. Solo Goldman slept.

In approximately eight hours, he would awake – at the bottom of the Atlantic Ocean, inside an Israeli nuclear submarine.

4

November 8th
New York City

Ella paced impatiently with both hands on her hips, constantly checking her iPhone for a return text. She had received dozens of texts in the last hour, but none of them had been from the sender that she'd so desperately desired to hear from.

Where is he?

"Ms. Franks, the Mayor is on line two," her crew-cut, female secretary announced from the office doorway.

Ella had decorated her office in modern, bright colors, the result of which had been that it in no way resembled a typical Manhattan-lawyer workplace. She picked up the phone on her desk and pushed the blinking line indicator.

"Good morning, Your Honor," she said.

"Ms. Franks, I'm amazed that you, of all people, got the police unions to publicly endorse my campaign with such ease," the mayor of New York City said in the default, matter-of-fact tone he used to discuss business and politics. "You certainly did deliver."

"Solo Goldman vouched for me, and I said I'd deliver. I'm just glad I've proven myself," she said, looking again at her iPhone for the hundredth time in the last five minutes. No texts. *What in the world could possibly be going on?*

Ella Franks had left the District Attorney's office three years ago to work for Goldman. Her former boss, Paul McLoud, was a man that she had simply despised, and could not stomach. McLoud, was the Chief Prosecutor for the City of Manhattan, and was a good-old-fashioned womanizer. He had used his powerful position to seduce as many young deputy prosecutors as he could get into his bed. Ella, however, had not been one of them, and her career had been quite limited by her unwillingness to jump into the sack with her boss.

At the D.A.'s office, she had climbed the ranks to Chief Deputy and earned a reputation as a tough, street-smart prosecutor, while at the same time successfully leading the division in charge of prosecuting police misconduct.

Ella Franks, all five-feet-eight-inches of her, could be simultaneously merciless and accommodating – which was why she had been ideally suited to being Solo's right-hand partner. But she was also a cycloptically *just* person. Being fair and reasonable, while prosecuting "cop cases," as they were known in the D.A.'s office, had allowed her to cultivate a close bond with the officers at the New York Police Department.

The local city cops trusted her, plain and simple. They knew she would aggressively prosecute dirty cops in their ranks; however, they also knew that she would descend into the depths of Hell to defend any of them that stood wrongly accused. She had, more often than not, outright dismissed the bullshit, politically-motivated cases that had been brought against her officers in blue. She never wavered nor flinched in doing the right thing, no matter the consequences.

And, now, she had just used her unique relationship with New York City's crime fighters in the mayor's favor.

The Mayor continued.

"I was hoping to have a chat with Mr. Goldman if he is available, Ms. Franks. I want to congratulate him on his spectacular win at the Naval Academy this morning, and I also think it might be prudent for us to begin to discuss some opportunities for service on my cabinet. That is, if my re-election goes as we think it will."

Ella glanced up from her phone. Before she could respond to the mayor, five men in dark-navy wool suits walked through the double doors of her office. She made the mistake of establishing eye contact with the tallest agent, who was clearly in charge. He immediately hung up his cell phone and walked across the room to address her.

She stared rudely at the agent as she continued her phone conversation with the mayor.

"*Mr. Mayor*, I assure you, as soon as Mr. Goldman walks into this office, you will be the first person I put him on the phone with."

The agent unabashedly listened to her conversation.

"Thank you, Ms. Franks. I look forward to speaking with him. Good day."

"Good bye, sir," Ella said, hanging up the telephone.

"Ms. Franks," the agent said forcefully, his experience in commanding people radiating through his voice. "I'm National Security Agent Paul Muldoon. I'm here to take Solomon Goldman into custody for questioning. If you do not tell me Mr. Goldman's whereabouts, I'm afraid my agency will simply issue a warrant for his arrest. My request here today is a mere courtesy."

The lead National Security Agent and Ella sized each other up.

Ella had not gotten as far as she had in the prosecutorial world by being easily intimidated, and she was certainly not afraid of barbarians dressed in dark suits, holding badges. Her prestigious, east-coast family pedigree had kept her out of a few prickly situations in the past, and she was no virgin to attempts to charm or bully.

"Mr. *Whatever-Your-Name-Is*, I am *not* Mr. Goldman's secretary. I am his partner," Ella said as her dark, almost-black eyes turned even blacker. She stepped around her desk and stood squarely in front of the agent, staring at the other four agents in the foyer. All of what she had just said was true. Nevertheless, she did know Solo's whereabouts at all times, since she, herself, planned his schedule, down to every last detail.

The N.S.A. agent obviously knew better. "I know you're much more than his partner, Ms. Franks," he said. "If you want to read in tomorrow's newspaper that your boss is being sought for questioning in a spy-ring investigation, then just keep on playing your little poker game."

"I don't think Mr. Goldman's family will take kindly to your accusations. When your father is a U.S. Ambassador and personal friends with the President of the United States, you don't shake in your boots every time some government minion mentions prison, or whatever it is that you're implying."

Agent Muldoon stepped forward and stared directly into Ella's eyes.

"Goldman's father went missing last night and has most likely fled the country," he whispered menacingly. "His brother has also disappeared in the Iraqi desert."

Ella's hard demeanor cracked. She had not seen Solo since the trial this morning at the Academy. She had felt instant alarm when he had missed the firm's private helicopter back to the city, and she'd been on the hunt for him ever since.

Solo Goldman was a wealthy and successful international businessman. He could occasionally be vain and self-serving, like any man, but overall he was extremely responsible and incredibly reliable. Furthermore, he was not the type that would just catch a ride home with some stranger. His mother had instilled in him a strong sense of balance between hard work and simple living, as compared to his father's world of prestige and wealth. Over the last three years, Ella had turned Solo's restless energy away from dating New York supermodels and directed it toward the city's much-needed philanthropic necessities.

Where is he, and why is he not answering my text messages?

If it were true that Solo's father had gone missing, and his war hero brother had also disappeared, something was desperately wrong. *Where could he be?* she wondered as her iPhone chirped, notifying her of her meeting with a new client in fifteen minutes.

5

November 9th
Latitude: 17° 34´ 60˝ S, Longitude: 168° 13´ 60˝ E

The 1,720-ton, Dolphin-class Israeli nuclear submarine departed the sovereign waters of Cuba under a moonless night. The submarine, carrying its crew of thirty-five, had been manufactured by Germany's leading shipyard, *HDW*, and it now increased its momentum to its maximum 48-knot submerged cruising speed. The boat was one of the fastest in service – more than double the speed of its non-nuclear sisters. Over the last several years, Israel had purchased multiple Dolphin-class submarines from Germany. Only three had been reported by the press as delivered, which had made headlines, as the German taxpayers had subsidized the Israeli acquisition. The first two submarines had been donated to the Israelis by the German government, free of charge.

Germany and Israel had kept the latest Dolphin a secret. It was similar to its sisters in every way, except for its propulsion system. This Dolphin, the pride of the naval arm of the Israeli Defense Forces, didn't operate primarily in the Mediterranean Sea, like its diesel-powered family members. Instead, Israel used the nuclear-powered attack and reconnaissance platform for missions that required longer range, like abducting a high-profile target in broad daylight from the eastern seaboard of the continental United States and transporting him back to Israel, undetected.

Eteye Azeb stood on the bridge, speaking to the Captain, when Solo Goldman began to stir in the far-aft quarters of the submarine. The young, Jewish corpsman, who had been put in charge of ensuring that *The Package* came out of his drug-induced coma as safely and comfortably as possible, radioed the bridge to inform Azeb that she should join him immediately.

Solo Goldman opened his eyes for the first time since the parking lot at the U.S. Naval Academy, almost a day ago. When he saw a large, nuclear-tipped harpoon missile silo directly next to his bunk, his already-groggy head hurt worse.

"Who are you?" Solo said to the young, pimple-faced sailor sitting across from him as he tried to sit up. However, the bunk directly above him in the cramped crew's quarters prevented him from doing so fully.

"Please, sir, be still. She will be here momentarily, and she'll answer your questions," the twenty-something sailor said. He shined a small penlight into each of Solo's pupils, which dilated and then returned to normal with the passing of the small light, as a woman walked through the hatchway and into the confined room. They were now cruising three-hundred meters below the surface of the warm, southern Atlantic Ocean.

"You!" Solo said as he recognized the woman from the parking lot of the press conference. "What is going on? And where the hell am I?"

She did not wear the uniform of the Israeli Navy. Rather, she was dressed in high-quality, custom-tailored khaki pants and a tight, form-fitting gray turtleneck sweater. She wore a thick, gold necklace, which resembled a young snake, tied around her neck. The two ends of the odd-looking necklace hung down from a square knot, which hung perfectly between her notably round and pointed breasts. The tightly-knitted metal reminded Solo of chainmail from a knight's armor. He had a strange premonition that he'd seen the captivating necklace before. Eteye's pants were tucked into her black combat boots, and her shoulder-length, sinewy hair matched their deep shine. Her face was warm and dark in color. She looked Middle Eastern, and her skin's complexion was tight and perfect. Her hair was brushed behind her small ears, and her high cheek bones glimmered in the overhead lights. Her lips were full and large compared to her nose, which was small and delicate. Her beauty was as powerful as it was stunning.

An affluent man himself, Solo immediately recognized that she was also a person of financial means. She was not a soldier, and she contrasted sharply with their current surroundings. Solo wondered if she worked for military intelligence, or if she was perhaps a spy of some sort.

"Mr. Goldman, please remain calm and let the medic see if you are okay before you try to stand," Eteye said, squatting in front of him.

The navy-dressed corpsman strapped the blood pressure cuff over one of Goldman's sleeves.

Solo simply stared at her, just like he had done in the parking lot before he'd passed out. His mind told him that he should be outraged and defensive – he'd just been kidnapped and drugged by a complete stranger, and he now found himself sitting inside what appeared to be a submarine. *A submarine? Am I really on a submarine?* his mind said, but he knew better. His past naval experience had instantly informed him that he was sitting next to a missile silo on a sub, similar to one he had been on for three summer months between his third and fourth year at the Naval Academy, some twenty years ago. Something deep inside of him told him that he was safe, despite his surroundings, and that he could trust the smiling woman in front of him.

She reached out and took both his hands into hers to reassure him. She had long, extended eyelashes, and there was not a blemish to her face anywhere. She didn't look like a typical olive-skinned Jewish woman from the Middle East. Her dark, oval eyes had an unusual depth to them, and they captivated Solo, calming his nerves. He almost felt like he knew her.

"All of his vitals look good, and – aside from a hangover from that sedative – he should be good to go," the youthful medic said. He began to pack his instruments while looking at the woman in charge, waiting for her next command.

"Thank you. You may leave us now," she said. She moved onto the bunk next to Solo in the spot the Israeli sailor had just vacated. Solo said nothing, and he noticed for the first time that he was not wearing his own clothes. He was dressed in a pair of blue jeans and a yellow, button-down Oxford polo. His expensive, black Italian leather wing-tipped shoes had also been replaced with designer boots.

"Where the hell are my clothes, and who dressed me in this outfit?" he demanded.

"Mr. Goldman, I know this is a lot to take in," she began, still holding on to both of his hands.

"Why are we on a submarine?" Solo tried to keep his voice calm.

"We just left Havana Harbor, and we should reach the Strait of Gibraltar in three days. From there, we'll travel through the strait and directly to Haifa," Eteye Azeb said, kindly.

"Haifa? As in Israel?" Solo asked, his confusion growing.

"I'm sorry, Mr. Goldman. Soon you'll be fully briefed on everything that has happened and why you are so desperately needed there. You will not need your tailored suit for the time being."

"Why did you drug me?"

"There was no time. We had a very short window to get you out of the States before they picked you up. My sincerest apologies, but we had neither the time nor the luxury of convincing you how grave the situation was – or of how much danger you were in," Eteye said, her hands still wrapped around his. "I need you to remember, if you can."

Old emotions, buried long ago, began to awaken in him. The energy from Eteye's well-manicured hands stirred sensations in Solo that he had sworn he would never let himself feel again. He could almost *see* his carefully suppressed memories traveling straight from Eteye's hands and up to his rapidly increasing heartbeat. Past sentiments and passions for another woman that he had secreted away. Feelings he would not even let himself experience with Ella or any other woman that had passed through his life since. Memories and recollections his mind knew were better left in the dead past. But his subconscious now called to him: *remember*.

"Jeans? Really?" Solo asked with a wrinkled brow. "I don't think I've worn anything but a suit for the last ten years of my life."

"Personally, I think you look very dapper in casual clothes," Eteye answered.

"You drugged me and kidnapped me and put me on a submarine?" Goldman said, attempting to get up from the canvas bunk on which he sat. As he stood, the blood rushed from his head, forcing him to sit back down.

"I know you want and deserve answers, Solo, and I will try to answer all of your questions the best I can, but first – try to relax. Let the drugs get out of your system and allow your head to clear," she said, a genuine concern rising in her eyes. "You and I are going to have plenty of time to get acquainted over the next few days."

Solo could not stop staring at her. He felt as though her eyes had told him an ancient story as soon as they had looked upon him. She was truly, blissfully captivating.

"Who are you?" he asked.

"My name is Azeb. But, please, call me Eteye."

Solo appeared puzzled over how, exactly, she had pronounced her name.

"My name sounds like 'bowtie,' only you say it with an '*Eeee*,'" she responded.

"Eeee—tie?" Solo asked.

She nodded, confirming his pronunciation.

"That is a very pretty and unusual name. Where does it come from?"

"It is an old Egyptian family name."

"An Egyptian on a Jewish submarine? For whom, exactly, do you work?"

"I work for many different people from time to time, and I am currently helping some friends in the Israeli government get you safely to their country, away from the hands of your government."

Her voice was gentle but commanding. She spoke as though she were no stranger to taking charge of a situation, and her calmness struck him, as though she knew her listener would obey and accept her instructions. She spoke like royalty, addressing one of her subjects. She buried the memories and fears of her former submarine days and the thoughts of spending eternity trapped on the ocean's floor.

"What are you? Some sort of secret agent?" Solo asked her.

"Oh my, no!" Eteye answered forcing a laugh, "I am the daughter of an important Egyptian politician, but I am not an *agent* for anyone, let alone a *secret* one."

She smiled and squeezed his knee with her hand, and Solo looked down at it as she did. Her touch made him feel good in a best-friend kind of way.

"I'm not going to Israel," Solo said, trying to sound resolute and break her spell over him. "I run an international law firm in New York. I can't just take a vacation and go tour the Holy Land with you."

"You have always been a very important man," Eteye said as she reached for a bottle of water that sat across from them in the cramped, steel room, crisscrossed with pipes and wires and large digital gauges. "Drink this. It will help with the headache."

"Please stop the nursemaid routine and give me some answers. Why are you taking me to Israel?"

"Solo, do you know that your brother was arrested two days ago and is currently being held – well, we are not sure where he is being held, exactly. Last we had word of him was when he left Iraq and arrived at Camp Arifjan in Kuwait," she said, attempting to get the facts out as quickly and succinctly as she could.

"Arrested? By whom and for what?" Solo asked in disbelief. "That guy bleeds jarhead! Why would the Marine Corps—"

She interrupted him politely.

"Your brother was working on a multinational project in Iraq that very few people knew about. It started as a search for suspected W.M.D.'s in the desert, but then he uncovered some very unusual and sensitive information that your government didn't want shared. And the only way to keep him from sharing—"

"—was to lock him up?" Solo interjected. "You said it *started* with W.M.D.'s? I assume you mean weapons of mass destruction?"

Eteye continued, pushing the water bottle towards Solo's mouth. "Did you know that Saddam Hussein had begun rebuilding the ancient city of Babylon?" she asked.

"I guess I remember hearing something about that."

"Israel suspected all along that his restoration of ancient Babylon was really just a guise to hide his W.M.D's. When U.S. forces took control of the country a few years back, they put together a multinational team, mainly comprised of undercover Israelis and Americans, who tried to sort through what Saddam had really been up to. Your brother had the right credentials to lead that military expedition."

"You mean because he was Jewish – and a Marine," Solo said.

"Exactly. And your father being the Ambassador to Egypt and thus well-connected politically made it easy for your brother to end up at the top of the list," Eteye said.

"So what did he find in the desert, or in Babylon?" Solo asked, cutting to the chase, as a skilled trial lawyer is prone to do.

Eteye smiled. "How well do you remember your lessons in Hebrew school?"

"Hebrew school?" Solo smirked. "What are you talking about?"

"It's a long story, and one better told by the people you will meet when we arrive in Israel," she said as she finally stood up. "You need to rest – to sleep and let your head clear. We will talk more after you have had a good night's sleep. We have many days to spend together in these luxurious accommodations," she said sarcastically.

"What did they find in the Iraqi desert? In Babylon?" Solo said, obviously intrigued. His mind raced through his early years in Bible school and the history lessons that had been drilled into his head by the rabbis dressed in black. His older brother had always been a better religious student than Solo. Even through later in their lives, his brother had remained the better disciple of Jewish history – and the more devout Jew.

Solo was not sure he believed in God at all, let alone a jealous, angry, and old Jewish God. He'd stopped believing in some sort of crotchety, ancient man in the heavens a long time ago, and he never really could bring himself to believe in a god who never did much about all the pain and suffering in the world.

It was not the same for his brother, Levi, and his father, however. They were both what Solo called *true believers*. They did not only believe in a divine God – they also believed their Jewish God was the *only* God. Solo had struggled with his views regarding a divine presence all his life. At some point, he had simply quit pretending to believe that his religion had all the right answers and everyone else's had the wrong ones. Eventually, he'd grown angry with God, his father, and his brother: *religion and the need for a God was for weak people who can't do for themselves*, he told himself. He'd stopped attending synagogue after he and the God of his youth had parted ways—after Abay had left him.

The weight of the drugs still in his system, combined with the trauma of his recent experiences, overtook Solo. He desperately needed to sleep. He had not thought about his brother or spoken to him in years. After that night on the beach, they'd never been close again – a stark contrast from when they'd been kids. *But how could they be – after what had happened?*

"What did they find?" he asked one more time.

Eteye turned and answered. Her necklace caught the light and flickered, like it was alive. "It is a story that started in Egypt with Moses' exodus and continued through King David, King Solomon, and, finally, to Jeremiah, the prophet. It is a story that defines Jews, Christians, and Muslims."

"And?"

"They found something that will consume all of mankind in a modern-day holy war, if we are not careful."

Solo lay down on the short, dark-brown canvas cot. He could feel the hum of the nuclear reactor through the thick, steel walls of his four-man-high bunk bed.

"You still didn't answer my question," he said as Eteye stepped over the shin-high lower portion of the bulkhead, into the passageway outside his bunkroom.

She looked back at him, her eyelashes fluttering and her white teeth appearing between her red lips as she smiled.

He was again struck by the sheer beauty of her perfectly proportioned face and her delicate-but-strong demeanor. She was the type of woman that a man would risk everything he had to possess.

She spoke with no inflection or emotion. "A map that reveals the secret hiding place of the lost Ark of the Covenant," Eteye Azeb said.

She closed the iron door behind her.

6

November 10th
United States Marine Corps' Birthday
Camp Arifjan, Kuwait

The dark-blue Nissan S.U.V. drove through the midnight rain and up to the first unmanned checkpoint. It came to a rolling stop as it turned ninety degrees to the right around the solid, three-foot-thick concrete tank barrier. There were seven more of these barriers to traverse before the unremarkable vehicle arrived at the first manned guard post. Water covered the road and the barren desert landscape surrounding it. The driver was alert to avoid hydroplaning.

It was the rainy season, which meant week-long rainstorms and floods throughout most of the Kuwaiti desert. U.S. military and political personnel traveled in Kuwait in non-military vehicles, and always in civilian clothing. The Muslim country had the largest U.S. military base in the Middle East, but the Kuwaitis did not want to be reminded of this fact by seeing camouflaged U.S. soldiers and Marines on their streets, or by seeing U.S. Humvees on their highways. Thus, all U.S. military personnel were instructed to keep as low of a profile as possible when off-post, and most military members weren't allowed to leave Camp Arifjan without explicit permission from the base's general himself. In effect, these policies rendered them quarantined to the base for their tour of duty.

Seven Kuwaiti soldiers greeted the three N.S.A. agents and their driver as they arrived at the guard shack. The native-born Kuwaiti soldiers were armed to the teeth with U.S. military weapons and hardware. As a result of the first Gulf War and the liberation of Kuwait, these soldiers were both keenly aware of and sensitive to the American military installation that they protected, and they knew many local, fanatical religious groups would love to cause them – and the U.S. military personnel they guarded – substantial harm. The guards noted that the N.S.A. agents had arrived on-schedule, and their security check-in was swift and efficient.

The agents exited the vehicle and proceeded through security into the base. Their S.U.V. remained on the outer perimeter as the men walked through the three-hundred-yard maze of concrete and barbed wire that led to the base's inner borders. After clearing two more guard shacks and enduring multiple body searches, they arrived *inside*, as the Americans called it. The agents were greeted by another waiting Humvee, driven by a young female M.P., who took them to the brig in the compound's center.

It was late, but the three agents were anxious to interrogate the man whom they'd just flown halfway around the world to question. They didn't stop at their temporary barracks; rather, they proceeded immediately to where the prisoner was being held. The heavy rain outside continued.

Levi Goldman, Colonel, United States Marine Corps, sat in the middle of a long, rectangular-brick room, his ankles shackled to the floor and his wrists handcuffed to the cold, gray, heavy steel table in the room's center. The table and its chair were a matching set. He was fully awake, despite having just been roused from a deep sleep five minutes ago by a military policeman.

As the three agents entered the room, the M.P. excused herself, leaving the four men alone to begin what would be a dozen interrogation sessions over the next seventy-two hours. Unfortunately for the National Security Agents, their interrogation efforts would always end the same way as tonight's would: futile.

"Colonel Goldman," the droopy-faced, long-nosed senior agent said, sarcastically flashing his N.S.A. credentials at the chained man sitting before him. "You have not been arrested, and you are not being held in this military prison."

The agent stared down Levi. Without so much as blinking or twitching, he continued.

"You do not exist anymore, and you will not exist until I say you exist. Depending on how I clean up this little mess of yours, your official record will either state that you were just another I.E.D. fatal casualty on some back road in Iraq – *or* we will get you back to your unit and to your men as quickly as possible."

The other two men, who were slightly shorter and more average-looking, clean-cut government agents, leaned against the back wall of the cellblock interrogation room, trying to get service on their smartphones. They remained indifferently passive as the lead agent continued.

"Colonel, let's start with what I know, and then you can help me with the parts I *don't* know."

The agent removed a thick, brown file from his worn leather briefcase and placed it on the table, closed.

"Several years ago, we began Operation Sand Storm. As I understand it – from reading this dense file while en route to this god-forsaken part of the world – the Israelis tipped us off a few years back regarding a secret military base south of Baghdad, where they suspected weapons of mass destruction were being stored or manufactured.

"However, when we got there, we found no W.M.D.'s at all – instead, we discovered that Saddam had turned himself into a real-life Indiana Jones, digging up artifacts from all around the desert. Apparently, he'd uncovered ancient historical and religious pieces, which dated back thousands of years, and he'd been obsessively distracted by them. We decided to investigate his little desert-digging operation further and at least protect the artifacts from local bandits – kind of like we did when we saved all the zoo animals in Bagdad. Am I on the right track?"

The agent stared at the Marine sitting across from him. Colonel Goldman remained stoically still, expressionless, and silent.

"That's okay. Let's jump to the important part – the reason I came to this mud-puddle in the desert," the agent said, continuing his monologue. "We now know that Saddam had uncovered the lost city of Babylon, and he was seeking some sort of ultimate weapon, which – if I have my Bible stories correct – had possibly been carried to Babylon around three thousand years ago. Can you believe that shit? The Ark of the Covenant, buried in the middle of a Muslim desert – I can't think of a better way to make the six-million Jews just a few hundred miles away in Israel lose their minds than to parade the ultimate symbol of Judaism around the Arab world."

The agent leaned back in his chair but retained his straight, professional composure.

"We all thought that was Saddam's end game, right? Humiliation of Jews around the world as he flaunted their holy box around his city streets. What I *didn't* know is that many people, obviously much smarter than I am, actually believe that that solid gold box—the *Ark*—really *is* some sort of mythical, ultimate weapon. A weapon that can lay waste to entire cities, just like in the movies, right? Now I get why Saddam put so much effort into trying to find it."

Colonel Goldman remained reactionless. His breathing had held steady, and he stared intently at the federal agent in front of him.

"Anyway, our troops get to Babylon, and with some help from our Israeli allies, we figure out what Saddam is really up to. But after cataloguing all of the uncovered artifacts, there was no Ark of the Covenant to be found, anywhere. Now *here* is where it gets interesting," the agent added, leaning over the closed, brown folder resting on the steel table. "Six months ago – for some reason I haven't quite figured out yet – someone on our side snuck into Babylon: an Israeli linguist, who'd been hired to help decipher some Hebrew scrolls we'd found. Top-secret scrolls. I understand we'd even sent copies of several of them to Israel for further research."

The agent opened the folder and pulled out a single sheet of paper, which sat atop the pile of photographs, reports, and maps contained inside. He read from the paper – a report, stamped "TOP SECRET" – aloud.

"*Message as follows: Israeli Field Agent Eteye Azeb made an unauthorized report to an unknown contact inside Israel four months ago. Her report stated, 'U.S. military has potentially discovered the original and authentic Book of the Dead. Have personally seen the golden book. Need direction on how to proceed.'*"

Silence hung over the brig room.

"A month ago, we intercepted a second unauthorized satellite transmission from Agent Azeb, which had again been sent to an unknown source in Israel," the agent went on after a few seconds. "'*Made contact. Solomon Goldman. Code remains intact.*'"

The agent spoke dryly, his tone devoid of inflection.

The two agents in the back of the room suddenly seemed to have received the same notification on their phones, and they immediately turned and exited the room. Neither the lead agent nor Colonel Levi Goldman made any indication that they'd noticed the men's departure. They stared at each other across the table, like two men in a high-stakes heads-up poker game.

The agent paused before removing another document from the folder. This one showed a computer data transfer report, which contained thousands of odd symbols with intersecting lines drawn through them. It resembled an adulterated tic-tac-toe game. The agent gave Colonel Goldman a puzzled look and continued.

"Three days ago, you go A.W.O.L. from your duties in the Babylonian desert, and Ms. Azeb is nowhere to be found. By the time some dip-shit finally figures out what you two are up to and pulls the alarm, we find out that the dusty old Bible scrolls have somehow walked off and disappeared – including a golden book, or *Book of the Dead*, or whatever the hell it is that everyone seems so interested in."

The agent began reading from another document in the brown folder:

"'*Missing Artifacts from Operation Sand Storm. J Source document: missing, P Source document: missing.*' And – finally," he said, "the only gold book that was ever found and catalogued

– *Jeremiah's Book of the Dead*, as your contact called it, is also missing.

"Then, twelve hours ago, we catch you at the Kuwaiti International Airport, just before boarding a flight to Germany. Of course, not one of these three-thousand-year-old relics is packed in your carry-on bag, and there are no hints as to what you did with them. What is also disturbing is the fact that we have no records of an 'Eteye Azeb.' I have photographs of her, right here," he said, sliding a picture of a pretty young woman posing for an Iraqi dig-team group photo across the table, "but, somehow, she doesn't exist. In fact, she has *never* existed. Now, how can that be?"

Goldman remained immobile and attentive, still silent.

"I'll tell you what I think, Colonel Goldman. *Goldman* – that's a Jewish name, right?" the agent asked, resuming his forward lean across the table. "I think that you're an Israeli spy, just like this Ms. Azeb – and probably your father, as well. Did you know that after 9/11 one-thousand foreign nationals were detained? Sixty of them were Israelis. Under the *Patriot Act*, we could conclude they were all active Israeli military agents, spying on the operations of the U.S. military, right in our own country. I think you are working for them – mixed Jewish loyalties and all."

Colonel Levi Goldman adjusted himself in his chair. His uniform made no sound as he squared his shoulders and sat up taller. His gaze remained a steady, respectful stare, and his mouth remained closed and still. His deep silence penetrated the small room.

The agent continued. "Colonel, did you know that the U.S. General Accounting Office has noted that Israel is the American ally that spies on the U.S. the most?"

The agent leaned back in his chair, unbuttoned the top button on his shirt, and loosened his tie.

"We know that you were working on breaking some sort of code," he explained, matter-of-factly. We've already interrogated all your team members, and they've confirmed that you and Eteye Azeb worked exclusively and secretively with the only book that was ever found, that you were trying to unlock some sort of code.

"But then, three days ago, you shut the entire operation down. They'd suspected that you'd finally broken the code, but they never saw it. And, suddenly, a small library of ancient scrolls goes missing, as do you and our cute little Israeli undercover agent. We still can't figure out how and where you hid all those documents, but we do know that they didn't leave the country. I'm guessing we'll find them shortly."

The agent paused for effect, but Colonel Goldman's icy stillness did not thaw.

"You do not exist, Colonel, to anyone in the outside world. You will never leave this brig – unless you tell us exactly what you found, and why you went to so much trouble to hide it."

Colonel Goldman did not look at the folder on the table or at the two agents as they returned to the room. He reverted instead to a practice that he'd learned as a young Marine Second Lieutenant at the Infantry Officers School, which he'd attended after Annapolis. The Marines called it the *thousand-yard stare.*

"I need answers, Goldman!"

Finally, Goldman spoke. His eyes stared straight through the National Security Agent as his lips formed the only complete sentence he would ever utter over the next several days.

"That's going to be difficult, sir, - since I no longer exist."

7

November 11th
Atlantic Ocean

The French research vessel never had a chance against the four Iranian quick-attack boats that surrounded it under the cover of night. The high-speed boats rapidly attached to each of its sides, and its men commenced boarding the ship. The marine commandoes, or *Takavar Daryayi*, as they were known in the Iranian military, had trained for this top-secret mission for over two years.

Capturing a relatively unarmed, civilian deep-sea recovery vessel in the middle of the Atlantic Ocean was not a difficult task for the superior military force. But the key to the success of the mission lay in the absolute need for zero communications to reach the outside world, for no emergency or distress signals of any kind to escape from the French ship. For this act of war to succeed without the knowledge of the French government – or the knowledge of any western government, for that matter – it needed to appear that the *Ile De Sein* had sunk, never to be heard from again.

Pirating the French ship was simple: overwhelm the crew in the middle of night, kill all non-essential crewmembers, and immediately depart the area at maximum speed for a location four hundred nautical miles southwest of the Azores Islands, on the eastern edge of the Sargasso Sea.

The most complicated aspect to the greatest Iranian military operation since the Persian Empire ruled the world, however, was not the successful takeover of the ship. Rather, it was the operation that would occur *after* the ship's capture: the successful recovery and tactical deployment of abandoned American nuclear weapons, meticulously recovered from the ocean's floor.

8

November 12th
Masada, Israel's West Bank

Rabbi Ziva Geller and Defense Minister Armando Koslov sat in the conference room of the underground bunker, which lay deep within the Masada Mountain Tourist Center. The center served as the anchor for the gondola that led up the mountain to the top of Masada. The military defense bunker inside the complex was functionally similar to the United States North American Aerospace Defense Command, located inside a comparable mountain in Colorado. But while N.O.R.A.D.'s exact location and military function were common knowledge, no one yet knew of Masada's military capabilities, or even of its existence.

It had been moderately easy to build the military command post within the mountains of Masada: its location in the desert, between Israel and Jordan in the Palestinian West Bank, had precluded voyeuristic neighbors.

The museum and tourist center had been completed in 2007, and the Israeli Defense Forces had conveniently enshrouded the complex's development within the ongoing commercial construction of the tourist center and the gondola to the top of Masada.

Every Jew in Israel was aware of the special meaning that Masada held for the Jewish people. It was where the famous nine-hundred and sixty Sicarii Jews had made their last, fateful stand against the Roman governor of Judaea, Lucius Flavius Silva, during the Jewish revolt against Rome in the spring of 72 A.D. The insurrectionist Jews had defied the Roman Empire with open rebellion, and Rome had feared that news of the uprising would spread throughout its empire and encourage similar outbreaks. Caesar himself had ordered no mercy for such a public defiance of his authority.

The Romans had surrounded the mountaintop fortress, laying siege to the rebellious Jewish population and constructing a 375-foot ramp to the summit of the refuge. The Roman Legion *X Fretensis*, whose name meant "the legion of the sea straits," had been uniquely suited to destroy the last remnants of the Jewish rebellion: its military symbol was that of a large pig – the ultimate insult to the Jews trapped upon the mountaintop.

As the Roman battering ram broke through Masada's stone wall, the nine-hundred and sixty inhabitants denied Rome its ultimate victory over them. Instead of being made slaves to Caesar and watching their families dragged through the city streets of Rome as an example to the world, they quietly took their own lives – their final act of rebellion.

Every new solider of the Israel Defense Forces climbs the long Snake Path to the summit of Masada after their *tironut* is complete. The ceremony, which commemorates the completion of the soldiers' basic training, ends with the declaration, *"Sheynit Masada lo tipul!" —Masada shall not fall again!*

With its constant presence of military personnel, civilians, tourists, and politicians, the secret bunker and military outpost at Masada's location was ingenious.

RABBI GELLER AND DEFENSE MINISTER KOSLOV ARRIVED at the same time for the top-secret meeting, which had been planned a week before when the current operation had been put in motion. Geller was an Orthodox, or Ultra-Orthodox Rabbi, as they were known in Israel. He did not look like a well-groomed modern businessman. He wore an ill-fitting, all-black suit and a wide-brimmed, black hat. His particular Jewish sect's idea of outward devotion to God had culminated from a decree made by community rabbis in the 18th century, which had stipulated that black outer garments be worn on the Sabbath and Jewish Holy Days. The historical rabbis had thought that brightly-colored clothes might arouse resentment amongst non-Jews.

Geller was considered a Kosher rabbi in Israel, but he did not participate in any state-run religious services of any kind. Instead, he mingled with the high-ranking political and military officials in the Israeli government and influenced their decisions. Rabbi Geller was single-handedly a cloaked institution, with access to powerful Israeli political and military figures.

The Ultra-Orthodox believed that their sole duty to the Almighty was to study holy scripture, which they believed would ensure the survival of the Jewish people. Geller's followers refused to serve in the military, despite the national mandate that all young adults serve a two-year stint in the defense of their country. The Ultra-Orthodox did not contribute to society around them. Rather, their large families lived on governmental welfare, and most of their employment-age young adults lacked basic educational skills, like elementary mathematics. Although ignorant in the ways of the secular world, the Ultra-Orthodox possessed significant political power, and they were often physically harsh and criminally brutal towards anyone who believed differently than they did.

The two men, one wearing the uniform of a general in the Israel Defense Forces and the other the garb of the Ultra-Orthodox, sat opposite each other and waited for the remainder of the attendees to arrive at the bunker in Masada's belly. Their topic: the status of Eteye Azeb and *The Package*, along with her scheduled arrival at the port of Haifa.

The base in Haifa was to be alerted one hour before the submarine arrived, and upon its docking *The Package* would immediately be off-loaded and placed in a large, white tourist bus, typical for the streets of Israel. The bus, covered in holy land tour markings, would then promptly depart Haifa and make the hour-long trip directly to the I.D.F. headquarters in Tel Aviv.

"This is going to be a complete waste of time and resources. You watch and see," Defense Minister Koslov said, leaning back in his leather conference room chair as he looked across the table at Geller.

The main conference room was square-shaped, with gray, concrete walls that had a single, flat-paneled T.V. mounted to each. A large, dark-wood conference table rested in its center, and two doors, located on walls opposite each other, were the sole sources of entry and exit. Aside from the conference table's chairs, the room held nothing except for the two men who sat in them.

"My colleague assures me it was worth the great effort and risk to get Mr. Goldman out of the States," Rabbi Geller said, sitting with his back straight and his legs crossed uncomfortably in front of him.

Koslov rubbed his forehead with his handkerchief. "We have risked too much and exposed too many of our capabilities – just to grab one American in your vain quest for some religious artifact," he said with a deep sigh.

Armando Koslov supervised all special military operations in Israel. "Special military operations" could mean any number of things, ranging from the assassination of a high-level government official in an enemy country to the creation of new psychological warfare models using Twitter.

"We are not seeking some worthless *artifact*," Geller shot back. "It is *the* most precious and divine artifact our people have ever been entrusted with."

"Rabbi, not everyone believes in your ideas of who God is and what He wants," the Defense Minister retorted.

"Nothing else matters, except finding it! It is divine providence that our blessed Lord has brought it so closely to our grasp. We must not fail in locating it – in restoring it to its rightful place in the Temple."

"I hate to bring you back to reality, Rabbi, but we lost the Temple a long time ago," Koslov said, staring at his religious adversary with disdain.

"It is you secular Jews who are costing us everything!" Geller countered. "You are either in the service of the One True God, or you are against Him. There is no middle ground."

"Of course, you and your fellow black-hatters will be the ones who determine what God's will is and isn't, I suppose?" Koslov sighed again. "There is a civil war coming to this country, and the likes of you are the ones who will destroy us all. You spit on secular little girls if they dare cross the street in your *holy* neighborhoods, you subjugate women in your synagogues, you act like terrorists if someone dares to put a photograph of a woman on a billboard in Jerusalem, and – worst of all – you refuse to serve in our country's military like the rest of us, because you believe your prayers will save us all instead," Koslov said acerbically.

"Your blasphemy is noted," Geller replied, swiveling his chair and turning his back to Koslov. "I welcome this bomb to our country. It is divine justice for you secular Jews, leading this country astray. Our Lord will use this bomb to His glory, and He will deliver the Ark back to us in order that we may rebuild our Temple on the Mount."

"You are a madman. You will bring destruction upon us all when you and your religious followers try to tear down the Muslim Dome of the Rock to rebuild your Temple," Armando Koslov said.

"You need to remember that you non-believing military types serve at the pleasure of the state – always have, and always will. And right now, *I* have more influence in our government than you do," Geller said matter-of-factly.

Koslov knew he was right. Geller's influence and his version of religious fundamentalism had enormous power in the Knesset. If the two of them went to war on the political battlefield, he knew Geller would prevail. Koslov changed the subject, as neither of them would ever change their world views.

"I refuse to wait around here much longer for an update on the status of your American. I have far more important duties to attend to, like verifying the potential nuclear threat."

"We will know shortly if our efforts were worth the cost."

"Who is this agent of yours that you sent to retrieve the American?" Koslov asked, calming down.

"She is not my agent, by any means, and she refuses to work for any one group or agency that I am aware of."

"Where did you dig her up, then?"

"She is part of an ancient culture, and her kind have been called on to serve the greater good from time to time. Tradition says that her people worked for King David and King Solomon directly."

"Oh, please," Koslov said, rolling his eyes. "You used our most-valued military naval asset to send some religious nut job to breach American sovereignty?"

"She is Egyptian. I am assured that she can be trusted, and she cannot be traced to our government. I thought you, of all people, would approve of that," Geller retorted.

Koslov again tried to change the subject.

"I am told the American has not spoken to his brother in years," he said. "They had some sort of falling out, long ago."

Geller leaned forward, breaking his perfect posture. "They are brothers. No matter what happens or happened, they will always be brothers. We must know what Goldman knows and does not know. Surely his brother deposited the ancient book with someone he trusted before the Americans captured him. His younger brother is the logical choice."

Geller explained to Defense Minister Koslov that Solo Goldman was a successful, wealthy businessman in New York City and that he had taken his father's law firm to an international level. Solo had represented numerous high-ranking military officials over the years, and – because of his repeated successes – he'd gained considerable connections and influence within the U.S. defense industry. They joked briefly about what a rude awakening his last few days on the submarine had likely been, compared to his posh New York City apartment.

But Koslov had a valid concern: someone like Solo Goldman did not disappear without a lot of people noticing. The more Rabbi Geller thought about the plan, which he had supported and pressured the military to put into action two weeks earlier, the more he worried it would blow up in his face.

"I thought your agent was going to just grab the book when she broke the code in Iraq," Koslov said with anxious frustration as the two continued to wait for news regarding *The Package*'s arrival in Haifa.

"We did, too. Something went wrong, though. They were never able to break the code, and all the source documents and the *Book of the Dead* simply disappeared one day, along with Colonel Goldman."

"Do you really think your magical Ark exists?" Armando Koslov asked. A controlled, professional sarcasm filled his tone.

"Yes, I do. We have been searching for it since it disappeared during our captivity in Babylon, over 2,600 years ago. Our people have never recovered from the first destruction of the Temple, from the loss of our most sacred national symbol. Those days were traumatic and catastrophic for our people – and for our way of life," Geller said, a genuine sadness creeping into his voice. "I hope this American has some answers for us."

Koslov said nothing. He found his mind returning, as it had every few minutes or so, to the vague intelligence he'd received earlier that day: about Iranian plans to smuggle a nuclear bomb into Israel – and to detonate it.

9

November 13th
Atlantic Ocean

The Iranian salvage crew worked nonstop for three consecutive nights, enshrouded by the absence of moonlight. Three of the Iranian marines had trained with their French shipmates, posing as part of the French crew as they learned how to operate the key equipment required for the mission, which would take place three thousand meters below the ocean's surface on the seabed floor. The three undercover commandos had had no problem slitting the throats of their French "friends" when the time had come, two days ago, when the rest of their commando team had arrived. The Frenchmen were *infidels*, and infidels all ended up in the same place, anyway.

The Iranian crew worked around the clock to unload the nuclear material recovered from the wreckage of the U.S. submarine. It was not an easy task, but they had trained specifically for this mission for over sixteen months.

The *U.S.S. Scorpion* had been declared lost on June 5th, 1968, and it was among the few U.S. Navy submarines to have been declared *officially* lost at sea while not at war. The U.S. sub had specialized in the development of nuclear submarine warfare tactics, often varying her role from hunter to hunted in the typical

Soviet cat-and-mouse games during the Cold War of the 1960's. The U.S. Navy had lost ninety crewmen aboard the *Scorpion* when it sank, and the boat had contained a treasure-trove of highly sophisticated spy gear and manuals, two nuclear-tipped torpedoes, along with a nuclear propulsion system – or at least that's what the official U.S. Navy reports had claimed.

The sinking of the *U.S.S. Scorpion* by a Soviet torpedo, along with the subsequent cover-up attempt by both the Soviet Union and the United States, however, was what had ultimately led Iranian intelligence down a path to the truth: the *Scorpion* had actually contained *eight* nuclear-tipped torpedoes, not two.

The U.S. Navy had always maintained that the nuclear material in both the torpedoes and the propulsion system had unquestionably been relegated to a useless ball of mud and metal on the ocean floor that was harmless to the environment. Despite this claim, though, Iranian scientists had eventually discovered how to utilize the abandoned U.S. nuclear material – to fashion a modern day tactical nuclear weapon.

Nuclear material from seven of the torpedoes, buried deep inside the hull of the *Scorpion*, had been removed from its skeleton and brought aboard the stolen French vessel. The precious material contained inside the torpedoes had proven difficult to retrieve, and one of the nuclear weapons had indeed fused so badly with the ocean floor that it had been rendered useless. The mission only required the contents of four torpedoes, however, so seven nuclear treasure chests had been more than sufficient.

The Iranian naval crew knew that the U.S. Navy often made unannounced visits, using both surface and submarine vessels to ensure that no one visited or tampered with the sacred *Scorpion* coffin and its innards as they rested in the ocean's deep. *Allah was surely with them*, the crewmen thought, as no U.S. Navy vessels had appeared over the last three days.

As far as the rest of the world knew, the French ship *Ile De Sein* had vanished without a trace, and the *U.S.S. Scorpion's* grave had remained undefiled. But the holy, nuclear material, tattooed with its indisputable American signature of origin, was now in the hands of the Iranian Revolutionary Guard.

They prepared to sail straight for Port Said, Egypt.

10

November 14th
Israel

The drive from the submarine port in Haifa to the Defense Ministry building in Tel Aviv was short and direct. The two cities, located on the warm Mediterranean Sea, were about one hundred kilometers apart from each other. Solo and Eteye sat in the back seat of the plain-white Mercedes-Benz van, which resembled a thousand other tourist-sightseeing vehicles driving throughout Israel. Although they were the only two passengers in its plush, VIP-trimmed interior, Eteye sat right next to Solo, unabashedly laying her head on his shoulder while she napped. The military driver, dressed in civilian clothes, made his way through the busy city streets of Tel Aviv.

Ever since they had met, Eteye had fostered a warm, physical and affectionate bond between the two of them. It made Solo trust her, yet, at the same time, he recognized that he did not know this woman at all. Eteye treated Solo like they were something more familiar: an old, married couple, long-time friends, or trusting lovers. However, his heart reminded him that he could not really know *anyone*, let alone someone he had just met a few days ago.

As the van approached the outside concrete barrier of the Defense Military Headquarters, Solo's mind flashed back to the vivid dream he had had on the submarine. He had woken up suddenly inside the steel tube that had been his prison for the last few days, still half-asleep and reliving it.

He was back on Cape Cod, where his father had kept the small beach house that they had all snuck away to—back when they had *all* been a family. It was an average, one-story house, which modestly overlooked the Atlantic Ocean. It was the most personal and private thing his father had ever owned, and it was the only location to which the family never brought guests. It was out of reach of the busy world of high-priced lawyers and the social circles of the big city.

Solo, his brother, and Abay had visited there often as young teenagers, frequently frolicking on the sandy cliffs that surrounded it. It was the three of them back then – before the weekend after Levi and Solomon's graduation from the Naval Academy, when their lives had changed forever and his relationship with his brother had withered away. He had never spoken of Abay again to anyone, not a single soul, since the night that she left him, and he had not talked to his brother since their graduation.

It's been a long time since I've said her name, he'd thought. But then he'd realized, upon waking, that he had not said it in that moment, either – at least not out loud. He had only dreamt it, and he was now even further away, now only *thinking about dreaming* it. Twenty years later, he still couldn't say her name aloud. She had been so much more to him than the girl next door – the beautiful, young refugee from a war-torn African country. He had loved her for as long as he could remember—if there even *was* a thing called love, which he now doubted.

"Where are we going?" Solo managed to say to Eteye. It was a conscious effort to escape the dream's painful memories.

"The Ministry of Defense."

"I don't suppose they are going to arrange to get me a flight back to New York City?"

"The International Airport is right over that way, and no, I don't think so," Eteye said, pointing over to her left and trying to cheer him up. "But you *are* going to meet someone very powerful in this country."

"Who would that be? Chief Rabbi of Israel?" Solo said.

"Good guess," Eteye said, "and close, but not quite."

They both were silent as they drove up to the heavily guarded building. The Israeli Defense Forces General Command Headquarters was striking; it didn't resemble any other military building he had ever visited. It looked to be twenty stories tall and designed by an artist, not a soldier. It was rectangular, higher than it was wide, and it was completely visible through its middle. There was an enormous matte silver tower that ran through the center of the office building and extended out its top with a flare, reminding Solo of a giant Olympic torch. There was an elegant and modern office structure that encircled it, yet somehow it did not actually touch the building or influence it in any way. Solo was amazed by its beauty. Never had he seen a military compound look so inviting, so aesthetically pleasing to the eye.

"Not what you expected?" Eteye said as she caught Solo staring out the van's window.

"Not at all," he responded honestly.

Eteye exited the van first, and Solo admired her slim, curvy figure as it climbed out of the vehicle. She wore a black-and-red wool mini-skirt with black, sheer pantyhose. He was amazed by her ability to climb in and out of vehicles and military vessels while simultaneously maintaining a sophisticated, fashionable air of feminine modesty. And her black, high-heeled shoes never slowed her progress in any way. Her face seemed to glow in the direct desert sunlight, and her beauty momentarily captivated Solo.

He felt comfortable in the new clothes that Eteye had picked out for him. He wore cozy, black dress jeans, with a white button-down shirt and a dark sports jacket. He couldn't remember the last time he'd dressed so casually for an important meeting.

Security was quick but extremely thorough. It was obvious that this was a country where security concerns were placed above all else.

Four military escorts led Eteye and Solo to the building's central elevator. When they entered it, however, they didn't go up, as Solo had expected. Instead, they descended fifteen floors beneath the street level. When the elevator door opened, Solo was shocked to see Ambassador Petur Goldman, his father, standing in front of him.

"Father?" Solo said in disbelief. "What in the world are you doing here?" He turned to Eteye. "You drugged me, kidnapped me, and smuggled me here to meet my *father*? You could have just scheduled a meeting for us at our New York City office."

"There is much for you to learn, Solo," Eteye said, again taking one of his hands into her own. Her touch immediately had the intended effect, and his blood pressure decreased slightly. "I am sorry to tell you that your father is also wanted for questioning by the American authorities, and he has taken sanctuary in this country for the time being."

"Ms. Azeb, what in the world is my son doing here?" Ambassador Goldman asked, equally as alarmed.

Solo turned incredulously to his father and saw from the look in his father's eyes that what Eteye had just said was true.

"Solomon, come. There is much for us to discuss and very little time," she said.

Solo's father took his son's free arm, stiffly, and they followed Eteye down the hallway. They walked through a beautifully decorated passageway, lined with brightly colored artwork. *What kind of military headquarters is this*? Solo asked himself.

They entered a large conference room, which appeared to be reserved for either high-ranking officials or other heads of state. Every electronic-media presentation device known to mankind sat in one corner, and what looked like a fully stocked bar rested in the corner across from it. There were plush leather chairs, stationed in separate one-on-one setups, in the other two corners, and dimly lit lights hovered over a thick, marble conference room table in the center of the room. On the wall opposite the door through which they'd just entered hung numerous flat-screen, high-definition T.V.'s, which displayed various in-progress military conferences.

There were two other people in the room, clearly expecting them as they walked in. Rabbi Ziva Geller sat at the conference room table, his hands folded neatly in front of him. Defense Minister Armando Koslov sat directly across from Geller, his body angling his chair towards the entrance. Eteye closed the door behind them, walked to the table, and lightly touched the screen of a silver iPad that had been stationed in the table's center. Immediately, on every TV screen in the room, a message appeared: *Private Conference in Progress—No Recording Permitted.*

"Solomon, this is my dear friend, Armando Koslov," Solo's father said, introducing the two of them.

"And this is Rabbi Ziva Geller," Eteye added, gesturing to the rabbi.

"Mr. Goldman, I have heard much about you, and it is an honor to finally meet your acquaintance," Geller said in a thick Middle Eastern accent. Solo surmised that the rabbi had to be at least in his late eighties, and he recognized the significance of his all-black suit from his early childhood days at Hebrew school. "I apologize for the manner in which we must meet today, but I'm afraid that these desperate days call for desperate actions."

"Mr. Geller," Solo replied, his exhausted nerves finally getting the better of him. Something about the old man's casual apology had irked the New York attorney. It was as though the rabbi were simply observing the formalities of a social nicety, like cancelling dinner plans or running late for drinks – not the kind of apology necessary to justify drugging and kidnapping someone before dragging him halfway across the world against his will. "I look forward to cutting through the introductions and getting some real answers – like what the *fuck is going on*?!"

Geller did not react in the slightest to Solo's outburst. Instead, he simply stood to offer a vacant chair to Solo. Solo sat, and Geller returned to his seat next to him. Solo's father sat on the opposite side of the rabbi, next to his friend Koslov, and the Defense Minister began to speak to the refugee ambassador.

"My friend, I am sorry that I was not able to tell you of our plans to bring your son here against his will. That was not my doing, and Rabbi Geller will have to explain those unfortunate actions to you," he said, turning to immediately to Solo before Rabbi Geller could interrupt. "Mr. Goldman, I will *cut to the chase*, as you Americans say. Currently, there is a vessel sailing to northern Egypt, which contains American nuclear fuel. Iranian commandos intend to deliver that nuclear package to their comrades inside of Egypt, and then Hamas will attempt to smuggle the cargo through their underground tunnels, into Gaza. We believe that they intend to set off a nuclear bomb, somewhere inside Israel. The fallout, if they are successful, would be devastating to the population of Israel. In fact, much of Israel would become completely uninhabitable."

Solo sat in shock as Koslov folded his hands in front of him, resting them on the table as he continued.

"We are aware of these horrific military plans only because of your father, and his dedication to the survivability of the State of Israel."

Solo stared across the table at his father, who had always been the poster-child for well-dressed aristocrats. He never ran, even if the building was on fire, and his impeccable manners had consistently been the first thing that people had noticed and liked about him, for decades. His father was the encyclopedia-photo equivalent of the word *gentleman.*

But now his father was seventy-eight years old, and he looked even older. Solo had not spent much time with him over the last several years, and he'd generally only spoken to him by e-mail when they had communicated. Ever since his father had deserted his family for *The Other Woman,* their relationship had been difficult, at best. *That was a long time ago*, Solo thought, looking at the aged, wrinkled man across the table.

Solo's father began.

"Solomon, not long ago, one of my dear Muslim brothers in Egypt came to me with the news that you have just heard. He is a well-connected businessman in Egypt's shipping yards and was a dear friend, prior to the recent overthrow of the Hosni Mubarak government. He knows that the consequences will be devastating to his people as well as the Jewish people, should Hamas succeed with its nuclear terrorist plans. As the former Ambassador to Egypt – when there *was* still an Egypt – I immediately reported this intelligence to our American government, but they were unable to verify the information. At this juncture, they do not believe the intelligence is valid, as they are incredulous that the Iranians possess the ability to salvage U.S. nuclear material from the ocean floor. Additionally, they have decided not to share this information with our ally, Israel, out of concern that Israel will make a pre-emptive strike against Egypt or Iran and spark another world oil crisis."

"How in the world could Iran or Hamas get access to American nuclear warheads?" Solo said incredulously. "That is just plainly impossible."

"In 1968, an American nuclear submarine sank. On board was the nuclear fuel from its reactor and its eight nuclear-tipped torpedoes," Ambassador Goldman said.

"1968? Certainly we've cleaned up our mess since then, right?" Solo asked.

"Not exactly. The U.S. Navy simply left the submarine and its contents on the ocean floor," his father said. "In fact, we have left nuclear material all over the world. It was inevitable that this day would come." Ambassador Goldman shook his head knowingly.

Solo's face said it all—pure, sheer disbelief.

Defense Minister Armando Koslov interrupted.

"I am afraid that what your father says is true. The U.S. Navy often passes by the wreckage of the submarine to check on it, but they've left everything right in the same spot since 1968. In 1950 as well, for example, an American B-36 bomber dropped a 30-kilo ton Mark 4 Fat Man nuclear weapon over the Pacific

Ocean before crashing due to severe mechanical difficulties. The bomb was never recovered, and it still sits somewhere on the ocean floor."

The Minister stood from the table and reached his hand across to shake Solo Goldman's hand. His grasp was firm but short.

"Please allow me to officially introduce myself," he said. "I have been the Defense Minister to the State of Israel for the last fifteen years, and our friendly Palestinian sources also have confirmed the intelligence that your father has brought to us. I'm afraid that it's true: recovered American nuclear material is currently on its way to Israel."

"We just left nuclear bombs on the ocean floor for anyone to find?" Solo asked, still in disbelief about his home country's actions over the past sixty years.

Koslov was the first to respond.

"Not just one or two," he said. "In 1957, a U.S. Air Force B-47 bomber flying from Florida to Europe with two 3.4-megaton capsules of nuclear material for bombs failed to meet its aerial refueling plane. Neither the plane nor the nuclear materials were ever recovered. In 1965, the *U.S.S. Ticonderoga*, in the Pacific Ocean near the Ryukyu Islands in Japan, had an A-4 aircraft roll off the ship, into the ocean!" Koslov smirked at the asinine nature of the error. "The aircraft contained one nuclear weapon, and it was never recovered."

Solo thought the Defense Minister had finished when he paused to take a contemplative breath. However, after exhaling, Koslov went on.

"In 1962, near the Johnston Atoll in the Pacific Ocean, a *U.S.S. Thor* rocket malfunctioned, and the rocket was destroyed after liftoff. Its nuclear payload fell into the ocean and, once again, was never recovered. They tried to launch another rocket, and the same thing happened. That makes two nuclear missiles, sitting somewhere on the ocean floor, just waiting for anyone to come along and scoop them up."

No one spoke, least of all Solo, as the impossibly long list continued for another few minutes.

". . . And the list of missing nuclear weapons from the Soviet Union is just as long," Koslov said, shifting to Russia. "In 1968, for example, the Soviets lost a Golf-II class submarine and a K-27 nuclear submarine. The first submarine, with at least three nuclear-tipped missiles, sank off the coast of Hawaii. We don't know for sure how many nuclear weapons were lost on the second one, but it has always been an unconfirmed rumor that the second one was on its way to make a rogue nuclear launch at the United States."

Defense Minister Koslov looked around the room before resting his gaze upon Solo. "My point is that there is an entire ocean, filled with nuclear missiles, torpedoes, and bombs, just waiting for the next terrorist to find them and use them."

"So you hauled me all the way to Israel, against my will, to give me a history lesson on a shitload of missing nuclear weapons?" Solo responded.

"Not at all, Mr. Goldman," Rabbi Geller said. "I have brought you here for a much more important mission than that."

"More important than *nuclear terrorism*?" Solo shot back. "I can't wait to hear what you have prepared for *me*."

The rabbi began to respond. "God's divine providence is at work, and we must have faith—"

The Defense Minister quickly interrupted Geller's sentence while rolling his eyes.

"The policy of the U.S. military is to *neither confirm nor deny* the presence of nuclear weapons in any accidents, so it's hard to tell exactly how much nuclear material the Iranians have recovered, even if this intelligence is accurate. But their chance of success in detonating a United States nuclear device inside the border of Israel is quite high. With the loss of Mubarak as President of Egypt, the border between Israel and Egypt has become alarmingly soft and difficult to monitor. Once those recovered torpedoes reach Egypt, it is almost certain that they'll be smuggled inside Israel, through one of Hamas' many underground tunnels."

"They don't even need to use the tunnels," Ambassador Goldman said. "Israel's southern border with Egypt is over one-hundred and twenty-five miles of mountainous desert, with no fence for most of its length. Bedouin smugglers ferrying drugs, along with thousands of African asylum-seekers, have crossed the border into Israel almost unimpeded for years."

Solo was concerned but confused. "Why am I here?"

"I have no idea, son," Ambassador Goldman said, as kindly as he could. "But the French government confirmed yesterday that their deep-sea recovery ship, the *Ile De Sein*, was in fact lost at sea, sometime during the last seventy-two hours. They have no idea where it sank or what happened to it – it just disappeared."

Koslov went to the bar.

"Anyone need a drink?" No one answered, so he poured himself a scotch in a short whiskey glass. "Until yesterday, Ambassador Goldman's intelligence was unconfirmed and seemed implausible. Today, however, with this news from the French Ambassador, I am afraid the I.D.F. will propose a full naval blockade over all of Egypt and the Suez Canal."

Solo interrupted him, turning to his father as he spoke.

"I still don't get it. You have a *friend* in Egypt – and, don't get me wrong, but a *Muslim* friend, at that – who whispers this unbelievable story in your ear, and now, just because the French say they lost a research boat, Israel is going to engage in the naval blockade of a sovereign Muslim country that has just recently imploded politically? The radical extremists are *looking* for a cause to take over the country, and the conservatives in Israel's military are just going to hand it to them? What do you think Turkey will do when you try to block off the Suez Canal?"

Ambassador Goldman spoke next. "Agreed. The intelligence is too thin at this juncture. And the Americans won't confirm or deny that there even *was* nuclear material left in the *Scorpion*, let alone that it's been removed by someone. That leaves a very conservative and nervous Israeli government with few options. If this intelligence turns out to be true, and Hamas sets off a dirty bomb inside of Israel, there will be nuclear war in the Middle East overnight. Israel has no practical way to stop the material from getting into Gaza, so they'll set up a blockade to try and stop it from getting into Egypt in the first place . . ."

Koslov finished the senior Goldman's thought.

". . . And that blockade may just be the act of war the radical extremists need to rally their war cry throughout the surrounding Muslim countries." He swallowed the last of his scotch and sat back down in his seat.

"And you need a trial lawyer from New York City to do . . . what?" Solo asked, still not understanding what any of this had to with him.

The two men on the opposite side of the table from Solo looked at Rabbi Geller: Ambassador Goldman's face revealed his puzzled intrigue, while Koslov's made no attempt to hide his irritation.

"As I was saying," Geller began, "we have a wonderful miracle, in the middle of this divine crisis, that requires your immediate assistance – and your faith."

"What are you *talking* about? It's been twenty years since I've been in the Navy. And I was a Navy J.A.G., not some missile or nuclear expert," Solo retorted, becoming rapidly more frustrated by the cryptic answers to his blatantly straightforward questions. "How many crises are there?"

"This entire region will be at war in the next week if we do not stop this madness. The I.D.F. will not hesitate to take any and all action against any country, Muslim or not, to ensure those nukes never make it into Egypt," the Defense Minister said. "And, if they do make it in – and Hamas detonates that bomb – Israel will retaliate without restraint against everyone who may have had a hand in this mission. They'll attempt to fully destroy Iran in a massive nuclear exchange, and then it won't be long before Muslim Turkey is drawn into a nuclear exchange with Israel – the Turkish politicians won't be able to stand by and passively watch Israel slaughter their country's Muslim brothers and sisters.

"For that reason, Israel will likely preemptively strike against Turkey, and then it gets even more complicated, since Turkey is a member of N.A.T.O. and has a treaty with the United States that requires your government's protection. Which side will the world's greatest nuclear superpower choose to defend? And how ironic that it all will have started because of American nuclear weapons."

"Okay, okay – I get how insanely dangerous things are going to get," Solo answered, exasperatedly returning to his single, basic question, "but why was I abducted and brought here?"

Rabbi Geller spoke up again. This time, no one interrupted him.

"Ms. Azeb was helping your brother search the Iraqi desert for the most divine object that has ever existed – in fact, you could even call it the world's first weapon of mass destruction," he said. "I believe your brother found, and then hid, the millennia-old map to the weapon's secret location, but – unfortunately for us – we could not get him out of Iraq before the U.S. grabbed him. We're uncertain of where he was taken, and we don't know what he did with the documents that he found in the desert."

"Levi was looking for an ancient weapon?" Solo asked in disbelief. "Does the Marine Corps know that?"

"Yes, they do," Geller answered. "He was the officer in charge of the operation. Ms. Azeb was brought in much later than the original team that began the project. We tried to keep the real purpose of her mission secret from both the Iraqis and the U.S. military. Our goal was to control the situation as best we could – and to obtain the results of the archeological digs."

"What kind of weapon were you and Levi looking for?" Solo turned to Eteye and asked. She had taken a few steps closer to the conference table as she'd listened to the rabbi speak. "I mean – how could any sort of caveman weapon stop the Iranians from detonating their nuclear package?"

Rabbi Ziva Geller calmly and efficiently interjected before Eteye could respond.

"We have much to share with you today," he said. He unbuttoned his suit jacket, exposing more of his starched-white dress shirt. "What do you know about the Ark of War?"

"Ark of War?" Solo said. "Never heard of it."

The Rabbi continued, looking first to Solo's father and then back to Solo, somberly. "Maybe you have never heard it called the Ark of War, but you most certainly know it by its popular Bible name—the Ark of the Covenant."

Solo abruptly sat up in his chair. "*The* Ark of the Covenant?" he asked, again turning to Eteye, his interest peaked.

Geller calmly and slowly began to recount the history of the Ark of the Covenant, or the Ark of War, as Solo had now come to know it.

"The Ark's saga is part science, part history, and part ancient lore," Geller said. "According to the Hebrew scriptures, the Ark was built by Moses, shortly after the great Exodus from Egypt. But our oral tradition tells us otherwise. It tells us that, during the Exodus, Moses and his followers took the secrets of the ancient Egyptians *with them* when they left, including Egypt's most valued and sacred treasure—a war machine, responsible for all of the Egyptian empire's military conquests."

"The Ark of War," Solo deduced.

"Yes. However, the Ark proved to be a dangerously erratic wonder-weapon – a double-edged sword, so to speak, quite capable of wiping out one's enemies as easily as one's own army. It was stubborn and refused to function at crucial military moments."

Solo sat back in his chair, still in disbelief that he was sitting inside a military compound in Israel, listening to old Bible stories and legends about the Egyptians and Moses. Eteye came and sat next to him, immediately taking his hand into hers. She leaned into him and pressed her shoulder against his.

"Tell him about Uzzah," she said, "about how he was instantly struck dead by a flash of energy, straight from the Ark."

Solo was intrigued by the strangely familiar story. "I remember that poor, dumb bastard from Hebrew school," he joked. However, he immediately understood from her silence that Eteye had wanted him to take Geller's words seriously. She ignored his comment and continued.

"How we have no idea what Uzzah did wrong in his handling of the Ark," she said. "Tell him about that part."

"She is right," Geller acknowledged. "In the current Hebrew Torah, which has been translated and re-translated over thousands of years, we have lost the original meaning of why Uzzah was killed, or *smote*, as it says. I guess, in the end, he was just another one of the thousands of unwitting victims to the Ark."

"So, you're telling me that this ancient Jewish W.M.D. killed this man, Uzzah, for some unexplained reason?" Solo asked in an effort to take the rabbi seriously.

"Let me tell you more," Geller continued. He reached under the conference room table and pulled out a large, blue book. He flipped to a page that had been marked with a yellow sticky note and began to read a passage from the Torah.

"' . . . *And fire came forth from the presence of the Lord and devoured them and they died before the Lord.*'"

The rabbi looked up from the book's Hebrew inscriptions. "Even the sons of Aaron tried to pay homage to the Ark," he said, "but they probably had no idea how to safely operate the Ark, and it devoured them."

He turned his attention back to the book and continued to read.

"'*And there came out a fire and consumed the 250 men that offered incense.*' When the King of Judah, attempted to worship in the Temple where the Ark of War was stored, '*the tumors even* rose up in his forehead.' As a precautionary measure, whenever the Senior Military General, Joshua, deployed the weapon against an enemy target, he established a half-mile safe zone around the Ark."

Rabbi Geller continued to recount biblical history for several minutes. He explained that the Ark had become treacherously unreliable when the knowledge of Egypt's scientists had failed to pass from Moses to the rulers after him. At one point, the Ark of War had been staged at Shiloh, in ancient Israel, with just two guards. But then, at the Battle of Eben-ezer, the Hebrews had lost four thousand men, so they'd sent for the Ark of War in a last-ditch effort to win the battle. However, the military weapon had failed to operate. Some 30,000 Hebrew soldiers were slaughtered, and the Ark of War had been captured.

However, the Philistines had had no idea how to control the Hebrew weapon of war they had taken. They'd paraded it back in triumph to their coastal city of Ashdod, only to have tumors break out on an epidemic level from exposure to the weapon. The captured war machine had eventually been moved from city to city—with the same disastrous results each time. Finally, the Philistines decided they'd suffered enough, and they'd sent the Ark back to the Hebrews on a cart, drawn by a pair of oxen.

When the Hebrews saw the return of their Ark of War, they had rejoiced. But then the war machine killed over fifty-thousand of them, simply because they'd looked into it.

"What do you mean, 'looked *into* it' – how do you look into it?" Solo interrupted.

Geller did not answer. He merely continued the story.

"The innocent man, Uzzah, was killed when he tried to prevent the war machine from falling off the Philistines' cart. After that, the weapon was locked away, out of sight, for the next twenty years."

Geller described to Solo how the Hebrews had lost the knowledge of how to properly use the Ark of War after Moses had passed.

The great warrior, King David, had wanted the Ark of War in his new capital city of Jerusalem, but he'd needed to first ensure the machine operated properly after the previous disasters. After three months of successful operations, he had summoned the Ark's guardians, the Levities, to bring it to Jerusalem.

Geller described the vault that King Solomon, King David's son, had built in Jerusalem to guard the dangerous war machine. King Solomon had called it the Holy of Holies, and he'd placed it inside the great Temple's fortress.

"*And God gave King Solomon wisdom and understanding exceeding much . . . And Solomon's wisdom excelled . . . all of the wisdom of Egypt,*" Geller read, his eyes meeting Solo's as he finished the sentence. "It's interesting that our scriptures felt the need to reference Egypt's wisdom. Don't you think so?"

Geller resumed his story, while his audience of four listened intently. He explained that, upon the completion of the Temple in Jerusalem, King Solomon had finished what Moses had begun. He'd built a fortress around a vault to house the most potent military weapon the earth had ever known—a war machine that contained pure energy, *the Face of God,* as it had been called by the ancients.

"*For he was wiser than all men . . .*"

But, even in the Jerusalem Temple, which had seemed to safely protect and guard the mysterious weapon, the Ark's operators had taken great care to protect themselves. Whenever they'd approached it, they'd cover themselves in thick garments, tying a rope to the operator's ankle to pull his body out of the vault, should he suddenly and mercilessly be killed by the Ark.

In 597 B.C., the world's newest super power, Babylon, had laid siege on the capital city of Jerusalem with the aim of capturing the infamous Ark. Geller explained that the Babylonians had prevailed, destroying both King Solomon's Temple and the city of Jerusalem in their frenzied search for the Ark of War. They removed everything of value from the Temple's vaults and then burned the temple to the ground.

"The second book of Kings and the Prophet Jeremiah's writings describe in great detail everything Babylon's king, Nebuchadnezzar, had pillaged from King Solomon's fortress," the rabbi said before returning to the story.

By the time the Babylonian soldiers finally secured access to the Temple's vault, however, the greatest war machine the earth had ever seen was *gone*. The weapon that had singlehandedly formed the Egyptian and Hebrew Empires had simply vanished.

The Babylonian king Nebuchadnezzar was furious at the weapon's disappearance. He killed the king of the Hebrew Empire in Jerusalem, and he took most of the Jewish population into captivity and marched them to Babylon. Those that escaped went to the prophet Jeremiah and asked them where they should hide. Before Jeremiah could give them an answer, he disappeared without a trace for ten days.

"Where did he go?" Solo asked as Geller paused to take a breath.

"A very good question, Mr. Goldman," Geller said excitedly. "Why would Jeremiah tell everyone that read his writings that he disappeared for ten days and then never mention where he went or why he disappeared?"

"Seems like he was trying to draw attention to his actions without fully explaining himself," Solo answered.

"Precisely. Jeremiah wrote that if all the remaining people went to Egypt, they would die there. But here's what's interesting. They all *did* go to Egypt, including Jeremiah himself, and they never returned. Jeremiah is drawing our attention to Egypt. He wants us to *look* in Egypt."

"Where exactly in Egypt did they go?" Solo asked.

Geller again began to read from the Torah in his lap, from a page labeled "Jeremiah the Prophet."

"*The word came to Jeremiah concerning all the Jews that dwelt in the land of Egypt, that dwelt at Migdol . . . *"

Geller looked up from the page. "In Hebrew, '*migdol*' means 'tower,' or a fortress," he explained.

Solo suddenly understood. "He got the Ark of War out of Jerusalem before the Babylonians got inside the Temple vault, and then he hid it in some *fortress* in Egypt?"

"Very good, Mr. Goldman," Geller said. "Almost all Hebrew scholars seem to agree that Jeremiah died in Egypt. Most suspect that he died wherever he hid the Ark of War."

"Some think the Ark of the Covenant is buried under the Temple Mount in Jerusalem," Koslov interjected.

"It's highly unlikely that Jeremiah would have buried it on the Temple Mount in Jerusalem as the Babylonians approached. If its location had ever leaked out to Nebuchadnezzar, the king would have had all the time in the world to simply dig it up," Rabbi Geller answered. "Also, there's no way that Jeremiah would have taken the risk of leaving the war machine in Jerusalem, which he knew would be overtaken soon by the Babylonians."

Solo spoke next. "Where is this Egyptian fortress where Jeremiah supposedly hid the Ark, then?"

No one answered.

"I'm afraid no one knows," Geller said, shifting uncomfortably in his chair. "But the time is now when all shall be seen. The Eternal, blessed is He, has created this wonderful opportunity for us – a threat, from our Muslim enemies, which will lead them to punishment, once and for all."

Solo stared at Geller suspiciously trying to understand his motives. Eteye quickly changed the subject.

"The key to finding the Ark of War is in finding the book with the gold pages – the one that your brother found in the Babylonian ruins inside Iraq. Jeremiah himself added his writings to that book after Jerusalem fell to the Babylonians. But now your brother has disappeared, along with the artifacts he'd found. We know the Americans are interrogating him in secret somewhere, trying to discover what he knows. We're hoping that he told *you* where he hid the scrolls—and the golden book—before he was captured."

The discovery as to why he had been secreted to Israel left Solo perturbed and exasperated.

"I'm sorry you've brought me all the way here for *that*," he said. "However, my brother and I haven't spoken in years. I have no idea where the book is, and I'd never heard of it until just a few minutes ago. Sorry to disappoint, but my brother has never left me any clues to *anything*, let alone clues to where he hid your ancient writings."

Everyone in the room stared at each other blankly. Geller's disappointment permeated the air, like fine dirt in a blinding desert sand storm.

11

November 14th
Egypt

The *Ile De Sein* reached Egypt's Port Said twelve hours ahead of schedule – another clear indication to all the elite marines on board the 140-meter ship that a higher power's blessing was on their side.

The Egyptian port had been founded in 1859, when the Suez Canal was built, and it served as a fueling station for ships that were passing through the canal's waters. It was a busy harbor, filled with foreign vessels from all over the world.

The *Ile De Sein* navigated to a prearranged docking slip, which had been reserved for a non-existent Turkish oil tanker.

The raging political turmoil in Egypt would prevent anyone from noticing the improper docking of a missing French vessel for at least twenty-four hours. By then, the custom-built, thick steel container, which fit perfectly in the back of a full-sized pickup truck, would be in the Sinai desert, on its way to a prearranged border crossing into Israel.

During the voyage, the men had carefully disinterred the nuclear materials from their warped and sea-ravished cocoons, packaging them safely and efficiently into heavy lead casings for their transport through the desert.

The Iranian marines changed into common street clothes, placing their compact automatic weapons throughout the front and rear of the truck, which had been parked directly in front of their docking slip the night before.

The Persian soldiers had abandoned all their radioactive protective suits at sea before entering Port Said—not that it would matter. By the time the local port authorities would discover the French deep-sea recovery vessel, and by the time anyone of significance would inspect the vessel and figure out that nuclear materials had been on board, the group of dedicated commandoes would be well inside Israel, close to accomplishing their mission.

12

November 14th
Tel Aviv, Israel

Solo was livid as he and Eteye walked out of I.D.F. Headquarters.

"What have you gotten me into?" he asked. They stood in the courtyard under the warm desert sun, with the military building towering directly behind them.

"I'm sorry this doesn't make sense to you right now, but there is someone else whom you must meet – someone that no one here can know about. I will tell you more when there are not so many listening ears around. I promise that you will fully understand why you were brought here then."

"I wish I knew what my brother was up to and what he did with your book. More importantly, though, I would rather not be here if the Iranians really do smuggle in a nuclear bomb."

"Solo, there are matters in this world that are far more important than our daily lives – more important than you and I, personally."

Solo looked up toward the hot sun overhead. "I bet my brother gobbled up your Ark of War legends with a spoon."

Eteye took two steps toward Solo to stand directly in front of him.

"You're right—he *did* believe the legends. And that is why your brother vanished before Geller could get his hands on the scrolls. It's also why Rabbi Geller and all of his resources will not stop until he possesses what your brother found."

"I just don't get it. Some golden chest our ancestors lugged around the Egyptian desert three thousand years ago has everyone turning into master spies and kidnapping people right off the street? Do you really think some cave-dwelling ancestors of ours from the desert could have built a modern-day weapon of mass destruction? I don't buy it."

"Soon you will understand. No one here can tell you what your part in this really is," she said. "You must hear the oral tradition directly from its source. The Hebrew oral scriptures have been passed down for generations—since the beginning of time. The ancient Hebrews only started writing down their traditions into Biblical scriptures twenty-seven hundred years ago. The oral tradition is far older. It contains the actual words of God."

"For heaven's sake. Just tell me the story, or at least tell me what it is that you want me to do. I don't need to hear it from some black-hat voodoo doctor. I need to get back to New York and back to my life."

"Solo!" Eteye exclaimed in a loud, shocked voice. "Your life in New York is not important right now! Your brother's life depends on you. This Jewish country needs you. *You* must complete the journey your brother started, and *you* must find the Ark of War before circumstances spin out of control and the world erupts into madness. Rabbi Geller and his self-righteous religious zealots wield enormous power inside the Israeli government. They have all the resources they need to pursue this matter to the very end."

"I'm a good lawyer, but I know nothing about Babylonian religious artifacts buried in the Iraqi desert. If Levi couldn't find your Ark, there is no way I could ever find it, even if I wanted to—and I *don't!*" Solo stated directly.

"Defense Minister Koslov will not say it in public, but he believes that if an Iranian bomb gets into Israel, Geller and his religious zealots will use it to promote their ideas of divine providence," Eteye said. "He thinks that they won't hesitate to let it detonate if they believe that it is God's will, as crazy as that seems. They have blind faith. Can you imagine what they would do with something far more powerful, like the Ark of War?"

Before Solo could respond, Defense Minister Koslov and Ambassador Goldman walked out of the building's entrance and joined them.

"I'm sorry you've been brought here at such a dangerous time," Solo's father said to him. "I had no idea what Levi was up to in Iraq, and I certainly had no idea that Rabbi Geller was planning to transport you here."

"I have just filled your son in on Rabbi Geller's plans as well," Eteye said before turning to Ambassador Goldman. "I can assure you that the rabbi believes this bomb to be part of God's will, and he has no intention of stopping it. He believes it to be the fulfillment of a prophecy that will lead to the rebuilding of the Temple and the tearing down of the Muslim Dome of the Rock. He'll use his considerable influence to ensure that his religious vision for this country is fulfilled."

Eteye's hand had gently grasped Solo's elbow as she spoke to his father. It soothed him, and his irritability began to subside.

"I know you both have much to do," she said to the two men.

"I'm staying at the French Embassy. The French Ambassador is a personal friend of mine," Solo's father replied. "I'll call him right now and ask that he make room for you as well. I'm sure he will take care of all your needs, and I'll arrange everything."

"Thank you, Mr. Ambassador," Eteye said. She moved her body closer to Solo's. They resembled a couple that had been married for several years, and she seemed strangely familiar with Solo for having only met him a few days ago. "We appreciate your assistance and kindness. We will follow you there now."

The drive from I.D.F. Headquarters to the French Embassy took about twenty minutes in rush-hour traffic. The Embassy sat directly on one of Tel Aviv's most popular Mediterranean beaches. Just as his father had promised, security and embassy staff had prepared for them by the time they arrived, and Eteye and Solo were immediately escorted to the embassy's high-ranking guest quarters. Their suite overlooked the sapphire blue Mediterranean Sea.

Standing on the balcony and looking south, Solo could see the old city of Jaffa. To the north, he watched the sailboats floating up and down the sea. Directly in front of the embassy grounds below them was a spectacular beach, a picturesque visage of sun and warm waters.

Eteye knew that the embassy provided absolute security and secrecy. No one, including the Americans, would ever know they had been there. For Solo's mission to have any chance of success, it would be imperative that no one know where he was or what he was doing.

Solo turned back to the room, where the two of them would be staying for the evening. It was decorated in a classic, elegant French style, and it reminded Solo of the Ritz in Paris. However, the spacious living quarters only contained one bedroom and bed. Eteye seemed to read his thoughts. She walked onto the balcony to join Solo.

"Don't worry, I don't bite, and I never sleep with anyone on a first date," she said, smiling.

Her necklace again caught Solo's eye, and this time he looked at it directly. "Your necklace seems very old to me," he said.

"It is very old, indeed – thousands of years old. Someone very dear to me gave it to me a long time ago. I have worn it ever since." She stared straight into his eyes as she spoke, as though she was hoping for some specific response from him.

"You were married?"

"Yes. A long time ago. He was a remarkable soul," Eteye said, still intently studying Solo's face.

"What made him remarkable?"

"He was my king, and I was his queen. Sadly, I keep looking for him. I have ever since he passed away."

"May I?" Solo reached out and gently took the golden knot into his hand. The weight of it struck him first, and then the sensation of touching Eteye so close to her breasts followed. "This feels like solid gold. It's very heavy."

"It's not the metal that makes it valuable to me," Eteye said, remaining still as Solo moved the necklace through his fingers. "It makes me glad to see it in your hands."

"Why?"

"Sorry—I didn't mean to say that. It just feels good to remember happy memories from a long time ago, when it was given to me."

"When are you going to tell me what's actually going on here?" he asked, changing the subject. "I've played along so far, but don't you, my abductor, owe me some answers at this point?"

Eteye moved into Solo while he examined the jewelry that dangled around her neck. Her warm body remained close to his, and she showed no discomfort or hesitancy about their closeness. To him, her proximity felt natural.

"What do you want to know, Mr. Goldman?"

"I want to know who you really are and how you fit into this bizarre story."

"Fair enough. I will try to answer your questions," she said, turning to look out at the sea. She watched the people below slowly leaving the beach to return to their homes and hotels for the evening. "My family has had significant influence in this region for many years. As I told you, my mother came from great wealth, and my father was a royal politician. My associates have continued to be people of influence throughout this part of the world for a long time. However, about six months ago, I was asked to help guide your brother while he performed his duties in the Iraqi desert. I enjoyed working with him. He is a good man, and he understood right away what was at stake."

Solo was struck by a wave of jealously as he heard Eteye's comment. He had not allowed himself to feel that emotion for a long time. So much pain had consumed him after Abay's death, and he had learned then how powerful and destructive his emotions could be. He'd thought he had subdued and buried them all.

As though Eteye could read his mind, she grabbed his hand, holding it with her fingers entwined in his as she continued.

"The Americans had no idea what Saddam had discovered— what he was really doing in the desert. They were content to just go through the motions, document everything that maniac had uncovered, and ensure that everything ended up in the next politically correct museum. But, when one of our undercover Israeli agents found some of the original source documents for the Torah at the Babylonian dig, everything changed."

"Why would a Torah scroll be so important to national security?" Solo asked. He left Eteye's side and walked to the fully stocked bar in the room's corner. He looked at her, his eyes asking if she, too, wanted a drink. She waved him off before answering his question.

"Not *a* Torah scroll—*the* Torah scroll," she corrected him.

"What does that mean – '*the* Torah scroll?'"

"You know, the very first one. Jeez, Solo, how did you ever get out of Hebrew school without knowing the history of Jewish scriptures?"

Solo smirked. "God, religion, and I don't really mix. We had a falling out a while back."

"What happened?"

"It doesn't matter anymore."

"Sure it does. Tell me what happened."

"Let's just say that there was one point in my life when I needed God more than I've ever needed anyone, and he never showed up. After that, I didn't believe in fairy tales anymore. Also, I just did not buy God *writing* the Ten Commandments with his finger on some stone tablet and then giving it to Moses on a mountaintop. Religion seems like the naughty-or-nice Santa Claus list."

"I think you are mixing up your religions," Eteye said. She walked to the massive, king-sized bed, which was covered in a gold-and-purple comforter and plush, matching pillows, and sat on its edge.

"So, what did you mean by '*the* Torah Scroll?'" Solo asked again. She waited until he had finished making his drink to respond.

"The Hebrew Torah, the first five books of the Hebrew Bible, has been passed down by oral tradition since the stories were first told. At some point, the oral tradition was written down. Some Jews even believe that Moses wrote the first five books himself, as God dictated them to him."

"Yep. I remember that story."

"Anyway," Eteye said, rolling her eyes in exasperation. "The stories were written by several different authors, and there were several different versions of the same story."

"Different versions?"

"Take, for instance, the first book in the Torah, Genesis. There are two completely different versions of the creation story, right in its beginning chapters," Eteye said, getting up and grabbing a large satchel that she had brought with her. She pulled out a copy of the Torah and turned to the beginning of Genesis before returning to the edge of the massive bed. For the next few minutes, she explained the two different versions of the creation story to Solo.

"As far back as the late 1600's, Biblical scholars have speculated that Moses wrote Genesis based on many different existing written and oral stories. Since then, scholars have uncovered numerous authors and versions, all edited together into the one Torah we have today."

Solo was amazed. "I never heard any of that in Hebrew school. How can you tell who wrote what?"

"It's not that difficult, when you know what you're looking for. Some authors only use a certain name when they speak of God. One author always calls God by the personal name, *Yahweh*, while another always uses the name *Elohim*. One author favored the Northern Tribes, another the Southern ones. Another writer was a priest during the Babylonian exile, and he focused on the code for priesthood and worship. The most important thing, though, is that at some point along the way, someone collected all the stories that had been written down by the various authors and edited them into one version—the Bible we have today."

Solo understood right away where she was headed.

"You found the original source documents for all these stories in the Babylonian library, didn't you?"

Eteye nodded. "We found much more than that, but I'll get to that eventually. When the Israelis realized what the Americans had uncovered in Iraq, there was a massive upheaval in the inner political and religious institutions of this country."

"Why? I thought they would be excited to find their original masterpieces," Solo said. He sat next to Eteye, his drink still in his hand.

"Bible scholars have known – or at least strongly suspected – for a long time that the version of the Bible we possess and use today is not accurate, compared to the original writings. They've understood that politics, religion, economics, war, and cultural evolution have changed the original stories into the ones we have today. You must remember, the world's three largest religions—Judaism, Christianity, and Islam—are built on the stories and the scriptures handed down from God as recorded in the Torah."

Eteye paused to let Solo mentally catch up before continuing.

"Now, imagine that you find the original source documents—the original versions of Genesis, the original Ten Commandments, the original stories as to who God gave the Holy Land to, and the original commandments from God as to who His chosen people really are. Then, imagine that the source documents tell a completely different story than the version in our Bible today."

Solo took it all in.

"How different could they really be?"

Eteye didn't directly answer his question.

"What if the original version said that God blessed Ishmael instead of Isaac, that God had made Ishmael's descendants the chosen people?" she asked. "What if the Hebrews conquered the Holy Land by sheer, brute force, and God never actually *gave* any of it to them—they just took it? What if the prophecies foretelling Jesus as the Messiah were never written by actual prophets?"

"My God," Solo said. "You'd have complete religious anarchy if those documents ever got out. Jews, Christians, and Muslims would consume each other overnight."

"Exactly," Eteye said. "But no one will actually know how different these original versions are unless we find where Levi hid them and actually read them for ourselves. That's where I was brought in. Someone needed to discreetly collect the source documents, to read and study them before revealing them to the entire world. There needed to be discretion as to what could be released and when. I was charged with covertly extracting all the documents from Iraq, without the blundering Americans becoming aware of what they really were, much less their absence."

"You convinced my brother to help you."

"He was not as difficult to convince as you are," Eteye said. "Your brother and I worked together closely over the first few months, cataloguing hundreds and thousands of artifacts and—"

"What is my father, a U.S. ambassador, doing working with the Israeli government behind America's back?" Solo interjected.

"What is he—some sort of spy?" Solo uncomfortably thought. However, he immediately looked at Eteye's face to see her reaction, hoping it would alleviate his fear. Unfortunately, it did not.

"Your father has helped the Israeli government from time to time, when a man of reason has been required," Eteye said, dodging his question.

"Helped? You mean he shared secrets. He spied for the Israelis!"

"I don't see your father as a spy, Solo. He has loyalties to both the United States and to Israel, and he has worked very hard over the years to keep those loyalties separate. But sometimes doing the right thing is not so black and white."

"Unbelievable," he muttered. He swallowed the rest of his drink in one gulp.

"In any event, once your brother realized what had been uncovered in the Iraqi desert and its possible impact on the world, he agreed to help me get the scrolls, along with the book that contains Jeremiah's writings, out of Iraq. But that's when all hell broke loose."

Solo was still in shock over the news of his father. He tried to turn his attention back to Eteye.

"What do you mean? What happened?"

"We found a book with gold pages and ancient writings. All of the words and wisdom of King Solomon and the ancients before him are contained within it. It is called the *Book of the Dead*."

"I heard you mention a book with gold pages back at I.D.F.'s headquarters," he said, getting up from the bed to make another drink. "But what is so significant about one book?" Solo turned from the bar and the silver ice bucket he was reaching into and looked at Eteye expectantly.

"It's not just any book," she said. "It's the *original*. Jeremiah added his writings to the very first Book of the Dead."

"You think Jeremiah's writings tell where he hid the Ark of War?" Solo asked.

"We know they do. We just have never had the original to decipher the clues he left."

Solo finished making his drink and walked back to the bed. She waited for him to sit back down next to her before continuing.

"In the 13th century, a Rabbi named Bachya mysteriously wrote of a code that he had discovered buried inside the Torah. It began with the first Hebrew letter in the book of Genesis."

"*Bet*. That's the letter, right?"

"Exactly. See, you do remember your Hebrew! You might not remember this, though. The Torah is made up of 304,805 Hebrew letters. Rabbi Bachya found that the letters *bet, hey, resh* and *dalet* formed a four-letter code that repeated itself, with *exactly* forty-two letters between each successive four-letter code."

"What did the code say?"

"As you know, the entire Hebrew calendar is based on the lunar cycle. The code mapped out the length and timeline of the lunar cycle to a five-decimal-place accuracy."

"Wow," Solo commented.

"Since then, scholars and rabbis over the centuries have found numerous E.L.S. codes buried in the Torah."

"What is E.L.S?"

"Equidistant Letter Spacing. The basic idea is that all the Hebrew letters in the Torah contain a series of equally spaced letters, or E.L.S., and they map out something that looks like a crossword puzzle. The codes get really complicated, but many believe the actual Torah letters contain the secrets of the ancient

Egyptians. Remember, the Torah was written at various stages and by many different authors *after* Moses left Egypt with the wealth and secrets of the mystical and technologically advanced Egyptians. Some people even believe these maps are the hands of God—God writing with his finger on the Ten Commandments, so to speak."

Eteye continued, "With modern computers, many more of these complicated codes have been uncovered. But none of the deciphered codes were the ones we were looking for because we didn't have the original. We had *versions* of original writings, but they had been altered over time. Thus, their codes and messages had changed, too. But, when we found Solomon's *Book of the Dead*—"

"—all of that changed," Solo finished, nodding.

"Levi found a book that goes back even further than King Solomon. It is a book of wisdom and magic. Solomon called it his *Acts of Solomon*. But much of the wisdom contained within it came from the ancient Egyptians and from civilizations *before* them. They had called it the *Book of the Dead*. It contained the knowledge of good and evil. The pathway to eternal life is within it. We originally suspected—and now *know*—that the prophet Jeremiah cared for and possessed Solomon's Book of the Dead and added his writings to that book. And we know Jeremiah died in the same place he hid the Ark. We believe he left a map to the Ark's final resting place coded inside that book."

"There's more to this Ark of War than just some sort of superweapon, isn't there?"

Eteye smiled.

Solo could still picture Geller describing in detail how the poor Israelite had touched the Ark to prevent it from falling off the cart, and God had killed the poor, dumb peasant instantly. "Why would God kill a man just for trying to help? After all, if God really lived inside the Ark, then the poor man should have gotten a reward or something for trying to keep God's house from falling into the mud."

"Whatever the origin of that story was, it was effective," Eteye said.

"What do you mean?"

"It made everyone terrified to be around the Ark or go near it. If the goal was to keep the masses away from the Ark of War, then don't you think some fantastic story about God instantly striking a man dead for his innocent gesture did the trick?"

"I see your point. Seems like a good way to keep everyone at a healthy distance," Solo answered.

Eteye answered his question for him quoting from the bible from memory, "*and the anger of the Lord was kindled against Uzzah, and he smote him, because he put his hand to the Ark: and there he died before God!*"

13

November 14th
Tel Aviv, Israel

Eteye and Solo left the embassy to find dinner in town. They wore casual hats and clothes, trying to make themselves resemble tourists as much as possible. Eteye had told Solo that Israeli intelligence indicated that the Americans had no idea where he was. So long as he didn't do something stupid, like use his credit card or cell phone in Tel Aviv, they were likely to stay under the Americans' radar.

"How is it that you have never been to Israel?" Eteye asked as they turned a corner and found themselves in a crowded local alleyway. Merchants covered both sides of the street, and goods hung from every nook and cranny of the entire alleyway for as far as Solo could see.

He saw two women standing at a table, where piles of spices had been poured into heaps, like fine sand on a beach. Every color imaginable rested on the table, and each mound of spice had a little stick with its name written on a card, which protruded from the top of the pile. The two women were haggling with the spice trader, and the three of them were impressively vocal and animated in their negotiations.

"I never saw a reason to come visit," Solo said as they walked past the pyramids of spices. They continued through the market to a row of food, meat, and a variety of fish.

"How can you be Jewish and not see a reason to come to Israel?"

"I'm not a big fan of fanatical religious fundamentalists."

"Your country has the same groups," Eteye said. She held his arm with both of her hands as she walked alongside him.

"You're right."

Solo had noticed that she was always close to his side, attached to him, no matter where they were. It was not as though she were attempting to be intimate with him, though. It was just her style, her personality. When she was with someone, she was fully *with* them. She was always in the moment, Solo noticed. As he looked over his shoulder at her, she smiled back at him and hugged his arm a little harder. It was as though her smile said, *I know*—like they were long-time friends who had recently reunited.

"My mother is not Jewish. She was a staunch Catholic. Her family disowned her when she married my father. Today she is probably what you would call a *mystic* Catholic," Solo said as they negotiated their way through the crowded street. "However, she wanted my brother and I to be raised in the Jewish tradition. She always said that God was big enough to accept her *and* her Jewish children and entire family. I think she embodies what real love and tolerance is all about. She had a huge impact on my concept of God, and, more importantly, on my concept of who God is not."

"Did she ever reconcile with her family?"

"No. Not even after my father divorced her, when she was all alone with just us kids. They never helped her in any way."

"That must have been incredibly hard and lonely for her. Raising two kids in the Jewish faith by herself and not even being Jewish?"

Solo stopped looking at the busy market and turned to Eteye.

"What kind of religion tells you to disown your own daughter just because she marries a Jew? What kind of God says that is okay?" he asked tersely.

"I don't have those answers."

"No one does. It was the beginning of the end between me and everyone else's idea of God."

"What was it like, being raised Jewish with a mother who was not? That would never happen in Israel."

"It was incredibly tough. In Hebrew school, my brother and I were considered half-breeds."

"Half-breeds?"

"Crazy fundamental religious teachings. They said that, unless your mother was Jewish, you weren't really Jewish. It didn't matter that our father was one of the most well-known Jewish politicians in New York City. We still were not considered Jewish by some."

"What happened?" Eteye asked, listening intently.

"My mother stormed the rabbi's office. I still remember it like it was yesterday. She had fully prepared for the meeting with the school's head rabbi. She began with, '*If Abraham, the Father of the Jewish nation, can have a Hittite for a mother, certainly having a Catholic for a mother can't be any worse!*' She then went on with a list of Jews whose mothers were not Jewish. I can't remember them all, but I remember that, when she got to King David, she reminded the rabbi that David was a descendant of Ruth, who was born a Gentile, and married a Jew, just like she did. She also demanded that the rabbi explain how Sarah could be Jewish since her mother was not Jewish. She then asked him if Isaac was Jewish since his mother was not Jewish. They argued in front of us for quite a while. But after that meeting, no one ever referred to us as half-breeds again."

"Tell me about Abay," Eteye said. She stopped at an outdoor coffee shop and sat down at a patio table. "You have mentioned her several times."

Solo began to open up to her as Eteye ordered two espressos from the waiter. "Her family members were Jewish refugees from Ethiopia in the early 1980's."

"Ethiopia?" Eteye asked.

"I guess they were being slaughtered by the thousands when the C.I.A. and the Israeli military took action to airlift all of the Jews out of Africa. I remember Abay telling me that the covert military action had been code-named Operation Solomon."

"Operation Solomon?" Eteye said, blankly.

"Obviously, that name always stuck with me. Thousands of Jews were rescued and taken to Israel. Abay lost her parents in the Sudan during the operation, I think, and our local synagogue took her in. I can't really remember any more. I think she was fifteen or sixteen when she moved in next door. I remember that she spent practically all her time with my family at my mother's apartment. It felt like she had always been with us. She was—" Solo speech broke off as he picked up a napkin from the table and held it in his hand.

"You were in love with her," Eteye said, her eyes not meeting his. She paid the waiter before standing and leading him by the arm to the next table, which was covered with colorful scarves.

"She died a long time ago, so I guess it doesn't matter anymore," Solo said.

"How did she die?"

"She drowned."

"Why don't you talk to your brother anymore?" Eteye ventured.

"I suppose Levi told you about that while the two of you worked together in Iraq?"

"Not really. He was as silent on the matter as you are. He said that the two of you had been very close growing up—*inseparable*, I think he said. But then something happened, and you blamed him for it. He said that you had both gone your separate ways after that."

Eteye paused. "You seem sad. Is it because of Abay?"

"I'm not sure," Solo said. He looked at the crowded market and reflected on that night long ago at the Cape Cod beach house – the night that life had changed in an instant, for all of them.

"Do you miss your brother?"

"Yes," Solo blurted, without thinking about it. "We have been apart for so long now, so I guess neither of us . . . well, really *knows* each other anymore, I suppose."

Eteye removed a pen from her purse and wrote several numbers on a napkin before casually placing it on the table next to them. The man sitting at the table slowly picked it up, stood, and walked away.

"So you both went to the same school?" Eteye asked, returning her look to Solo.

Solo watched the man walk off and shook his head in disbelief. Nothing Eteye did surprised him at this point. He continued, ignoring the stranger to whom Eteye had just given the napkin.

"Yes. With my father's connections and his strong sense of patriotism, he made sure both Levi and I served our time in the military. We had always been very competitive with each other growing up."

"Because you were fraternal twins?"

"I don't know. I think we both just liked to win. Levi always reminded me he was born six minutes ahead of me, though."

"Yes, he told me that several times when we were together," Eteye laughed.

"He chose the Marine Corps after graduation and did several combat tours, ultimately landing in Military Intelligence."

"And you chose to go to law school and make the big bucks," Eteye joked jovially.

"Yes. I went into the Navy, and then I was a Navy J.A.G. officer after law school for two tours. I got out as soon as I had paid the Navy back for my schooling. I started with my father's law firm and worked my way to the top. Believe me, my father did not give me any special handouts just because I was his son."

"Oh, I don't doubt that for a second, from what I've heard about your father."

"My father *was* a good man once. He has been lonely for as long as I have known him, though. He left my mother and us a long time ago to go screw his secretary. That didn't last, and he has been different ever since."

"Different how?"

"He split our family apart. Tore it in half to be with some woman—whom everyone but him knew just wanted his money. I wanted nothing to do with him for a long time. I still hate him for what he did to Mother, but I can also see the massive regret he carries over what he did."

They drank their coffee and continued through the market. Eteye stopped at another stand of scarves and picked out one that was deep purple. She tied it around the top of her head before weaving it through her hair, down to the bottom of her black ponytail. She handed the merchant fifty shekels and smiled as she looked at Solo, wanting him to approve of her purchase.

"I like it," he said. "Purple is very much your color."

"Thank you! I have heard purple is the color of royalty."

"Maybe you are some long-lost queen," Solo said, taking her hand as they resumed their walk through the crowed marketplace. "That seems to fit you. A beautiful queen in a past life?"

"Who knows," Eteye said. "Maybe you were a famous king in another life, too. You do have the name of the most famous king of all, you know."

Solomon smiled but said nothing in response. It had been a long time since he had been so open about his feelings, and his memories of his family. Eteye had an obvious effect on him, and he knew it.

They walked through the alleyway and exited the market directly in front of the beach. They followed the coastline hand-in-hand as they made their way back to the French Embassy. To anyone who noticed them, they looked like a happy tourist couple that had been together for a long, long time.

When they reached their room, Eteye excused herself to the restroom, and Solo sat on the brightly colored bed, contemplating the turn of events that the last few days had taken. He realized he was no longer angry about being kidnapped and secreted away to a foreign country.

Eteye walked out of the bathroom in her thong underwear and a thin, white t-shirt. Her brown, erect nipples stretched its cotton fabric, and her unusual golden serpent necklace hung between her breasts, visible beneath the see-through shirt. She walked into the bedroom and climbed into bed.

"Mr. Goldman, you have a very busy day tomorrow, so you should come get into bed and get a good night's sleep."

Solo smiled at her as she crawled under the covers. Her figure was lean and curvy, and the sight of her erect nipples made his heart beat faster. Her beauty and her comfortable nature aroused Solo.

"Now, don't tell me you have never slept in a woman's bed before without engaging in extracurricular activities?" she asked. "We are going to share this bed and get some sleep. Nothing more. Agreed?"

Eteye fell asleep as soon as her head hit the pillow. She spooned Solo all night long. He couldn't fall asleep right away as he honored Eteye's wishes but eventually drifted off in her arms.

14

Solo knew his father would be waiting for him in the lobby of the French Embassy at exactly the time he had told Solo he would pick him up: *twelve o'clock, noon.* His father had always been obsessively punctual. Eteye had elected to remain in their suite.

She had told Solo to make up the excuse that she would meet up with him after lunch with his father and take him to some of the tourist sites around the city. However, her actual plan was to bring him to a meeting with a man named Dav'd. She had instructed Solo not to mention this meeting to anyone, including his father.

As Solo dressed himself in the other room, wearing clothes that had been brought to him the night before, his mind wandered. He had had strange dreams the night before about the ancient Bible stories his head had been filled with at I.D.F. Headquarters. In his dream, he had been with King Solomon at his magnificent, golden towering Temple. He hadn't actually *seen* the king during the dream, but he remembered seeing the Temple. Eteye had been there, too wearing purple. He'd been passionately in love with Eteye in his dream, and Solo felt there had been more to his slumber's imaginings. However, the memories had quickly evaporated after his conscious mind had taken over and he'd opened his eyes.

Eteye indicated that she had some other tasks to attend to, but she would be waiting for him back at the Embassy when he returned from lunch. She kissed him on the lips as he left their room to meet his father. Solo liked how she tasted, and he found himself aroused and distracted.

"Good afternoon, son," Ambassador Goldman said, setting down his newspaper and standing to greet Solo as he walked out of the elevator and into the lobby. Ambassador Goldman had been sitting with his close friend, the French Ambassador, and they both walked over to greet Solo. The elder Goldman introduced his son to the Frenchman, and they shook hands. Solo and his father were then escorted to the basement of the building, where another tourist van was waiting for them. The driver departed the embassy grounds promptly.

"Where are you taking me for lunch?" Solo asked.

"Jerusalem."

"How far away is that?"

"Not far at all. The entire country of Israel is smaller than the state of Hawaii. We'll be there in less than an hour."

The van left the modern city of Tel Aviv and began to climb the small mountains of the eastern half of the country. Olive trees, stone walls, and settlements covered the hillsides, appearing and vanishing in rapid succession as the van cruised by them.

"I am taking you to the most holy location in all of Judaism. It is at the heart of God," Ambassador Goldman said, looking out the window as the van left the city streets and turned onto the highway leading to Jerusalem. "Even your mother said so, when I first brought her here."

"What did she think of Israel?" Solo asked.

"She loved everything about the country. She loved the people, the culture, and especially the history. There are few places in the world where you can see four thousand years of living history and the beginnings of the world's three major religions. Jerusalem especially intrigued her because it was such a holy place for Jews, Christians, *and* Muslims. She said she could feel God's presence in the city. She especially felt the hearts of the Jewish people in the stones of Solomon's Temple. She said 'she felt their longings for a new Temple.'"

"Sounds like mother," Solo said.

"Yes, it does, doesn't it? A lot has changed between your mother and me that we need to talk about."

"I would rather not."

"I hope you will reconsider your feelings toward me," his father said quietly.

Solo's memory haunted him when he remembered the day his brother had told him that their mother and father were splitting up. For some strange reason, any time he smelled freshly cut grass, it reminded him of that painful day. He must have been mowing the lawn, although he had no memory of doing so. For some reason, he remembered the kitchen—his brother putting his hand on his shoulder, his mother's tears and father's absence. He could still smell the damn grass.

His father had moved out of the house that next weekend. He had immediately started living with the girl from his office, who in short order had become his second wife. Solo had never met the woman, or even heard of her, prior to that day.

He remembered his heart physically hurting all throughout that next week. His mother had cried a lot, and they had all hugged a great deal. But it had never been the same after his father left. An air of loneliness had hung throughout the family home. His father had always been the life of the party—the man with dramatic stories about his clients and the cases he worked on. His mother and father had always thrown such galactic, social holiday parties, and they'd climbed the New York City social and political ladders quickly. They had all loved the excitement his father added to their lives. Then, suddenly, the house had fallen silent.

His mother, overnight, had gone from being the wife of a rising political star to a penny-pinching miser. Solo knew his father had treated his mother fairly in the divorce, but she would always worry about money from that day forward. Father had continued his extravagant social lifestyle, albeit with a newer and younger wife. Mother had kept the same family apartment. But every now and then Solo had seen a distant, pained look in his mother's eyes, and he had felt that she missed her soul mate. She had never dated or even looked at another man after Father left.

His hatred for his father had taken some time to sink in. *Hate* was too strong of a word, really, and it was not completely accurate. However, it was the word that Solo preferred to use. *Anger* was probably a better description of how he had felt toward his father for most of his childhood. *Anger* could be managed, whereas *hate* ate a person from the inside out.

Their mother had ensured that her two boys' Hebrew education continued in earnest. Every day after private school, they'd attended to their Hebrew studies at the neighborhood *shul*.

However, she had never fully abandoned her Catholic roots. She'd talked about mystical ideas in the church, and she'd attended mass every Sunday morning. Abay, who had joined their fatherless family after the divorce, spent more time than any of them with Mother in church, although Mother had never asked her to attend.

Solo, generally avoided anything he was not forced to do. His growing disdain for any religion had kept him to the bare minimum he had to attend. Hebrew school was enough; he did not need a second religion.

By the time a few years had passed, life had become that of a typical divorced family. Every other weekend and two weeks a summer, Solo and Levi had been forced to hang out with their new father's wife at their penthouse apartment. *Number Two*, as she had become known to everyone back at Mother's house, had been nice enough, but it had felt like everyone just tolerated each other in an attempt to make it through the weekend. Frequently, Number Two had been absent—gone shopping or away for a girls' weekend—when Solo and Levi had been forced to visit. Their father had taken them to ball games, Central Park, and occasionally to his office. He'd kept them entertained, but their time together had lacked any real depth.

Whenever Solo and Levi would come home, their mother would never ask what they had done or how their father was doing, and she'd certainly never wanted to hear about Number Two. The off-limits subject had always created awkwardness when one of the boys would forget and mention some interaction they'd had with the woman while at their father's house.

The only time Solo could remember Mother, Father, and Number Two together was at he and his brother's high school graduation ceremony. The three adults and Abay had all sat together, and no one would have guessed there were ill feelings floating over their heads. Everyone was civil and smiling, and Solo remembered feeling that it had been a genuinely great day. He'd been so wrapped up in the ceremony and the after-graduation parties, however, that he'd never noticed his mother's iron smile, her pure grit, and her refusal to show any signs of pain in front of her ex-husband and his new wife. Abay had later told him about how Mother had cried for two days straight, alone in her bedroom, after that event. *Father was such an asshole.*

The van swerved around a slow moving car, jerking Solo back into the present. "What made you decide to start helping the Israeli government *while* serving as a U.S. Ambassador? I can't imagine you're very popular with your friends back at the State Department right now."

"Time will tell how my actions should be judged," Solo's father said. "Some will call for my head and call me a traitor, others will understand that I do what I do for the safety of both Israel and America, and for the protection of all people in this region. I have been and always will be an American first, but I can't just blindly wrap myself in my country's flag when I know something must be done for the greater good. Your mother taught me that, first-hand, when her family rejected her for marrying a Jew."

"And then you proved their prejudices true, when you left her for another woman," Solo said flatly.

"Yes, I suppose that's true."

Solo shrugged off his father's agreement: *too little, too late.*

"Where do you think the Americans are keeping Levi?" Solo asked.

"I don't know yet, but I'm working hard with my connections to find out."

"So he really smuggled all of those ancient biblical records out of Iraq? These *source documents,* as you call them?" Solo glanced at his father.

"Rabbi Geller has no idea what he did with them. Geller says he has a couple of pages that were copied and sent to him from one or two of the scrolls that had been uncovered, along with an outline of the remaining scrolls that have yet to be photographed and interpreted."

"Are the scrolls they found really *that* different from the Bible we have today?"

"While they were in Iraq, the Israeli team fully translated and documented two minor scrolls found at the dig."

"What do you mean by 'minor?'"

"Geller told me yesterday that the two scrolls they'd interpreted were not from the actual Bible itself. However, the differences between them and the modern versions are staggering and fully support what scholars have suspected about the Hebrew scriptures."

"And what have they suspected?"

"That a massive rewrite of Jewish history took place in Babylon – that the original stories were all buried in the king's library, so they wouldn't compete with the new, politically correct version of Jewish history."

"Rabbi Geller is really going to piss off his followers when they find out that they've been studying a rewritten version of scripture for the last several thousand years."

"No one is ever going to find out," Solo's father said in his usual, diplomatic tone. "That's why Geller is going to such great efforts to retrieve the documents that Levi smuggled out of Iraq."

The statement shocked Solo.

"You mean he's going to bury the truth? Geller is going to let all these religions keep believing a history and a version of God that he knows isn't true?"

"That is *exactly* what he intends to do. Geller and his religious political wing are highly influential in the Israeli government. He is someone to be feared, and if you *are* working with Levi somehow, you should let me know right now. Koslov and I can help you, but you need to tell us what Levi did with those scrolls and the gold-paged book," Ambassador Goldman said sternly.

"I am not working with Levi! I haven't seen him or talked with him in years. He didn't leave me any information about any scrolls that he may have been smuggling. Besides, it's obvious that Koslov hates Geller, and vice versa. I'm guessing that if Koslov got hold of those ancient scrolls first, he would use them to control Geller and keep his religious cronies at bay."

"Koslov is a good man. I have known him a long time. He is genuinely worried about the theocracy that Geller wants to create in this country. If those scrolls could prevent a religious takeover of the government by Geller, then I fully support him," his father said.

"I don't understand why Levi went to all the effort to hide them from everyone."

"Levi would never betray his country or the uniform he wears," his father replied. "It's likely he felt that if he turned over the documents to Israel or any another foreign government he would be committing an act of treason."

"Once a Marine, always a Marine," Solo replied.

"Exactly. You know your brother. He has always bled red, white, and blue. Koslov told me that once Eteye had shown Levi what his team had actually uncovered—once Levi knew the consequences to the world if those documents were suddenly thrust into Iraqi Muslim hands, or even crusading Western Christian hands—he'd understood that he could not just follow his military orders and transfer the religious antiquities to the Iraqi government. Levi probably had no problem accepting the personal consequences for his failure to follow orders, but he would not betray the Marine Corps by working for another country. My guess is that he made his own secret plans without anyone knowing about it."

Solo did not reply. He looked out the window at the rolling hills and the red-roofed buildings that lined the highway. It was beautiful out there, in the towns and trees leading up to the hills of Jerusalem.

"So he hid them from everyone, including the two of us?" Solo asked.

"I think that was the only way he could keep his honor clean, so to speak."

"Makes sense. If no one has the scrolls and the Book of the Dead, then he certainly can't be a traitor. Maybe a thief, but not a traitor."

"I think you're correct, son. The problem is, the Americans now know those documents are valuable. They want them before anyone else can get them, so they can use them as leverage as they see fit. Imagine what the U.S. could do behind the scenes with just a hint or a whisper of what is contained in those documents. Israel would become a pathetic lapdog to the American bureaucracy."

"You mean they plan to blackmail their allies with the contents of the scrolls?" Solo scoffed.

"It wouldn't be the first time we arm-twisted an ally or made veiled threats to get what we want. As an ambassador, I did it all the time. That is called *politics,* pure and simple."

"It's bullshit, if you ask me. So, in the end, Levi just disappears into some C.I.A. prison camp, until they beat the information out of him?"

"Something like that."

"I still think Levi is smarter than that. Marines are notorious for obtaining whatever equipment they need to accomplish their mission."

"You mean stealing?" the Ambassador asked.

"They prefer the word *commandeering*, but it's part of their Marine history. What I mean to say is that Levi would have had numerous assets at his disposal to get those documents and himself out of Iraq. I don't believe he just dug a hole in the desert, buried them, and then was grabbed boarding a flight out of Kuwait. Makes no sense."

"I agree. Your brother is much smarter than that, and he—"

"—always had a plan," Solo finished.

"Exactly. He has a plan," his father agreed. "We just have to figure out what it is."

"Levi is a true warrior. He won't think twice about sacrificing himself for what he thinks is the greater good."

"That's why we have to find those documents—and trade them for Levi."

Solo was initially surprised. But then he realized his father was not working for *anyone*—not the Israelis, nor the Americans. He was simply working to find a way to save his son.

"So you're using the Israelis to find their scrolls, and then you're going to make a secret deal to get Levi back?"

"Something like that," his father answered vaguely.

15

November 15th
An Najaf, Iraq

The helicopter left its well-guarded hanger on the remote, private airfield in southern Kuwait at exactly two in the morning. Shielded by the darkness, it crossed the border into Iraq in complete radio silence. The helicopter was a technologically advanced Boeing/Sikorsky RAH-66 Comanche stealth aircraft. It was a five-blade, armed, reconnaissance and attack machine that had been designed for the U.S. Army, but full production of its prototype had been canceled in 2004, after nearly $7 billion had been spent on its design. At least, that was what had been reported to Congress and the American public. The stealth helicopter was the only one of its kind, and it had been built specifically for the civilian conglomerate that owned it—a conglomerate that controlled the purse strings of Congress.

The black-ops pilot and his one-man crew were owned by the ruling international corporate aristocracy. Corporations, banks, and monetary funds had long since replaced the nobility and lords of the former ruling class. A handful of these commercial leaders controlled the world, in all practicality, from a single headquarters in Switzerland, where both their financial institutions and privacy were still the most guarded secrets across the globe. Their small military unit was never mentioned in any newspapers. The U.S. Congress did not even know about it. The conglomerate never attended fancy state or political dinners, and it was never mentioned in the media. Its aim was to operate in secrecy at all times, and it accomplished its goals without fail. Profit above else, by controlling public opinion.

Their private secret army was an unimaginably well-funded surgical scalpel, used from time to time to further, or protect, its masters' interests. Formed from the clandestine operators of the world's traditional armed forces, its organization was lean and mean, and it was impressively effective at committing corporate espionage, stealing highly valued intellectual secrets, and discretely assassinating high-level C.E.O.'s when the economic nature of a situation required it.

The privatized soldiers never made mistakes. They were highly paid and discreetly recruited, and their army of mercenaries remained small and tactically perfect. No one in the media knew of the private army's existence, and embarrassing public blunders were nonexistent. In short, the exclusive garrison of elite and advanced warriors operated as the strong-arm of the capitalist industrial conglomerate.

The two-man flight team on the stealth helicopter worked in complete silence. They had been well-briefed before their departure from their fortress in southern Kuwait.

The helicopter landed on the flat rooftop of a three-story building in the middle of an abandoned town in southern Iraq. The town's infrastructure had been decimated in one of the past Gulf wars, and it was obvious in the daylight that no one lived in the insignificant, deserted settlement. The G.P.S. coordinates they had been given were exact, and they'd taken them directly to the rooftop of the squatty, burned-out structure that was now directly beneath them.

The pilot landed the aircraft on top of the building, slowly and cautiously letting its weight bear down on the rooftop. The building did not budge. *Whomever picked this landing site had obviously checked it out and confirmed that it was structurally sound enough to handle the aircraft's dead weight*, the pilot thought to himself.

The two men found the black, watertight, and virtually indestructible polycarbonate container in the southeast corner of the building, exactly where they had been told it would be. It was two feet high and five feet long, and it had been secured with two harden locks. A camouflage net had been bolted to the building's roof, and the small container sat hidden underneath it. No one could see it from the air, and given the thousands of desolated buildings throughout southern Iraq, no one would have ever found it on the rooftop of this one, inconspicuous edifice without precise G.P.S. coordinates.

The crewman used four taut, short cables to attach the container to the belly of the helicopter, along with a high-strength nylon net, which he wrapped delicately around the container. He noticed that it was remarkably light, and therefore he encountered no problems securing it to the helicopter. The pilot watched as the crewman attempted to read the markings that had been stamped on all sides of the container.

"It doesn't matter what it says or what is inside!" the pilot yelled into the microphone of his headset.

The sound of the five rotor blades spinning overhead and the two turbines, operating at twenty-percent power, were minimal as the black helicopter idled by itself on the flat concrete of the roof.

"We are here to pick up and deliver this package. That's it. Got it?" he commanded. The newest soldier nodded his head and immediately stopped looking at the side of the crate.

"Today, we are the U.P.S. delivery man. *What can Brown do for you?*" the pilot laughed into his headset.

The crewman double-checked the connection points. Then, like the smooth ticking of a Swiss watch, he climbed back inside the aircraft, and the pilot spooled up the turbines to one hundred percent.

The helicopter was airborne again, after having only been on the ground for nine minutes. The container rode snuggly beneath as it ascended a hundred feet in the air, facing its southwestern course. In less than an hour, it would rendezvous with the rest of their team at another set of G.P.S. coordinates in the Saudi Arabian desert, where the crate would be transferred.

A lean, mean operating machine.

16

Solo and Eteye rode through the Dung Gate in the Old City of Jerusalem and into the roundabout, which led them directly to the Dome of the Rock and the Western Wall. The late afternoon sun was just getting ready to fall below the horizon up the hill. Their yellow cab resembled any other taxicab in the free world. The large, golden dome sitting on top of the obviously ancient and massive stone platform was nothing short of astounding. Solo had seen this picture a thousand times during his younger years in Hebrew school, but seeing it for the first time in person and actually standing on the *holy ground* of Islam, Christianity, and Judaism's epicenter moved him.

It was seasonally warm for November, and he could feel the desert heat as it sought to be noticed but lacked the intensity to force itself upon anyone.

A large, bulky man, dressed entirely in black with a long, white beard and a black yarmulke on his hairy white head, greeted them. Hair stuck out from beneath the small, rounded hat, like a bush that had been neglected by its gardener. The stranger looked like the thirty-five other orthodox Jewish men waiting in line at the security gate to get into the inner perimeter of the security zone

that led to the foundational stones of King Solomon's Temple. He
bowed to Eteye.

"We must not delay," he said. "Darkness is coming, and there
is much to do before it arrives."

Solo followed Eteye and the hairy guide, and the three of them
stepped to the right side of the security gate, skipping the long
line of men waiting to get into the Temple's heavily secured zone.

Preparations for evening prayers were beginning, and after
the three of them had cleared the security checkpoint, they
headed straight to the Western Wall.

"How was lunch with your father?" Eteye asked.

"Surprisingly, I had a nice time. He and my mother have moved
in together, and they're a couple again. Weird."

"Good. I am happy for them."

Solo stopped in his tracks when he saw the foundational
wall that had subtly served the past two Jewish temples. His
eyes briefly tried, but they failed to absorb and comprehend the
significance of the wall before he continued walking with his two
escorts.

They walked with the masses for a short stretch, toward
what appeared to be a ten-story stone wall, which reached up
into the blue Israeli sky. The beautiful and massive Dome of the
Rock, with its gold cupola, sat on top of the wall in front of them,
protruding from the top of the massive rock foundation like a
beacon straight to heaven. Solo began to grasp why the Koran
said that God took Muhammad to heaven from this spot, and he
could see why King David had chosen here to build his capital
fortress for his expansive empire.

As he stood looking at the Temple's foundational remains
and the surrounding hillsides that sloped down into the desert

valleys, he remembered his tactical military lessons at Annapolis. The elevated ground was an advantage in any military battle. Solo could see what his ancient relative had seen: the key to defending this region lay in Jerusalem's high ground, specifically the pinnacle at the Temple Mount.

Eteye observed Solo's expression. Many pilgrims shared the same look during their first visit to the holy site.

"I see why he picked this spot," Solo said.

"Please, follow me," their wild-haired escort insisted.

Solo and Eteye resumed their pace and followed the man, straight to the far left side of the holy wall. Its right side was reserved for women only, and next to it was the section for all of Geller's ultra-orthodox men. Solo quickly noticed the women tourists being asked to wrap a colorful cloth around their exposed legs protruding from their shorts, so they could approach the Western Wall with modesty.

The three of them entered a door next to a ticket booth with a full line of tourists in front of it. Once inside, they walked down a well-lit hallway that journeyed down a long stone ramp before leading them directly to a section of the holy wall that had been unearthed deep underground. At the end of the tunnel, they arrived at a large, active archeological dig. Lights were clamped to tall, steel tripod stands all over the cavern. Solo stopped when they reached the wall at the front of the cavern, and he observed the large stones, stacked like massive bricks all the way up, until the darkness engulfed it. He tried to imagine the skill and ingenuity required to cut such massive stones into perfect squares, transport them from a quarry located miles away, and then somehow lift them a hundred feet into the air. It reminded

Solo of the same skills that must have been necessary to build the great pyramids in Egypt.

"We must hurry," the escort said with impatience.

He turned left and entered another, smaller cave, which had been carved out of the base of the interior hillside, directly to the left of the hill from which the Western Wall protruded, beneath Old Jerusalem.

Solo followed Eteye, who in turn followed their rushed escort into the cave. It was not at all what he'd expected. As they entered, Solo saw massive bookshelves to his left. They had been crafted from thick, dark wood. Directly in front of them, Solo saw dozens of Orthodox Jews, praying and rocking backwards and forwards in their traditional manner as they whispered their Hebrew prayers earnestly.

They continued to follow their guide around several rock corners lined with bookshelves, all the way to the rear of the prayer cave. They then entered another room with a ceiling that had been carved higher than the rest of the facility. As soon as they turned the corner to enter the final cavern, Solo saw two massive men whose muscles bulged from their clothing at every seam.

They sat on either side of what looked like the entrance to a smaller cave at the rear of the cavern. There was a long, rectangular rock that acted as a massive mantelpiece close to the smaller cave's entrance. Solo could not see anything but darkness emanating from the small hole, but the two large men were obviously guarding whatever was held inside.

The men stood and stepped forward to physically block the three arriving people from the dark hole they protected.

"They are expected, and we are short of time," the escort barked to the two guards.

The elder of the two told Solo and Eteye to stand still and hold out their arms like a cross. After a detailed body search, he added, "Only the American."

Solo looked at her. She nodded and gently patted him on the shoulder, as if to say, "*It's safe.*"

Solo stepped forward, taking in a deep breath before exhaling slowly. He ducked under the massive stone ledge in front of him and into the small, black cave opening.

17

"We need more time," Ambassador Goldman said into his cell phone as he and his chauffeured van left the Old City of Jerusalem and headed back to Tel Aviv.

"I am sorry, my friend, but we are out of time. The Prime Minister gave the orders this morning to the Israeli Navy. They are preparing a naval blockade of all northern Egyptian ports, and . . ."

Defense Minister Koslov paused in mid-sentence.

"And what?"

"It is worse than we feared."

"Worse how?" the former U.S. Ambassador asked.

"Israeli defense forces are also preparing to seize and take over the Suez Canal."

"Oh, no," the ambassador whispered. "By trying to prevent World War III, we'll start it."

"I know. I received the preparation orders this morning. I'm sorry. Rabbi Geller is trying to inflame the situation as much as possible. Unfortunately, he has more influence than I do. He says he speaks for God. That is hard to compete with."

"How much time do we have?"

"Maybe a few days. Our preparations are moving forward as quickly as possible," Koslov answered. "You should also know that Geller plans to detain Solomon until he gets the information that he's convinced your son possesses about the missing scrolls. I convinced him that he is still at the French Embassy, and since that is sovereign France, Geller can't grab him until he leaves. It was the best I could do."

"I understand, and thank you," the ambassador said as he hung up the cell phone.

A few days? He knew it was not enough time. And now Solomon's fate was about to become the same as Levi's. *What was the God of Fate up to?*

18

As Solo entered the cave, his eyes slowly adjusted to the dim light. He found himself in a greeting room that had been carved into the mountain. There was a plush carpet on the floor, and several large, leather chairs were stationed throughout the cave. Multiple small lamps hanging from the ceiling provided some light, but only enough for Solo to identify the chairs. At the rear of the tiny room, Solo was surprised to see a thick-looking door with a large, ornate metal handle on it. He wondered how such a large door could have gotten so deep underground. Solo walked up to it and immediately noticed that it had no hinges. Its handle resembled a snake, humped over and stretched out. When he touched it, he could tell it had been crafted from bronze or another type of similarly heavy metal.

He turned the handle, and the door silently opened inward. *The craftsmanship is remarkable*, he thought, watching the heavy door appear to exert no effort as it opened on its mysteriously hidden hinges. He walked into another dimly lit room and saw two sets of wrought iron staircases. One set spiraled downward, and the other spiraled upward in the same manner on top of it.

There was no one in the room. Solo approached the two spiral staircases and saw what looked like natural light emanating from the steps that rose upwards. The one that traveled downward also had a faint glow of light coming from somewhere deeper within Jerusalem's holy mountain.

Without consciously contemplating the choice in front of him or his complete lack of guidance as to which staircase he should choose, Solo instinctively grabbed the railing of the heavy iron that went upward. He put his foot on the first rung and began to climb toward the light above.

"Solomon. Would you please join me down here instead?"

The voice had a formal English accent, and it rolled up from the darkness below his feet. Solo froze, somewhat startled. He waited a moment to make sure the sound really had come from below, even though he felt quite sure that it had, before answering. However, the sounds in the solid mountain cave played tricks on his ears, and Solo could now hear someone moving but could not tell where, exactly.

"Sir?"

"Please, Solomon. Do not be alarmed in any way. You have traveled a long way to see me. I think it is time we formally met," the unknown voice said from the shadows below.

Solo began the rounding climb down the staircase. At the bottom, he found himself standing in front of a tall man, who was dressed in a very proper three-piece suit. Solo quickly looked around the rectangular room to see if anyone else was with them. The room had much better lighting than the floor he had just come from, and it was also very small. There was a desk and two chairs, with some large shipping crates stacked on one side. A curtain covered a wall to the rear. The man standing in front of Solo extended his hand in a gentlemanly gesture.

"Mr. Solomon Goldman. What an absolute pleasure it is to meet you," the man said.

He was old—at least over eighty, Solo estimated, if not older. He had large, thick ears that hung down each side of his head, and the glow from the light made his skin look olive-colored. The stranger's free hand held a cane with an intricate design, and his full, gray hair had been combed back and meticulously oiled to the sides and top of his head.

"I'm sorry for all the drama, but there are not many places in Israel these days, what with all of the terrorist monitoring systems and all, where two gentlemen can have a truly private conversation. Please, let us sit for a minute, and then I would love to give you a tour of this magnificent structure."

"You know my name, but I did not get yours?" Solo queried as he sat down in the hard-backed wooden chair opposite the man with the ancient-looking face.

"I offer you two things this afternoon, Solomon. The first is this: I will not deceive you in any way. I will answer all of your questions that are appropriate *at this time* to answer. If I cannot answer a question, however, then I will be direct with you, and I will let you know that I cannot answer it. Is that fair?"

"Seems fair," Solomon answered. "My first question, sir, is who are you?"

"I would take great pleasure if you addressed me as Dav'd. It is a very special family name, and it is the one that inspires me the most. Who I am," Dav'd said as he leaned back in his chair and rested his cane against his right leg, "is a long and complicated conversation. But it is a question that I will try to answer during our meeting this afternoon. Fair enough?"

"Fair enough," Solomon answered, studying the man like he would contemplate a potential juror. The man's face appeared honest, and he exuded genuineness from his body language and mannerisms. His demeanor conveyed a sense of military orderliness. Dav'd kept eye contact with Solo and did not fidget. *All signs of honesty,* Solo thought. *Or signs of someone well-schooled in the art of deception.*

Solo relaxed, and as he did so he realized that he was strangely *aware* that he had noticed himself relaxing.

"Where are we?"

"Indeed, a great question, my son. Later, I will take you into the tunnels below the city that *Dawidh ben Yishai* and his men built over a millennium ago."

"Who?" Solo asked.

"You may know him as King David. *Dawidh ben Yishai* is his Hebrew name. He was a good military general, trained in the art of war by some of the world's greatest fighters."

"I thought David was a shepherd, whose claim to fame was killing a lion as a small boy with his bare hands," Solo said trying to not be serious.

"We speak only non-fiction here, Mr. Goldman. No bedtime Bible stories. King David was a well-trained and impressive military general of one of the greatest armies that ever spanned the ancient world. His united monarchy extended all the way from the Red Sea to the Euphrates River. By the time his son *Sh'lomoh ben Dawidh,* or King Solomon, as you know him, took over the kingdom, the Hebrews had amassed more wealth than your Bill Gates and Mark Zuckerberg combined," he said with a chuckle.

"We are sitting in the basement of the capital city King David built for his massive empire," Dav'd continued as he stood and walked toward the curtain. "I want to show you something truly remarkable."

He flung aside the curtain and walked through a narrow doorway carved into the stone. Solo followed Dav'd for several minutes through what appeared to be an archeological dig. There were piles of rubble everywhere, and large overhead lights lit up the entire underground excavation site. Dav'd led him to a stone wall, which continued in both directions for as far as Solo could see.

"Where are we?"

"Beneath the Muslim Quarter in the Old City of Jerusalem. The wall you are standing in front of is the same Western Wall that you saw outside. Except this part has been buried underneath the city for hundreds of years. Israeli archeologists continue to find amazing things down here. I'm sorry I cannot give you a fully proper tour today. I brought you here to show you this stone." He pointed to a location directly in front of Solo.

Solo looked at the wall in front of him, unable to identify the stone Dav'd had referenced. "It just looks like one giant wall," he said.

"Indeed, you are correct, Mr. Goldman," Dav'd answered. "Please walk to your left and stop when you find the end of the rock. It will be a seam that goes from the ground to as high up as you can see."

Solo walked to his left with his hand rubbing up against the rock, like a blind man searching for direction. After twenty steps, he came to a seam in the rock, just like Dav'd had said. Solo realized the wall in front of him was not like the outside rock wall, where he'd seen the Orthodox men praying. The stones outside were about five-feet-high by six-feet-long in size. The section of the wall where Solo was currently standing was nothing like them.

"Did you find the seam?" Dav'd asked from about forty feet away. Solo looked down the wall and saw the old man standing with his hand against it. "This is the other end to the world's largest building block."

Solo looked back at the seam before him. If Dav'd was correct, then the carved stone piece was about forty-five feet long.

"The stone you are standing in front of weighs 570 tons, and it is the size of a city transit bus."

"A city bus? How in the world was a building block that heavy and large created in the first place?"

"No one knows, Mr. Goldman."

"What do you mean?"

"That is exactly what I mean. This massive stone is suspected to have been quarried miles from here, and no one has any idea how the ancient Hebrews could have moved something that weighed almost six-hundred tons and then lifted it a hundred feet in the air to place it in the foundational wall in front of you. There is no explanation for such a feat."

Solo stood in amazement, looking from his position to where Dav'd was standing and then back again. The sheer size and mass of the mysterious rock was incomprehensible.

"Follow me. I need to show you something else before I tell you what you must hear," Dav'd said. He then turned to his left and began following the wall into the darkness.

Solo followed Dav'd. After several minutes of crawling through small, dark tunnels, and then climbing down two aluminum ladders, they arrived at a narrow corridor. Solo had no idea where exactly underneath the city of Jerusalem they were, and he was surprised by the physical agility of the old man in front of him.

"Just before the pending siege by the Assyrians in the 8th century B.C., one of the most amazing building projects of the ancient world was completed. I think it was as good as anything built in Egypt, personally, but others debate me on that point," Dav'd said.

"In order for Jerusalem to withstand an enemy siege, which was a common military tactic of the day, it needed a source of fresh water. One tunnel team started from the water source at the Gihon Spring, where we are standing, and the other team started from the other end of the city, below the natural spring at the Pool of Siloam. These two teams dug an *S*-shaped tunnel that was over five hundred meters long beneath the city. When the two tunnels met beneath the city streets of ancient Jerusalem, they matched up exactly.

"Did you know that when the English and the French dug the Chunnel under the English Channel, even they did not perform as well as these craftsmen did? How could these ancient builders perform feats of greater engineering precision than our most advanced computers and G.P.S. systems are capable of today?"

Solo did not answer. He only listened.

"They used sound waves to direct their underground construction," Dav'd said, answering his own question.

"Sound waves?"

"The ancients were incredibly knowledgeable about sound and its dynamics. They used it as a tool for many things. Walk through these tunnels. Feel them with your hands, and you will understand the rest of the story I am about to tell you."

19

Dav'd and Solo continued their slow journey through the tunnels underneath the Temple Mount in Jerusalem.

"What do you know of ancient Egyptian history?" Dav'd asked.

"I saw the King Tut display when it traveled through New York several years ago, but I have never visited Egypt or the pyramids. I guess that about sums it up."

"You never visited Egypt while your father was the ambassador?"

"No sir. We have had a difficult relationship, to put it politely," Solo Goldman said, following Dav'd on their slow walk deeper into the Jerusalem mountain.

Dav'd smiled as he turned and looked over his shoulder at Solomon. "I am sorry to hear that about your father. Father and son relationships can be quite difficult."

Solo felt an unusual connection to the man who was in front of him; a sense of déjà vu he could not quite place. They continued through the dark, empty tunnel.

"Somewhere around 1500 B.C., there was a great famine in the Middle East, leading all the way to Egypt and her rich delta agriculture. A group of wealthy shepherd families were forced to relocate to Egypt, where they could purchase food for their families and livestock during the great famine. The pharaoh of Egypt treated them very fairly and probably saved these families from certain death."

"I've heard that story before many times in Hebrew school— Joseph and his coat of many colors. Then he became the prince of Egypt and moved his entire family there," Solomon answered.

"Very good, Mr. Goldman. The story I am going to tell you is where your Bible story originated from, and it is different than the one you were told as a child."

Solo listened, intrigued.

"You see, one of these shepherd tribal leaders was a man named Yu-seph—or YuYu, as the Egyptians called him. He later became a close business advisor to Pharaoh Amenhotep III, and then he became his formal vizier. The foreign shepherd Yu-seph and his family became very prominent under the Egyptian system of commerce, and over time their tribal numbers multiplied enormously.

"Yu-seph's people were an extremely loyal group, and they swore their allegiance to the pharaoh for saving them from certain death during the great famine. They called themselves *servants* of the pharaoh because they felt obligated to pay back the pharaoh's kindness from the time of the famine, and they said they would not leave Egypt until the pharaoh had released them from that debt. Yu-seph and his desert people were honored to be treated like real citizens in the Egyptian Empire."

Dav'd bent down and slowly crouched his way through a rock tunnel that was only about four feet high. Solo followed. Dav'd continued speaking as they made their way through the cramped space.

"Yu-seph became such a trusted servant to the pharaoh that eventually he was promoted to great status. He and the pharaoh grew to be close friends, and eventually Yu-seph's monotheistic religious beliefs rubbed off on the pharaoh himself. However, what later became a real source of conflict between Egypt and the foreigner shepherds from the desert was not the wealth that Yu-seph's people had accumulated. Rather, it was Yu-seph's God."

"His God?" Solo asked. "Didn't ancient Egypt have hundreds of gods?"

"Exactly. But, Yu-seph and his people believed in and worshiped only *one* God—an extremely jealous God that tolerated no others. Egypt, on the other hand, had many gods and many royal temples."

Solomon listened intently.

"Yu-Seph and the pharaoh's children eventually married, and their oldest son, Prince Amen, adopted the religious zeal for the monotheistic beliefs of his mother's ancestors. Eventually Prince Amen became pharaoh, and he made the beautiful Nefertiti his queen.

"New to the throne, Pharaoh Amen took drastic and controversial steps. He closed the temples of the many Egyptian gods throughout Egypt, and he replaced them with temples to his One True God. His brazen actions created open hostility with the Egyptian religious establishment.

"During the fourth year of his reign, Pharaoh Amen decided to build a brand new city in Middle Egypt—a city dedicated to the One True God. He even moved the Treasure of Egypt there from the Great Giza Pyramid.

"However, the pharaoh had a tragic flaw: he took away his peoples' freedom to choose and worship the gods they had always worshiped, and he forced the population's allegiance to his God. With the backing of a large military force, the religious establishment rebelled and marched on the pharaoh's new capital city.

"Around 1344 B.C., after seventeen years as pharaoh, Amen was forced to abandon his beloved City of Gold and Light and lead its entire population into the Sinai territory of Egypt.

"The city's inhabitants had refused to abandon their wealth in the well-planned exodus, so they carried away all their riches and possessions with them. They believed the items were their blessings from the One True God, and they left the city completely empty.

"Eventually, the military seized the throne of Egypt and engaged in a purification of the entire Egyptian Empire. All official records, temples, and tombs that mentioned the name or existence of the One True God, Pharaoh Amen, or Vizier Ay were forever wiped clean from Egyptian memory and official records."

They walked through the last turn in the long tunnel maze.

"It would be three thousand years later, in 1714 A.D., before a Jesuit priest named Claude Sicard would discover the artifacts of the abandoned City of Gold and Light, along with the remnants of Egypt's most mysterious religious reformer."

Solomon paid close attention to the old man's words.

"Archeologists later confirmed that the city had been abandoned, not conquered. The population had taken anything and everything of value from the city with them when they left."

The two men emerged through a metal security gate somewhere at the southern end of the Temple Mount. Solomon realized that they had crawled and walked through a vast network of hidden tunnels as Dav'd had spoken to him. They entered a large outdoor area that resembled a miniature Roman coliseum.

"Please, sit with me," Dav'd said, sitting down on a large stone staircase.

They sat and observed the clear nighttime sky and stars above them. Solo was the first to speak.

"That's a remarkable story. It sounds like a story I heard told at the dinner table on every Passover, ever since I was a small boy. Yours has a much more Egyptian flavor to it than the Hebrew story of Moses leading the Jewish slaves to freedom during the exodus, though."

"Yes, it does," Dav'd answered. "It is not that hard to see how history morphed from an Egyptian story into a Hebrew story."

"How so?"

"Once the population settled in the land of Canaan, most of their Egyptian identities faded away. Their monotheistic beliefs and their devotion to the One True God made them distinct from the local desert communities. Over the next several centuries, they became known as the Tribe of Israel. About a thousand years later in Babylon, when the Hebrew traditions were being written down as scripture, the ancient story of the pharaoh and his religious conversion of Egypt had evolved to become the story of Moses, the Prince of Egypt, who led the shepherd slaves to freedom, away from the Egyptian capital city. All of the parts of the Bible story you have heard dozens of times are there: the exodus, the jealous One True God, the pharaoh, the burning pillar of fire, and the Ark with the power to level entire cities."

"That *is* quite the story," Solo said, deep in thought.

"You know, there really are no Jews or Egyptians or Arabs. We really are all one family. Brothers and sisters at some common point in our history."

Solo pondered the implications of his companion's comments. "You said there were two things you wanted to offer me when we first met: truth, and what was the second?"

"I did not say *truth,* Solomon. I said that I would not *deceive* you. There is a big difference. I do not possess truth like it is some sort of book that I can simply hand to you for you to then preach to others. Real truth is far different from that."

"What was the second thing you wanted to offer me?" Solo asked as he contemplated the meaning behind Dav'd's comment.

Dav'd did not reply.

They sat for several minutes in silence, gazing at the peaceful lights of the city of Jerusalem and listening to the Arabic prayers that floated over the Temple Mount. Finally, Dav'd answered Solo's question.

"The ability to save your people from this current madness that has swept over them. And maybe the ability to save your brother," he said simply.

Part II

20

November 15th
Egyptian-Israeli Border

The Bedouin shepherds and their camels crossed the Egyptian-Israeli border under the thick darkness of night.

The large crate had been disassembled at a makeshift staging area on the Egyptian side of the border. There, the six bulky nuclear packages had been strapped to the desert animals that would haul them to the waiting team of Hamas commandos near the Mountain of Ramon in Israel.

An unmanned Israeli surveillance drone had flown by once, soaring within five kilometers of their position. Otherwise, their journey proceeded uninterrupted.

The desolate mountain terrain and the deep dark night sky obscured them.

21

Dav'd and Solo sat on the steps of the southern Temple Mount as evening prayers ended and the multitudes began exiting the surrounding area.

"Mr. Goldman, you should know that the Egyptian people did quite well after the exodus," Dav'd said. "They had a sizeable military, tradesmen of every sort, bankers and businessmen, high priests, and a royal family to lead them. They also had tremendous wealth, which they used to buy and conquer this very land on which we sit today. From their not-so-humble beginnings, we were given the likes of King David and his strategic empire-building, along with his son, King Solomon, who later attempted to form an economic alliance with the pharaoh of Egypt."

As Solo stood and stretched out his legs, he caught a glimpse of the cane that Dav'd carried. A snake's body had been carved into the wood of the staff, and the handle, forged out of some sort of metal, appeared to be the serpent's head.

"Wasn't King Solomon the wisest king of Israel?" Solo asked.

"He sure liked to think he was," Dav'd laughed, "but the Bible's version of King Solomon is much like your legends of George Washington."

138

"What?"

"George Washington, the first President of the United States, was known for his truthfulness, even as a child. The legend tells that young George chopped down a cherry tree, and when his father asked him about it, he told his father the truth. George was not punished because of his truthfulness."

"That does sound like a fabricated politician's legend."

"It was the same for King Solomon. His domestic and foreign policies threatened the country's unity. He spent the country's tax revenues disproportionately on military defenses and navies in the south, and the Israelites who lived in the north, ended up funding the South's security. Solomon was not exactly the beloved king that most people think of today."

"I've never heard any of that."

"How much do you remember about Hebrew scripture?"

"I'm not really a religious man."

"Really?" Dav'd looked at Solo intently. "I wouldn't be so sure about that. That is why you were chosen."

When Solo did not reply, he resumed his lecture on King Solomon.

"We know that the king's empire extended from the Nile in Egypt to the Euphrates River in Mesopotamia. The Hebrew king shared a strategic border with the pharaoh, much like modern Israel does today with Egypt.

"The book of the Bible called First Kings says, '*And King Solomon became allied to Pharaoh, king of Egypt by marriage, and took Pharaoh's daughter, and brought her into the city of David.*'"

Dav'd looked at Solo, letting the pieces of the ancient puzzle come together. When again Solo did not respond, he continued.

"But it is common knowledge that the ancient pharaohs *never* gave away their daughters in marriage to foreign kings. In fact, except for this brief mention in the Hebrew scriptures, there is no other claim in all the histories of the ancient world that an Egyptian princess was ever married off to a foreign ruler."

"So the Bible got it wrong?" Solo asked. Dav'd ignored his question.

"This marriage between King Solomon and the Egyptian princess was singled out in the Hebrew scriptures. None of Solomon's vast harem of women, wives, or concubines were ever mentioned in detail, except for this very specific account of the marriage of a Hebrew king into the royal bloodline of Egypt.

"You know," Dav'd continued. "Most scholars today recognize that the love poems written in the Bible's Song of Solomon were written about the pharaoh's mysterious daughter. Their love for each other was much more than a political marriage. They really were deeply in love. Some even say they were soul mates."

"Soul mates?" Solo inquired. "Who was she?"

"The Hebrew writers of the Bible kept her exact identity a secret. But to answer that question, Mr. Goldman, we must look to another passage in the Bible—one that describes a politically influential princess who attracted the attention of King Solomon."

"Another princess? From where?" Solo asked.

"Theologians say that this princess came from Ethiopia, while historians instead believe that she came from modern-day Yemen. However, both of these versions are incomplete. She actually came from—"

"—Egypt?" Solo blurted out.

"Yes, Solomon. Egypt. You see, the Bible describes another Egyptian princess who visited King Solomon. She was called the queen of Sheba and the book of First Kings says, '*King Solomon gave the queen of Sheba all she desired and asked for.*'"

"'Anything she asked for' sounds like a lot." Solo stated.

"Yes, anything. Not something a king would do for just any visitor. Wouldn't you agree?"

Solo nodded. "It does seem strange that the Bible would say King Solomon agreed to give away anything that this visitor asked for or wanted. Why would he agree to do something like that unless . . ."

Solo trailed off, deep in thought, and Dav'd did not interrupt. Rather, he waited patiently, letting Solo connect the dots of the mystery.

". . . Unless this queen of Sheba wasn't just some foreigner visitor. Unless she was someone incredibly important to him," Solo said.

"Like his soul mate?" Dav'd asked.

"Yes—his soul mate. It makes sense that he would give his soul mate anything she asked for."

"The Ethiopian Bible eventually disclosed the secret identity of the *pharaoh's daughter* as the queen of Sheba, and we have long known that she really was an Egypto-Judaean princess who married King Solomon, who was himself a distant relative of the royal Egyptian bloodline. Thus, King Solomon was actually *not* a foreign ruler. His bloodline dated back all the way to Pharaoh Amen. If you go back far enough, King Solomon and Sheba both came from the same royal Egyptian family."

"That means the Hebrew scriptures are accurate when they say that King Solomon married an Egyptian princess?" Solo asked.

"They are if you know how to connect the entire story. It was the queen of *both* Egypt and Africa who visited King Solomon, and he fell madly in love with her. The reason this mysterious woman's identity was kept secret is another story altogether. Maybe next time we are together I will tell you that one," Dav'd said.

"Why was she called Sheba?" Solo asked.

"Sheba means '*star*' in Egyptian."

"And King Solomon really loved her?"

"It was a political marriage that had been an attempt by both sides to form an economic alliance. However, it was actually a ruse by the pharaoh."

"A ruse for what?" Solo asked.

"To recover the Ark," Dav'd said, pausing for effect.

"It was always about the Ark, wasn't it?"

"That's correct, Mr. Goldman. King Solomon had just recently placed the Ark inside the Temple's vault in Jerusalem—the same national treasure that Pharaoh Amen had taken from Egypt during his exodus."

"What vault in Jerusalem?"

"The Bible called King Solomon's vault the *Holy of Holies*. It was the most well-guarded vault in the entire Hebrew kingdom."

"I'd never thought of the Temple as a military fortress or a vault, but now that I think about it, that's exactly what it was."

"I told you that Pharaoh Amen removed the treasure from the Giza Pyramid and brought it to his new capital city, the City of Gold and Light," Dav'd began.

"Yes," Solo said. "That national treasure really is the Ark of War that I heard so much about yesterday?"

"That is what some people call it—those who see the Ark's use for military conquest, much like I used to. The Treasure of Egypt is said to have exuded a pillar of fire that went all the way to heaven and could be seen throughout the entire Egyptian empire."

"I remember that story, too. The Bible says the same thing happened during the exodus that Moses led, doesn't it?"

"Exactly," Dav'd answered. "The Bible's book of Exodus says, *'God went ahead of Moses and the Hebrew slaves. God guided them during the day with a pillar of cloud, and he provided light at night with a pillar of fire . . . Neither the pillar of cloud by day nor the pillar of fire by night left its place in front of the people.'*"

"So the Bible was describing the Treasure of Egypt, wasn't it?"

"The treasure, or Ark, is what protected Pharaoh Amen and his people as they traveled through the new lands and eventually built their new Egypt in Jerusalem. And, fast-forwarding to King Solomon centuries later, the pharaoh orchestrated civil war in Jerusalem as an attempt to take back the Ark," Dav'd said.

The two men locked eyes for a moment, briefly and wordlessly conveying their thoughts and emotions. Feelings of long ago foggy memories.

"Have you ever found someone that you would trade your entire world for, Mr. Goldman?"

Solo looked away in silence. Dav'd's question penetrated him deeply.

"What happened to King Solomon and his Egyptian queen? His soul mate?" he asked after a moment.

"King Solomon died and civil war broke out in his empire. The Ark and the pharaoh's daughter disappeared from the pages of history. Ever read the story of Romeo and Juliet?"

"Not a tragic lovers' end?" Solo said.

"'Show me a hero, and I'll write you a tragedy,'" Dav'd quoted. "At least, that's what F. Scott Fitzgerald said. Some legends say that the queen found the fountain of youth and lived forever. No one really knows for sure, as there are no existing records about her. She simply vanished."

"I get the tragedy part now," Solo said. "She lived forever, while her soul mate died. That *would* be a lovers' tragedy."

"It is a great legend, indeed. I think the queen lived on in obscurity to care for the Ark, and the king passed away and faded into the religious history books."

"So why did King Solomon's plans for an economic alliance fail?"

"For the same reasons Pharaoh Amen had to flee ancient Egypt—religion and politics."

Solo smirked. "Nothing has changed," he said. "Religious politics are still alive and well in my country today. They still divide Americans against Americans."

"King Solomon instituted religious freedom throughout his Hebrew empire," Dav'd explained. "He began to allow many other religions into his empire. He allowed the gods of Egypt into his realm, and he no longer excluded them like the Hebrew kings before him had done. He tried to learn the lessons of the past, and he set out to create religious freedom and tolerance throughout his kingdom.

"However, the Bible describes how the wealthy and influential High Priests in Israel were outraged at their diminution in power. Put simply, their monopoly of the kingdom's religious practices had been threatened. They ensured that King Solomon's empire fell into civil war at his death."

Solo changed the subject. "Why was the Treasure of Egypt, or Ark of War, originally kept in the world's biggest pyramid?"

"What do you know about the Great Pyramid of Giza?" Dav'd asked.

"Nothing close to what you're about to tell me, I'm sure."

Dav'd laughed. "I'm sorry that I am forcing you to take in so much tonight. However, our time together today is short, and you need to understand your place in history."

"It's okay. I'm a quick study."

"Inside the heart of the Giza Pyramid in modern-day Cairo, at its center, is what has become known as the King's Chamber. This chamber was not a tomb. Rather, it too was a vault."

"Another vault?" Solo remarked. "Like King Solomon's vault in the holy temple in Jerusalem?"

"They were almost identical. At the center of the Giza Pyramid sits a large, lidless stone chest that is seven-and-a-half feet long by three-and-a-quarter feet wide, with sides averaging six-and-a-half inches thick, made of dark, black granite. It's estimated to weigh more than three tons. It is the only object inside the vault, and it sits exactly in the center of the room. There are no hieroglyphics or markings on the vault's walls or on the stone chest."

Dav'd paused to let Solo's mind keep pace with everything he was being told.

"The vault inside the Great Pyramid and the stone chest that sits inside of it are over ten thousand years old," he said. "Now, do you remember the stories about Moses building the Ark?"

"A little bit, I think."

"Again, according to the Bible's book of Exodus, the Hebrew God instructed Moses how to construct and build the Ark. Its dimensions were very exact and precise, and it was to be covered in gold from bottom to top."

Dav'd looked at Solo, anticipating him to making the connection, as he went on.

"What if I told you, Mr. Goldman, that the measurements for the Ark of the Covenant, handed down from the Hebrew God to Moses, and written in precise detail in the Bible, *exactly match* the interior measurements of the stone chest found inside the vault of the Giza Pyramid?"

Solo reacted by standing up and stretching again looking out over the city's twinkling lights. He then looked back at Dav'd and asked, "How do two radically different objects, from two very different cultures, separated by thousands of years of time, end up fitting precisely together?" But then Solo's quick courtroom mind understood.

"It's impossible," he said. "Unless the Ark of the Covenant came from the Giza Pyramid. Unless it's the same object that Pharaoh Amen removed and took to his new capital city—the same object that led the exodus from Egypt that the Hebrews later wrote about in the Bible and renamed the Ark of the Covenant."

"Well done, Mr. Goldman." Dav'd smiled at his new student's interest. "The Great Pyramid of Giza looks very different today than it did when Pharaoh Amen visited it and removed the Treasure. Back then, the pyramid was encased in highly polished, white limestone, and, according to legend, it was capped by a perfect pyramid of black onyx stone."

"What happened to the white casing?"

"The beautiful limestone was removed by an Arab sultan in the 14th century, to build mosques and fortresses in nearby Cairo."

"Where in the world did the Egyptians obtain an object like the Ark?" Solo asked.

Dav'd looked away from Solo as he answered, gazing out on the city as he spoke. "My son, that is again another story altogether, and one for which we do not have time tonight. However, I think a major clue as to its origin lies in its use of God's Number at its mathematical core."

"What are you talking about?"

"The interior vault of the pyramid, where the Ark resided, is precisely expressed in the mathematical proportion known as the Golden Mean, or *phi*."

"The Greek number *phi*?" Solo asked.

"It has been called many things—The Golden Ratio, Golden Proportion, and Divine Proportion."

"Divine?"

"Yes. However, my favorite—and its most accurate—name is *God's Number*. It is a number found throughout creation and extensively in the human body and face. You find this perfect proportion in animals, plants, and the solar system. It is no coincidence that the vault inside the Giza pyramid and the Ark itself were designed using God's Number."

"So you're saying that the Ark of the Covenant, this Treasure of Egypt, came from God?"

"We need not concern ourselves with where the Ark came from. Its *current* location is our only concern."

"Tell me more about the Pyramid's vault," Solo said, intrigued.

"It is built of enormous blocks of red, solid granite, weighing as much as fifty tons, that were transported by a still-unknown means from the quarries of Aswan, six hundred miles to the south. The first recorded entry into the vault was by an Arab, Abdullah Al Mamoun, in the 9th century, and he found the vault completely empty."

"It was empty because Pharaoh Amen had taken the vault's Treasure with him a thousand years earlier," Solo said. "I'm guessing that whoever taught the Egyptians how to build the pyramids also taught the Hebrews how to place that bus-sized stone you showed me into Solomon's temple."

Dav'd nodded his head. "The builders of the Giza Pyramid were extremely advanced mathematicians, engineers, and scientists. In order to house the Treasure of Egypt, the greatest object the world would ever know, its vault had to be just as magnificent as the treasure it guarded. The pyramid builders understood the dimensions of our planet with the same precision as modern-day satellites."

"I had no idea," Solo remarked. Dav'd could detect Solo's sense of bewilderment in his voice.

"Recently, scientists used robots to crawl through some very small passages inside the pyramid. They found out that the layout of the three pyramids on the Giza plateau precisely mirrors the position of the three main stars in the Orion constellation. They have even discovered new, previously hidden doors and caverns that have not been unsealed or opened yet."

"What does this all mean?"

"The ancient builders of the Giza pyramids encoded an enormous amount of precise mathematical, geographic, and astronomical information into the pyramid. But the vault was a focal point for the Ark."

"Focal point?"

"Did you know that the French Emperor Napoleon himself spent a night alone inside the Pyramid's interior vault? He emerged the next morning, pale and dazed, and he refused to speak of the powerful experiences that happened to him during his night inside. The only thing that was ever recorded was what he told his men: '*You would not believe me if I told you.*'"

"I've never heard of Napoleon sleeping inside the Great Pyramid," Solo commented.

"Most people haven't heard any of what I'm telling you, Mr. Goldman. My favorite stories about the Ark, though, are about its abilities to prolong life."

"How so?"

"There are legends that tell of the Ark's keepers living forever."

"The Fountain of Youth and eternal life—another bedtime story?" Solo said.

"The Ark seems to choose some over others to grant its most precious gift to," Dav'd explained, ignoring Solo's' sarcasm.

"Eternal life to those who are worthy, huh?" Solo asked. "Like when the Ark chose the queen of Sheba and not King Solomon?"

"I think it is more like who is *ready,* rather than worthy. Who really knows? That is what makes it a great legend."

Solo gazed out over the early evening twilight of Jerusalem and contemplated the magnificent story he had just been told. He wanted to reject it completely, but something inside him would not allow it. His cynical character was slowly shifting, and he found himself filled with *what-ifs.* He felt himself becoming aware of a much bigger world than his own. Inside his mind, he could see the details of the vault of the Great Pyramid of Giza, almost as though he had actually been inside it before.

"The Treasure of Egypt that Pharaoh Amen took with him into the desert"—Solo paused to rephrase his statement—"I mean this *Ark of War* really is something that could be used as a weapon of mass destruction then, just like Rabbi Geller said."

Dav'd did not answer.

"Imagine what the Americans or the Israelis or even Iran would do if they obtained such a weapon," Solo reflected.

"Now you see why *you* must find it first."

Dav'd stood, grabbing Solo's shoulder to steady himself.

"Come," he said. "There is much to do."

22

The return ride from Jerusalem to the French Embassy passed in complete silence. Solo was the only passenger, and neither he nor the driver spoke each other's language.

Solo's mind reeled from the conversations he'd had with the mysterious man inside the Temple Mount. He suspected that Dav'd was somehow connected to the original keepers of the Ark of War, but he did not understand exactly how. Dav'd had intentionally left his questions in those regards unanswered.

He began to see the impossible task that had been laid at his feet: *Recover the greatest scientific weapon and treasure the world has ever known – a weapon capable of destroying an entire city, or instantaneously healing a man's wounds, or making its keeper live forever. A treasure that had been removed from its protective vault, inside Egypt's Great Pyramid, by an ancient pharaoh—or by Moses, depending on whose name you preferred. He was being asked to find the Ark of War!*

Solo sat in silence as the night team street lights flashed by outside his van's windows. He reflected on everything that Dav'd had told him. He thought about one guardian of the Ark—Jeremiah the Prophet—with his mysterious ties to Egypt. Jeremiah had gotten the Ark out of Jerusalem before the invading Babylonian army had arrived and laid siege to the city.

Jeremiah hid the greatest weapon that the world had ever known somewhere in the ancient lands of Egypt, and he'd left a coded road map inside King Solomon's *Book of the Dead* for future guardians to follow.

Colonel Levi Goldman's archeological team had found the golden paged book and he understood the historical significance and military implications of his discovery.

Solo was impressed by how readily Levi had sacrificed himself to ensure his country remained protected from the world-conquering weapon.

And now the race had begun. Finding where Levi had hidden the book, was only the beginning. It would only be a matter of time before the Americans retraced Levi's path and recovered the artifacts themselves. Solo would have to pick up the responsibility that his brother had briefly carried. He needed to find where Levi had hidden the ancient book before anyone else could. He knew that his brother had a plan, that he likely would have left clues, but he had no idea how to begin or even where to look.

He struggled to truly comprehend the task that he had been asked to undertake. Without being noticed by the C.I.A., the U.S. military, Rabbi Geller's religious thugs, or the incredibly adept Israeli intelligence community, he needed to find the golden book, and unlock its coded map. A map that would lead him to a hiding place that had eluded treasure seekers and world conquerors for over three millennia.

Impossible, Solo thought to himself.

23

November 16th
French Embassy Elevator, Tel Aviv, Israel

Eteye was waiting for Solo in the lobby of the French Embassy. She wore a short, colorful, flower-print dress that ended at the middle of her thigh. After noticing her athletic legs in her black, knee-high boots, Solo's attention was quickly drawn to her breasts, which her dress greedily clung to. Eteye's mouth spread into a large smile the second she saw him come through the inner security checkpoint.

Solo was attracted to her in a powerful way. There was something so *different* about her. She affected him in a way no woman ever had. He knew that, if he was capable of love . . . but he then quickly dismissed the thought. Seeing Eteye made him feel something he liked.

She moved across the lobby and hugged him, squeezing him close. Her warm, firm breasts pressed against his chest. She looked at him for a moment before kissing him hard on the mouth. She tasted salty and sweet.

Solo wanted to make love to her, right there in the lobby. Eteye realized the same and reached up and ran her fingers through his moonless-night dark hair. His eyes met hers, and she answered his question with her second, longer kiss. *Soon.*

"I can't wait to hear all about your meeting with Dav'd," she said in a hushed tone. She began to lead Solo across the lobby towards the elevators. "However, we need to grab our bags. We have a plane to catch."

Solo stopped Eteye in the exquisitely decorated elevator before she pushed the button to their floor. The door closed, and the two of them were alone as it waited for the command from its passengers telling it where to go.

"Tell me what is going on. Why do you seem to be leading me around? Who are you, and who are you working for?" Solo asked. He had about another hundred questions as well, but he thought these would be good ones to start with.

Eteye moved to push their floor button and smiled in an attempt to avoid answering his questions. Solo pulled her hand back and stopped her. He pulled her close and stood in front of her.

"I need to know where we stand, and how you fit into everything I've heard over the last two days. Things are happening fast, and I need some answers."

Eteye seemed to know that this time he would not take no for an answer. She relaxed in his arms and let out a deep breath. Her warm, feminine face turned serious, and she answered his question.

"I'm not an Israeli spy, and I'm not an American spy. I don't work for any corporation or country. I don't work for anyone."

The trust she exuded convinced Solo to relax. He knew he would stay and follow her, regardless of how she answered his questions.

"My story is a very complicated one," she said, "and I don't think you would believe me if I told you."

"Try me." Solo stared into her eyes and didn't budge.

"I know that you trust me. I can see it in your face. You can trust Dav'd, too. He has been like a father to me. Trust me, Solo. I will do everything I can to make sure you get home safe and sound when this is all over."

"I *do* trust you. That's what bothers me. I don't even know you, but I trust you."

"I simply believe that you can complete what your brother started, and that you can find the Ark of War before anyone else does. I believe you are a man who will do right by history if you should discover the final resting place of this sacred, lethal artifact. I am only here to guide you. You can dismiss me any time you like."

The two of them moved in closer, and Solo held her arms. His emotions were clouding his judgment, but he felt there was much more to Eteye Azeb than she was telling him.

"All that I can tell you is that I am a part of all of the world's religions—and none of the world's religions. The One True God cannot be labeled with such simplistic labels like Jew, Muslim, or Christian. No one *owns* God."

Solo answered her. "I am certainly not religious. It is clear to me from looking around the world that if there really is a God, he is either not all-powerful—or he is not at all about love. I quit praying when it was clear to me that no one was going to answer my insignificant prayers." Solo said, stepping away from her in the elevator.

"What prayer didn't get answered?"

Solo had not thought about that night on the beach in a long time. He had worked hard to forget it. It had been the beginning of the end between the Almighty God of his childhood and him.

"It doesn't matter."

"I'm sorry you feel that way," Eteye said. "Regardless, though, our concern is not the theological justification for world religion. Right now, we must hurry to catch a flight out of this country as quietly as we can. The Israelis aren't convinced that your brother didn't leave you with a map to the book. However, Geller plans to hold you until they make a decision one way or the other."

"Everyone talks around me and assumes I am part of some big plan to uncover this ancient secret. My brother did *not* leave me Jeremiah's book, or any clues to what he did with it!"

Eteye smiled as they walked out of the elevator toward their top-floor suite. She turned back to Solo in the hallway and warmly pressed herself close to his side.

"I'm sorry I could not tell you sooner," she said, "but I needed you to be convincing to the Israeli officials if they grabbed and interrogated you today."

"Tell me *what* sooner?"

"Your brother *did* leave you the book, and I need to take you to it—right now."

"What are you talking about?" Solo said with frustration. "How did he leave it? And where in the world could we possibly be going now?"

Eteye answered in a quiet voice. "Do you remember the man at the coffee shop earlier?"

"No. What man?"

"When we walked by the coffee shop, a man was sitting alone. He made sure I caught his eye. There were three coffee cups on his table, with their handles all pointing to its center. He was the only one at the table."

"I never saw any of that."

"The man had written a note on a napkin and placed it in the center of the cups. He made sure I read it."

"What did it say?" Solo asked.

"It said, '*Your Iraqi orphan awaits its parents. Need a home address.*'"

"What home address did you give him?"

"Shhhh," Eteye put her finger to her lips. "We can't take the chance that someone will overhear this conversation. Let me grab my bag. We have a driver in the basement who's waiting to take us to the airfield. I will tell you everything once we are on our way to Frankfurt."

"Frankfurt? As in the Frankfurt in Germany?" Solo said, following her out of the elevator to their suite.

"Shhhhhh," she repeated.

She motioned for him to follow.

24

Their private flight departed from the airfield at Tel Aviv's Ben Gurion International Airport without incident.

The white General Dynamics *Gulfstream G550* business jet, with no identifiable markings except its tail number, had been fueled prior to Eteye and Solo's arrival. Solo carried no luggage, and Eteye only brought a small, black Hermes duffle bag with some personal effects in it. Solo noticed how easily she traveled and he'd realized how tired he was and desperately needed sleep.

The flight from Tel Aviv to Frankfurt took three hours and forty-seven minutes, and by the time they'd landed at the Frankfurt International Airport, Solo had gotten a shower, a shave, a decent nap, and an elegant meal of sushi and seaweed salad, which Eteye had prepared in the aircraft's galley. During their flight, Eteye had explained to Solo that she'd given the man at the coffee shop an address to a safe house in Frankfurt, as well as her secure cell phone number. Prior to Solomon's arrival back at the French embassy, she'd received a telephone call regarding Levi's plan to courier a package to Levi's brother. Levi's standard U.S. Marine Corps five-point mission plan had been far simpler than anyone had expected, which was probably why it had worked so well.

Over their exquisite meal, Eteye described how Levi had met with one of their old Naval Academy classmates in Baghdad. *Ike Duggan.*

Ike was six feet two inches tall, two hundred and sixty pounds, and had dark, thick hair. He looked like every other Arab trader in the Middle East. In fact, that was why Ike had been promoted so quickly in the intelligence community—he'd looked the part. However, Ike was not an Arab, he was Irish.

Solo reminisced over how Levi had worked with Ike every weekend at the Naval Academy pool when they were all midshipman. Ike had been so big and muscular that he couldn't swim—as soon as he hit the water, he would sink straight to the bottom of the pool. And no one who couldn't swim graduated from the United States Naval Academy. Ike and Levi had become more than classmates during their first year together, a result of Levi's dedication and perseverance in getting the large Duggan across the academy pool. The two of them had become very close friends, and Solo knew that Ike would have done anything for Levi after that.

Remembering Levi's unselfishness and friendship in those early days at the Academy, reminded him of something he hadn't realized: he missed his brother.

"So all this time the documents have been sitting in a crate, waiting for us to direct them to a safe address?" Solo asked as they finished dinner.

The cold sake that Eteye had chosen to pair with his fish was exceptional, as were the clothes that she'd purchased for him while he'd met with Dav'd. He liked the feeling of casual clothes. *At least I was kidnapped by someone with good taste*, he thought.

"Ike said he wanted to wait until we were sure I could get you out of Israel before he contacted me. I've met him once before, I think in Baghdad, when he visited Levi there," Eteye said.

"Does Ike have any idea what he's smuggled out of Iraq for Levi?"

"No. And he said he could care less."

"Sounds like him. However, I'm a little curious what you and I are going to do with a crate of 6,000-year-old Hebrew documents once we get there. I'm afraid my reading of Hebrew is a little rusty. I also doubt the great prophet Jeremiah simply left a map with a big 'X' on it as to where we could find the Ark of War."

The pilot announced over the intercom that they would be touching down in thirty minutes. The weather was stormy in Frankfurt, he said, and they should expect a rough and bumpy descent into German airspace.

25

November 16th
Frankfurt, Germany

The drive from Frankfurt International Airport to downtown Frankfurt was slow and tedious. The rain was coming down so hard that traffic backed up on the highway in both directions, even though morning rush hour was just beginning. Solo sat intentionally close to Eteye in the back seat of their black Mercedes Benz G550.

He knew he had fallen for her some time back, but he did not want to think about the implications of those feelings. He knew this treasure hunt was only a brief distraction, and that it would all end soon. He had to return to New York and pick up the pieces of life.

My real life, Solo remembered, staring out the window into the rain. *What is my real life?* He barely had any relationship at all with his father, and he hadn't spoken to his brother in years. His bond with his mother was efficiently conducted through text messages. And then there was Ella. He genuinely liked her, and knew she wanted something more from their relationship; however, he also knew for some unexplained reason that he would likely always keep her at a safe distance. Solo could sense that a storm of trouble was forming—a category-five, hurricane kind of storm—and it was heading straight towards him.

As they arrived downtown, the rain stopped completely. The thick, dark clouds passively rolled by, opting to withhold the dispensing of their moisture. Eteye and Solo were dropped off at the entrance to a large, open-air street market, surrounded on both sides by two stretches of alternating skyscrapers and commercial buildings.

As they walked, Solo kept their shared umbrella held over them even though the rain had let up, utilizing the opportunity to hold Eteye close. His free arm rested across the back of her shoulders, and she snuggled close to him in the cool German air.

They walked four city blocks and passed a sizable coffee shop with outdoor seating that was in the middle section of the street market. Its patrons had moved from the outside seating area inside due to the morning rain, and they sat sleepily drinking their various espressos and coffees and looking through the large glass walls that made up the entire shop's structure.

Eteye led them several more blocks to the front entrance of a large, stone high-rise building that contained no address or signage of any kind. Its two large, stainless-steel entrance doors contained no windows or peepholes, and Solo could not figure out how Eteye knew this building was the correct one. Looking up, he noticed that the building had no windows on at least the first three floors. The bland, flat, and gray blocks that made up the edifice had been jointed so tightly and neatly that a casual passerby would likely not notice that each block was the size of a small automobile.

As he absorbed his surroundings, he also noticed that the building was completely surrounded by vacant parking lots—an unusual feature for the area. It then dawned on him that Eteye hadn't needed any maps or directions to the ominous building: she'd been here before.

One of the steel doors opened outward on its own as they stood before it. The door was thick, with multiple security bolts on both its top and bottom. He was looking at a modern castle, not an office building. There was no other way into the building except through the two massive front doors, which looked as though they could stop an H1 Hummer's impact, and there were no windows to break and climb through for at least thirty feet overhead. And the parking lots around the perimeter meant there were no neighboring buildings that someone could use as a platform to stage an assault. Right here, in the heart of a modern busy German city, was an impenetrable fortress, and no one was the wiser.

A tall man wearing a suit stitched from dark wool instantly greeted them. He looked German, and he seemed extremely serious about his duties. He immediately shepherded Solo and Eteye through a modern-looking security apparatus that looked like a large, man-sized shoebox. A green light came on as they emerged, and the man briskly escorted them to an elevator at the back of the dimly lit first-floor lobby. As Solo stood in the elevator, he realized there had been several other men standing in the lobby's shadowy corners as they'd passed through. Their stillness and silence made them appear as though they were human statues, and he only barely noticed them as he glanced back out into the room through the elevator's closing doors.

Eteye remained silent until they reached the top floor of the building. When the doors opened, she grabbed Solo's arm, yanking him out of the elevator like an excited schoolgirl pulling her date out onto the dance floor.

"Solo, I want to introduce you to a dear friend of mine. He's also one of Dav'd's closest advisors."

"Mr. Goldman," a man said, stepping forward and holding out his hand. "I have heard much about you. It's pleasure to meet someone so vital."

The nameless man was old. He had dark skin, but Solo could not place his thick accent. He walked hunched over with a cane, which Solo immediately noticed resembled the one Dav'd had used. He was almost completely bald, and he seemed to be in poor health.

Solo held out his hand, returning the old man's gesture.

"It is a pleasure to meet you, sir," he said.

"Eliam Giloh," the dark-skinned man said as he shook Solo's hand firmly. The strength of his grip surprised Solo. He smiled.

"Mr. Giloh, it is a pleasure to meet you. I'm sorry you have been so misinformed, though –I'm afraid I'm not vital or important at all."

"I beg to differ," Eliam said.

"I enjoyed my time with Dav'd in Jerusalem," Solo said, opting to leave the man's comment unaddressed.

"He is the greatest man the world has ever known. I wish you could remember him when he was in his prime, as I do," Eliam said, his facial expression shifting as he reflected on the memory fondly.

"You were pretty great back then, too, you know," Eteye said, hugging her long-time friend.

As Solo watched Eteye and Eliam, he noticed that they shared a brief, meaningful glance—a mutual reminiscence, perhaps—and he felt a moment of inexplicable déjà vu.

Eliam politely returned his attention to Solo.

"There is a gentleman waiting to see you. He's been anxious for your arrival," he said.

He began to walk toward two closed French doors at the far end of the room. The blinds on the opposite side of each glass panel had been tightly shut, obscuring any indication of what lay behind them.

"I was admiring your building when we arrived," Solo said. "It reminded me of some of my past military training, where we learned how to defend a perimeter. A modern-day castle! It seems to just be missing the moat at the front door," Solo joked.

"Indeed, Mr. Goldman. It is a rather unique building. It serves our purposes well."

The two French doors opened. Ike Duggan appeared from behind them and walked toward the group. He grinned massively.

"Son of a bitch!" he roared. "Solomon the Jew! It has been a long goddamned time." He grabbed Solo in a burly, giant bear hug.

Solo had not seen Ike Duggan since . . . well, he couldn't really remember the last time. Certainly they had bumped into each other since their four years together at the Naval Academy, but maybe not. *Had it really been over twenty years ago?*

"You drunk Irishman!" Solo shot back, returning the embrace from his brother's most trusted friend.

"I look more like a wealthy Arab trader these days!" Ike again grinned as he extended his arms to show off his expensive, custom-tailored suit. "It's what allowed me to get Levi's dusty old box of junk out of Iraq."

"Dangerous work?"

"Nothing I can't handle. I work for some well-funded people these days—unlike my time in the Marine Corps, when I had to beg, borrow, and steal for everything we ever needed."

The three men followed Eteye through the French doors and into a large living room. In its center sat a bulky, black carbon-composite container.

"I thought Indiana Jones crated all his artifacts around the world in a wooden box," Solo joked. "This looks pretty high-tech."

"Mr. Goldman, we have yet to open this box. We were waiting until you arrived. Its contents were meant for you, and we felt it wouldn't be right to intrude upon your brother's wishes," Eliam said, motioning for Ike to open it.

Ike began unlocking the eight clasps that secured the lid to the one-piece, watertight box. They all helped to lift off the top. Everyone looked inside in unison.

Ike spoke first. "Levi told me the contents were non-flammable, non-toxic, and inert. He said it was a bunch of religious writings that needed to be protected at all costs. I told him that was all I needed to know."

"Did he say why he wanted you to deliver them to me?" Solo asked.

"You're his fucking brother! Who else would bail him out in a jam?" Duggan laughed back. "Besides, I got the impression it had to do with some Jewish thing, and, well, this Irishman isn't very kosher."

Ike turned to Eteye, who immediately gave him a big hug and kiss on the cheek. Solo felt a twang of jealously pulse through him, and he made a mental note of the sensation. Jealously meant his feelings for Eteye had certainly evolved into something greater than any of his other current relationships.

"Everyone thinks I'm in Venezuela. Not here, dropping off your little package," Ike said.

"Thank you," Eteye answered. "We all owe you tremendously."

"You owe me nothing. There is nothing I wouldn't do for these two. Levi has saved my bacon more times than I will ever be able to repay," Ike said, grabbing Solo around the shoulders. "Sorry about the bacon comment, Jew Boy."

Solo laughed. "You haven't changed a bit."

"Sadly, I have, my friend," Ike joked back. "I work for *The Man* now, and when they say jump, I jump. Someday, though, I'll only have myself to answer to," Ike said. "Whatever I can do to stick it to those Washington, D.C. politicians who have Levi tied up somewhere—count me in."

Ike rubbed his hand on the black container's surface. "So what's so damned important that everyone's risked their lives to get this here?"

Eliam Giloh spoke up first. "Your friend Levi found the original writings that formed the Bible."

"What do you mean, *that formed the Bible*?" Ike asked, puzzled.

Contentment spread across Eliam's face as he peered into the container. *Oh, how I miss my library*, he thought wistfully.

"Today's Bible is a compilation—or an edited version—of many original Hebrew stories and legends," he explained. "The version of what you call the Old Testament that we possess today was created by ancient editors who made a politically correct version for us from the original sources."

Ike's face reflected concern as he frowned. Mr. Giloh walked over to him, reaching up to put his hand on his shoulder to calm his obvious unease.

"Mr. Duggan," he said, "you must understand, the authors of the Bible lived in an age when they believed that sickness was a divine punishment and mental illnesses were caused by demonic possession. They believed that solar eclipses were divine omens." His voice was even-toned and reassuring. "When you speak of the Bible, you are speaking of someone's *translation*—the edited version of many different ancient writings. There is a very big difference between a translation and an original story, Mr. Duggan."

"Translation?'" Ike asked.

"We have no original manuscripts of any book in the Bible. No original Hebrew or Christian writings ever survived. All the original books of the Bible themselves have been lost or destroyed over the centuries. All we have are copies of copies of copies, most of them made hundreds of years after the original texts were written."

Ike crossed his arms in front of his chest, deep in thought.

"I hope you see why these original documents you brought here from Iraq are so incredibly valuable," Eliam continued.

"Priceless," Eteye added. Ike turned to look at her as she spoke. "There are literally *thousands* of differences in the surviving copies of the biblical manuscripts—many of them are simply minor spelling differences or different word orders, but some of them are quite major."

"Tell me how they are different?" Ike asked.

"Whole sections are missing in different versions of the Bible, and entire other sections have been added by political editors over the past several thousand years," Eliam explained matter-of-factly. "Some of the Hebrew words occur only once in our modern-day Bible and appear nowhere else in ancient literature, so their exact meanings are unknown. And some biblical phrases are ambiguous, with more than one possible meaning."

"How can there be words we don't know the meaning of in the Bible?" Ike asked, looking around the room. "I'm no theologian, but my priests made damn sure we all knew that the Bible was the *word of God.* And I'm pretty sure that God wouldn't write a Bible with errors in it!"

Eliam continued explaining calmly.

"Take, for example, the passage in the book of Genesis that describes when Joseph was made second only to the Pharaoh in Egypt," he said. "'*Abrek*' was shouted out in front of Joseph as he rode in a chariot. The exact meaning of the Egyptian word *abrek,* translated into Hebrew, is uncertain."

The concern on Ike's face spread.

"The Bible is really an evolving story of folktales, heroic narratives, and royal propaganda. Take, for instance, my favorite character in the Bible, King David," Eliam said, an air of pride in his voice. "One version of the Bible story in I Samuel claims that the shepherd boy who became King David killed the giant warrior Goliath. Later in the Bible, however, II Samuel tells the same tale—only in this version a different man altogether, a man named Elhanan, is said to have killed the Philistine Goliath."

Ike objected. "How can that be? How can the Bible be the word of God when we don't even know what all the words mean, or what really happened?"

Eliam answered.

"Mr. Duggan, all I can say is that there are many uncertainties and unknowns in the actual words and meanings of the Holy Scriptures. It is just that simple."

"Unbelievable," Ike said. "I see why they left those lessons out of Sunday School. But why is *this* strange-looking book so special?"

Eliam stooped over the crate and put his hands on top of the plastic bag that protected the dirty, brown book and its gold-colored pages. He lifted it gingerly out of the container and set it on the conference room table in the middle of the room.

"About three hundred years after King Solomon died, a mysterious book was found by a priest in King Solomon's Temple."

"Book?" Solo said interrupting.

"Yes, Mr. Goldman," Eliam said. "The Bible states in II Kings that the High Priest Hilkiah said, '*The Book of the Law, I have found in the temple.*'"

"Why was it called the *Book of the Law*?" Solo asked, Solo asked, staring at the leather book on the table in front of him. Its brown cover was intertwined with metal gears and latches wrapped around the golden pages inside.

"Some translations call it an instruction book."

"An instruction book?" Ike asked. "They found an *instruction book* hidden away in King Solomon's Temple?"

"That is correct, Mr. Duggan," Eliam said patiently.

"An instruction book for what?"

Solo added up the pieces and realized where Eliam was heading with his story.

"It's the Book of the Dead. An instruction book of ancient knowledge and wisdom," he exclaimed. "The book was lost or hidden away in King Solomon's Temple until it mysteriously appeared . . . if I had to guess . . . right before Jeremiah secreted the Ark back to Egypt?"

Eliam smiled at Solo like a proud father. "The Bible says that the priest who found the mysterious Book of the Law was none other than Jeremiah's father. Quite a coincidence, don't you think? But right at the same time this book was found, the Babylonians destroyed Jerusalem, and most of Israel's population was exiled as captives to Babylon. King Solomon's temple was destroyed, the Ark of War disappeared, and this mysterious book vanished from history just as quickly as it had arrived. The Bible never mentions it again. What was left of the population in Jerusalem and Judah fled to Egypt with the prophet Jeremiah as their leader."

"What's so special about this book?" Ike asked.

"This book was originally called the *Book of the Dead*," Eliam said. "It was written before the time of the Egyptian empire and was taken by the Hebrews when Amen"—the old man paused, catching himself— "when Moses, I mean, left Egypt in a great exodus. Legend says the book contains the secrets of creation— the magical enigmas of eternal life and God's knowledge of good and evil."

Eliam paused, and Ike, Solo, and Eteye stood in obedient silence, waiting for Eliam to continue his story.

"King Solomon, the wisest man to have ever lived, renamed it the *Acts of Solomon*, and he added all of his wisdom and secrets to it. It disappeared in the civil war that erupted after King Solomon was killed."

"My guess is that it was hidden in the Temple along with the Ark," Solo added.

"Yes, Mr. Goldman, you are correct. We have always believed that Jeremiah added his own writings to the book as well, leaving a code, or *instructions*, if you will, to where he hid the Ark of War," Eliam finished, still resting his hands on the ancient book's cover. "Jeremiah was exceptionally clever. He added a single reference in the Bible about a mysterious book, which had been found in the Temple at the same time as when the Ark disappeared with him to Egypt. We have always believed that it was Jeremiah's coded way of telling us where to look for his map to the Ark. We have been searching for this book ever since."

"And you think the Ark of War went with Jeremiah to Egypt?" Solo asked, looking intently at the book in front of them.

"Ark of War?" Ike Duggan asked, clueless.

Solo smiled. "It's a long story, my friend."

Ike did not reply, his countenance still indicating his concern.

"I think we're going to need your help again. Can you stick around for a day or so?" Eteye said as she walked over to Ike. Her question jolted him back to the present.

"Not a problem. I need to make some arrangements and go drop my guys off. They're waiting for me in the basement garage."

"I'll walk with you to the basement," Solo said, following Ike to the elevator.

As he and Dugan rode down past the street-entrance floor and into the basement two floors lower, Solo explained what the Ark of War was to his friend. As they emerged from the elevator into the underground garage, Solo saw a large FedEx truck thirty feet in front of them. Four massive men, all wearing FedEx uniforms, stood around it, and each carried a small, black sub-machine pistol in a sling around his neck.

"Nice disguise," Solo remarked as he walked with Ike towards the waiting armored truck.

"It helps us keep a low profile," Ike said. He turned abruptly and stopped in front of Solo.

"What do you really do these days?" Solo asked, his eyes scanning Ike's tactical team and truck.

Ike's face grew serious. He turned his head to survey the garage around them before answering in a whisper.

"It's best that you don't know what I do these days—for your own protection, so to speak."

"My protection?"

"I work for someone very serious and who values his privacy and anonymity more than anything. I'm not proud of what I do, but you can't just resign your commission and leave."

"What in the world are you talking about?" Solo asked, his voice now a whisper as well.

"Let's just say I'm in the asset-protection business. And the rest is none of your business," Ike said with a smile. He intentionally changed the subject. "I hope you figure this shit out and get your brother out of the pickle he is in. If I have to go in guns-a-blazin' to rescue him, I will. I owe him at least that much."

"I hear you. I hope I can finish what he started."

Ike moved in closer, and his face turned even more somber.

"Levi told me in Iraq what happened to Abay after we all graduated. I'm very sorry. All these years, I never knew."

Solo tried to physically pull back from the uncomfortable conversation, but Ike grabbed his shoulders and held him where he stood.

"You need to let it go," he said sternly. "You can't blame Levi all of your life. The two of you are better than that." He turned and walked to the fake FedEx truck and jumped in, his men following suit behind him.

"I'll be back tomorrow," he added. "Think about what I said."
They drove away.

Solo would wonder who his friend actually worked for, right
up until the moment of Ike's death in three days.

26

November 16th
Frankfurt, Germany

By the time Solo returned to the top floor of the chameleon-like Frankfurt castle, Eteye and Eliam had removed the contents of the carefully packaged plastic crate. The items were laid out on the large conference room table in front of them as Solo walked in.

Six large scrolls, resting inside six thick, clear-plastic vacuum-sealed bags, lay spread before them. The scrolls were at least three feet long, and they looked heavy and incredibly aged. Solo was amazed at their pristine condition, though, given that they were supposedly over six-thousand years old. Each bag had a big, black letter that had been handwritten on the outside of the plastic. Solo could see the word *Yahweh-Judah* written on one of the scrolls and the large words *Elohim-Israel* written on the bag of another.

"I'm sorry we didn't wait for you," the old man said as he gently moved one of the scrolls from one side of the table to another. "I have been waiting so long, and I just could not stand to wait any longer. These six scrolls each tell their own version of—and form the basis of—the first five books in the Bible."

"The Egyptians could preserve a body for thousands of years with their embalming process," Eteye said. "They taught the

Hebrews how to preserve their sacred writings for eternity as well."

Solo studied the gold-paged book. It's leather was covered in metal gears that interconnected and opened and closed locks on its side. The gold pages made it heavy. It had been wrapped inside a thick, puncture-proof, vacuum-sealed bag. The bag had no description of its contents within, but this book needed no identification. It was unlike anything Solo had ever seen.

"I confirmed that this was the original *Book of the Dead* before I sought out your brother's assistance," Eteye said.

"It is just as you described it. There is no rust anywhere," Eliam remarked, peering through the unopened bag. "Remarkable preservation skills."

"Will you be finished by tomorrow?" Eteye asked him.

"Yes, I hope so. I know you must depart quickly."

"Where are you going?" Solo asked. "And *what* will be done by tomorrow?"

"Not me—*we*," Eteye answered. "Eliam's associates, who are skilled in this kind of archeological work and who are also loyal to keeping our secrets, will carefully open the book and make an electronic copy of the entirety of Jeremiah's writings inside. You and I will then take that electronic copy to someone in Tokyo who is expecting us."

Solo did not object to Eteye's news. The impending doom, should he not see through what his brother had started, had a lot to do with his lack of protest, but he also knew his desire to spend as much time as he could with Eteye was also a reason. Secretly, he feared his newfound feelings for Eteye would end poorly for everyone involved.

"What's in Tokyo?" Solo asked, trying to escape his thoughts.

"Mr. Goldman," Eliam answered, "a supercomputer has recently been built—a computer that can decipher the code that Jeremiah the Prophet left for us."

"They told me about the hidden codes in the words of the Bible when I was in Tel Aviv," Solo said.

"They were searching for simple word-intersection codes. Bible scholars and religious priests have known of these types of codes for a long time. However, we're looking to unlock something much more complicated than a Bible crossword puzzle," the elderly man said, gently removing the book from the thick plastic bag that protected it.

"The Israelis I met in Tel Aviv spoke of a fortress in Egypt. They believe this book points the way to it," Solo said.

"We have always believed that this book contained the clues and the map to where Jeremiah hid the Ark of War. However, the book was only mentioned once in the Bible, and no one has seen it since," Eliam said. He placed the book on the table gently.

"After all of the archeological digging in Egypt and all of the tombs that have been uncovered, no one has come across the tomb for a Jewish prophet named Jeremiah?" Solomon asked incredulously.

"Mr. Goldman, ancient Egyptian history is being uncovered every day in modern Egypt. Tombs of pharaohs we have never heard of are discovered each year. It's not at all surprising that the tomb of an obscure foreigner has gone undiscovered."

Solo looked at the book on the table and imagined Jeremiah creating a hidden mathematical code within the writings inside. He wondered about the skills and understanding it would have taken to design such a complex system, one that scholars even today were unable to break without the use of a supercomputer. *Amazing*, he thought.

"Why do you need a computer in Tokyo?" he asked.

"The Egyptians remain the most advanced society of mathematicians and expert builders to have ever walked the earth. Even today, we lack the technology to build the pyramids with the same precision they had thousands of years ago. But the greatest architectural achievement the Egyptians ever built—the one that guarded their most prized national treasure—was built in a very specific and unique way."

"Dav'd told me about this. The Great Pyramid of Giza, where the Ark originally came from," Solo said with excitement. "It's another clue, isn't it?"

"Indeed, Mr. Goldman," Eliam said. "The divine pyramid was built using a very special number—one that has no end."

Solo understood the old man's reference. The original vault for the Ark of War had been built using God's Number at its core, he remembered. The number, Phi, held the key to unlocking the code contained in the book as well. The never-ending number had been the D.N.A. to the perfectly crafted pyramid; it was the secret that Bible scholars had overlooked for centuries, and all along it had been sitting right in front of them like a giant lighthouse in the Egyptian desert.

It was so ingeniously simple: Jeremiah had chosen a number so unique, embodied in a landmark that he knew would survive the ravages of time. He had known that the pyramid and its holy number, Phi, would still be there when mankind was ready to discover and reintroduce the Ark into civilization.

"Now that we have Jeremiah's writings, we need the supercomputer to generate the almost-infinite mathematical intersections of Jeremiah's words, using Phi as the key to the code," Eliam explained. "The computer, we believe, will be able to analyze his code in all of its possible combinations and will hopefully show us the Ark's final hiding place. To answer your question, Mr. Goldman, Tokyo has the only computer in the world powerful enough to run all of the potential word intersections on an infinite scale."

"They're just going to let Eteye and I walk in and borrow the mainframe for a few hours?" Solo asked.

"No, Mr. Goldman. No one can know that you were even there. We have someone on the inside."

"Of course you do," Solo said.

Despite himself, he grinned.

27

November 16th
Haus Römer, Frankfurt, Germany

Solo and Eteye ate dinner in an old German restaurant that overlooked the original Frankfurt City Hall. The six-hundred-year-old municipal building and city square resembled a photo on a Christmas card. The medieval building, with its stair-stepped roof, had been put into use as a functional city hall in 1405 and was still used by the local city government to this day. The town's center was rounded, and it was strewn with ancient structures that had been converted into modern-day restaurants and shops.

The restaurant Eteye had chosen was at the far end of the town square. It had been built with thick, dark timbers from bottom to top. Inside, the restaurant was small, and the tables rested quite close to one another. Solo chuckled to himself, remembering how he thought New York City was the best at cramming as many tables as possible into a restaurant. The Germans were far better.

The host recognized Eteye right away, kissed her briskly on both cheeks, and motioned for them to follow him. They worked their way through the maze of tables and chairs and climbed a tiny spiral staircase to the second floor, where a table for two, overlooking the lights and the tourists in the town square, waited for them.

"This is my most favorite restaurant in the city," Eteye said after ordering meals for them both in fluent German.

"I didn't know you spoke German," Solo said, wondering what she had just ordered for him.

"You never asked!"

"What else should ask I you, Ms. Azeb?" Solo said.

A server poured them each a glass of wine, and Solo watched Eteye swirl her glass and then take a large sip. She paused as if thinking about the wine dancing with her taste buds and then smiled.

"I know what you would *like* to ask me," she said, a grin on her face. She reached across the table and squeezed his hand. "You have been thinking about it ever since we shared a bed together back at the French Embassy. Am I right?"

"I was a perfect gentleman back there. Even your father would approve of my conduct."

"I was surprised by the depth of your self-control," Eteye teased. "I had hoped that you would have tried something terribly inappropriate with me."

It was not what Eteye said at that moment that made Solo realize he had always loved her. Rather, it was the realization that his heart never slowed when he was in her presence. He had been with strong, exotic women before, and many had increased his heart rate, at least for short periods of time. But after watching his father decimate his mother and their family over another woman, and after the loss of Abay and eventually his brother, he had never let anyone near his heart again. Not even Ella, who was the most dear person in his life. Despite that resolution, however, here he was—somehow in love with the mysterious woman sitting directly across from him.

The candle on their table flickered and danced in the cramped, dark German tavern. Solo gazed intently into Eteye's eyes as she held his hand across the small table. There was something genuinely different about her—different than anyone else he had ever met. Memories or emotions or *something* itched in the back of his brain somewhere, and Solo felt as though he would eventually go mad, should his developing love affair with Eteye continue. Or maybe he would go mad if it didn't continue—he couldn't quite tell which one.

He changed the subject, even though he wanted to stay in the romance of the moment. "What's the plan for Tokyo? Are we going to be doing some *B and E*?"

"B and E?" Eteye asked.

"Breaking and entering."

"Has anything I have planned so far been that crude and lame? I got you out of the U.S. right under the C.I.A.'s nose inside an Israeli submarine, for heaven's sake!"

He smiled. "Everything you have put in motion has worked flawlessly. I am thoroughly impressed."

"As you should be. My sister works for the president of the company that operates the supercomputer. She has prepared for our arrival. We will have access to the mainframe for several hours during its evening backup process."

"Your sister? Come on! Your sister *just happens* to be the right-hand man—or woman, I mean—to the one person who can get us access to the only supercomputer in the world that can unlock this code?"

"My closest friend, not sister by birth," Eteye corrected herself. "We have been preparing for this day for a long time. We knew were we close."

Their food arrived, as if on cue, as she finished her sentence. Solo noticed Eteye's necklace again during their dinner, and it dawned on him that he had never seen her without it on.

"You never take it off, do you?" he said, motioning to the serpent around her collarbone. It hung heavily on her neck, and one could instantly tell that its weight was substantial. It was the most unique object Solo had ever laid eyes on, and the itching in the back of his brain started up again as he stared at it. Solo noticed that the square knot in the center of the necklace seemed to be closer to her neck than the last time he saw it. It appeared to be tighter around her neck. *Odd*, he thought to himself.

"Never," she answered.

"He must have been very special."

Eteye did not answer for several seconds, and a strange smile spread across her face.

"It helps me to remember," she said, finally.

"I'm sorry you lost your husband. You don't ever talk about him, though?"

"Why would I talk about a man from so long ago, when I have such an amazing man sitting right here in front of me?"

Solo could see sensuality flickering behind her eyes, and his heartbeat quickened. Her stare caused his senses to inflame, and he knew that he would make love to her tonight. In fact, the entire universe knew that they would make love that night. Solo tried to remain dapper.

"I liked how you described him as your king, and you his queen," he said.

"When did I say that?"

"I don't exactly remember. Maybe back on the submarine or the embassy?"

Eteye smiled and nodded.

After their plates had been removed from the table, their waiter brought them rich, dark coffee in small, white porcelain cups. The waiter's presence abated their sexual tension, and he waited for the young man to leave before returning to the topic of the journey before them.

"So, in a few hours, this computer is going to print out a location to Jeremiah's tomb and the resting place for the Ark of War?" he asked incredulously. He took another sip of his coffee.

"That is the weakness to the plan. We have no idea if this computer can even do the job, let alone whether the computations will take a minute or a month to work through. This has never been done before."

"I guess we have to try. God only knows where the recovered American nuclear material is by now. If the Iranians have gotten it into Egypt, then I don't suspect we have much time."

"Yes. Sadly, once the Egyptian government dissolved and the American Embassy closed, we lost most of our best intelligence. There are a few American soldiers stationed in the Sinai as part of a U.N. peacekeeping force, but they have not been much help. We really are running blind at this point."

"I love unwinnable cases."

"I know you do, Solo. I watched you win your last case."

"What do you mean?"

"I was at the Academy."

"You were in the courtroom?"

"I loved how you ignored the judge and that lawyer who was yelling at you to stop, and how you kept focused on the jury and their absorption of your pictures."

Solo liked knowing that she had watched him. He reached into his pocket to grab some money and pay the check that had just been delivered to their table. But then he realized his wallet and cell phone had never been returned to him. *The easiest way for him to be located*, she had said, *was for him to use his cell phone or his credit card.*

Eteye giggled, pulled out some euros, and set them on the table.

"When do I get my wallet and phone back?"

"Come with me," Eteye answered, ignoring his question.

They window-shopped along the central pedestrian street, looking like any other local couple out on the town. Eteye held on to Solo's arm with both hands, and she told him the story behind every local trinket in the windows they passed. At least it seemed that way to Solo.

"I thought the girl sitting at your table during the trial was very pretty. I understand the two of you are very close?" Eteye asked casually as she looked into the window of a store filled with colorful shoes.

Solo was surprised that Eteye was asking him about Ella. How much did she really know about the two of them?

"It's complicated," he answered.

Eteye stopped, turned, and kissed Solo hard on the mouth, which prevented, for the moment, his tongue from speaking any additional words. She then pulled back quickly and gazed at him intently. Her voice was a near-whisper.

"I want to make love to you, Solo—if you will have me."

He looked squarely into her face. Her perfect skin was darker at night, and her large, full lips beckoned him to her. He kissed her softly at first, and then slowly he allowed his tongue to enter her mouth. She tasted like the ocean on a hot and sunny day. Salty and sweet. His hands fell to her waist, and he reached lower behind her and cupped her round, soft curves with both hands. He felt Eteye respond as she moved her leg in between his and pressed herself against him. He kissed her harder, and their tongues swirled together as he caressed her long, black hair with one hand. His other hand had moved to the curve of one of her perfect breasts.

Without a word, they turned and hastily walked back to their private room at the modern-day fortress.

28

By noon the following day, the Book of the Dead, or Jeremiah's instruction book had been expertly opened and electronically photographed.

There had been seventeen Hebrew words in Jeremiah's writings that were unknown to the Hebrew scholars that worked at the modern fortress. They had photographed and scanned every one of Jeremiah's Hebrew words into a digital document.

Solo had been concerned that there were too many ancient words the scholars did not recognize, but they had assured him the unknown words would not impede his mission.

"We will do our best to decipher them while you are on your way to Tokyo. If anyone can interpret them, it's the men here," Eliam Giloh reassured him.

A man handed Solo what appeared to be an ordinary iPhone. When Solo turned it on, it operated like a standard smartphone, and he couldn't find a single unusual quality to it. Eliam instructed him to hold down the center button for fifteen seconds. Solo obliged, and a small, hidden USB port opened from the phone's side. The phone was a massive flash drive, which contained all the data from Jeremiah's writings that they would need in Tokyo—data that was protected in an encrypted format.

"Thank you, my dear friend. Send anything new to my phone. I will let you know when we get there," Eteye said. She kissed Eliam Giloh on the check and hugged him.

Solo was smitten. Last night had been the most romantic night he had ever spent with a woman. They had made love three times, well into the early morning hours. Their last tryst had been an enlightening experience for him, and it had caused him to unpack his inhibitions toward love and to share his heart with Eteye. *What was it about her that had so dominated his thoughts and feelings?*

"Mr. Goldman, there is one last thing . . ."

Solo turned to look at the old man, the disguised hard drive still in his hand.

"Yes, sir. What is it?"

"These scrolls and this book belong to you now. *The Almighty* has entrusted them to you. You are responsible for their safety and protection. We will keep them here as your stewards and guard them, but in the end you will have to decide their fate."

"Why should I decide their fate?"

"We have not touched the six source document scrolls, Mr. Goldman, other than to identify them. And we will not, unless we are directed by you to do so. The God of Fate has made you their keeper and master, and you must carry their burden forward," Eliam said. He moved his head in what appeared to be a bow of some sort.

Solo did not respond. Eteye grabbed his arm and pulled him to the elevator hurriedly.

"I will let you know what he decides. We have a plane to catch!"

29

November 18th
Tokyo, Japan

Ike had arranged for his company's G650 private jet to take them into Tokyo's Narita International Airport undetected. The 5,820-mile flight took just under eleven hours. Ike's military access and high-level political connections rivaled Eteye's, and she was appreciative of the extra pair of hands to assist with their clandestine logistical needs.

Solo and Eteye made love in the rear stateroom of the private jet as it whisked them from Europe to the comparatively small island of Japan. Solo wondered for the first time whether he could ever fit into Eteye's world once her need for him—once their mission—was complete.

Japanese customs did not meet them on their plane, as was typical for travelers under diplomatic license. Nor did they go through the long immigration lines like the commercial passengers did.

It was morning in Japan, and Eteye informed Ike and his team that they had eight hours to kill before their appointment with her friend in downtown Tokyo. Ike and his men remained onboard the aircraft while Solo and Eteye departed via the city's subway system while they waited for the evening to arrive.

The streets in Roppongi, where they exited the subway, were narrow and lined with brightly lit billboards. Even in daylight their flashing lights and neon colors made the streets resemble a T.V. game show. Eteye pulled Solo's hand along as she led him down the street. A large grin spread across her face. Young Japanese girls in traditional school uniforms passed by in groups, giggling and laughing as they made their way through the crowds.

Solo noticed that absolutely everyone on the street corners waited for the green *walk* lights to appear before crossing. *How unlike New York City*, he thought to himself.

Eteye guided him across the street and into a stark white lobby. A line of people waited to pay or check in at the front counter, and dozens of others sat on the various couches that were speckled throughout the area.

Amazingly, they reached the front of the line in less than a minute. *Classic Japanese efficiency,* Solo thought to himself. Eteye spoke to the two men behind the counter and held up three fingers. Whatever she had just ordered, he discerned, she had ordered three of them. He still could not figure out exactly what the place was.

Eteye received a plastic card with the number 345 stamped largely on it. He followed her to the elevator in the corner of the lobby, and they soon found themselves on the third floor, standing in front of room 345. Solo could see waitresses with large serving trays of glasses and beers making their way down the hallway several feet away from them. Eteye laughed loudly and threw her head back as she opened the door and pulled him inside.

"I purchased three hours," Eteye said. She immediately took off her shoes and ran to the front of the room, stepping across pillows that had been neatly lined along the floor for guests to sit on. In the front of the room sat a large projection-screen T.V., a thick book, and two microphones. Solo laughed and shook his head as he realized that they were in a karaoke room. Eteye was already punching in the numbers to select her first song.

"I can't sing!" Solo protested jovially as he plopped down on a pillow and crossed his legs.

"*Everyone* can sing," Eteye said, barely able to control her excitement. "Some better than others, is all."

A waitress entered the room and bowed to them slightly before setting a large, blue bottle of cold sake and two tiny glasses on the end table in front of Solo. She bowed once more and left, closing the door behind her as she exited.

Solo poured the sake as the music to Eteye's first song began to play and the lyrics appeared on the screen. Eteye jumped up and walked across the room to grab the microphone.

"*I used to rule the world . . .*" Eteye sang, facing him.

The music was loud, and Solo found himself drifting into a trance-like state. Eteye swung her hair from side to side and danced to the beat like no other woman he had ever seen. She was completely, exuberantly absorbed in the moment and the words of the song. Her uninhibited energy filled the room, saturating Solo's consciousness.

He leaned back against the wall and smiled. The wrinkles on his face from his grin felt good. He drank his sake and relaxed as the most beautiful woman he had ever seen performed a concert for him that he knew he would never forget.

Eteye grasped the microphone in the palm of her hand, performing like a polished rock star as she continued to sing with her eyes closed.

"... *I hear Jerusalem bells a ringing, Roman cavalry choirs are singing ...*"

She sang well past their allotted three hours, and Solo ate up every moment greedily. He watched her intently, drinking up her soul as his mind excavated who the wonderful creature before him really was, beyond her songs and performance. That afternoon, her soul and her heart were his for a few precious hours.

Suddenly, in the middle of one of her songs, she stopped singing. Solo had just poured the last of the sake into his glass. As he looked up to see why she'd stopped, Eteye stepped over the cushions and straddled him, sitting across the front of his lap. She leaned into him and kissed him. He liked how she tasted on his lips, and she smelled of sweet perspiration. He held her face with both of his hands and kissed each of her closed eyelids.

"You have the most beautiful face I have ever seen," he said. "I catch myself trying to get a glimpse of it whenever I can."

Eteye kissed him back, hard. Solo undid her blouse as calmly and quickly as he could. She wore nothing underneath it. For as long as Solo had known her, which was only a few days, she had never worn a bra or camisole. He cupped her small, round breast, and she threw her head back as she arched her back, making both breasts elevate and become taut. They made love passionately on the plush, square cushions of room 345.

They made their way back to the subway station from the karaoke bar and boarded a train heading for downtown Tokyo. It was rush hour, and the train car was packed with people.

As they stood together in the crowded car, Eteye's body suddenly tensed, and her eyes and face rapidly changed their demeanor.

"We are being followed," she said quietly under her breath. Solo resisted the urge to look around.

"Where?" he whispered back.

"We picked someone up back at the airport. I saw the same man last night, smoking a cigarette outside the restaurant in Frankfurt when we left."

Solo tensed. "What does that mean?"

"It means someone knows we have the data, and they are following us to the treasure. Letting us do all of the work for them."

"Are you going to kill him?" Solo asked in earnest. He kept his back to the unknown man that had caused their alarmed conversation.

Despite her concern, Eteye laughed.

"You have seen too many James Bond movies," she said, her voice returning to a whisper. "I don't kill people. But we need to figure out how to play this out. We can't go through all of this only to have Mr. Double-Oh-Seven back there come in and grab the Ark once we find it."

"*If* we find it, you mean. Maybe we should just let him tag along for now, until we figure out how to give him the slip."

"It's not just *him* following us. There's likely an entire *team* on our trail. Helicopters, surveillance aircraft, drones—the entire package."

"Who would know we are here?"

"Does it really matter?" Eteye said, sitting down as the train stopped and a seat opened up. Solo continued to stand, but he moved to Eteye's right to try to identify their tail. However, no one looked out of place, and he wondered whom Eteye had recognized.

"C.I.A., I.D.F., N.S.A., Geller's soldiers—they're all the same to you and me. None of them is ready to possess the Ark of War," she went on.

"How do you think they found us?"

"Again, it doesn't matter. What matters is that our meeting occurs without unwanted company."

"Tell me what you want me to do," Solo said. He tried to appear casual, like someone who rode the subway every day to and from work.

Eteye leaned in and casually whispered instructions into his ear.

As the train slowed down to arrive at the next station, Eteye stood and walked directly over to a man that was standing in the back corner of the car reading a newspaper. She reached into her purse, pulled out a modified Taser, and dropped him to the ground with a single shot before he could react. He fell face-first onto the floor right as the train came to a complete stop. As the doors opened, Eteye began screaming and pointing at the man in what sounded to Solo like perfect Japanese.

Two uniformed men wearing blue-and-white suits and white gloves rushed in to help the man, who was still lying face down and convulsing on the train's metal floor. One of the train conductors pulled out his defibrillator and prepared to use it. The entire train remained stopped at its last station until the paramedics could arrive to help the heart-attack victim.

Solo had exited the train as soon as the doors had opened. He went up a flight of stairs, crossed over the tracks, and got on a train going in the opposite direction, exactly as Eteye had instructed him to do. He then immediately exited at its first stop and ran into the first men's bathroom he could find. She had told him to wait at the sink for five minutes, washing his hands, to see if anyone followed him into the bathroom. If no one did, then there was a fair chance that he had lost his tail.

Seven minutes passed, and no one entered the bathroom. Solo then caught the first taxi he saw. "*Tsukiji*," he said to the driver.

A few minutes later, he arrived at the world's largest international fish market—the Tokyo Metropolitan Central Wholesale Market, also known as the *Tsukiji* Market—located near the downtown Tokyo wharf.

As soon as he walked into the massive warehouse and saw the gargantuan piles of raw seafood sitting on ice, sitting in buckets, and sitting in water tanks, he was concerned that he would never find the place Eteye had said she would meet him.

Loud forklifts sped through the tiny alleyways between the vendors' displays. Solo watched as two men argued over what looked like a long, black eel. He heard the English word "radiation" and assumed they were fighting about whether the eel was contaminated. Solo remembered the recent nuclear disaster north of Tokyo—a tsunami had struck the nuclear reactor and knocked out its electricity and cooling pumps.

The sheer size of the market and the smell of raw fish was overwhelming, as Solo wandered throughout the maze of ocean creatures. The warehouse felt like it was the size of Yankee Stadium.

After about thirty minutes, he found what he was looking for. On the outside of the maze of vendors was a large ice-cutting shop, which looked like it had been built before World War II. A forklift lifted ice blocks the size of washing machines and placed them onto a vertical conveyor belt, which then sent them up to the visible second floor. Four men guided the blocks through a massive, steel band saw, which cut the huge chunk into smaller pieces. The ice then travelled down another conveyor belt, back to the first floor, where workers and their wheelbarrows waited. As soon as they filled their wheelbarrows, the runners would immediately take off to deliver the quickly melting ice to the vendors.

The operation amazed Solo, and for a moment he forgot Eteye's instruction to not stand in the middle of the market like a lost tourist. He looked around for a remote place to stay out of sight. He found a parked truck near the ice mill, climbed into the passenger seat, and waited for Eteye. He paid attention to everyone who approached and left the area and he did not sense that anyone was looking for him. He felt he was safe, but he also knew that he lacked the training to support that feeling.

An hour passed. Solo was deep in thought, watching the activity around him and looking for Eteye, when suddenly the driver-side door opened. He turned his head, his mouth already open to apologize for trespassing, when she jumped in. Eteye immediately started the small truck's engine and began to pull out of the parking lot. She glanced at him briefly and smiled, acknowledging that she had found what he had thought was his covert hiding spot without him seeing her. Solo returned her grin.

"Just borrowing this truck, I assume?" he asked.

"It was clever of you to pick out our getaway vehicle. We'll dump it at a mall just up the street. Our ride is waiting for us there."

She shifted the manual truck into gear as they left the busy downtown Tokyo streets and entered a highway, which had been built on stilts and ran the entire length of the city. They rode in silence, and Solo found himself constantly feeling for the fake iPhone disk drive in his front pants pocket.

They arrived forty-five minutes later at the Odaiba commercial district, denoted by its large Ferris wheel, which circled passengers above the city's skyline. Eteye drove into a parking garage and headed down to the first-floor basement level.

"I didn't see anyone tailing us. That is a good sign. We can't tell what or who is watching us from above, though, so I guess this is the best we can do for now."

"Why did we take the subway from the karaoke bar in the first place?" Solo asked as Eteye circled the garage, looking for her contact. "Why not a private car, so no one saw us?"

"We needed to know if we had a tail or not. It was only a matter of time before someone tracked us down, and the subway was the best way to find out. Our plans haven't changed at all. We just need to be aware that they are close. We can't afford any mistakes from now on."

Eteye pointed to a dark blue taxicab that was waiting in the corner of the parking garage, nestled between two parked cars.

"There she is!"

"Who?"

"My sister! I mean, my dear friend!"

"Your friend drives a cab?" Solo joked before realizing that Eteye had planned their inconspicuous getaway vehicle long before they had even gotten to the parking garage. She parked the small cargo truck, and they got out and walked to the taxicab.

"Don't we need to wipe down the truck to get rid of our prints? Or set it on fire or something?" Solo asked as Eteye took his hand and quickened their stride toward the waiting car.

"You watch too many American T.V. shows, Mr. Goldman. I'll have someone return the truck with a full tank of gas within the hour, and no one will care or be any the wiser that we *borrowed* it for the greater good."

An elegant, tall Japanese woman wearing a bright red evening cocktail dress got out of the taxi. She was thin and had long, straight black hair that fell to her waistline. She beamed when she saw Eteye, and her smile spread from ear to ear. The two women embraced, squeezing each other firmly. The Japanese woman kissed Eteye on both cheeks, and Eteye did the same, smiling warmly with satisfaction.

"It is so good to see you again. It's been so long since we were last together," the woman said.

"It has been *too* long!" Eteye said, still holding the woman's hand "The captured gold from the Solomon Islands?"

The Japanese woman nodded.

"That long ago?" she said, shaking her head in disbelief.

"Solo, this is my closest friend, Ashki. I have known her for what seems like forever. We have been through a lot together."

The attractive woman shook Solo's hand and then hugged him. As she released Solo from her embrace, she looked seriously into his eyes, as though she were studying and testing him.

"So this is Mr. Solomon?" Ashki asked as a warm smile returned to her face. She turned to Eteye, and the two of them exchanged a knowing nod.

"It is Mr. Goldman, actually. Solomon Goldman," Solo said, trying to understand the look that had just passed between the two women.

"Of course it is!" Ashki said. "It's so good to see you. I wish we had time to catch up, but we are behind schedule as it is. I need to get you into the building before it closes and the nighttime security procedures kick in."

"I know. We can chat in the car. I think we're in the clear," Eteye replied.

Solo and Eteye sat in the back of the taxi while Ashki drove them to an office complex. She pulled into a public parking spot, and the three of them exited the cab.

They entered the complex and took the public elevators up to the third floor, which led to a pedestrian bridge that connected them to the office building on the other side of the street. Within minutes, they had walked through a maze of buildings and parking structures, and they found themselves in the parking garage for the Tokyo Institute of Technology. Ashki had planned their arrival route flawlessly.

As they stood in the small private lobby, she removed a credit-card-sized I.D. badge and inserted it into the elevator's security station access panel, which was labeled "Executives Only" in both Japanese and English. Ashki's photograph, name, and title appeared on a large H.D. screen in front of them: *Executive Assistant to the Vice President of Research and Development.*

Ashki punched in a lengthy numeric code. She then withdrew a Q-tip from a dispenser on the security console, wiped the swab inside her mouth, and placed it inside a plastic container the size and shape of a cigarette. The entire container withdrew into the machine like an A.T.M. card. A few seconds later, a green light appeared, and the elevator door opened. They quickly stepped inside.

When the door closed, however, the elevator did not move. Instead, a set of instructions appeared on the interior screen, and

Ashki spoke to the computer in Japanese. A few seconds later, Solo heard a hum, and the elevator started to rise.

"What just happened?" he asked.

"The exterior elevator security requires D.N.A. analysis to ensure that only high-ranking executives use this particular building access point."

"The elevator can analyze someone's D.N.A. in seconds?"

"Of course. There are many technological marvels here, which is why this entrance point is so well-secured," Ashki said. "When we stepped inside, it could tell I had two guests with me. I had to say a special "panic word," and the computer analyzed my voiceprint to ensure there was no stress in it—to make sure I was not being held hostage or under duress. We had to use this elevator, as it's the only one with no video or audio recording devices inside it. The executives like to have their own *discreet* entry to their offices, away from the watchful eyes of the employees—and their own wives, if you know what I mean."

Solo knew exactly what she meant.

"When we get to the main floor, I am going to stash you in my office, which is conveniently being remodeled," Ashki said. "No one will go in there. I'll come back when the mainframe computer is in hibernation mode and the servers are backing each other up to take you to the computer access terminal."

"You will only have three hours on the mainframe. I am sorry, but there was no way to get you more time. I hope it is enough."

"So do we," Eteye said.

The three of them exited the elevator and entered a round reception area. Office doors surrounded the exterior of the circular room, like spokes on a wagon wheel. They followed Ashki to the left and into her office. It was massive.

"Wow! And I thought I had a great office in New York City," Solo said.

"I take very good care of my boss, and he makes sure I am rewarded for it."

Ashki led them through a door at the rear of her office that opened into another room, which looked like a small day spa in the process of being remodeled.

"Everything works, so I hope you are comfortable for the next few hours until I return."

"You have done a magnificent job assimilating yourself here. Will you be sad to leave?" Eteye asked as she hugged Ashki goodbye.

"It's been nice being back home again," she said with a shrug before turning to leave the room. "I will lock this door, and no one will bother you. I'll see you at eleven p.m."

Just before Ashki closed the door behind her she smiled wryly.

"I get the sense you two will have no problem passing the time," she said with her eyebrows raised. She shut the door.

Ashki's assumptions about them were correct. However, she had no idea how terribly wrong their plans were about to go.

30

November 18th
Tokyo Institute of Technology

The locked door to Ashki's executive washroom opened at exactly eleven o'clock. Ashki entered, still wearing her full-length cocktail dress, which plunged deeply between her breasts. Its high-rising slit highlighted her slender, athletic legs. *She is striking*, Solo thought.

Solo and Eteye followed her back to the elevator, where they traveled up another five floors to the research headquarters. They walked toward a glass door in front of them as they emerged from the elevator, and Ashki knocked on it quietly. Nothing happened. The three of them looked at each other, and Ashki knocked again, just as quietly as the first time. Again, they waited. Just as she raised her arm to knock a third time, the door slid open mechanically.

A young Japanese man wearing a white lab coat smiled when he saw Ashki. She walked beside him and put her arm around his shoulder as she turned to introduce him to Eteye and Solo.

"This is my dear friend, Hito. He is going to help us with the mainframe tonight," Ashki said.

Hito bowed to them and then looked at his watch.

"Not much time," he said. "We should hurry."

The three of them followed Hito into the entrance of the research facility, which opened out into a circular platform that was protected by a stainless-steel fence. The platform overlooked the floor beneath them, which was shaped like a giant cereal bowl. Wisps of white gas obscured most of whatever lay inside the bowl below them.

"Is that the supercomputer?" Solo asked.

"Yes, Mr. Goldman, this is *Ah-Dee,*" Hito answered.

"Ah-Dee? What is that?"

"It stands for Advanced Dynamic Intelligence. She can think for herself on a scale difficult to understand, and, yes, she takes up this entire floor. She has to be cooled with liquid nitrogen because she generates so much heat. You are looking at only part of her. That part, down there, is like the Intel chip inside your laptop. There is nothing more powerful or faster in the world, I assure you of that."

"I believe you."

Hito walked them to what looked like an expensive, modern kitchen countertop made of glass. It was about two feet wide by four feet long, perfectly smooth, and dark-colored. It connected to a matching glass piece behind it that was about four feet tall and resembled a kitchen back-splash. Neither had any markings. Solo, Eteye, and Ashki watched as Hito walked directly up to the strange-looking station.

"Good evening," he said.

The machine recognized his voice, and the entire station came to life. The opaque glass in front of them lit up, like New York City at night, and a 3-D projected image of a keyboard appeared out of thin air and seemed to float just above the crystal countertop in front of Hito. Hito began moving his fingers in the air above the machine, typing something into the non-existent keyboard. After a moment, he turned and asked Solo for the flash drive.

Solo removed the device from his pocket and handed it to the Japanese man in the lab coat. Hito then plugged the it into a port on the top of the counter—Solo swore he had not seen one there before—and resumed typing with impressive speed on the mysterious, holographic keyboard.

"The mainframe is supposed to be backing up its daily work on the servers down on the seventh floor. However, I ran the backup earlier today, so we have a small window in which to use her without interruption," Hito said, still typing away at the air.

"How, exactly, are you going to use the data with this computer?" Solo asked.

"I have been working on this problem for months, hoping we would get a chance to unlock the riddle," Hito replied. "First, I'm going to compare the words that you recovered from your instruction book with the words in our traditional biblical sources to see if ADI can detect any patterns in the differences. Frankly, I don't suspect that it will give us any real data, but, logically, it's where we should start.

"Next, we'll access the series of Equidistant Letter Spacing in Jeremiah's coded writings. We'll be looking for all types of patterns, but especially for patterns wherever the Hebrew words "*aron*" and "*brit*" intersect. However, what has never been done before—and what this computer can do—is look for intersections on a 3-D scale."

"How do you take a two-dimensional page of writing and turn it into something three-dimensional?" Solo asked.

Hito did not immediately answer. Instead, he hit the imaginary *Enter* key, and the entire piece of glass lit up as words whirled across its screen. To Solo, it looked like the computer was scanning through the entire Tokyo phone book.

"I built this program a month ago, when Ashki told me of the Iraqi discovery. ADI is now running it."

He stared at the rapidly scrolling numbers for a moment before answering Solo's question.

"Mr. Goldman, do you remember those collapsible plastic cups we had as children? Think of them as two-dimensional objects when they are collapsed. However, they turn into three-dimensional cups when you pull the wide top away from the narrow bottom. A better example is the paper pinwheels we used to play with. They are flat, two-dimensional pieces of colored cardboard until you pin the corners to the center. Then they become pinwheels and spin like windmills in the wind. We are going to do just that. We'll take the linear string of Jeremiah's words and spiral them up, into a corkscrew, looking for all possible intersections of the words on a three-dimensional plane."

"How will you know when we've found the hidden map?" Solo asked.

Hito pointed to a section at the top right of the computer screen.

"My program just verified that your book contains the same passage that the Book of Jeremiah contains in the Bible: '*No one will ever say again: Where is the Ark of the Covenant of God?*'"

Solo stared at where Hito was pointing on the screen.

"It's such a striking passage in Jeremiah's book," Hito said slowly. He was contemplating something. "I'm going to use our brief time to search for all possible three-dimensional intersections of those words and see what we find. I think Jeremiah meant for us to look where he bluntly asks the pivotal question that his code answers: 'Where is the Ark?'"

For the next hour, the four of them fidgeted and conversed. Solo tried to figure out the complexities of the relationships between Eteye, Ashki, and Hito without asking them directly—a skill he had employed often while cross-examining witnesses.

Suddenly, the computer screen went blank, and the massive amounts of data that had been scrolling by disappeared. Solo's heartbeat picked up as he watched Hito type on the floating keyboard.

"I think it worked!" Hito said. "That was much faster than I thought it would be. Let's hope ADI found something of value."

The three of them peered over Hito's shoulder as the entire screen filled with a list of Hebrew words.

"Wait one second. I need to reformat the data, so you can *see* what she has found," Hito said, smiling to himself with pride in the program he had created as he typed. "Hmmm . . . She uncovered something very different than what I was expecting. In fact, she stopped using my program altogether almost immediately!"

He continued to stare in silence at ADI's raw-data answer for a moment.

"Oh, my!" he exclaimed finally. "Give me a second to reformat this."

They waited, anxious to see what the world's most advanced and self-aware computer had found. Then, on the screen in front of them, a page of text, filled with original Hebrew words, appeared. As they watched, the words began to lift off of the page in what appeared to be random fashion and then move to the bottom center of the screen.

"I should have thought of this. It is really quite extraordinary!" Hito said as he watched the computer work.

"Tell us!" Ashki said, trying to prod Hito along.

"Okay. ADI went in a totally different direction than I told her to go. Remember Legos?"

Solo and Eteye glanced at each other, wondering where this was going.

"They make large Legos for young children. They are the size of an apple, and they mostly come in only two shapes: a rectangle and a cube. Now, if I gave you four pieces of these large Legos and asked you how many geometrical shapes you could make from those four pieces, your answer would be two or three shapes— probably a square or a bigger rectangle. But that would be it.

"Now, imagine that we try this exercise again, only I give you a box with one thousand pieces of the most advanced Legos on the market today—Legos with hundreds of different shapes and sizes—and then I say, 'Show me every possible shape you could build with these thousands of pieces.'"

"The shapes would be infinite," Solo said.

"Oh, no, Mr. Goldman! You are incorrect. The amount of shapes you could build would *not* be infinite. Rather, the different shapes that could be created with the pieces would only *appear* infinite because of the limits of our minds' computational abilities. This is not the case with ADI, however. She could build every different variation and tell you exactly how many different possibilities there are."

"Okay, I follow you . . ." Solo said, nodding.

"What ADI found this evening is truly amazing. She discovered that the writer of your magical book was an exceptionally well-versed mathematician and builder, and that—if she applied the integer *phi* to each of the Hebrew words contained in the instruction book's writings—she could transform each Hebrew word into a Lego-type building block."

"You mean, God's Number—*phi*?" Solo asked.

"Exactly, Mr. Goldman. *Phi*, or the divine number, as you say, because it is the perfect ratio. It is a number that never ends. ADI applied this perfect ratio to each of the Hebrew words in your flash drive and made them into three-dimensional building blocks. Instead of looking for every possible combination that you could build with the blocks, however, she first analyzed them linearly—that is, in the order as they appear on the original pages," Hito said.

He pointed to the screen, where the first page of instructions from the book was still displayed. The group watched as ADI morphed each word from the book's pages into small blocks of words. Some were long rectangles, and others were short and only consisted of two letters.

After a minute or two, a block materialized in front of them in the space where the holographic keyboard had been. It was also a holograph, and it formed a three-dimensional, rectangular shape that was roughly an inch tall and the size of a hand.

ADI then began moving each word block from the screen to the holographic simulation in front of them in sequence. The first few blocks moved slowly, as though the computer were intentionally trying to give them an opportunity to grasp what she was doing. She gradually picked up her pace, and the blocks began attaching to the holograph in a manner that resembled the pitter-patter of falling raindrops.

"She found the design and building blueprints hidden inside this manuscript for something you are not going to believe!" Hito said as he took a step back from the computer's rapid activity. "You will have to see it for yourself."

The 3-D Hebrew building blocks began to fall into place, like a perfect, three-dimensional puzzle, and a shape started to form in front of them. When ADI had finished placing all the puzzle pieces, the floating holographic image slowly came into focus as it rotated around in front of them.

Solo's jaw dropped as he recognized the treasure map that the supercomputer had successfully unlocked from its millennia-old hiding place.

Floating right before his eyes was an exact replica of the Great Giza Pyramid.

31

"That is quite the map," Solo said with amazement. "Jeremiah picked a hiding place for the Ark that he knew would survive the ravages of time."

"There is more," Hito said. The holographic keyboard reappeared, and he began to type. Four Hebrew words on the cornerstones of the floating pyramid in front of them briefly glowed blue before enlarging.

"See these four words at the base of the pyramid?" Hito asked. Everyone nodded, and Hito glanced up at them briefly to ensure their attention before continuing. "Jeremiah highlighted these cornerstone words from four key sections of his writings."

He hit *Enter*, and the screen flashed to a shot of outer space. It then zoomed in, first to the continent of Africa, then to Egypt, and then straight down, into the city of Cairo, where it hovered over a satellite image of the Great Giza Pyramid.

"Your ancient writer was so advanced that he actually left you the exact coordinates of where to find your treasure," Hito explained. "The four Hebrew words that he used for the cornerstones are translated as "where," "is," "Ark" and "Lord.""

"Unbelievable," Eteye said as she looked over Solo's shoulder and said, "Where is the Ark of the Lord."

"There was one flaw in ADI's pyramid-building model, however," Hito said. "She found a string of words that don't fit anywhere in the three-dimensional pyramid construction. She could find no meaning or place for them in her model, so she discarded them."

"What were they?" Eteye asked.

Hito typed again on the hovering keyboard, and a verse appeared on the screen:

סעה ועיריו רפושה לוק־תא סעה עמשכ יהיו תורפשב ועקתיו סעה עריו
ודכליו ודגנ שיא הריעה סעה לעיו היתחת המוחה לפתו הלודג העורת
ריעה־תא:

"Translate to English," Hito said. The screen went black for a moment, and then the English translation appeared:

And the people shout, and blow with the trumpets, and it cometh to pass when the people hear the voice of the trumpet, that the people shout— a great shout, and the wall falleth under it, and the people goeth up into the city, each over-against him, and they capture the city.

"She did a cross-reference for this verse and found that it comes from the book of Joshua. The Ark is also mentioned in that scripture. Other than that, though, she was unable to apply *phi* to its interpretation, and she therefore couldn't fit it into the rest of the pyramid model."

Solo looked more closely at the three-dimensional pyramid, rotating and floating in front of him. It looked so real he felt as though he could reach out and grab hold of it. He noticed that the model reflected numerous interior chambers and small tunnels that led upward from the pyramid's center to the outside of the pyramid.

"Hmm . . ." Hito said to himself as he pulled up more data onto the large screen in front of them.

"What is it?" Eteye asked.

"There is a footnote to ADI's model," he said.

"A footnote?" Solo and Eteye responded in unison. They looked at each other briefly in mutual recognition: the more time they spent together, the more they had increasingly been thinking the same thing. Their mutual glance only reinforced the notion.

"Notice the large, square chamber—the one with a long exit out to the Nile, deep below the pyramid," Hito said, pointing at the holograph in front of them.

"ADI compared her *Jeremiah model*, so to speak, to the known structure of the Great Giza Pyramid, and she discovered that that exact chamber does not exist on any current maps. That's the footnote."

"Maybe no one has discovered it before?" Solo suggested. "We need to figure out how to get into that basement." He looked around at the group, trying to gauge their thoughts.

"I think you're right," Eteye answered. "We know that the book of Maccabees and the Hebrew oral tradition state that the last person to possess the Ark was Jeremiah. And we know that Jeremiah disappeared into Egypt, along with the remnants of the Jerusalem population . . ."

Solo finished her statement for her.

"It looks like he returned the Ark and hid it in a secret space directly below the original vault—the vault that Pharaoh Amen had removed it from centuries before."

"ADI, thank you very much for your assistance this evening," Hito said, calmly and succinctly.

"You are quite welcome," she responded in an impressively human-like and feminine English-Japanese accent.

"Erase all records regarding this project, and erase your usage log for this project, please."

"I am ready to proceed with your command," ADI replied.

"ADI, please proceed."

"All files and logs have been deleted."

"Thank you, ADI. You may now return to your primary duties. We will speak again in the morning. Pleasant dreams," Hito finished with a slight tone of affection in his voice. He turned to Ashki. "We should get you all out of here. I'm afraid I have assisted as much as I can without creating a record of our presence."

"The computer is really going to erase all of the work she just did?" Solo asked as they followed Hito out of the central computer room.

"She has already erased all of the records," Hito said. "Only the four of us will ever know what she uncovered." He handed the iPhone flash drive back to Solo as they waited for the elevator.

"I doubt anyone in the world could have done what ADI did tonight," he mused to no one in particular. "Her abilities are growing every day."

They entered the elevator and rode back down to the floor of executive suites that contained Ashki's office in silence. As the elevator doors opened, Hito and Ashki stepped into the plush, round foyer first, and Solo and Eteye followed behind them, hand-in-hand. Solo had taken two steps into the lobby and was staring down at the iPhone, still in his free hand, when he bumped into Hito, who had stopped suddenly.

He looked up and realized everyone had frozen. Looking left, he saw three American men, all holding black assault rifles, exiting Ashki's office. It was apparent that the armed men had just seen the four of them as well. For a split second, everyone froze. To Solo, it felt as though time briefly stood still as his brain raced to figure out what they should do.

Two cracks, which sounded like two chalkboard erasers smacking against each other, suddenly rang out through the small lobby, and Solo watched in slow-motion as Hito's throat instantly erupted in an exploding spray of blood. He collapsed, his hands desperately attempting to put the parts of his throat back into his neck as he fell. When he hit the ground, his body crumpled, and he lay slumped and motionless against the left front wall of the elevator door, blood still gushing from his trachea and his wide open in terror.

Like dominoes, Solo watched as Ashki instantly collapsed next to Hito. The iPhone fell from Solo's hand as he lunged to catch her, mid-fall. Both Solo and Eteye watched in horror as the iPhone bounced away from them and landed on the floor, just outside of the elevator.

Eteye reacted the fastest and saw the next chess move before anyone else. She shoved Solo and Ashki back into the elevator just as its doors began to close. She dove for the small, black phone lying on the lobby floor, which lay just beyond where Hito and Ashki had stood moments before.

"Finish the mission!" she yelled, sliding the iPhone across the floor and into the elevator just before its doors closed around

Solo and Ashki. Solo heard her continue to yell from the foyer above him as the elevator started its descent.

"That's all that matters! Nothing else!"

He fell to the floor of the elevator as it automatically descended to the garage. Ashki's body lay limp in his lap. His mind raced. *How could he leave Eteye up there?* He knew he couldn't go back to help her. *He had to leave her! He had to get out of this building.* He knew that she would do her best to ensure that no one followed him. *How would he complete the mission without Eteye?* He knew she would not survive. That was a certainty. He yearned to go back for her, but he knew that whatever was going to happen to her had already happened, and a similar fate would almost certainly await him. *He had to get back to Ike and the plane and get out of Japan.*

As soon as the elevator opened in the parking garage, Solo scanned the area. He heard no engines and saw no one. He carefully placed Ashki's body on the elevator floor. "Thank you," he whispered and briefly touched her pale, pretty face.

Run! his mind told him.

He darted out of the elevator and began to sprint back down the same path that he and Eteye had traveled earlier that afternoon. He had to force his mind to focus. He couldn't think about what had just happened to Eteye. *He could not take another loss in his life. First Abay, now Eteye.* He could feel the dark clouds of panic and despair beginning to form in the back of his mind. He had to focus. *One step at a time,* he told himself. *First, find a way out of here. Get back to the plane. Stay alive.*

It took Solo twenty minutes to find a running construction truck parked on a city street. He stole it without even thinking to look around and headed for the airport. As he drove, he feared that flashing police lights would appear in his rear view mirror at any time, but none did.

When he reached a bridge, he pulled the truck over and got out. He threw the iPhone as far as he could, over the bridge and into the black mass of water below him. He then drove to the main highway, where he followed the airplane symbols on its signs to make his way back to the airport.

When Solo arrived at the private airfield connected to the airport, he parked the truck in a remote parking lot and walked the rest of the way to the private aviation entrance. He dialed up Ike's aircraft from the business lobby, and Ike Duggan and his team appeared five minutes later. Ike immediately saw the blood on Solo's sleeves and knew that something had gone horribly wrong.

"Where is Eteye?"

"She's dead," Solo said matter-of-factly. "We have to get out of here. We picked up a tail earlier, but we thought we had lost them. Somehow they found us at the computer lab downtown."

"Who tracked you?" Ike asked as he twirled his hand above his head to give the signal to his team and their pilot: *wheels up as soon as possible.*

"I don't know. I was the only one who got out alive."

"Where is your flash drive?" Ike asked as they walked to the waiting jet. "Did they capture it?"

"No, but it doesn't matter. I know where we're going next. We don't need it anymore," Solo said. He climbed up the ladder into the cabin of the Gulfstream. "Just get us in the air."

"Where are we going?" Ike asked as he pulled the private jet's door closed and pushed the interior handle into locked position.

"Cairo," Solo said. He slumped into the first leather seat on the aircraft and stared numbly out the window.

The twin Rolls-Royce BR725 engines spooled up to takeoff speed. Although they could produce 17,000 pounds of thrust each, the plane's small payload required much less.

Minutes later, Solo stared out the small round window and watched the nighttime skyline of downtown Tokyo disappear as the jet climbed to cruising altitude and headed east, over the South China Sea towards Africa. His mind violently wrestling with the fact that he had left Eteye behind.

32

November 19th
30,700 Feet above the South China Sea

The trip from Tokyo to Cairo was long and eerily quiet. Solo hardly spoke during the nearly 6,000-mile flight, and he resisted Ike's inquiries, electing to keep the details of ADI's discovery to himself. Focusing on the mission at hand was impossible, and Solo found himself incapable of processing the grueling pain he felt over leaving Eteye behind to die. How could this happen to him twice? How could he have deserted the only two women he'd truly *loved* in life in their greatest hour of need? *What kind of man am I?*

The long-ago memories of his last night with Abay on the beach at Cape Cod flooded into his mind as an unwelcomed visitor. He took another gulp of scotch, curled up in his reclined seat, and pulled his blanket over his head. Abay and Levi stood before him clearly, even though his eyes were shut tight. The memory of celebrating their graduation from the United States Naval Academy consumed his mind.

Abay, Levi, and Solo had headed to the family beach house on Cape Cod that weekend. Unaware that their lives were about to change forever. Levi was heading off to the Marine Infantry Officers School, and then who knew where the big, bad Marine

218

Corps would send him. Solo was about to begin law school, and
Abay had been content to spend the summer by herself at the
beach house to try and figure out where she wanted her life to
take her. She had often talked to Solomon about returning to
Africa. Her parents had died long ago, and everyone else she had
known during her childhood in Ethiopia had been relocated to
Israel during the multiple secret military operations.

Solo had been attracted to Abay since the very first time
they'd met. Her exotic, dark skin and micro-braided hair had
drawn him to her in some inexplicable way. Solo remembered
their first meeting at the neighborhood synagogue when they
were both sixteen. It was the first time he had learned of her
terrible tragedies in the Sudanese refugee camps. She had told
the Sabbath gathering of Jews in her choppy but understandable
English that her name was Abaynesh, which meant "like the Nile."
She had described how the Nile River was the central river in
Africa and how it was a source of water and life to everyone there.

Solo's mother had taken in Abay as one of her own from the
very first moment they'd met, and to Solo it had seemed that their
mother-daughter bond had blossomed out of nowhere.

Solo and Abay's lives had become intertwined over high school
and college, but they'd both felt the same looming sensation
when they'd arrived at the Cape Cod house that weekend for
the graduation celebration with Levi—the feeling that their
lives would inevitably float apart in the years to come. The three
of them had planned this one, last weekend together: a final
celebration before the treasured present transitioned into the
untouchable memories of the past.

Solo had still enjoyed the smell of the musty old Cape Cod
house their father had bought when they'd been small children.

It had been the family escape from the busy city life and the increasing demands that his father's law practice had placed on his time. Levi and Solo had spent almost every summer of their young lives bicycling around the beach town's slow-moving streets, and they'd played every day on the sandy cliffs that overlooked the Atlantic Ocean.

Abay and Solo had made love for the first time in that house, upstairs in her bedroom, one hot, summer night during college. They had been in love with each other for a long time, all throughout high school, and she had been a great comfort to Solo during the years after his father had left. Over time, they had grown inseparable.

Under his blanket on the flight, Solo could remember it like it was yesterday: watching her young body grow from that of a teenager into a curvaceous young woman. In high school she had loved to drive Solo mad by walking around the house wearing as little clothing as possible. When Solo's mother had yelled at her to put on some clothes, she had just giggled and asked *why*?

Solo took another sip of scotch before giving in and letting his mind wander where it wanted to go. In some ways, it felt good to remember the things he had pushed out of his memory for such a long time.

The first time he and Abay had made love, it had been a new experience for both of them. It wasn't that Solo had held any puritanical beliefs about waiting to have sex until he was married. Rather, he'd just never been all that impressed by any of the girls he'd known growing up. In high school, however, he'd eventually understood that Abay was the one he wanted to *be with*.

Looking back on it now, Solo almost laughed aloud as he realized that both his mother and brother had known exactly how he'd felt about Abay, long before he had.

During the only week-long break that Solo and Levi received during their first year at the Naval Academy, the family had planned to meet at the Cape Cod house. *The family* meant everyone but Father during those days. Abay and Solo had arrived at the house on a Friday night, a day ahead of his mother and Levi, who would not arrive until the following morning. *Had his family intentionally orchestrated some time alone for the two of them?* Solo now wondered.

Abay had cooked them a small, simple Sabbath meal. They'd lit the candles, blessed the bread, and opened a bottle of wine. However, before Solo had even picked up his fork, Abay had said to him, "I want to make love to you, Solo—right now."

They'd never returned to their meal that night, and his mother had instantly known what had happened once she'd seen both of their smiling faces the following morning. After that week, they'd been a couple.

Solo had longed for his father desperately during those years. His absence had caused him to miss out on so many moments of his children's lives. He'd never had any children with Number Two, and every time that Solo had been forced to visit he'd refused to speak to his father about anything of substance, which had only increased the void.

Levi had been even more distant from their father. But somehow, several years ago—Solo was unsure when—Levi and his father had reconciled, and now they seemed close.

How strange it was that his father was now *dating* his mother. His mind couldn't really comprehend it. He had watched his mother live an enormously lonely life over the twenty years of his father's absence. Contemplating his mother genuinely welcoming his father back into her life after two lost decades made Solo uncomfortable.

The waves of the Cape Cod ocean again crashed into his mind, sweeping him back to the night he had tortured himself for so long to forget.

A fierce storm had blown into the cape that final weekend, but Levi and Abay had wanted swim in the ocean one last time. Solo had thought it was a dumb idea. The rain was coming down sideways outside their sturdy, little house, and he'd known that rain like that meant rip tides—not a good combination for three drunken college kids swimming at midnight.

Abay had stripped naked at the front door and yelled to them, "Come on!" Her dark, slender athletic body had run out the front door and skipped down the steps that led straight out to the beach in front of their house. Levi had run out next, a bottle of vodka in his hand, and he'd been screaming something derogatory back at Solo about being a *squid.* Solo had finally stripped down to his white boxer shorts, stamped *Property of the United States Navy*, and run out after them. They had all been exceptionally drunk.

He remembered seeing Levi sitting in the sand at the bottom of the stairs, trying to get the vodka bottle to his mouth as sand and rain pelted his face. He'd sat down next to his brother and taken a few swigs of the clear liquor. Their obliterating intoxication had masked the cold. They'd sat there, drinking vodka, as the waves crashed violently in front of them. It had been high tide, which meant that there hadn't been much beach for them to sit on, and the big boulders that normally littered the coastline had been temporarily overcome by the dark night's rising water.

The next day, Solo remembered, neither one of them could remember how long they'd sat there, waiting for the free spirit they knew as Abay to come back ashore. Solo finished his scotch as he held back a gasping sob under the blanket.

I'm so sorry, Abay, he thought. *I'm so, so sorry I left you there.*

She never did come back.

Sitting in the luxurious jet as it soared 30,000 feet over the South China Sea, Solo's heart broke all over again. He missed Abay so, *so* much, and he hated himself and Levi for just sitting there for God knows how long, drunk on the beach, as the sea swept Abay away from them, forever. He could feel the stabbing pain again as he remembered the look on the Search and Rescue officer's face: *there's simply no sign of her body, anywhere. I am sorry but she is gone.* The anger he felt towards his father for deserting his family, Solo felt even more fiercely towards himself and then towards Levi for their reckless stupidity that night.

After that night, Solo and Levi did not speak again for ten years.

33

November 19th
Cairo, Egypt

Somewhere over the course of the fifteen hours from Tokyo to Cairo, Solo tried to pull himself together—to remind himself that he had to finish the mission at hand. The loss of Eteye clung to him like a dark, heavy thunder cloud, ominously surrounding a mountain peak.

He'd at first tried to sleep but had quickly given up. Instead, he searched and read everything he could find on the Internet about the Great Pyramid of Giza. He wanted to confirm what Dav'd had told him at the Temple Mount in Jerusalem. He verified everything he could about the pyramid, reconciling it with Dav'd's story.

He discovered that the Great Pyramid was the largest pyramid ever built, with a total mass of more than 6.3 million tons: representing more building material than all of the Christian stone buildings built in England since the time of Christ. And now he was heading right back to where it had all started.

He encountered numerous articles explaining how the number *phi* had been woven into the mathematical proportions of the pyramid and its interior rooms. It seemed to Solo that everything about the pyramid flowed in and around this magical number—*God's Number.*

224

It amazed him to find out that, even today, Egyptologists had no idea how the approximately two million limestone and granite blocks—which weighed between two-and-a-half and fifty tons each—had been cut and shaped to form the outer shell of the pyramid. The known tools of the age could only barely cut through limestone, and they would've been useless against granite.

Solo was stricken by the fact that modern archeology had no idea how the blocks had actually been quarried. But the mystery of the Great Pyramid did not end there. The unsolved problem of how the two million, heavy blocks had been transported to the pyramid's building site was mystifying. *How had the massive blocks possibly been lifted five hundred feet to the pyramid's summit?* Solo read an article by a Danish civil engineer, who calculated that a ramp built to the top of the pyramid would require more than seven times the amount of material used for the pyramid itself. *Where would all the ramp material have gone, since it's nowhere to be found near the Great Pyramid?*

Solo also discovered that no one had ever solved the riddle of how the fifty-ton blocks that made up the vault in the pyramid's center were lifted and positioned into place. The working area for the vault's blocks only allowed four to six workers to stand in the vault's working space at a time. However, at least *two thousand* workers would have been needed to lift a single granite block. *It didn't add up.*

He was fascinated by Herodotus, who had visited the pyramid in the fifth century B.C. and reported that engravings of strange characters had completely covered the pyramid's exterior at the time. In the 12th century, the Arab historian *Abd el Latif* had noted that these strange inscriptions were so numerous they *could have filled more than ten thousand written pages*. William of Baldensal, a European visitor to the pyramid in the early 14th century, had also reported that the stones were covered with strange symbols, which were arranged in precise rows.

However, later in the 14th century, following an earthquake that leveled Cairo, the local Arabs robbed the pyramid of its beautiful casing stones to rebuild their primitive mosques and fortresses in the city. As the stones were cut into smaller pieces and reshaped, all traces of the mysterious ancient inscriptions that covered the outside of the giant pyramid were removed and lost forever.

Solo wondered what great library of wisdom had been inscribed on the pyramid's outer shell. *What had all the exterior writings said? What had they meant?*

Solo's mind ached as he attempted to figure out what all the mysteries meant. *Why had the ancient builders of the pyramids encoded such a vast amount of precise astronomical, geographical, and mathematical knowledge into the structure of the pyramid?* It almost seemed as though they'd wanted mankind to have a library of knowledge that would last forever.

When Solo confirmed that the exterior measurements of the Ark of War precisely matched the interior measurements of the stone chest that had been found in the vault in the pyramid's center, he knew he was on the right track.

Solo felt certain that the Ark had been there at one time. In addition, Jeremiah's code, along with the three-dimensional model that ADI had created, pointed to the unexplored and unknown subterranean chamber of the pyramid. Solo was convinced that Jeremiah had hidden the Ark there.

He next searched through information about the Battle of Jericho and the strange reference from the book that ADI had not been able to fit into her 3-D puzzle.

"... *And it cometh to pass when the people hear the voice of the trumpet, that the people shout—a great shout, and the wall falleth under it...* " Solo knew it was a clue, and he started to believe that it was the last piece to discovering the Ark's final resting place.

Ike's voice interrupted Solo's reflection.

"We'll be landing soon," he said as he sat down in a charcoal leather chair next to Solo.

Solo nodded his head in acknowledgment.

"What did you mean by asset protection work?" he asked Ike.

"What?"

"Back in Frankfurt. You said you were in asset protection. From what I've seen so far, you have access to means and equipment that most countries in the G20 don't have access to. What do you really do?"

At first, Ike said nothing.

"I don't think you would care for my line of work these days," he finally answered, gazing out the window. "Initially, I got paid a lot of money to protect the secrets of some very powerful corporations around the world."

"Initially?"

"I think that's how they suck in guys like me. You know, money beyond belief and a cause you can believe in. Back then I really thought the people that I worked for were some of the most honorable men in the world. I thought they were true leaders and patriots—not the politicians or the whores we see bankrupting our country on Wall Street. I saw that these men really *did* run the world, and I felt excited to be part of something that could actually get the job done well."

"I'm guessing the paycheck probably didn't hurt, either?"

"They definitely bought me."

"And now?" Solo ventured.

"I'm just another hired gun, in too deep to ever get out."

"So for whom do you really work?"

"The *Fat Man*," Ike answered bluntly.

"What?"

"I've never met him, and I have no idea who he really is. What I've been told is that he used to be a priest. They call him the *Fat Man* for some reason. I don't know why. Maybe it's because he's actually obese, but I think it's some sort of code name."

"How are you in too deep to get out?"

"You don't leave an organization like this. You can't retire or walk away, ever. Be careful, Solomon. This organization really does run the world." Ike stood back up. "Put your seat belt on, my old friend. We'll be on the ground in Cairo in a few minutes."

Solo didn't reply as Ike walked toward his men at the rear of the plane's main cabin. He wondered about the abundant wealth and power of an employer that could grant Ike permission to land his private Learjet on a military base in Egypt.

The G650 Learjet touched down at the military airfield known as the 222nd Tactical Fighter Brigade at Cairo West, just outside of Cairo proper. Although Ike's plane had been cleared to land, two Egyptian F-16's scrambled and escorted the jet all the way to the runway. As it landed, they throttled back up and circled around above them.

As soon as Solo and Ike exited the aircraft, they were greeted by an armed escort and immediately whisked away to meet with the commanding general of the airbase himself, Air Marshal Hafez. Ike's influence around the world was nothing short of presidential.

The Egyptian military had taken control of the country right after the civilian government had collapsed in an effort to keep the rebels from destroying it from within. This military had always been a separate entity and power source within Egypt, with its own assets and an ability to generate income for itself. However, times had changed as chaos had run through the country, and the military's standard of living had gradually become threatened.

Ike had told Solo about how his employers had used large sums of cash to gain crucial influence and create strategic alliances around the world. Solo and Ike had planned to utilize Ike's international corporate slush fund access to help them get inside the pyramid.

Solo and Ike were led to the base commander's posh headquarters, located to the far east of the military complex. The rest of Ike's crew remained with the aircraft and awaited further instructions.

"Ike Duggan!" the Egyptian air marshal said in fluent English as he walked out the front door of his headquarters to greet the two American visitors.

"Marshal Hafez," Ike said. He embraced the man and kissed him on both cheeks. The marshal returned the greeting, and both men briefly smiled at each other.

"Please, come inside. It's much too hot for you pale and sun-shy Americans to be out in the winter desert sun," the air marshal said, motioning to his two guests to follow him inside.

The marshal's office was well-furnished, but it was not extravagant, like Solo had expected. He obviously liked the Dallas

Cowboys, as trophies and trinkets bearing the N.F.L. team's motif were scattered everywhere throughout the room. He even had a large, poster-sized photograph of himself and Roger Staubach that had been taken at some American football stadium.

Ike and Solo sat on a thick, brown leather couch that was identical to the one that the marshal sat on directly across from it. Ike rested his stainless-steel briefcase at his feet. Between the couches lay a large rug, which appeared to have been made from the hide of a Texas longhorn.

It was obvious to Solo that the marshal and Ike had done this negotiation dance before. He remained quiet, as Ike had instructed him to do, and he listened as Ike did what Ike did best: *bullshit.*

"My good friend. Thank you for the courtesy of allowing me to land in your wonderful country," Ike said, leaning forward and resting his arms over his knees.

"You are always welcome in my homeland," the marshal replied. He nervously stole a glance at the briefcase on the floor and then looked back up at Ike. Ike had told Solo that it would take a lot less money today than it would have a few years ago to buy the proposal that Ike was about to make to the marshal. The people's revolution had made even a small amount of cash - king.

"This is a dear man I have known almost my whole life," Ike said, gesturing to Solo, who sat beside him. "He is somewhat of an amateur archeologist, and he would like some private study time in your great Giza Pyramid."

"I'm afraid there are no treasures buried there anymore. Many people have been through the Great Pyramid over the years. I am sorry, but it is empty," the marshal said, leaning back into the couch as he unbuttoned the top button of his uniform. "The thousand new tombs and pyramids discovered by your American infrared satellites are all north of Cairo, at the ancient city of Tanis. However, there are no new discoveries here in Cairo. If your friend would like a private tour of our national landmarks here, we can certainly accommodate him, but I do not want him to be disappointed or to seek a *refund* if he is hoping to find treasure."

"I am wondering what a fair fee would be for me and my eccentric friend to have a night of exclusive time inside your wonderful Giza Pyramid—and to be allowed to take with us whatever little trinkets he *might* find?"

Ike pulled the briefcase off the floor and sat it on his lap. He waited for the air marshal to speak before opening it.

"Ike, my friend. There is no fee for a private tour of our great landmark. I owe you that much as a gratitude for the handsome and generous Ramadan gift you sent me last year. It drives very fast. But, should your friend find some ancient crumb of antiquity that he wishes to keep for himself and deprive us of our national treasure, well, then . . ." the marshal trailed off, slowly nodding his head up and down as he contemplated an acceptable price.

"Marshal, there is no amount that my friend could compensate you for such a loss. I propose instead that you accept this gift from my friend as a mere deposit for your permission to allow him the privilege of removing whatever he might find, so that he might study it further in private and then return it *someday* for the benefit of all the Egyptian people."

Ike flipped the tumblers on the briefcase's two numerical locks and handed the marshal the closed briefcase before leaning back into the couch.

Gaining permission to land at an Egyptian military base and garnering red-carpet treatment from their military host had not cost them anything. The history between Ike and the marshal had paid for that. However, the price tag for the privilege of removing an artifact from the great Giza Pyramid was $250,000 US dollars—a small pittance of the cash that Ike kept in his aircraft's safe for situations just like this one.

Marshal Hafez opened the briefcase but did not touch the cash inside. He seemed to be computing how much cash it contained simply by looking at it. After a moment, he looked at Ike and smiled largely. That amount of money was obviously more than what he had planned to ask for. Ike had played the situation masterfully. The marshal picked up the phone on the blue-and-white end table next to him and barked orders into it.

"Gentlemen, you shall be treated like kings while you are visitors in my country—*pharaohs*, I mean," he said with a grin. "My men will escort you to the pyramid immediately. They will call ahead and close the entire grounds at all three of the pyramids. You will have all afternoon and all evening to roam the grounds and study them as you deem fit. No one will disturb you. My chief of staff will ensure that you will have whatever assistance you require. However, I expect that by morning, when the prying eyes of the city awaken for morning prayers, you will no longer be with us?"

Ike stood to shake the marshal's hand.

"Yet again, your generosity is too much," he said. "We thank you. We will be gone before the morning sunlight."

They returned to their aircraft and retrieved Ike's three companions, who had remained behind to guard the jet. The pilot disabled and locked the aircraft with a G.P.S.-looking device that he kept in his pack and joined their expedition. The five men were then transported in a black Range Rover to the other side of the city, where the pyramids awaited them.

The city streets of Cairo were mayhem. None of the traffic lights worked, at least as far as Solo could see, and people, bicycles, animals, and vehicles all seemed head in random, different directions. There was no discernible order to any of it. When Solo first saw the pyramids in the distance as they drove through downtown Cairo, he was amazed at how close the city was to the giant stone structures. It was as though the city had grown up around the three ancient fixtures.

As they drove through the entrance to what Solo guessed was a visitor's center, he saw two Egyptian military trucks pull up. Armed men jumped out of them and began to erect a simple, wooden blockade across the street they had just driven down. A large barrier circled the entire pyramid complex.

"Where would you like us to take you?" a large Egyptian soldier asked as he drove the Range Rover onto another side street and pulled up close to the largest of the three pyramids.

Solo got out of the car and stood, looking up at the mammoth structure of stone. It looked nothing like the postcards and posters he'd previously seen. From afar, the pyramid looked smooth and precise; up close, however, the stones were rough and ragged, and they formed what looked like a gargantuan monster's staircase.

Solo walked up to the pyramid. As he touched the base of one of the massive stones, he realized that he had seen these building blocks before: their size and shape were identical to the stones that formed the foundation of Solomon's Temple in Jerusalem.

"We need to go all the way down, into the subterranean chamber inside this one," Solo said to their Egyptian escort as he pointed to the largest pyramid, directly in front of them. He grabbed an oversized duffle bag that he'd brought with him from the jet out of the back seat of the car.

"There is nothing in there but rubble," the Egyptian soldier replied as he passed out flashlights to everyone. "The ancients did not finish their work down there."

Ike's three team members, all well-armed and ready for any contingency, looked around the parking lot, passing tactical messages to each other through simple facial expressions. The three of them were dressed in their casual civilian-military gear: olive-colored, canvas pants, with black Kevlar bullet-proof vests that fit snugly over their tight, black, short-sleeve shirts. The tallest and most senior of the three men wore a dark-blue Detroit Tigers baseball cap, and the shortest of the three wore a dirty, straw cowboy hat. The third team member's bald head gleamed in the direct sunlight. They followed Ike, Solo, and their Egyptian escort through the maze of sidewalks and climbed up the tourist staircase, which led to the entrance of the heart of the Great Pyramid of Giza.

As soon as they stepped inside the well-lit tunnel and out of the hot Egyptian sun, they could feel the coolness of the massive stone structure. It was a natural air-conditioning unit, resting in the middle of the desert. Solo and Ike hurried behind their guide to keep up with him. The tunnel took the party of five downward on a steep slope. Eventually, they reached a plateau that felt like the middle of the pyramid. He remembered Dav'd's story about Napoleon and a shiver went down his spine.

"This way," their escort said, and they began descending again, deeper into the heart of the timeless beacon.

They crawled through tight spaces and walked down long, stone staircases before finally reaching the very end of a long tunnel, thirty meters below the base of the pyramid. The ground leveled out for several feet in front of them, but the tunnel remained tight and narrow.

"This is the chamber you seek," the Egyptian said as the party of five followed him into a large room, filled with stone rubble. "You cannot go any deeper, unless you crawl into that one-meter square hole over there."

The five men looked around the subterranean chamber. Lights had been attached to the front portion, where they stood, and Solo could now see first-hand what he'd spent the last eight hours researching. A square pit, surrounded by a metal handrail, was directly in front of them. And the square hole that the Egyptian soldier had just pointed out—or the *microphone tunnel*, as Solo now called it in his head—was just beyond the pit in front of them.

"The tunnel runs for about fifteen meters, and then it ends," the escort added. "The ancients never finished this part of the tomb. We have no idea why it was built."

To their right, several feet away, was a large, raised platform that appeared to have been carved from the floor on which they stood. It resembled a stage, towering above them, with several rough-looking stairs in the middle, which ascended from the ground floor to the platform. Although there were no lights attached to the walls near the area, Solo could make out several rock protrusions extending from the floor of the platform to the ceiling above. The area was dark and shadowy due to the lack of direct light, and it appeared far too difficult for anyone to successfully climb.

"Thank you," said Solo as he set down his duffel bag. "We'll be fine by ourselves. We'll meet you at the entrance when we're through looking around."

"As you wish," the escort said. "The marshal has instructed me to give you anything you desire." He turned and vanished back up into the tunnel.

Solo continued to look around the underground chamber, and the man in the cowboy hat followed him. The chamber was almost two stories high in some places. Solo examined the hole in the ground that the metal railing surrounded, and he used his flashlight to peer down at the rubble at the bottom of the pit over ten feet below him. However, his primary interest was the small tunnel that the Egyptian soldier had pointed out to them, which apparently proceeded straight into pitch-black darkness before ending for no reason. The lights, which had been strung together and hung along the cold, stone walls, did not extend illuminate the small tunnel.

Later, Solo would realize that he had instinctively turned towards the stone stage *before* he'd heard the voice resonating from it. It had been as though he'd known he was about to hear it.

"We've been double-crossed."

The feminine voice echoed from behind the protruding rocks. It was as though Solo's mind had heard the words before his ears had. Ike and his three men instantly jumped and turned to face the rock stage.

"Ike has been working against us all this time," the calm voice said as it echoed and bounced off the underground chamber walls.

Ike looked back at the two men standing directly behind him, and they immediately moved to separate tactical positions in front of the platform. Baldy and Baseball Cap each attempted to point their automatic pistols toward the unseen voice, looking around them in quick, fluid-like motions. They never spoke, yet each seemed to know the other's thoughts and movements at every instant. They wanted to advance on the unknown stranger up on the stage, but the high stone wall in front of them that formed the platform's front blocked them.

Solo's heart crashed and leapt in the same moment when the voice again spoke.

"I am sorry, Solo, that I let you think I was dead."

"Eteye?!" Solo said, taking a step toward the voice in front of him. "Is that you? How is that possible?"

Before Solo realized what they were doing, Ike and Cowboy Hat moved to close the gap between Solo and the voice emanating from the top of the stage.

"We don't need you anymore, Ms. Azeb," Ike said as he leaned against the wall and drew a pistol from his jacket, pointing it toward the still-unseen person above him. "You should have stayed in Tokyo and played dead."

". . . Ike?" Solo asked as he watched his friend point his gun in Eteye's direction.

"Ms. Azeb, there are not many hiding places in this small, rock tomb," Ike said, holding his pose.

"You fucking bastard! It was *your* men at the computer lab?" Solo shouted as he began to move toward Ike, scanning the floor for a weapon to use against him. Cowboy Hat pivoted and pointed his gun's muzzle towards Solo's face.

"Relax, Solomon. There's no need for you to get in the middle of this and get hurt," Ike said. He kept his gun and eyes aimed at the platform. "We still need your help to figure out why we're all standing in this god-forsaken pyramid."

"Fuck you!" Solo said. He took another step towards Ike and the staircase leading up to the stage, ignoring the gun that was now less than two feet away from his head.

Eteye carefully and slowly walked out of the darkness and down the stairs, her hands raised over her head. Her snake-like golden necklace glimmered in the shallow light, and her hair, which she'd pulled back into a ponytail, blended in with the shadows. The memories of the evil woman who had locked her away in the deep dark dungeon flooded back. Panic and fear tried to weasel their way into her thoughts. She took a deep breath and focused on the present, refusing to give into the dread.

"I think we would draw unwanted attention from our Egyptian hosts if we had a gun fight down here, don't you think?" she said.

"I'm genuinely impressed," Ike replied as he dropped his arm that held his gun. He motioned to Baseball Cap across from him. "I thought my crew took care of you back in Japan. I should have known something was up when they never reported back to me before we took off. However, I certainly never expected that you'd get the better of *three* trained assassins. Besides"—Ike gestured at the miserable chamber around them— "we are buried in solid rock so deeply that you could set off a tactical nuke down here, and no one up at the surface would hear you."

"I suspected you were playing both sides on this one," Eteye responded. She stood just at the edge of where the chamber lights penetrated the darkness.

"I did everything Levi asked me to do, God damn it! I delivered those ancient documents to you, just as he asked. I didn't double-cross anyone, and I don't see any downside in turning over to my employers whatever Solo finds buried under this pyramid," Ike shot back.

Ike's betrayal hit Solo like a fist to the face. As he listened to Ike and Eteye, he tried to figure out what his next move would be. He thought he had a small chance of getting the jump on the soldier pointing the gun at his head. *A small chance—if he could close the gap between the two of them.* However, if he made a move, he knew the other two men, who were still pointing their automatic weapons at Eteye, would have no problem shooting her instantly. *Why had she just given up?*

"So you're just some corporate lap dog, huh? Whatever they say, you do?" he yelled at Ike as he ventured one more step forward, closing the gap between the gun and his head. Ike turned to look at Solo as he continued to yell. "That's it? You're just going to turn over the world's most powerful weapon to some Fat priest, or whoever the fuck it is that you work for?"

"Fat priest?" Eteye asked reacting quickly to the mention of that description.

"Not at all, Solo. The Fat Man really *does* run the world, and his organization will be able to ensure that your weapon—or whatever it is you find down here—is safely guarded and kept out of the hands of all the religious lunatics running around *up there*," Ike said, pointing to the ceiling.

"How do you know he won't use it for his own purposes? Just like he uses *you*!" Solo said, trying to simultaneously draw a reaction from Ike and distract the man aiming a gun at his head.

"Ha! And you sit in your million-dollar Manhattan office doing *what* every day? You're a hired gun, just like I am! Last time I checked, Solo, you sell justice to the highest bidder."

"Unlike *you*, I'm no one's pathetic little lap dog. I decide who I work for, and, more importantly, who I *don't* work for," Solo shot back. "You can't trust these people with the kind of weaponry we hope to find. *No one* can be trusted with it. I don't think you comprehend the gravity of the mistake you're making."

"I'm not here to debate with either one of you," Ike said coolly and authoritatively, turning back to Eteye. "Solo is going to figure out where that *Book of the Dead* leads to, and then we'll all dig up this Ark of War—*if* it's here—and get it back to my aircraft before morning. I'll tip the marshal handsomely for the courtesy of helping us pillage his national monument, and then we'll all share a drink, knowing that no lunatic religious nut-job out there will get their hands on this W.M.D."

"I'm not doing it," Solo said, closing the distance between himself and Ike and ignoring the gun, which was now twelve inches from his face. "I'm not going to tell you about *anything*. You can figure it out on your own. Go to Hell."

"I know you think I'm just a dumb Marine and not some smart trial lawyer like you, but even I can see how you feel about this bitch," Ike smirked, gesturing toward Eteye. "You look at her like you used to look at Abay. I can see the lovesick, puppy-dog look in your eyes. I bet if I just *hinted* at hurting her pretty, little face, all those secrets in your head would come flooding out."

Solo knew instantly that his expression had betrayed him.

As Ike again turned to face Eteye, he missed the split-second in which she'd winked at Solo. Baldy, who was closest to her, however, did not, and he immediately tensed, recognizing that something was about to happen.

Baseball Cap raised his pistol. The shot, even with a silencer, was shockingly loud in the small, encased tomb. Baldy went down instantly as his head exploded and his body crumbled. Blood spattered onto Ike, who had been standing two feet away from his now-dead guard only a moment before.

Solo immediately lunged at the man wearing the cowboy hat, blindly grabbing for the gun that was pointed at his head as he leapt. As his fist struck the arm holding the deadly firearm, he noticed he hadn't heard gunfire. *They have no intention of shooting me*, he realized as the two men fell to the ground. *They need me alive.* He and Cowboy Hat writhed and wrestled on the stone floor.

Ike, still mid-turn, raised his weapon toward Baseball Cap. His traitor had the jump on him, though, and the bullet caught Ike low in the chest, just below his right shoulder. Its impact spun Ike's body around before he could shoot, and he dropped his firearm as he fell to the ground and grabbed his chest.

As Baseball Cap fell to the ground, Eteye had instantly moved to recover the dead soldier's machine pistol. She grabbed it off the ground in a single, fluid motion before making a dead sprint toward Solo and Cowboy Hat.

Baseball Cap moved in on Ike and jabbed his foot into his back to keep him down. Ike screamed in agony from the ground with a sucking chest wound.

Solo slammed his forearm into Cowboy Hat's throat as they rolled over the straw hat that he'd ripped from the man's head in the frenzy. Cowboy Hat had just wrestled his way on top, his fist raised to strike Solo, when he felt the barrel of a gun shoved hard into the back of his neck. He froze.

"Let him go," Eteye said, her hand pressing the firearm forcefully into his skin. "Now."

Cowboy Hat placed his hands over his head slowly.

"Are you okay?" Eteye asked. She used her gun to push the man off of Solo and into the ground. With her free hand, she helped pull Solo from the floor. As he stood, Solo stared at her in complete disbelief.

"I thought you were dead," he said. "I really thought you were gone. How in the world did you get here?"

"We can share flight records later," Eteye said with a grin. She quickly kissed Solo's lips. Her attention, however, remained focused on the man kneeling in front of her. "First, we need to tie him up, just in case some of those Egyptian soldiers you rode here with heard our little gun fight and come to investigate."

Eteye handed Solo her weapon and then picked up Cowboy Hat's gun, which had landed on the floor near Solo's feet. She dropped the magazine and emptied the chamber. She then threw the empty gun down the hole in the ground that Solo had examined only a few minutes earlier.

The mysterious baseball-hatted man who had saved them both left the motionless Ike lying face-down on the ground and quickly moved to the captured bodyguard, who was still kneeling in front of Solo and Eteye. He had just begun to pull his wrecked cowboy hat from underneath his legs when Baseball Cap stuck him in the neck with a syringe.

"What the hell is going—?" Solo began, but Eteye's mouth pressed hard onto his, and he stopped trying to speak. She smiled and caressed his face, like she had done several times before over the last few days.

"You're smiling, Solo." She said. "I haven't seen much of that from you."

Solo *was* smiling, and the false sense of confidence he had gotten by with for so long evaporated.

"I can't tell you how bad it was when I thought you were dead," he said.

"I can't die, Solomon. I love you too much. I always have."

Solo felt the response inside his stomach at the exact same time the words came out of his mouth. He never thought consciously about the words that had just brought a smile to both of their faces. They were spoken on instinct, not through rational thought. They were like the mysterious force that gently guides flocks of geese south in the winter—words you didn't need to think about to know they were true.

Solo had never told anyone those three words. Not even Abay. He had planned to tell her, but she had left him before he could. The words *I love you* rolled out of his soul and off his tongue in the cold, dark basement of the Great Pyramid of Giza. Eteye's large, dark eyes moistened, and they hugged each other. Solo's smile grew larger.

The mysterious man who had just stuck the cowboy interrupted the moment. "He'll be out for six hours, at least," he informed them.

"Who are you?" Solo asked as rational thoughts returned to his body.

"He works for Mossad," Eteye answered. "Institute for Intelligence and Special Operations. They're the national intelligence agency of Israel. He's a long-time undercover plant, and we lucked out tremendously by having him on this detail today. Ike had no idea he was working with us."

"I thought you said we couldn't trust Israeli intelligence any more than we could trust U.S. intelligence?" Solo asked.

"I guess we don't have a choice now," Eteye answered.

For the next three minutes, Eteye tried to treat Ike's wound and stop the bleeding as Ike rested against the wall, writhing in pain. The Israeli agent stuck a syringe in Ike's neck.

"What're you giving him?" Solo asked.

"Extremely refined marijuana. It's the best pain manager out there," the agent said as Ike laid his head back against the wall. A few minutes later, he began to relax, and his breathing calmed.

"Solo," he whispered.

Solo squatted over Ike and watched the Israeli soldier plug his gunshot wound with a clean bandage.

"I'm right here," he said.

"They will find you. There is nowhere you can run or hide. They will own you, like they own me," Ike said as he winced in pain.

"Who will find me?"

"The Fat Man."

"I'm not worried about someone you have never met and aren't even sure is real," Solo said.

"You should be," Ike answered. "He knew all about the Ark of War, before I ever sent him the information. And he knew about *her*, too, once I described her necklace," Ike said, pointing to Eteye.

"Eteye? How could he know about her or the Ark?" Solo asked.

"He knows much more than you think," Ike said. "His organization runs everything and everyone—governments, presidents, economies. They never make mistakes, and they never leave any loose ends. They will come looking for me, and they absolutely will not hesitate to kill anyone around you to get what they want."

"We'll worry about that once I find what we came here for."

Solo could see that the plant-based medicine was taking effect. Ike's eyelids began to grow heavy, and he started to drift off to sleep.

"They will find you . . . I'm sorry, Solo."

"Solo, it's time we get back to why we're here," Eteye interrupted. "We don't know when the Egyptian soldiers will be back, but you're not going to have the same reception from them without Ike as you did when he was leading this expedition."

"I think I figured it out!" Solo said. He again smiled as he sensed that he was about to actually *contribute* to their mission for the first time.

"Tell me," Eteye said, moving her body close to him, as usual.

"Remember that extra reference from scripture that we found in Jeremiah's writings—the one that didn't fit into ADI's three-dimensional model?"

"The one about the battle at Jericho and the walls falling down?"

"Exactly," Solo said. "I read the Book of Joshua several times on the plane ride over here, particularly the story about the Walls of Jericho."

He reached into his pocket and pulled out a piece of paper that had a section of scripture from the book of Joshua scribbled on it. The paper's margin was filled with scattered notes.

"Joshua takes over after the death of Moses, and he uses the Ark of War to cross the Jericho River, on *dry land*—just like Moses did when they left Egypt," Solo read. "That's how we know that Moses took the Ark from Egypt in the first place. The entire book of Joshua is all about the early military campaigns of the Hebrews. However, the bizarre scripture reference we found in the book doesn't make any sense. It says, '*when the people hear the voice of the trumpet, that the people shout—a great shout, and the wall falleth under it.*'"

Eteye read the reference from over his shoulder as he spoke.

Solo explained. "It reminded me of an Army colonel I represented a while back who had a gambling problem. He was part of a military campaign to develop a weapon using sound waves. He told me that they used it mainly for crowd control, but they'd created a laser-type pulse of sound that could kill people, like a sniper's rifle. I began to think that, somehow, the ancient Hebrews developed the very same sound-wave technology six-thousand years ago—that the sound from the ram's horn in close proximity to the Ark of War had created a sonic weapon, one that crumbled the defensive walls of the City of Jericho."

Solo and Eteye walked to the far end of the chamber, opposite the tunnel entrance where they had entered. They stood in front of the ominous hole that crept straight into the solid-rock underbelly of the pyramid.

"So you think the reference to the ram's horns is another clue to finding the Ark?" she asked.

"Not another clue—the *key* to opening the door," Solo said. He motioned to the tunnel in front of them.

"What is this?" Eteye asked, squatting down to peer into the ground-level, pitch-black tunnel carved into the massive rock wall. She shined her flashlight inside but could not see the tunnel's end.

"No one knows," Solo said. "The tunnel goes straight back into an abyss of nowhere for fifty feet, and then it just ends."

"What do you mean, 'no one knows?'"

"Just exactly that," Solo said. "No one has any idea why this entire subterranean chamber was built, let alone the reason for this weird offshoot of a tunnel that just dead-ends in the middle of solid rock. We are incredibly deep under the pyramid, and this unfinished chamber and tunnel here are the most mysterious parts of the entire structure to this day. No one knows why they're here or what they were meant to do."

Solo walked across the chamber and picked up the duffle bag he'd brought with him into the pyramid. He pulled out a laptop and a portable speaker system that he'd borrowed from Ike's executive cabin on the plane.

Eteye watched him in silent curiosity as he placed the three speakers in a row just inside the small, square tunnel at their feet, facing them into the darkness.

"I couldn't figure out why Jeremiah left a dangling reference to Joshua's sonic weapon at Jericho in the *Book of the Dead*. What could Jericho possibly have to do with a chamber a hundred feet underground—a chamber that remains unexplained to this very day? But then I got it," Solo said, standing up. "I think they came up with a sonic device that, when magnified by the power contained in the Ark, was able to wreak havoc on the walls of their enemies' fortresses. The number *phi*, sonic waves, and the map all led us straight to this dead-end rock chamber."

"I still don't get it," Eteye said as Solo powered up his lap top. He opened up the application and showed her a string of musical notes.

"I created a fractal string of ones and zeros in the form of what's called the *golden string*—a musical representation of the number *phi*. Actually, I didn't do it—some really smart math guys on the Internet did. I just copied it. It looks like this."

He showed her a string of numbers:

01001010010010100101001001010010 . . .

"So those numbers are God's Number—what Hito was talking about back in Japan?" she asked.

"The number *phi*? Yes, exactly. I'm going to play it through these speakers into our tunnel to nowhere here. I think this little tunnel here is a microphone."

Eteye smiled as he plugged the speakers into the computer's audio jack.

"I think Jeremiah led us here because the Ark is buried somewhere in this chamber. He referenced what happened at Jericho because it holds the key to unlocking the entrance that's hidden somewhere in all of this rock."

He stood and looked at Eteye and the Israeli soldier next to her.

"I think the Egyptians, or Hebrews—whatever you want to call them—played a sonic version of the number *phi* at Jericho, and the Ark of War magnified it into a sonic weapon that brought down the walls of the city. I plan to play the same sonic version into this little tunnel, and if the Ark of War is really here—"

"—the walls will come falling down?" the Israeli soldier wearing the Major League Baseball hat asked.

"They very well might. However, my hope is that Jeremiah designed a sonic *entrance* into the last resting place of the Ark—not a musical booby trap."

They both looked at Solo and understood what he was asking them. They nodded in unison, giving their consent for him to proceed. He took a deep breath, bent over, and pushed *Play*.

Instantly, a strange beat emanated from the speakers. The sound was incredibly quiet. They could hear the beat, but it seemed as though the small tunnel was greedily sucking up every last note from the speakers. They waited. Nothing happened.

"Turn it up," Eteye said.

Solo turned the computer's volume to maximum. However, the volume in the chamber did not change. Solo and Eteye looked at each other: *what now?*

Suddenly, the beat's rhythmic echoes began to bounce off the walls of the chamber. The echoes seemed to be playing a rhythm all their own. For the first time, Solo realized that he really had stumbled onto something.

The Mossad agent looked around the room, and his eyes grew wide as the ground began to rumble.

When the first part of the stone staircase fell inward on itself, panic struck the three of them. They huddled together as the entire staircase that Eteye had descended from earlier disappeared into the darkness below. The dust and dirt momentarily blocked out the light, and Solo grabbed Eteye and pulled her to the ground with him. They sat with their backs pressed against the hard rock wall.

The deafening roar from the crashing rocks over the rhythmic beat of the sound of *phi*—now blasting from the room's amplification—was overwhelming. They cowered together, trapped, waiting for the chamber to crash down upon them and bury them forever in their own, pharaoh-less tomb, deep beneath the Great Pyramid of Giza.

Part III

34

The dust cleared faster than expected.

To everyone's amazement, the lights had never flickered or gone out, and the room had not collapsed around them. Solo unplugged the speaker cord from the laptop, and the chamber was silent once again. The three of them stood and looked around. Aside from the collapsed staircase, nothing looked any different than it had just moments ago.

Eteye walked over to check on Ike, who was still curled up on the floor next to the wall by the stage.

"He's dead," she said. No one responded, and Solo realized he was unsure how he felt about his friend's death.

"Solo, come look!" Eteye exclaimed suddenly. She pointed to where the stairs had been. Solo and the Mossad agent quickly walked over to her and immediately saw what the loud crash of rocks had revealed.

The rough staircase that had led upward to the stage only moments before now led in the exact opposite direction. At their feet, they could see a perfectly formed staircase, which led deeper still into the depths of the pyramid's mysterious underbelly.

"We need Ike's bag. I saw him put some lanterns in it before we came down here," the Israeli soldier said as he turned and began searching.

"I can't believe it," Solo said. He looked at Eteye, and a proud smile spread across his face.

"You did it, Solo!" she said squeezing his hand. "You added up the clues and solved the riddle—just like one of your courtroom trials."

"I found two Maglites, a few glow sticks, and one lantern that the Egyptian guide left for us," the Israeli man said as he walked back to them.

"What's your name?" Solo asked, truly acknowledging the man for the first time.

"Minkoff,"

"Nice to meet you, Minkoff. Hand me the lantern, please."

Solo was the first to go down the stairs. Rocks from the formerly ascending staircase lay everywhere, but the walls lining the downward staircase were smooth and polished. The massive stones that had crafted them formed perfect planes. *They're just like the stones in Giza's vault*, Solo thought.

Solo's lantern was high-powered, and he could see that the splendid stone staircase that continued downward, flaring outward as it went deeper, like stairs from an old, southern plantation house. He saw the bottom of the staircase, which he estimated was about two stories below him. His mind struggled to comprehend everything that had just happened.

He continued down, staying near one side of the wall, and ran his hand across the smooth stones as he stepped over and around the large, broken boulders that had fallen all the way down to the bottom of the stairwell. Eteye and Minkoff followed behind him.

They were about halfway down the stairwell when Solo reached the bottom and stopped, holding his lantern above his head.

"What is it?" Eteye asked, quickening her pace down the stairs to join him. She felt claustrophobia's brush up against her and her long battle with the fear of dark closed in spaces. *Another deep breath*, she told herself as she continued.

Solo didn't answer. He just stood there, frozen.

As Eteye neared the bottom of the staircase, her face went blank as she saw what towered in front of Solo.

35

The New York Times was the first worldwide news agency to run a story of the pending nuclear doom that faced the small nation of Israel. Many facts were still missing, but the article did say that unnamed sources had confirmed that nuclear material had been or was about to be smuggled into the country. The Israeli Defense Forces had been placed on their highest alert, and their naval forces were descending on the Suez Canal and Israel's southern border with Egypt in a last-ditch attempt to prevent the successful smuggling operation by unknown terrorists.

The Turkish Ambassador to the United States was quoted as saying that his country would not allow Israel to invade Egypt and control the Suez Canal. He even hinted that the nuclear bomb rumor was likely just a ploy by the hardliners in the Israeli military establishment to justify their Egyptian invasion plans.

The article also implied that U.S. military forces had been placed on increased alert, and an American aircraft carrier group was moving deeper into the south Mediterranean Sea.

36

They were inadvertent archaeologists.

Eteye, Solo, and Minkoff stood in amazement as their searching flashlights exposed more and more of the massive room before them. It was a large, underground complex, and it extended as far as their eyes could see. Directly in front of them were two sets of dump-truck-sized stone sphinxes, perched on intricately carved rectangular platforms. The glaring, four-legged sculptures, each with the head of a human and the wings of a bird, had been staged two to the left and two to the right at the end of the stairwell—the obvious entrance to whatever lay hidden inside.

To the left and to the right of the four Egyptian beasts were four Roman columns that connected to the ceiling above. Solo estimated the columns to be at least twenty feet in circumference, and they were covered in what looked like hieroglyphics.

Just past the sphinxes and between the round columns were two black obelisks, which also reached all the way to the ceiling two stories up. Whomever had designed the entrance to the massive underground chamber had clearly intended to awe his visitor, and he had succeeded.

They walked in silence between the stone sentries and past the obelisks. Solo wished he could read the writings on the stone columns as they passed them. For some reason, he had the strange sensation that Eteye could.

As they reached the edge of the final, surrounding columns, they came upon a new set of stairs, which looked to be a hundred feet wide and descended downward at least another fifteen feet.

Solo's sensory intake systems were reaching critical mass as he held the lantern above his head and walked even deeper into the pyramid. He slowly crawled further into the unknown darkness in front of him, revealing another massive room the size of the biggest aircraft hangar he could imagine. Two 747 jetliners could easily have fit into the shadowy, darkened warehouse. As he looked around, he saw every shape and object imaginable: shelves, tables, full-sized boats, small pyramids the size of a car, chariots, steles, animals, carvings, furniture, and stacks of weapons. There were shadows of objects he couldn't make out, which rested so far back into the complex that he had no idea where it ended.

"It's a museum," Solo breathed as Eteye grabbed his hand. Solo's lantern only illuminated about a hundred feet in front of them—nowhere even close to the back of the stadium-sized room.

"It's much more than that. It's the world's first university and library," Eteye said.

They walked down the stairs and into the room. Her face radiated both sheer amazement and curiosity as she looked around them.

"So this is what Jeremiah was up to," she said. "Look at all the scrolls on the shelves and all the stone tablets over there."

"How will we ever find the Ark in a place this big?" Minkoff said, bringing them out of their bedazzlement.

"If Eteye's right, there must be some sort of organization to all of this. You can tell that everything has its place. Nothing in here has just been randomly dumped," Solo said.

"And, clearly, no tomb robbers have been here," Minkoff added.

"We need to spread out and see if we can figure out the organization system," Eteye said. She started down the middle of the gargantuan room.

"You go right, and I'll go left," Solo instructed Minkoff. Solo's lantern provided the most light, and he tried to absorb as much as he could possibly see as he walked through the dark.

It became apparent to him several seconds later that he had walked into a medical section. He found a full-sized skeleton, still hanging from some sort of metal structure. He couldn't tell what held the bones together, but its reflection in the lantern's light made him think it was some sort of precious metal. He saw all kinds of small jars, lined up neatly on rows of shelves, and he found a large, limestone tablet that was as big as a king-sized bed, held upright by some sort of rock base. A complete diagram of the human circulatory system had been carved into the massive stone. Solo couldn't read the hieroglyphics that labeled each part on the diagram, but he was amazed at how accurate the life-sized carving appeared.

He heard Minkoff's and Eteye's voices in the distance as he continued past the medical section and found himself in an astrological partition of the ancient university. Surrounded by shelves, which also reached two stories high and were covered with scrolls, Solo found a model of the solar system the size of a small car. Rounded stones of many different sizes, held together by bronze and copper rods, had been fastened into an antique prototype of the sun and its planets. The sight of it rendered Solo motionless as he held his lantern up to it, his mouth open in awe.

He remembered what his mother had taught him as a child as he stood in front of the model of the planets orbiting the sun. She had said to be guarded when it came to the teachings of the church, while at the same time professing an unshakable faith in her Lord and Savior. One evening at the dinner table they'd had a heated discussion about St. Augustine and the church fathers who had formed the early Christian religion. Levi was upset; he had just learned of the anti-Semitism and hatred many of the early church founders, including St. Augustine, had held toward the Jewish people.

"How can you believe in a religion whose founder, Augustine the Saint, asks God to slay all the Jewish people with his divine, two-edged sword?" young Levi had blurted out at the dinner table. Their father's chair had been vacant. "Augustine wanted his god to kill your own children!"

Solo couldn't remember his mother's mystical response, but he remembered that Levi had been calmed by it. His mother had always made sure nothing came between her and her two children—not even God, and especially not her religion.

Solo smiled while looking at the solar model as he recalled that St. Augustine and his peers, in the throes of creating their new religion, had rejected the science of the day, believing instead that they lived on a flat earth, where hell boiled below and heaven floated above.

"Over here!" Eteye's voice bounced through the quiet arena.

Awakened from his reverie, Solo looked up and saw a faint glow a long way off, towards the rear of the cavern. He could make out Minkoff's flashlight and the shadows it casted from across the room on the opposite side, and he could see that it was quickly making his way to Eteye's location.

Solo walked hastily but carefully, and his heart began to beat faster with excitement. He hoped Eteye had located the Ark. He had no idea that he was about to see in this most magnificent historical discovery of all time.

Ahead, he saw Minkoff's light reach Eteye's position, where the two lights stopped moving and focused on whatever it was that they were looking at. He quickened his pace. Nothing could have prepared Solo for what he saw once he reached them.

Eteye and Minkoff stood motionless, their flashlight beams fixed on what looked like a dozen golden mummy coffins. Solo slowly approached and counted nineteen large, gold coffins, lined up perfectly in a row. He could see that the entire rear section of the warehouse—or university—that they'd just walked through was a completely distinct area from the rest of the arena-sized space. The rows of ornate sarcophagi had been raised up on a platform three steps above them, and Solo realized they all looked just like the coffin of King Tut that had traveled the world on exhibition after its discovery in Luxor, a mere 419 miles from their current location.

Solo's lantern further illuminated the area, and the three of them could now see a long line of sarcophagi laid out before them. In the center were seven small coffins; three on one side of two large, full-grown sarcophagi, and four on the other. It appeared that a king and queen had been buried here, surrounded by their seven children. To the right and to the left lay numerous additional coffins, similar in design and stature.

Solo walked past Eteye and Minkoff and started up the wide, granite stairs that led up to the golden human containers. He reached the top and looked back down at them, about five feet below; they, too, began up the steps. When they arrived at the top of the platform, they could see all the way to the rear of the perfectly proportioned stone platform on which they stood. The golden sarcophagi continued around its sides. Sitting in the exact center of the platform was a rectangular chest, approximately the size of a small office desk. Solo's emotions immediately recognized what he saw, but his mind had not yet caught up.

Each sarcophagus had been positioned with its head closest to the rectangular object. The large box in the center appeared smooth, yet the light from Solo's lantern did not reflect off of it, despite its glassy appearance. It was dark in color, not golden or ornamental. It had no hieroglyphics or writings of any kind that he could discern, nor did it have a lid or any handles. It was a plain strongbox that seemed about two and a quarter feet wide, almost three feet high, and six and a half feet in length. Something inexplicable about it pleased Solo as he stared at it.

For a moment, Solo forgot that he'd already known it would be in the perfect dimensions of *phi*. Slowly, though, he understood: there, right before him, sat the original, divinely proportioned Treasure of Egypt. He was standing in front of the Ark of the War!

Strangely, though, nothing about it made Solo feel as though it were the world's most powerful weapon of mass destruction. *Maybe its reputation as the Ark of War is all a legend and a myth?* he thought.

Standing only a few feet away, looking at The Ark in real time, Solo realized that he had no idea what to do. *Should he approach it? Should he stay a safe distance away? Bow to it? Worship it?*

Shivers flooded his mind as he finally began to comprehend that he was looking at the long-lost Ark of the Covenant.

Solo felt Eteye's warm, soft hand curl up inside his. Peacefulness always followed whenever she was near. *Is it possible my consciousness is magnified?* He was suddenly very much in the moment of the situation, and he could almost see the love and affection he held toward the woman standing at his side. He felt as though he had known her for an incredibly long time. It was then that he understood that he was standing in the presence of the divine. *The God of Fate?* he wondered. He was on holy ground, and he felt as though he should remove his shoes.

"Pharaoh Amen and his Queen Nefertiti," Eteye said as she looked over at the two massive, parental coffins. Solo followed her gaze and realized that one had carvings of an Egyptian king's face and the other held the face of his beautiful, royal queen. The king's face was unusually long, and Solo immediately noticed his lengthy nose and knobby chin. The golden face was far different from any other pharaoh's face he had seen in history books. He also noticed that, instead of a crook and flail, the king's golden arms and hands wrapped around a long, wooden staff, which had been carved to resemble a snake's body. A bronze serpent circled the uppermost part of the staff and protruded from its top. The carved staff appeared to be very old and worn, and he realized it was a separate piece from the coffin. It could be pulled right out from the golden king's carved hands.

"Their six daughters, I presume?" Solo said, looking at the three coffins on either side of them. Almost as soon as he'd said it, however, he realized that there were actually *seven* coffins, not six. He saw that the seventh sarcophagus, the farthest out from the left side, had no lid. He released Eteye's hand and walked over to the large, hollow box, which had the shape of a small body. He looked inside the lidless coffin; it was empty. No lid lay anywhere in sight.

"He was their only son. They had to leave him behind after the great plague and the exodus from Egypt," Eteye said, approaching Solo and the empty coffin. "Their boy king was killed before he even had time to grow into a man."

Minkoff stood on the far right side of the platform, holding his flashlight so that its beam fell on one of the sarcophagi.

"Come look," he said, his eyes remaining on the tomb, which came up to his waist.

Solo made his way around the coffins to Minkoff, avoiding the Ark in the center. When Solo reached him, he instantly recognized Hebrew letters that covered the top and sides of the tomb. Minkoff pointed to the two tablets on either side of the headdress.

"It says in Hebrew, *Yirmeyahu ben Hilkah ha-Levi*," he said.

"What does that mean?"

"Jeremiah's tomb," Minkoff said, matter-of-factly.

"He led us right back to where it all began."

"He's buried with all of our ancestors," Minkoff said reverently, walking to the next coffin.

Solo could feel Minkoff's excitement and awe, and then the realization of what they had discovered started to sink in: a direct link between the Jewish and Egyptian people. They really were *one*—not two distinct peoples that had merely shared the same backyard; they had started as brother and sister. Solo wondered if the knowledge of this discovery today would draw their descendants closer or push them farther apart.

Solo followed Minkoff around the platform until they stood opposite Eteye. She hadn't moved from her initial position, and he felt her gaze as it turned to the Ark in the center of the platform. She did not attempt to move, but he could feel her apprehension about being in the Ark's presence.

Solo looked at the perfect box sitting in the middle of the giant platform, guarded by the ancient pharaohs, kings, high priests, and prophets. It rested in perfect silence and waited. It felt to Solo as if it could wait for all of eternity, if necessary. He felt a strange sensation and emotion crawling inside of him, and he realized that he was more conscious than he had ever been in his whole life. He had heard people say that they were *in the moment* or *in the zone* before, but standing there, in front of the Ark, he knew that he was fully awake and in *this* moment. His thoughts and feelings did not wander, and his whole being was part of the scene they were living out. The Ark had focused him in a way he had never experienced.

Solo felt the urge to walk over to it, and his feet began to move before his thoughts instructed them to do so. As he reached the Ark, he experienced an overwhelming sense of reverence, and slowly, without explanation, he dropped to his knees and put both hands on the top of it. The Ark began to glow dimly. The dull light emanating from its interior, directly below Solo's hands, didn't seem to come from a direct light source. Rather, the light resembled a large, chemical glow stick that kept getting brighter.

Sixty seconds later, the Ark glowed bright enough to light up the entire platform, along with the surrounding section of the massive chamber. Eteye and Minkoff took a few steps back as they watched Solo continue to hold his hands on the Ark while bowing his head. He was in a trance.

With the increased light, Eteye and Minkoff could see a large, formal entrance, or exit, built into the wall directly opposite the platform where they stood, opposite the direction from which they'd just come. It had been carved into the stone face of the stadium's back wall and was similar to what they'd seen at the first entrance, with large columns, sphinxes, and monoliths.

Solo rubbed his hands on the Ark's surface, and he realized it was not really an *ark* after all. It had no seams on its sides or top. Whatever it was, it was a single, solid object—it didn't *contain* something, it *was* the something. Solo felt a magnetic force growing from the Ark, and a slight sensation of heat. His exact feelings were unclear, but he found himself acutely *aware* of exactly what was happening around him. He felt his mind kick in, like the pull of a turbo charger on a race car engine, as though its capacity was growing from its exposure to the Ark. Solo suddenly felt an acute awareness, not just of himself, but a growing consciousness of all of his surroundings—with the pyramid, with Egypt, with Africa, and with the—

He lifted his hands from the Ark, and its glow slowly began to fade. He felt his thoughts and mind begin to calm.

"What happened, Solomon?" Eteye yelled, not moving from Minkoff's side.

Solo looked at them with large eyes.

"I woke up!"

Eteye smiled.

"What do you mean you *woke up*? You weren't sleeping. I was watching you the entire time." Minkoff said.

"I woke up in my being—my consciousness. I started to see and understand everything. I was part of entire continents of people, and my mind began to understand . . ." Solo stopped talking and swallowed hard.

"Understand what, Solo?" Eteye asked.

After a long pause, Solo answered her.

"Everything."

"I was afraid we'd all be killed by our Lord," Minkoff said excitedly, taking off his baseball cap and rubbing his head erratically.

"It's nothing like that," Solo said.

"Don't be afraid," Eteye said. "You are becoming a part of something much bigger than yourself. You need to continue."

Solo looked at her and knew that she was right. The glow from the Ark had barely dissipated, but its intensity had decreased slightly. Solo smiled and put his hands back on top of it. The Ark's mysterious internal generator began to work again, and the platform's brightness again increased.

Solo inexplicably understood some of what was going on inside the Ark. Atoms swirled around electric currents. Powerful magnetic fields and electrical forces attracted and repelled.

He suddenly understood that the emergence of substance from pure energy, of which light was the purest form, was biblical in scope. Pure energy could change from one form to another— electrical, chemical, and kinesthetic—and pure energy could transubstantiate into both matter and anti-matter. Good versus evil, yin versus yang, positive versus negative. North versus south and east versus west.

Solo became aware of massive currents of electrically charged plasma circulating in patterns inside the Ark. The currents gave rise to massive magnetic fields. He could see with his mind that the Ark's interior was a collection of regions, which possessed unique combinations of temperature and density. There were gravitational pressures that compressed and heated the thick gases inside. Atoms collided so furiously that some fused together at temperatures of fifteen million degrees centigrade. Every second, six hundred million tons of matter inside the Ark converted into pure, radiant energy, creating a pressure that literally held the Ark up against gravity. Some of the energy leaked out in the form of light and created Solo's awareness.

He saw positrons inside the Ark bumping into electrons, generating a counterbalanced opposite that disappeared in the flash of a gamma ray. He now understood that the glow that emanated from it was really the result of anti-matter being produced and annihilated, deep within its heart.

He thought he saw protons and anti-protons engaging in a brief dance of friendliness. The dance only lasted a hundredth of a second, but as soon as they became spellbound by the strong love between them, their mutual annihilation was almost instantaneous. The revelation of their forbidden love traveled at the speed of light, and within a billionth of a billionth of a second they were both gone, leaving gamma rays and pions to tell their fabled story. Then, he saw they, too, disappeared; the pions turned into quarks and anti-quarks, self-destructing before becoming more gamma rays or electrons, positrons and ghostly neutrinos, all of which the Ark transformed into pure energy from their annihilations.

Solo saw the mysterious field that permeates the universe: pure, massless energy that interacted with everything and everyone. Somewhere in his memory, he heard a scientist call it the *God particle*. Its long fingers and infinite reach wove everything together. He now understood that outer space was not a vacuum; rather, it was saturated with God's invisible and unknown handiwork.

Solo saw himself, kneeling on the stone floor in front of the Ark, and he understood the fear that had lived inside him ever since his father's absence during his childhood. He saw his pain and terror float by, like a raft on a slow-moving river. He saw the suffering he carried over the death of Abay, and how he had shut off his heart to everyone and anyone after that. He saw his love for Eteye floating as well, like a sailboat under full power from the wind.

Solo understood his feelings for the first time in his life, and he became aware of who he really was. He realized that the source of his lifelong conflict with his father had not been from his father leaving his mother; rather, it'd been because, all along, he had *wanted* something from his father that he had never gotten. He wanted time with his father and his father's love. His father's absence had allowed his fear to take root. He saw clearly that the source of their conflict over the past many decades had not actually been his father at all. *It had been him!* He realized how much of life and time had passed by while he had been wrapped up in his love affair with his own pain.

He saw the religions he had grown up with and grown apart from. He saw the struggle he had with the religion of the One True God, and his mother's religion as well. But he now realized that all religions were equally true and false at the same time. Yet each, in its own way, attempted to point to the truth. He now realized the difference between pointing at something and *being* something.

He saw the attachments in his life. Power, money, reputation, winning at all costs, beating the other side, jealousy, fame, and above them all, fear of love. He could taste each one in his mouth, like a cold, rusty metal on his tongue. He could see that his attachments wanted to define him, but they didn't and couldn't.

He was awake! And he never wanted to sleep again for the rest of his life.

37

November 19th
Vatican City, Italy

The Holy See, John Paul III, awoke from his dream covered in sweat. His bed sheets were soaked with perspiration that had seeped all the way through to the mattress. He sat up straight and took a deep breath. The air reached all the way to the bottom of his lungs, and he held it there for a short pause. *A deep breath?* he asked himself.

The 59-year-old man, sitting halfway in his bed with his legs dangling over the edge, exhaled heavily. He felt no wheezing or shortness of breath. The Vatican doctors had secretly told him that, the older he got, the more his childhood injuries would take a final toll on his lungs. However, he was not afraid of death or the suffocating manner in which the doctors had promised him it would arrive. Rather, he was disappointed—disappointed that he would not see all the fruits of his labor in his beloved Church. *There was so much to be done.*

But sitting up straight on the edge of his bed in the middle of the night, John Paul felt no pain. In fact, it seemed to him that he could run a long race. He felt ashamed that *he* of all people did not recognize the miracle when it happened. But then he remembered his dream. *Or was it a vision?* Ever since his first communion, he had always doubted his religion's idea of miracles, but now he no longer doubted anything. His vision had changed all of that.

His feet missed his slippers and he felt the cold tile floor on his toes. He felt the dampness from the thick, square slabs working its way up through his ankles. He breathed in deeply again. Tonight, everything was different. *Tonight he was aware of the cold in a way he had long since forgotten.* He breathed in and out. *Luxurious gulps of air.*

He remembered the ice and the sensation of not being able to breathe when he was a child. He remembered the cold. Wet, damp, German mountain cold. He was thirteen when he'd fallen into the frozen winter lake, and when it happened he'd thought he would never experience warmth again. The cold had crushed his body and sucked the life right out of his lungs.

Sitting on the edge of his bed, curling his toes on the cold marble below, reminded him how alive he had felt just before the God of Death had come for him as a boy.

But no more thoughts of death and his childhood. There was so much to do before his guests arrived. There was much to prepare before *it* arrived.

The Holy Man in Rome was awake!

38

When Eteye heard shouting voices echo down the staircase and across the large coliseum basement, she cautiously approached Solo and grabbed his shoulders, forcefully shaking him out of his trance. Solo released the Ark and immediately fell to his hands and knees.

"The Egyptians are coming, and I don't think they mean to welcome us!" Eteye said as she and Minkoff helped Solo up from the floor. The three of them listened across the vast underground room they'd woven their way through. Solo could hear voices in the far-off distance as the soldiers made their way down the newly exposed staircase that had led them into the entrance of what Solo now mentally called the *University of the Ancients*.

"We need to get out of here," Solo said, turning to the Ark in the pitch black of the platform. It had shut down instantly as Eteye had shaken him, its internal light completely vanishing. In addition, Solo's lantern and the two flashlights in Eteye and Minkoff's hands had gone out with it.

"How did you do that?" Minkoff asked, fiddling with his flashlight in the dark.

"I just understood what needed to happen, and then somehow I saw it happen," Solo answered confidently. "There's an exit through those columns, over there." He lifted his arm to indicate where before remembering that no one could see it.

"Minkoff, break one of your glow sticks. We'll use it to get out of here. They won't be able to see something that small from all the way over on the other side, and it will take them some time to get orders from a superior before they start trampling through a major archeological discovery."

Minkoff broke a red glow stick from his pack. He watched Solo walk over to the Ark and stand on one side of it.

"Eteye, I need you to grab the other side of the Ark and help me carry it out of here," Solo said.

"I can't!" Eteye said. "Once is all that you are allowed."

"Okay," Solo said, "I understand. Minkoff, today you will assist me with the greatest treasure our people have ever known. Do not be afraid. It will not harm you—"

"But the scriptures tell of the man who was killed by the Lord instantly for just touching the Ark . . ." Minkoff said, trailing off as his mouth dropped open. However, he realized there was no other choice, and he handed Eteye the glow stick and silently walked over to Solo.

Eteye watched them bend down and pick up the Ark of War effortlessly by simply placing their hands on the side of the chest. The rectangular box appeared to float in the dim, red glimmer of the glow stick. They hastily walked through the golden coffins and back down the steps at the rear of the platform that led to the main floor.

Eteye moved ahead of them to illuminate their path. They passed through the rows of columns and followed a wide, cobblestone ramp, which angled upwards and appeared to be leading them back up to the surface. Solo wondered how he and Minkoff could miraculously carry the weight of the sun without breaking a sweat. Several hundred feet up the ramp, they reached a wall.

"It's a dead end," Eteye said as she walked up and placed both hands on the it and pushed. Nothing happened.

"Set it down and step behind me," Solo said to Minkoff. He instantly did as Solo had instructed, and the men lowered the feather-light Ark to the floor in unison.

Eteye stepped back as well. Solo again rested his hands on the Ark, lowered his head, and closed his eyes. He seemed to be praying to it. Suddenly, the wall in front of them crumbled before their eyes. The wall's massive, square granite blocks that had been stacked on top of each other thousands of years ago simply fell backwards, revealing a short tunnel in front of them. They saw the morning sun rising from the east at the end of the short tunnel that was large enough to drive a semi-truck through.

"I know where we are," Eteye said, amazed. "This is what was called the Sphinx Temple. This long tunnel connects the two pyramids to the Nile River when the Pharaohs used to travel by barge."

Solo answered. "Jeremiah planned this like a Russian chess master."

They carried the Ark out of the tunnel to the entrance and briefly paused for a second to catch the sun rising over the Nile River. It was an astonishingly beautiful morning.

"Now what?" Eteye asked, wishing she had a thought-out plan.

"It's your turn, Minkoff," Solo said. "That's why the Ark brought you here. Am I right?"

Minkoff squinted his eyes and nodded slightly. He, too, now understood what the God of Fate required of him. His brief, physical contact with the Ark had shown him exactly what it wanted him to do. He reached into his pack and pulled out a lightweight satellite phone. He punched in some numbers and began speaking in Hebrew. Solo couldn't understand what he was saying; however, he already knew exactly what Minkoff planned to do. Minkoff nodded as he listened to the voice on the other line and then hung up the phone.

"In fifteen minutes, an Apache Longbow and one of our long-range Ospreys will cross into Egyptian airspace and land on that courtyard, over there," he said, pointing to a flat, open area about a hundred yards away. "However, they likely will not be able to avoid Egyptian radar. You two and the Ark of the Lord will load into the Osprey. I'll board the Longbow."

Eteye and Solo listened intently as Minkoff unveiled their escape plan.

"The Egyptians and their military are in great disarray these days," he explained. "We hope their Air Force's response time will be compromised accordingly. Right now most of their attention is directed at the Suez Canal and the approaching Israeli and American fleets to the north. The two aircraft will fly close enough to appear as one unit on the Egyptian radar, and the Osprey will take you straight back across the border to Israel—hopefully undetected."

"And yours?" Eteye asked, understanding the plan's implications.

"I will fly straight down the Nile, gaining elevation and hopefully drawing everyone's attention away from you."

Solo smiled, appreciating the simplicity of Minkoff's solution. *It was a good plan. Levi would have approved.*

"They'll shoot you down," Eteye said, alarmed.

"They will chase me, not you," Minkoff countered. "I will be an easy and obvious target, and that will buy you time to sneak back across the border."

He walked up to Solo, put both hands on his shoulders, and looked into his eyes.

"I know you are not a *believer,* Mr. Goldman. I saw it when our thoughts mixed together as we carried the Ark. You have many doubts about God, but today you are in His service. My brother will pilot your aircraft, and he'll take you wherever you command."

Minkoff leaned in close to Solo's face.

"*Wherever you command,*" he repeated. "He will never speak to another soul about this mission, even if it costs him his life. It will never appear on any records, and no one will ever learn of your destination. Do you understand what I am telling you?"

Solo embraced his new friend.

"I understand. I will never be able to thank you, my brother."

"My journey and service to God is almost complete," Minkoff said, placing his hands on Solo's shoulders. "However, mine is a simple mission and easy to obey. Yours is much more difficult. You must decide the fate for all of us—Jews, Christians, Muslims, perhaps the entire world. You must decide what is true and what is best. I cannot carry such a burden. I was not chosen—I saw it when we carried the Ark. I am sorry that you must carry that burden."

He released his hands from Solo's shoulders.

"Today, I must play the role of a radical Zionist—a result of serving too long in an undercover position for the West. Today, I commandeered an Israeli aircraft and illegally flew it into Egypt to provoke them and give our Navy cause to seize the Suez Canal. Hopefully, no one will ever know of your second flight out of here."

They had just sat down on the ancient Egyptian remains when the giant tilt-rotor aircraft with its oversized, three-bladed propellers, attached to the end of each stubby wing, became visible on the horizon.

39

The two aircraft approached low from the east. Their propulsion and rotor blade platforms were physically distinct, but they were difficult for an untrained ear to distinguish. As the sun rose behind their silhouettes, Solo could see their hot turbine gases streaming behind them. They glided in such a tight formation that they resembled a giant, mutated insect flying straight at them.

The two helicopters had taken off from the Ramon Air Force Base, just southwest of Beersheba, near the town of Mitzpe Ramon, deep in the Israeli desert. The base had been built as part of a joint operation with the U.S. Government after the 1978 Camp David Accords, when the entire Sinai Peninsula had been handed back over to Egypt. The 113th Squadron, or the Hornet Squadron, as it was known to the local air force pilots, had been reformed in 1990, and then again in 2005, to be the exclusive helicopter squadron in Israel. Minkoff saw the AH-64D Apache Longbow appear first, flying point in the hot Cairo sun.

The four-blade, twin-turbine Boeing attack aircraft touched down with only a single pilot inside. Although the cockpit had a tandem space for a crew of two, the rear seat had remained

279

empty, as Minkoff had instructed. The pilot, wearing a solid-black flight suit, locked down the collective control arm, forcing the helicopter to remain on the ground, and lowered the turbine power to twenty percent. He jumped out of the helicopter and sprinted to guide the second aircraft into a landing position.

The Osprey landed several dozen meters away from the Apache shortly after. Solo had never seen a V-22 Osprey up close. The fifty-seven-foot aircraft—half-helicopter, half-plane—hovered and then rested on the large, rocky pad where they waited. Solo could see a single pilot in the cockpit as the two massive turbines and rotor systems, attached to the end of each wing, winded down slightly. The pilot in the black flight suit crossed his arms in an X motion above his head to indicate that the Osprey was on solid ground. Solo was shocked at the size of its eighty-four-foot wingspan and the roaring noise generated by the two idling aircraft's engines.

Minkoff and Solo moved the Ark to the rear ramp of the Osprey. The back cargo bay door had been lowered to the ground prior to the aircraft touching down. They loaded the Ark effortlessly into the rear bay and quickly strapped it down. The large, rear cargo bay was empty, with the exception of a few headsets and two sizeable, internal fuel tanks, which were used to extend the heavy combat radius of the aircraft from 685 kilometers to over 3,590 kilometers with a light, ferry-type payload.

Eteye walked up the Osprey's ramp and joined Minkoff and Solo. She kissed Minkoff on the mouth lightly and hugged him.

"None of this could have happened without you," she said loudly into his ear over the engines.

He smiled as he picked up a headset and said something in Hebrew to the pilot. She couldn't hear him over the engines, but she guessed he was saying his last goodbyes to his brother. The black-suited pilot ran up the Osprey's ramp, passing Solo, Minkoff, and Eteye as he headed into the cockpit of the Osprey. Minkoff pointed to the massive ramp button labeled "CLOSE" and then pointed to Solo, who nodded his head in acknowledgement of his instructions. Minkoff then ran down the ramp, disappearing as he turned the corner in a sprint to the front of the Osprey. They never saw him again.

When Minkoff reached the nose of the massive helicopter he twirled his hand above his head in a circular motion, gesturing to his brother and the black-suited pilot, who now sat in the Osprey's co-pilot seat: *get in the air!* He raced to the empty, idling Apache and climbed in.

He flipped several switches, rolled the collective lever to take the turbines to one-hundred-percent, and pulled up the lever next to his left knee. The helicopter shot into the air. The whine from the twin turbines was deafening, like an air raid siren. Minkoff let the torque on the transmission and rotor system exceed their normal, safe operating parameters to gain altitude and airspeed more rapidly. Exceeding the safe mechanical limits of his helicopter did not matter today.

He rose straight up into the air and briefly hovered over the Great Pyramid of Giza. He was amazed to see all of the military activity headed towards the pyramids. He would miss hearing about the discoveries found in the ancient chamber that would soon be broadcast to the world.

He circled the three pyramids and headed south, following the Nile River away from the Osprey and the Ark. He switched on his radio to the preprogrammed frequency of the Egyptian Air Defenses and began to speak the fanatical, religious rhetoric that he had despised all his life. As he heard the air raid sirens west of Cairo begin their droning wail, he realized his only real sadness was that he would be remembered as a religious fundamentalist. Minkoff loathed fundamentalists.

Solo and Eteye sat in the cargo bay of the Osprey next to the Ark as they headed towards the Israeli-Egyptian border, flying just over the rooftops of the local city on their easterly route out of Cairo, towards the Sinai Desert.

After fifteen minutes, Minkoff's brother, the Osprey's pilot, spoke into the headsets.

"My brother is no longer with us."

Eteye hung her head, and Solo took a deep breath. Neither spoke a word.

The Osprey landed just across the Israeli border in an open dirt field. As soon as the helicopter stopped moving, the co-pilot walked back through the cargo bay past Eteye and Solo, keeping his eyes on his feet, as the rear bay door opened and he jumped out. He never said a word, and he never looked at either of them or the Ark.

The Osprey's pilot, now alone in the cockpit, pulled the aircraft up into a hover and then quickly transitioned into forward flight. As they reached an altitude of five hundred feet above the ground, he spoke in a well-trained military manner into the internal intercom system.

"I will take you anywhere you wish to go. I swear on my brother's memory that no one will ever know your location."

Eteye looked at Solo, wondering what he was thinking. *Where would he tell the Israeli pilot to go?* She had protected so many secrets for so long. Now it was up to Solo, just like it had been in the beginning.

The most elaborate and secretive hiding place for the world's most powerful weapon had just been discovered. For millennia, the Ark of War had remained safe from the likes of Mao, Hitler, Stalin, Genghis Khan, and Attila the Hun. Now it sat in an Israeli aircraft, entrusted to the one soul who would have to decide its fate—and the fate of the rest of the world.

Eteye smiled to herself as she contemplated the large, black chest next to them in the cargo bay. She was amazed by how the Ark had helped her find Solo; she had been looking for him so long this time. She knew that he would make a selfless decision for the benefit of the rest of the world. She felt glad to be in his company.

"Solo, have you decided where we're going?" Eteye asked into her headset.

Solo moved the small microphone attached to his headset closer to his mouth to speak as he looked at Eteye.

"There's only one place we can go, and only one person we can trust," he said. Solo looked in the cockpit's direction as he addressed the pilot through the microphone. "We are going to Rome."

The pilot was about to object when he remembered his vow to his now-lost brother. *No questions asked.* He pulled out the charts next to his seat and switched the Osprey, with its large, blue Star of David on its side, to autopilot as they cruised over the Mediterranean coastline north at two hundred and seventy miles per hour.

"Our G.P.S. says that Rome is just over two thousand kilometers away," he said calmly and coolly into the intercom system as he calculated his fuel-to-weight ratio, comparing the maximum range of the aircraft with its extended fuel cells. It would not be easy, but his vow to his brother was a vow that he could not break. So long as they didn't hit any headwinds or need to divert, he estimated that they would have a small amount of fuel to spare. The Italian Air Force's reaction to an unauthorized Israeli military aircraft was another matter altogether, however.

He hoped his passengers had a plan.

40

The air marshal walked past the corpse of Ike Duggan and down the steps that had led upwards for the past three thousand years. By the time he'd arrived, his men had strung lights all the way down the staircase and into the newly discovered basement.

When he saw the sphinxes and the monoliths, he momentarily lost his breath. When his men shined a large, portable, handheld spotlight across the ancient university stadium, his breathing stopped altogether. He knew the archeological find would make the discoveries at the Valley of the Kings look like amateur hour.

He would be the one to announce the discoveries to the world, and any mention of the American visitors who had arrived the evening before would evaporate. He ordered Ike's body and the tied up man wearing a crumbled cowboy hat to be discreetly disposed of and their aircraft to be secreted away in a military hangar. Although he wondered where the rest of Ike's team had gone, it was only for an insignificant moment.

Hafez was so deep underground that his radio didn't work, nor did the radios of his military subordinates and he did not receive the radio transmissions requesting permission to engage the Israeli helicopter that had intruded on Egyptian airspace and

285

was being chased down the Nile River. One of his soldiers had to physically courier the frenzied request to him in person.

Egypt was about to resume her role in the center stage of the world, but not because of the approaching Israeli Navy and their threats to seize the Suez Canal. Rather, the discovery would prove that Egypt had been the birthplace of civilization, of all religions and culture. Her prominence had been swept away over time, buried in the swirling desert sand. Today, however, it would be restored. Today, everything would change. Air Marshal Hafez was about to become a wealthy and influential world leader as he announced to the world his newly discovered treasures.

41

"Why didn't you just take the Ark? I am sure you had a plan for it like you have had a plan for everything else?" Solo asked Eteye as they sat in the Apache's rear cargo bay.

"It's not mine to take from you."

"You know what I mean," Solo said, leaning back into the helicopter's nylon, cot-like seat. "You have the means and the ability to orchestrate all of this, yet you let *me* decide what's best to do with the Ark?" He pointed to the mysterious-looking black object strapped down in the middle of the cargo bay as he spoke.

"The Ark has never been mine to possess," Eteye said emotionlessly. "The god of fate chose you a long time ago, before I ever was."

She smiled, leaned back, and laid her head against his shoulder. Solo said nothing. He had just cleared his mind for the first time in a long, long time. Somehow, he could still see himself separately from his thoughts and feelings. He knew that the Ark had affected him—that it was changing his consciousness the longer he remained in its presence.

"I know where Levi is," he said calmly.

Eteye sat forward and looked at Solo.

"You know where they have him?"

"He's in a safe house in Turkey."

"In Turkey?"

Solo nodded. It should have been impossible for him to know the exact location of the C.I.A. prison where his brother was being held. *Simply impossible.* Yet he knew it, and he knew the best way to attack it. He could see a clear picture of the compound in his mind.

"And you still think you are not chosen?" Eteye asked, leaning back on the uncomfortable bench.

He did not reply.

It had only taken Eteye five minutes on her satellite phone to make the necessary arrangements for their landing in Italy. It was obvious that an Israeli tilt-rotor Osprey, landing at Rome's Leonard Di Vinci International Airport, was not the unobtrusive arrival they'd all wanted. Eteye hung up and unplugged the large headset she'd worn from the phone's adaptor cord. She then re-plugged it back into the cargo bay ceiling, where Solo's headset was also plugged in. She turned the small, yellow switch from *Cargo* to *Cockpit* and began to speak in Hebrew to the pilot over the intercom.

Solo could not understand what that they said, back and forth, but he could definitely discern that the pilot was shocked by what Eteye was telling him to do. He heard the pilot say, *"Yes, ma'am"* in English, and the conversation ended.

"Our pilot didn't like the idea of landing in Rome, but he agreed," Eteye said, putting away her phone. "Do you think he's actually going to see you?"

"Yes. He'll see me," Solo answered matter-of-factly. He saw she was smiling at him, and he did the same.

"He is waiting for us."

"And how do you know that?" Eteye asked.

"I just know," Solo answered glancing over at the Ark.

Eteye understood his gesture.

Solo unstrapped himself from his seat belt which was attached to a canvas cot that served as their seats. He stood and walked to the Ark. The Osprey bounced around quite a bit, as they were flying close to the ocean's surface.

Solo carefully placed both hands on the Ark, this time in a slower manner. At the pyramid, things had moved rather quickly, and he'd had no idea what he'd gotten himself into when he'd walked up and simply touched the Ark for the first time. Now, though, he realized that it had been several thousand years since the Ark had had any intimate contact with another living being. He could tell it was hungry for companionship. He began to grasp the immense depth of this moment in time and the impact that his actions would have on the future of humanity. *How in the world had he gotten to this place? No, that was not the right word—moment. How in the world had he gotten to this moment?*

His hands rubbed the smooth, black surface of the Ark, and this time, through Solo's mind, it caressed his skin gently and kindly back. He could feel the awareness in the Ark's dense core—a consciousness that interacted with his own. He felt keenly awake again, and he became aware that every part of his body was *alive*. He felt life inside of every one of his cells, and then he saw the moment of creation.

Solo closed his eyes and let his thoughts go. He let his feelings end, and he became aware of the *Eternal Being* that resided inside him. *Hashem*, as his Hebrew schoolteacher would call it. *Father*

God, according to his mother, and *Allah* to the majority of the world's believers.

Solo could feel the energy that ran through him, the Ark, the airplane, the ocean below, the continent they were approaching, the people in the cities, and the earth as a whole. And then his awareness began to take him beyond the earth. The same energy that ran through every cell of his person also ran through the vast emptiness of space, and only now did he realize that space was simply a different form of energy than that which existed in his physical world.

Solo saw the earth, and realized that it was one large organism, similar to the way he'd been made. The earth and all the people and creatures that relied upon the planet for their survival had also been constructed from the exact same energy. He could see how everything was connected, and he could feel the planet breathing in and breathing out.

He turned his awareness back to the Ark as he began to grasp what lay inside of it, what it was made of, and where it had come from.

"Solo," Eteye said as she squeezed his shoulder, causing him to open his eyes and remove his hands from the Ark. "We have a problem."

Solo followed Eteye to the Osprey's cockpit, where they plugged in their headsets to speak with the pilot.

"What's going on?"

"Big problem," he said in English, pulling out an aviation chart that showed the entire Mediterranean Sea. He pointed his finger to a location over the water, halfway between Cairo and Rome. "There is an American carrier group directly in front of us. They're jamming my radio, so I couldn't contact them, even if I wanted to. We have two inbound fighter jets that will attempt to force us away from their location—or shoot us down."

"Can't we just go around them?" Solo asked.

"We lack the fuel to divert that far around them. There are lots of ships in this group, and they're headed to the Suez Canal in response to the Israeli blockade that's about to go into effect."

"We can't let them report to anyone who we are," Eteye said.

"If the Americans report contact with an Israeli aircraft, your secrecy will be lost," Minkoff's brother said. "We have no fuel to spare. We'll barely have enough to make it to Rome. If I divert from our course now, we'll have to turn back because there's no other place to land."

No one spoke for several moments. Solo heard the demand for identification coming in from one of the American ships over the internal radio.

"I need your satellite phone," Solo said, turning to Eteye.

"It's in the back."

"Let's get it, before we run out of time."

They both jumped up and headed to the cargo bay, where Eteye handed him the phone and plugged it into his headset. Solo dialed a cell phone number he knew well.

Five minutes later, they were back in the cockpit.

"Climb to an altitude of fifty-thousand feet and stay clear of the main aircraft carrier by fifty miles. That's the best I can do," Solo said to the pilot. "If we deviate in the slightest from our heading or altitude, they will blow us from the sky."

The pilot looked up in disbelief, but when he saw Solo's face, he immediately started plotting on his chart and punching numbers into his handheld fuel-to-weight calculator. After a minute of calculations, he looked as Solo.

"It will be close," he said, "With the carrier heading south and us heading west, though, we might just make it."

Eteye's eyes grew large as she contemplated crashing into the ocean if they ran out of fuel shy of the Italian coastline. The memories of her fear of being trapped in an underwater coffin began to flood into her mind.

"How did you get permission for us to fly straight over their carrier group?" the pilot asked.

"I have a friend who is an admiral at the Naval Academy. He owed me a big favor. It just so happens he was classmates with the admiral onboard that carrier group down there in front of us, and he vouched for me. If we stay at this altitude and maintain the minimum safe distance away from the carrier, they'll let us pass with no questions asked. However, if we deviate in the slightest, they will not be able to allow the risk to the aircraft carrier."

"Won't the Israelis see us at that altitude?" Eteye asked.

"Maybe, but they're too far away for them to try and intercept us. With the Egyptian blockade about to begin, they have far more pressing engagements," their pilot responded. "Besides, there's so much electronic jamming going on within a hundred miles of the carrier that it's likely no one but the Americans will see us as we pass."

Solo felt the Osprey climb rapidly and bank left as the pilot changed their course and altitude. The commandeered Israeli aircraft continued onwards towards Italy. Two F-18 Hornets shadowed them, and they heard the American carrier group's radio chatter with other vessels that were heading to the Suez Canal.

They sat in silence as they bounced along at almost three hundred miles an hour, soaring toward the Holy Man in Rome.

42

A private limo, sent by the Vatican City, was waiting for them at *Aeroporto di Roma-Ciampino*. The Italian airport had opened in 1916 and was one of the world's oldest airports still in operation. It had been Rome's main airport until 1960, but now it handled almost exclusively charter and executive flights.

Eteye was still shaking her head in disbelief that a private meeting had been set up with the Pope, inside his private quarters at Vatican City, no less. The limo had been waiting for them when they'd touched down, unimpeded, at the executive airport in front of the Vatican's private hanger.

Several Swiss Guards waited with the limo. They informed Solo and Eteye that they had strict orders to let no one near their aircraft. They opened the enormous Vatican hangar immediately and moved the Osprey, with its distinct Star of David, indoors, safely tucking it away from the public eye. Although there were only six guards, Solo felt confident that no one could board the Israeli Osprey without significant effort and violence. It wasn't an entirely secure defensive perimeter, but somehow Solo knew it would be enough.

Their twenty-minute ride to the center of Rome passed in silence; Solo and Eteye were each consumed by their own thoughts. The limo took them through a back gate that looked more like a service entrance than the entry to one of the most sacred locations in all of Christendom.

Vatican City was a walled enclave within Rome, Italy—a one-hundred-and-ten-acre, sovereign city, ruled by the Bishop of Rome, the Pope. Solo could feel Eteye's discomfort as soon as they entered the walled, Christian fortress.

"What is it?" he asked, sensing her discomfort.

"Nothing," she said. She looked out the window as they drove through a small alleyway with massively high stone walls.

"Tell me," Solo insisted. He grabbed her hand and squeezed it twice.

"It's a long story."

Solo gave her a raised-eyebrow look: *What—like the last couple of weeks haven't been enough of a long story for you?*

"Let's just say there are some in my family who have long memories—who still don't trust Roman men who wear large crosses on their chests."

Solo did not immediately respond. He watched Eteye as she looked out the window, staring at a massive, ornate stone as the car cruised past it.

"Are you one of them?" he finally asked.

"It's just strange, being here, at the center of Christianity. I remember orders coming from the Pope himself during the Crusades," Eteye said.

"What orders?"

"There was a pope who raised an army of over twenty-thousand knights, and they slaughtered their way through Europe hundreds of years ago. When the Christian soldiers asked the pope how they could tell the difference between the faithful and the infidels, they were told, '*Kill them all. God will know His own.*'"

"Every religion has its bleak moments, including ours."

His mind took him back in time. He remembered standing in the living room of his mother's apartment once, when he was in high school.

"I'm going to mass. Be home in an hour or so," Solo remembered his mother saying as she'd grabbed her coat and gloves. "Has anyone seen my rosary?"

"It's here, in the bathroom!" Abay had yelled down to her from upstairs. "Wait up. I'm coming with you!"

"Hurry up, then! I'm not going to be late for mass. Please bring my rosary when you come down!"

Solo had looked at his mother in her conservative Sunday dress and blurted out, "Why did you marry a Jew? I thought Catholics didn't like Jews?"

"I love Jews!" his mother had smiled back. "There are three that I especially adore."

"Do you wish you had never married him?"

Solo's mother had answered without missing a beat.

"Heavens, no. I have the dearest family because of your father."

"Levi and I were called half-breeds at Hebrew school last week. They said you're a Catholic mystic. They said Catholics love to slaughter Jews."

"Is that where Levi's black eye came from?"

"Yes, but I swore I wouldn't tell you about it," Solo had said as his mother stood by the front door, waiting for Abay.

"I suppose they're right. At one very bad time in the church's history, some evil men did slaughter many Jews. In fact, the

Church probably has not done right by the Jewish people for a very long time."

"Is that why you work so hard to ensure that Levi and I get through Hebrew school? Why we have Sabbath every Friday night?"

"It may be part of the reason," Mother had said to him as Abay came running down the stairs. "I think a religion is only as good as each person that practices it. I certainly can't atone for all the sins of the Christians during the Crusades, or for when they kicked all the Jews out of Spain and Europe. I can, however, show the world that Jews and Catholics can live together as a family—that they can support and love each other like a family should."

She'd looked around for her coat finding it on off the back of a chair.

"Let's go, Abay!" she'd said cheerfully before looking back at Solo. "You are not a half-breed, no matter what that orthodox rabbi says."

"What are you guys talking about?" Abay had asked as she hurriedly tied her long, tiny braids into a big knot behind her head and then grabbed her coat. She'd been walking to the front door with the rosary in her hand just as his mother had leaned in to kiss him on the forehead.

"I was just telling my favorite little Jewish boy how adorable he is."

Solo remembered hugging his mother.

Three Swiss Guards approached their car, jarring Solo back to the present moment.

"I suppose you're right. We all have our bleak moments of history, but I just feel great apprehension being here. I can't quite explain it," Eteye said.

A Swiss Guard on each side of them opened the car doors at exactly the same time. Eteye and Solo stepped out of the vehicle and into the warm, dry air of the courtyard.

"Please, follow me. Welcome to the Apostolic Palace," the lead Swiss guard said as he gestured to the stone steps, which were protected by six two-story-tall Roman columns. Solo looked at the courtyard around him and surmised that they were at a back entrance of some sort. There was no one around, aside from a few visitors and military guards.

Eteye shuddered, grabbed Solo high up on his forearm, and pulled him close. She pressed her breasts against the back of his arm and nuzzled in closer. Solo pulled her alongside him, putting his arm around her, and whispered into her ear.

"These are not the same people who committed the atrocities against your family so long ago. Trust me. I know what I'm doing."

Eteye squeezed his arm twice: *okay.*

They followed their escort up the stairs and into a grand foyer that was a spacious, open room with identical front and rear entrances. In fact, standing inside it, one could not tell which formal-looking entrance was the front and which was the back. The ceiling rose three stories above their heads and had been painted in the most beautiful colors. Between the doors was a large, grand staircase that led up to a second floor. Large pictures of past pontiffs lined the walls all around them, and thick, long pale-yellow curtains hung down around the few windows that displayed the outside world. Solo immediately recognized this as a place of solitude, where one could retreat from the busy and prying world outside.

The guard stepped into the center of the room.

"Your patience is most appreciated," he said. He turned and walked out, leaving Solo and Eteye alone in the middle of the luxurious foyer. Eteye shuddered again, and Solo rubbed her shoulder and held her tight with his arm around her. They stood in the room, alone, for several minutes, before a voice from behind them spoke.

"I apologize that I kept you waiting."

Solo turned around and saw a man dressed in a form-fitting, dark-blue wool suit walking down the magnificent staircase. The silk, white skull cap on his head matched perfectly with the nicely folded pocket-square in his left breast pocket of his suit. As the tall, well-dressed gentleman walked casually toward them, Solo saw that he was slim and athletic, with a full head of brown and gray hair. His eyes were blue and warm, and they crinkled when he smiled.

He was just as his mother had always described him—the new generation of the Catholic Church. He looked more like a former European model than a priest. Had Solo not seen the man's picture in his mother's living room for the past five years, he would have thought he was about to shake the hand of an investment banker, not the Pope himself.

"Your Holiness," Solo said as he bowed his head and looked down. He noticed the Pope's stylish Italian-leather shoes.

Eteye did not move.

The Pope walked up to her, held her gently around both shoulders, and pulled her face to his, kissing her once on each cheek. Eteye saw kindness in his eyes, and his presence put her at ease. She let out a deep breath. He then turned to Solo, grabbed his hand, and shook it firmly and crisply.

"Please, call me John. We should not begin this momentous occasion with labels that serve our egos or the egos of our religion. I am no more holy than you are, Mr. Goldman."

Solo felt himself relax as John Paul continued to hold his hand. He had not realized until that moment how anxious he'd been about his meeting with the Pope. He also realized that the Pope was doing more than being polite; he sensed that the Pope was reading him. He felt calmness and kindness flowing through the man's arm, and he knew right away that the Ark had told him to do the right thing.

"We are alone here today. I have prepared some tea for us," the leader of over one billion Catholics said, letting go of Solo's hand. He held out his elbow to Eteye, indicating that the three of them should walk to the adjoining room. She took his arm and smiled, her cautious demeanor softening as the moments went by.

They sat down in what looked like John Paul's personal library. Books, which had been meticulously organized on wide oak shelves, lined all four walls in the perfectly square room, creating a mosaic of paper, marble, and heavy wood all around them. A beautifully crafted wooden desk sat in the room's center, and was also covered in literature. Stacks of more books, of all shapes and sizes, covered the floors. The Pope was clearly an avid reader.

Two dark-brown, leather couches faced each other, and a wooden table rested between them. The Pope sat next to Eteye on one sofa, while Solo sat on the other. John Paul began to pour tea into three cups that were on the table in front of them.

"Does anyone care for sugar or milk?"

"Sugar, please," Eteye answered.

"None for me," Solo said, still looking around the room.

"Hmmm, I thought so," the Pope said as he poured the tea. He looked at Eteye as he dropped two lumps of sugar into his saucer. "I like mine like just like you do. The sweeter, the better."

Once he had handed Solo his tea, the Pope stood politely.

"Please, bring your cups and follow me to my desk," he said, smiling at the two of them before he turned. They followed.

Solo noticed handwritten papers, notes, and dozens of open books spread all across the desk. The Pope reached down and picked up an oversized piece of paper that was covered in neatly spaced, handwritten letters.

"Can either of you read Latin?"

"No Sir," Solo said shaking his head.

"I do," Eteye said.

The Pope smiled and handed her the paper, holding it as if it were an ancient document.

"It is not complete," he said, "but it is a start. Let me know where you think I could improve."

Eteye began reading. After a few lines, she paused to look up at the gentleman next to her with large eyes, her mouth dropping open briefly. She looked back down as John Paul III and Solo walked over to a large window that overlooked the Vatican complex.

"Mr. Goldman, Our Father showed you and your precious cargo to me in my dreams. I have been anxious to meet you ever since."

"In your dreams?" Solo asked.

"Yes. The dream was both wonderful and horrible, all at the same time."

Solo paused as he turned to look at the man standing at his side. The Pope also turned, and his blue, moist eyes were calm as he met Solo's stare.

"I needed to meet you to know if I could trust you or not," Solo said. "My mother spoke very highly of you, but the matter that we must speak about—"

"—requires much more than a mother's religious devotion." John Paul finished his sentence.

"Yes, sir."

"I understand completely. I think we should have your companion read the draft of my soon-to-be-released edict to you. It's time for our world to begin to heal some old wounds, don't you think?" he said. He had a glimmer in his eye that Solo did not yet understand.

"Is this real?" Eteye asked as she walked over to them, still holding the handwritten note.

"I assure you, it is quite real. I wrote it just last night, in a cold sweat," John Paul said. He motioned for Eteye to join them. "Would you be so kind as to read some of it to my new friend here, Mr. Goldman?"

Eteye stared at the Pope in disbelief and then slowly began to read.

"*Ioannes Paulus III, Episcopus, Servus Servorum Dei, Sicut Judaeis . . .*" she began. She translated the rest to English aloud as she read:

"*Our faith has been part of an unfortunate and sad history towards our Jewish brothers and sisters, and, also, at times, it has been a poor example of the love shown and lived out by our Lord and Savior Jesus Christ. It should be without a doubt that the Jews are already in communion with our One True Father. We should remember that it is only through our Jewish Savior, the Lord Jesus Christ, that the gentiles of the world may come into communion with the Father. Therefore, it becomes the mission of the One True Church to continue that cause and to bring the new peoples of the earth also into communion with the Father.*

The Vatican hereby annuls the Bull of Pope Clement VIII, the Cum Hebraeorum Malitia, that, among other dreadful deeds, decreed that all copies of the Talmud and Kabbalah be turned over to the Inquisition for burning. May our terrible transgressions of that age, and our indifference in other ages, be forgiven by the blood of our Lord and Savior.

May the Jewish people continue to grow in love of the Father's name and in faithfulness to His eternal covenant with them."

Eteye stopped reading and looked at the Pope, her eyes round and glistening. Solo had never seen her on the verge of crying before.

"There is more to be added. But we must talk about why you have come to see me first," John Paul said as he gently patted Eteye's arm. Solo did not fully understand the centuries of pain that the Pope was undoing in his simple proclamation, but Eteye clearly did.

The three of them walked back to the couches and sat down. Eteye still held the Pope's letter, as though she were afraid it would vanish into thin air if she handed it back to him.

"I don't really know where to begin or how to explain the events that have gotten me here," Solo said.

"Mr. Goldman, please drink your tea," the Holy Man interrupted. "Do you remember accompanying your mother to confession when you were a boy?"

"Of course, many times. I have never experienced confession personally, since I am not a Catholic, but my mother always seemed to feel better after she attended."

"Yes, it is good for the soul for a man to share his secrets with someone in whom it has complete faith and trust. Please, just start at the beginning. After all, you are simply talking to a priest right now, and we have been keeping the secrets of mankind for the past two thousand years."

Eteye sat next to Solo, with one hand on his knee and the other on his shoulder. The Pope sat opposite them, across the coffee table, and listened without judgment. He sat perfectly still, and his face remained stoic and non-reactionary as they spoke. Solo and Eteye took turns telling the priest about the events that had led them to Rome, starting with the backdrop of the U.S. military expedition into Babylon-Iraq, the discovery there, and Levi's abduction to Turkey.

His Holiness sat back in the plush leather sofa and took it all in. The only time he interrupted was to ask more questions about Solo's visions when he had touched the Ark, both in the tomb beneath the pyramid and on the flight to Rome. Solo and Eteye spoke for almost three hours, leaving out only the intimate details of their relationship.

". . . Actually, it's sitting in the cargo bay of the helicopter that flew us into Rome," Solo said, answering the Pope's last question.

"A truly fascinating story, Mr. Goldman. A *miracle*, I would dare say," the Pope replied. "And why have you come to see *me*, Mr. Goldman? I do not find you in need of spiritual advice. In fact, I find the spiritual guide who traveled here with you to be more than adequate."

Solo looked at Eteye. *His spiritual guide?* He had never thought of her that way, but that was exactly what she had been to him over the last several days. She had awakened his soul, bringing him to life on so many different levels. She had kindly allowed him to recognize the sufferings of his past that had continued to play in his mind like a broken record. She had granted him the oblivion of true love, of true compassion, and she'd enabled him to remember his relationships with Abay and his father as some of the best moments of his young life, rather than shutting out their memories as painful recollections. She had brought him back to life.

Solo turned back to John Paul.

"I can still remember five years ago, when you became Pope. It was a very big event for my mother," he said.

The pontiff looked at Solo and nodded.

"I would very much like to meet her someday," he said. "We must arrange for her to visit."

Solo laughed. "She would faint before she got up the steps outside."

"Your mother planted the seed for this visit a long time ago," Eteye pointed out.

"I realize that now," Solo answered, turning to look at Eteye, the Pope's letter still clutched in her hand. "I'm starting to think much of this has happened by design."

Eteye smiled, and Solo turned his attention back to the Pope.

"Sir, that's why I'm here," he said. "I have seen what you've started with the Church over the last few years, and the letter Eteye read only confirms my beliefs about you. My mother said that you were chosen to be the Pope at such a young age so that you could lead the next generation into true partnership with the

Almighty. She's made note of every headline you've been in over the last few years. I especially remember the heat you took over the changes you implemented in the Church's view towards gays and lesbians."

The Pope smiled proudly.

"I know that wasn't easy," Solo said.

"And to us non-Catholics, it has been very noticeable," Eteye added.

"What I brought to Rome is something that I have only begun to understand," Solo said. "It is so old that no one can even begin to speculate where it could have come from."

"Maybe the beautiful lady at your side has more answers than you have asked for?" the Pope said, kindly and gently.

Eteye's lips curled into a small smile, unnoticeable to anyone but John Paul—and he only noticed it because he had already known it would be there. Solo missed it as he continued speaking.

"I believe we have in our possession the greatest religious icon of antiquity," he said. "Jews, Christians, and Muslims all recognize this symbol as some sort of direct link to God. However, it is not at all what our scriptures have made it out to be."

The Pope again stood and motioned for Solo and Eteye to follow him. Solo walked at John Paul's side as Eteye trailed behind them.

John Paul picked up where Solo had left off.

"The Ark is so much more than the beginning of your religion or some sort of a symbol for mine," he said. "We both know that our religions will not accept what is in the cargo bay of your aircraft as the *true* Ark of the Covenant. It does not fit the description of a golden box built by Moses, as described in our scriptures."

They left the expansive library and began to climb the staircase at the center of the residence to the next floor. They climbed slowly to the third floor and entered a great, glass room with large French doors that led to an outside balcony.

"It certainly is not some sort of wooden box covered in gold that holds the ten commandments," Solo said as he stepped out onto the large, open-air porch.

The view was beautiful. The entire Vatican City could be seen from the perch, and much of the city of Rome lay visible over the walls that guarded the holy territory.

"You are correct, Mr. Goldman. Legends last a long time, especially religious legends," the Pope said. He looked out at the sprawling city landscape with Solo and Eteye.

"I'm not certain that the Ark, or whatever it is, even comes from this world. Regardless, it was fashioned by a civilization that understands this earth on a far greater level than we do," Solo said.

"How so?"

"I know that the Ark *can be* an Ark of War in the hands of men who desire to use it for that purpose. But I have . . ." Solo paused, searching for the right word.

"Communed?" the Pope asked.

Solo thought it about it for a second.

"Yes, *communed* with it, and it changed me."

The Pope turned his head and watched Solo, as if inspecting him to discern whether what he had just said was true.

"Changed you how?" he asked.

"It woke me up. That's the best way I can explain it. I became aware that I was so much more than my thoughts and feelings. I was so much more than all the fears I have been carrying for so long. I felt alive and conscious of a world and a universe that I had never even begun to imagine. I saw creation."

"You saw creation? *The* creation?"

"Yes, I was there. The serpent, the two trees, the Ark."

"Fascinating," the Pope said. He continued to stare at Solo, riveted.

"I saw God. Not His face, so to speak, but He really is both there *and* right here. But He—or She, or *It*—is just like the Ark. The Divine is not the jealous old man we have been taught to believe in over the centuries, who wants us to live on our knees, singing songs to Him every week. I saw levels of physics and science that Einstein himself could not even begin to understand. But the greatest thing I experienced when I became one with the Ark was the awareness of all of mankind. I saw us all as one, and then I understood the source of the Jewish pledge of allegiance, *The Lord is One.*"

"The *Shema*?" John Paul asked.

"Exactly. God, us—we are all one. One people, one world, and one God."

"Very true and very wise."

"I believe that is what the Ark is for—to bring people together, to bring the world together. To show us all that we belong *with* one another and that we are part of each other. The we need one another. The Ark was meant to be our partner in creation."

"Ah, but the Ark has not always been used for something so noble as that," John Paul stated.

"No, sir. In fact, I fear that, even today, we are not much farther along than King David was when he used the Ark to battle the enemies of ancient Israel."

"I am sorry to say I would have to agree with you there. Very troubling times continue to occur in your homeland of Israel, even today. I am afraid the headlines bear witness to your thoughts more than you think. You fear the Ark will be used against man, rather than to bring mankind together?"

"I fear it because I saw it," Solo said simply.

"I think Solo is right," Eteye said. "There is no doubt in my mind that if the State of Israel or the Americans were to possess this weapon of mass destruction, they would use all of their energy to harness its military power."

"Weapon of mass destruction?" John Paul said, again turning back to look out at his small kingdom and the Italian city beyond. "I see. What is it that you seek from me?"

Solo paused before answering and gazed at the Pope. He had thought long and hard about this decision, ever since the Osprey had landed in Cairo. He was not positive that what he was about to propose to the Pope was the right decision, but remembering the inauguration from years ago reassured him. *Could the Ark really be planning its own destiny?* It was too much to attempt grasp at this juncture.

"Mankind is not ready for the responsibility of this treasure yet," Solo said.

"From what you have shared with me, it seems you are correct," John Paul agreed.

"Pharaoh Amen knew that, and he took the Ark with him out of Egypt before the coming civil war erupted and before the military generals could take over Egypt and get their hands on it. King Solomon's followers hid the Ark when the country broke out in civil war. Jeremiah saw the Babylonian King Nebuchadnezzar's desire to conquer the world on a scale never seen before. He knew he had to hide the weapon away from the war mongers. He knew what would happen to our world if he didn't."

Solo could see Jeremiah's plan very clearly now.

"I think Jeremiah's plan was for the Ark to remain safely hidden away in its vault-like tomb, until we had evolved past our desire to use the Ark as a weapon," he continued. "But mankind has found the Ark too soon, and we are not yet ready for it."

The Pope cut to the chase.

"How can I be of service to you and to the One True God, whom we both serve?"

"I think you need to finish what Jeremiah started," Solo answered.

"You are referring to Vatican City? A new, modern vault for the protection of the Ark?" the Pope asked.

"Perhaps. But I think I am referring to you, personally. *You* need to protect the Ark and decide how and when we will all be ready for it. Your church has evolved over the last five hundred years in ways that other religions have not. You no longer have or seek a military, yet you inhabit one of the safest and most secure fortresses in the world. You have set about trying to erase hunger and disease instead of acquiring new lands. Although it's imperfect, your desire is to heal the world, not conquer it."

"He is right," Eteye said. "You have become a partner with the One True God, as He designed it to be in the Garden of Eden— man and God working alongside each other, in partnership, to take care of the earth."

"When my eyes were opened by the Ark inside the tomb, I became aware of your speech to the United Nations. Maybe I'd heard it somewhere before and the memory came back to me, or maybe I heard it for the first time then—I can't really tell, to be honest."

John Paul took a slow, deep breath.

"I meant what I said," he replied. "Our church has become a *religion*—and that is not what our Savior was all about."

"I was there," Eteye said

"You were where?" Solo asked.

"In New York, when he gave his speech."

"You are far more than you appear, Ms. Azeb," the Pope said. "Our Savior had no possessions, and He taught us to give away whatever we owned. How do you align that with the western capitalist world, which runs unchecked? Capitalistic greed has become the new religion of the 21st century."

"You lost popularity in America after that speech," Eteye said.

"No doubt, I did. But our Savior was also a pacifist. He was against all forms of war and violence. He certainly would have spoken harshly of the American pre-emptive strike doctrine, for example."

For the first time during Eteye and Solo's visit, the Pope became agitated and animated as he shared his views with them.

"We have lost our way," he said, shrugging and shaking his head. Solo could hear the frustration in his voice as he spoke. "We must live our values around the world, in all contexts, not just in church on Sunday mornings. Governments can't bomb five Muslim countries a year and then wonder why there is no peace in the world; we can't build an oppressive military empire, only to feign surprise when colonies revolt. Nor can we continue to sacrifice our neighbor in the never-ending pursuit of more black oil.

"Until we return to the roots of our Savior's message and follow the example of His life, I am convinced we will continue down this self-defeating path. There can be no room in our ranks for greed, for *profiteering*, above the needs of the poor. We simply cannot look the other way when it comes to the suffering of our brothers and sisters around the world who are infected with AIDS and other social diseases. We cannot pretend that equality does not matter and let the rich take advantage of the poor, merely because the rich have the means to exploit their fellow brothers and sisters."

"The money changers in the temple?" Eteye asked.

"That is what I called them at the United Nations," the Pope continued. "The foundation of the Christian religion is love—love for *all* of mankind, sinner and saint alike—and we have lost our way. Now we worship entrepreneurs, and we judge those born into poverty. Our heroes are megalomaniacs, from egocentric celebrities to C.E.O.'s who make their stock options more important than the people that sacrifice for the company every day. We have moralized the capitalist into a saint, and we've demonized the homosexual couple seeking to adopt a child. We turn our young boys and girls into war heroes, and we mock those who wish to protect the earth from the effects of mankind's pollution."

"Your Holiness, *you* are meant to protect the Ark. I know it inside of me—you are meant to follow in Jeremiah's footsteps, to protect us all from ourselves," Solo said. "I know this sounds strange, but the Ark told me to come see you."

"You are asking for the Church to risk a lot," he said. "My attempts to heal our Jewish-Christian relationships would be destroyed if the world were to ever discover that I'd hidden the Ark of the Convent inside Vatican City."

"Certainly you have religious and historical treasures here that you have been entrusted to protect over the millennia?" Eteye asked.

"You are correct," John Paul answered. "However, the Ark is something far different than the 9th century *siddur* that we just released to the Jewish Museum in London."

"I agree. But if not you, then whom?" Solo asked his voice raised.

"I am still not certain that Vatican City is the appropriate place for the Ark," the Pope said, "but I do see your point. If we do not intervene in the destiny of the Ark now, who will?"

Solo and Eteye watched the holy man hopefully, waiting for him to make the decision that would affect the rest of the world. His face wrestled calmly with his reply for several seconds before finding peace.

"My friends, I believe your wisdom to be sound, and this matter is of grave importance for both the survival of the Christian Church and the good of mankind. I do not yet know how or what I will do to safeguard the Ark, but I accept the burden, all the same."

Solo exhaled heavily in relief. He hadn't realized how much weight this journey had placed on him until the Pope had accepted the mantel of this quest. Suddenly, he realized he was tired. *Extremely tired*. He also realized that over the last few weeks he had completely walked away from his entire life. He began to remember all the people who had no idea where he was or what had become of him. He was sure his recent actions had hurt most of them, and he now felt the burden of those relationships. He had just traded the burden of the Ark for several others.

John Paul turned back toward the French doors that led inside.

"Let's go back in and have something to eat," he said. "I would love to hear more about your devoted-Catholic mother."

43

November 20th
Vatican City, Italy

    Solo and Eteye supervised the Ark's midnight transfer from the Vatican's private hangar at the *di Roma-Ciampino* Airport to the vast, underground network beneath the streets of Vatican City. Only the Pope, his most trusted Swiss security advisor, and three members of his holy council knew what the large, wooden crate that had arrived in a borrowed, brown U.P.S. truck contained. The crate had been carefully unloaded and placed on a forklift, where it was whisked off into the rear shadows of the vast, underground bunker. Solo wondered if this would be the last time he would ever see the world's most magnificent treasure. As the forklift turned the corner and disappeared into the blackness, he felt the Ark's presence leave him, and a sad *goodbye* and a *thank you* floated through the air to him.

    John Paul had offered quarters to Eteye and Solo, but they'd wanted to be on their own and, more importantly, on their way. The fate of the world and the Ark of the Covenant was now the responsibility of the modern-day holy man and high priest—just as it had been for the ancient holy man and high priest Jeremiah and those before him.

For better or worse, Solo had negotiated this mysterious and spectacular journey as best as he could. He knew that he didn't want see the woman next to him go. *She was his soul mate.* Somehow, he knew she had always been. They had always been together, and he wanted to be with her now.

They turned right out of the front gate of St. Peter's Square and into the calmness of Rome's streets as dawn inched over the horizon. They didn't grab a taxi but walked, like a couple that had been together for a long time, silently and hand-in-hand.

44

November 21st
Zurich, Switzerland

They caught an early morning sleeper train from Rome to Zurich. The instant Solo crawled into the bed inside their private car he fell into a deep sleep. The mental and physical exhaustion and jet lag from the last several days had finally overtaken him. He slept face-down on the train mattress for the seven hour, thirty-six minute train ride, and he was still sound asleep when they arrived at the *Zurich HB* train station during the afternoon rush hour.

Eteye woke him and led Solo into the massive, stone train station in the heart of Zurich, and he followed her down two more floors. His head still ached from the first deep sleep he'd had in weeks. The dull pain at the back of his head made him a little disoriented and out-of-sorts, but he followed Eteye like a well-trained and loyal bloodhound. Somewhere amongst the bustling people and glittery tourist stores that covered the underground streets and tunnels of the central train station, Eteye purchased two train tickets from an automated kiosk. They then boarded an afternoon train, which was just getting ready to pull out of the station.

"Where are we going?" Solo asked.

"Somewhere I have never taken anyone else."

They eventually found two empty seats next to each other, and Eteye parked Solo next to the window. He fell asleep again, resting his head back and forth between Eteye's shoulder and the window, before the electric train had even reached its top traveling speed.

The two seats opposite Solo and Eteye were occupied by an elderly couple that smiled at her. They politely ignored the fact that Solo's knees were taking up most of their space.

Eteye watched the changing Swiss countryside pass by as the train slowly made its way along a wide, gently sloping mountain. Autumn was over, yet winter had not quite arrived. Solo never woke as the gentle swaying of the train, along with Eteye's kind shoulder, encouraged the continuation of his much-needed slumber.

As Solomon had drifted off, he'd begun to dream almost instantaneously. Strangely, though, he was consciously aware that he was both dreaming and sleeping. In his dream, he'd travelled to the coast of Spain.

He saw a village in Barcelona, full of merchants, traders and businesses that spread up and down the coast as far as his dreamlike vision could see. He saw horse-drawn carriages grunting through the crowded city streets, and townspeople crammed everywhere. He felt worry and alarm as he stood at his second-story living room window, looking out at the seaside harbor below.

He was aware that there was someone behind him, madly rushing around the exquisitely furnished home; however, he continued to look out the window at the people amassing by the docks below.

The horde of people carried everything they owned on their backs or in wooden carts, which they pushed, pulled, or dragged, as needed. He could see several large schooners docked in front of the growing crowd below. Sea gulls barked their never-ending, beseeching squawks overhead. The ships sat at the docks, hungrily awaiting their passengers. Their tall, wooden masts pointed to the blue sky above, and their myriad of spider-web ropes, glistening in the morning's dew, covered the tall timbers in every direction.

Still aware that he was dreaming, Solomon turned from the window and saw several maids running around his house, packing everything of value into four heavy, wooden chests that sat open in the middle of the room. He felt great apprehension.

"Please make sure these get packed with my personal belongings," the lady of the house instructed her maidservant, who immediately turned and placed the books into one of the wooden chests. "Put them on top, so I can easily get to them."

Her back was to Solomon, and he couldn't see her face.

"How much time do we have?" she asked the eldest of the girls, who was busy packing.

The lady's colorful dress was covered in shiny beads all along its seams. The beads glimmered in the morning sunlight coming in from the window behind Solomon. Even a person uneducated in the throes of fashion could tell the dress was incredibly expensive, and the woman wearing it was someone of great means.

"The edict of expulsion from Queen Isabella was read in the town square this morning," the maid said. "The queen says that we all have to leave or convert."

The wooden floors creaked underneath her as the well-dressed woman turned around, and Eteye stood in front of him. Her black hair was pulled up into a bun on top of her head, making her presence seem prestigious and serious. Her golden, serpent necklace was prominently displayed over the lace of her dress, which reached her neckline.

In his dream, Solomon said nothing to the beautiful Eteye.

"What do you mean—*leave it all*?" she asked, responding to something he'd said to her but somehow had not heard himself. "You want to leave all of our possessions in Spain?"

Solomon turned and looked back out the window. The crowd had doubled in size, and it was beginning to frantically press upon itself. Everyone was trying to get out of the seaside village by any means they could.

He still could not *hear* his own words to Eteye, but he felt exactly what he said in his dream and could tell that she loved the idea. The two of them would ignore the mass exodus from Spain that was headed across the Mediterranean Sea to Africa. Instead, they would head for the *New World*, where freedom was rumored to be as real and as powerful as the queen's edict of expulsion. Eteye joined him at the window, and they kissed passionately.

—

Eteye woke Solo as they arrived at a small station, which had only a single, white building to account for the official part of the train stop. The mountainside on both sides of the track was lined with large trees that extended upward into the blue, calm sky. The red-and-white Swiss flag flew atop an old wooden pole next to the boarded-up, white depot building. It looked to Solo like the building had been shut down for some time.

No one else got off at their stop, and thirty seconds later the train pulled away with a short whistle of goodbye. Solo realized he had slept the entire ride, and by the time he'd woken up there'd been no one on the train but the two of them.

Eteye took Solo's hand, and they walked down the gravel road that followed the train tracks for about a half mile before veering off into the wider part of the valley, between the small, rolling hills located on either side of the road. Solo heard one last, short whistle from the train as it worked its way farther down the mountainside. A small town appeared through the trees in front of them.

They walked along, holding hands but not speaking much. Solo was still miserable from the lack of sleep, or from being woken up in the middle of a deep sleep—he couldn't really tell which. He just plodded along, not really paying attention to anything, and enjoyed the lack of drama in his life, for a change. The air was cool and brisk. He smiled as they walked out of the thick, tall woods and into the brown valley.

Directly in front of them was the smallest and neatest-looking town he had ever seen. Two rows of buildings lined up tidily on both sides of the gravel road. There were simple, one-story, white-and-gray homes with reddish-brown, stone-tiled roofs lining the main street. Solo felt like he was looking at a Swiss postcard from two centuries ago.

A dozen sheep grazed in the field in front of them, and he watched as two young lambs ran away from the group, darting back when they realized they had ventured too far. *Where in the world am I?* Solo wondered to himself.

"Fräulein!"

The greeting came from the man across the street, who was sweeping off his porch with an old straw broom. The old man wore suspenders and brown trousers, and his white button-up shirt was neatly tucked into his pants. His collar had been buttoned at the top.

From his greeting and countenance, it appeared that the elderly man knew Eteye quite well. *Strange*, Solo thought to himself. He had the sensation that he could feel the man's feelings.

"Herr Zugler!" Eteye yelled and returned his wave. "*Guten morgen!*"

They walked across the road to his porch.

"*Mein Herr*, this is Mr. Goldman. A very dear friend of mine," Eteye said.

"*Grüetzi*, Mr. Goldman," Mr. Zugler replied in a thick German-Swiss accent. The old man spoke to Eteye again in what sounded to Solo like German.

When Eteye answered, the man laughed aloud but continued to sweep to ensure that his efficiency for the day did not waver. She again spoke to him in German, but this time Solo could tell the conversation had turned serious.

Solo looked around the small town and noticed the river on the other side it for the first time. There were larger buildings, several stories high, that followed the river on its winding path.

"*Sehr gut! Guten tag!*" she said after a few minutes.

"*Guten tag*," Herr Zugler answered, and he went back to sweeping with full devotion as she and Solo continued down the town's gravel-laden main street.

"What was that all about?" Solo asked.

"Herr Zugler takes care of my horse when I am gone. He has a marvelous little farm just outside of town."

"I've never thought of you as a horse person before."

"He's not just *a* horse. He's an Egyptian Arabian. If you are nice, maybe I will introduce you."

Solo saw a general store, a hardware store, and a shop that looked like it sold tractor parts. There were other various establishments for provisions, but Solo couldn't read the Swiss or German labels on their signs. When they reached the end of the two-block main street, the road came to a four-way intersection. Eteye turned left, and they continued their leisurely stroll down the road that headed towards the larger apartment-looking buildings nestled along the meandering river.

They passed a wooden water trough that had been carved by hand from a giant log a long time ago. Clear water poured into it from a shiny, brass spout attached to a pipe. Solo walked up to it and looked at Eteye. She nodded—*go ahead*—and he drank from the spout with both of his hands greedily.

They walked in silence along the vacant street between the river and the five-story buildings, stacked tightly side-to-side. Solo again realized that he had no idea what town he was in or where, exactly, he was.

The almost-winter air was cool, and the sun poked in and out from behind the white, puffy clouds. They paused for a moment to watch some ducks begging for food in the river. Eteye clung to Solo's arm as they continued down the street for a few more minutes.

"What are you thinking?" Eteye asked him.

"For some reason, I was thinking about my father and my mother."

"Happy thoughts?"

"Yes," Solo continued. "I was thinking about how unpredictable life is. My mother and father dating again?"

"How crazy is that? After all they've been through," Eteye said.

"It was like the universe would not let them be apart."

"So true."

Solo stopped walking and turned to Eteye.

"In spite of themselves, they were meant to be together," he said.

"Soul mates," Eteye agreed.

Solo looked at her and thought about her statement. *Yes, soul mates*, he thought himself.

"I didn't think you believed in those kinds of things," she said.

"I didn't believe in a lot of things, before I met you."

"Yeah, I guess I have always had that effect on you." Eteye smiled as she guided Solo down the street.

"Seriously. I didn't understand a lot of things until you took me on this journey. John Paul was right. You've been like some sort of spiritual guide to me. Like an—"

"Next, you are going to call me angelic," Eteye interrupted, laughing.

Solo left the last word unspoken.

"So now what happens? You kidnapped me from New York City, stashed me on a submarine, flew me all over the world, almost got me shot in Tokyo, and *Cairo*, and now you bring me here?" Solo said, looking around. "Exactly where are we?"

"There is one thing I have left to show you, and then you can be free of me."

Solo hugged her. "Maybe I have that syndrome where I have fallen in love with my captor?"

Eteye kissed him and then continued their walk.

The hill on the opposite side of the river rapidly inclined upwards over a city block's worth of space. The housing complexes packed in along the riverbank were of a myriad of design and color. They all shared the classic Swiss architecture: a brown, wood-shingled roof, with several dormers neatly arranged on the rooftop, sharing space with a tall, lean chimney. Some of the buildings were only three stories tall, and then, directly attached to their right or left, was a building two or three times higher. The different masses created a landscape of puzzle pieces, with corners jutting out here and there and rooftops intersecting at random, odd locations.

Eteye held Solo's hand as they passed an arched bridge that crossed over the river. In front of Solo was a large, run-down hotel structure, which took up an entire block of riverfront property. The Swiss hotel was covered with wooden shutters, married to both sides of each of its petite windows. Green trees lined the street between the river and the hotel's entrance.

To the far left of the hotel, a single-story, flat-roofed apartment had been sculpted into the hotel's second-story space. It looked more like an out-of-place barn than a residence. The apartment sat on top of the far-left, first-floor section of the hotel. Six-foot trees peaked above the railings and lined its front entryway. The apartment was dark-brown and contrasted against the hotel's tan exterior. It had three sheltered windows on its front that faced the river, and its odd-shaped roof crested and rolled forward like an ocean's wave. It, too, was covered in the traditional wooden shingles. Sitting like a small, dark-brown appendage to the hotel's light-colored foundation and structure, the apartment was the most beautiful Solo had ever seen.

A man on a bicycle rode by with two skinny greyhound dogs. Their lean, muscular bodies ran next to the bicycle in perfect unison and form.

"Who lives here?" Solo finally asked. His dull headache reminding him that he still needed more sleep. He knew he needed more downtime before he could return to normal again.

"You will remember," Eteye said. She told Solo to put his hand inside the mailbox-looking metal can next to the front door. Solo reached inside and felt the top half of a smooth, round ball with a handprint molded into it. He put his hand on top of the mold, lining up his fingers with the mold. After a second, the finely crafted front door, made of steel and wood, opened on its own. *A handprint security lock*, he realized. *How had his handprint opened the door?*

He followed her inside, and the front door closed on its own after a few seconds. He meant to ask her about the security device, but he found himself immediately distracted: he had just stepped into the home of Eteye Azeb.

She gave Solo a tour of her house, which did not take long, given its size.

"It is an amazing place," Solo said as they walked upstairs and entered the only bedroom in the apartment. He saw a small, red bag made of silk lying on her bed, along with a bunch of cards covered with drawings and symbols.

"Yes, isn't it divine?" she said. She picked up the cards and placed them in the bag, which Solo noticed had a large eye on its front. She noticed him watching her and held the bag up. "These were my mother's."

Before Solo could answer, Eteye pointed to the bathroom.

"Mr. Goldman, I want you to take a hot bath, and I am going to make us some dinner. Then you are going straight to bed to catch up on your much-needed sleep."

"That sounds perfect," Solo answered. "How long have you lived here?"

"Oh, I've had this place for a long time. It's my sanctuary. Now, run some water and clean up. I'll bring you up some tea. It'll help you relax and sleep better."

Solo turned to ask another question, but Eteye had already left the room. He walked into the bathroom and turned on the light. There was a large, white claw-foot bathtub in the center of the room. The floors were covered in yellow pinewood planks that each looked to be over a foot wide. As he settled into the hot bathwater, Eteye appeared with hot tea. It smelled of tree bark. She sternly ordered him to drink it all.

That was the last thing Solo remembered before waking up in her bed a day later.

45

When he woke, the sunshine streamed in through the bedroom windows, and the shutters and curtains were wide open. For a few seconds, Solo had no idea where he was or even *when* he was. He looked up at the ceiling overhead. Attached to it was a dark canopy, covered in gems. The sunlight bouncing off them made the canopy twinkle like the nighttime sky. Déjà vu hit Solomon like a bag of bricks: *he had seen this place before.*

He crawled out of the feather bed and stood, looking around the bedroom. On the wall above the bed's headboard was a beautifully hand-painted, Impressionist-style oil painting of a young couple, walking arm in arm through a cityscape. It was the only thing hanging on any wall in the bedroom. He was groggy and disoriented, but when he heard Eteye's voice singing to herself from outside the balcony he remembered where, and who, he was.

He stood at the window completely naked and let the warm Swiss sunshine rejuvenate him. He saw Eteye watering her trees below and he watched her care for the diminutive trees. Her open blouse hung loosely, and he saw flashes of her bare breasts as she moved back and forth.

327

"Good morning," Solo said from the balcony, stretching and yawning.

"*Gut nacht,* you mean."

"Is it evening?"

"You've been asleep for a full night and almost a full day. The sun is setting, not rising."

"I'm starving," Solo said, looking around. "I was going to suggest ordering in some pizza, but . . ."

"Dinner's almost ready. Maybe put some trousers on and join me on the patio." Eteye laughed and then went back to her plants.

She had prepared a fabulous candlelight dinner for the two of them. How she'd found fresh salmon in the middle of the Swiss forest Solo would never know, but he had given up trying to figure her out. The sound of music caught his attention, and he walked over to where a vinyl record was playing and listened attentively to the words of the song.

"I love this song," Eteye said as she walked over to him.

Eteye turned the music up louder, and the lyrics from *The Whole of the Moon* floated throughout the room:

> *. . . I pictured a rainbow,*
> *You held it in your hand.*
> *I had flashes, but*
> *You saw the plan.*
> *I wandered out in the world for years,*
> *While you just stayed in your room.*
> *I saw the crescent,*
> *You saw the whole of the moon . . .*

"Does it remind you of anything?" Eteye asked, searching his dark eyes for a spark of recognition. His bewildered look answered her question. She changed the subject. "Let's eat. Dinner is ready."

Solo followed her to the plain sturdy, hand built dining room table.

"You have much to do, back in New York City," Eteye said, avoiding his eyes for the first time since they had met.

Solo did not reply as he tried to slow the pace of his ravenous eating.

"I wanted to show you my place. My sanctuary, as I like to call it."

"You said on the train that you've never brought anyone else here?"

"Only you. It's the only place in the world I can go when I need to be alone and at peace. I wanted you to remember it. In case someday—"

"What do you mean, *someday*?"

"Solo. We both know that you're going back to New York. You are going back to your life. You have a mother and father who are worried sick about you. You need to go find your brother and reconcile with him. You have a law firm that needs you, and . . ."

Eteye paused as she looked at him. She took in a deep breath and then finished what she had to say.

". . . there are many things you need to remember."

"You keep saying that," Solo said, concern shadowing his face. "What do you so desperately need me to remember?"

Eteye did not answer.

Solo didn't like being told what to do, but he knew Eteye was right. He had to return to New York and the real world. His whirlwind Indiana Jones fantasy had come to an end, and the real world demanded his attention and presence.

They finished their dinner, each lost in their own thoughts. Solo moved his chair closer to the corner of the small dinner table and put his arm on Eteye's shoulder. He leaned over and kissed her on her neck and ear, and he began to unbutton her blouse. Eteye pulled back for the first time since they had met.

"Solo, there is nothing more I'd rather do than be with you right now. *We will always have Paris*. But you have to leave."

Solo pulled her close again.

"Paris? What are you talking about?"

"It's nothing."

"No, I can tell it's something," Solo said.

"It's just a line from a movie, but it doesn't matter—you have to go back to New York."

"I'm going to think about what I want from my life over the next few weeks, while I'm here with you. Maybe you can put me to work gardening or taking care of your horse while I figure it all out."

"No, Solo. I'm sorry, but you have to leave, right now," Eteye said, freeing herself from his embrace and getting up from the dinner table. He was not prepared for her suddenness.

"What do you mean, *right now*?"

Eteye walked through the house and waited for Solo at the front door. Three minutes later, Solo slowly found his way to her.

"Wow. When you mean right now, you really mean *right now*," he joked.

They both smiled. Oddly, there were no tears. They just stood in the doorway, looking at each other, holding each other's hands while they spoke in silence. Solo could feel the warmth of her grasp and remembered the first time she had touched his knee on the Israeli submarine. His heart still enjoyed the adrenaline she caused in his body. He was drawn to the necklace that she never took off, and he wondered if she would ever tell him its secrets.

Eteye opened the door and walked Solo outside. She kissed his lips once, briefly, then let him go. On the street in front of the old hotel, a dated utility vehicle idled with its headlights on. Eteye pointed to it.

"Mr. Zugler will take you to the airport in Zurich. You can catch a flight home from there."

"You've made one mistake in trying to get rid of me," Solo said.

"Oh, really?" Eteye smiled. "What's that?"

"Well, my hand knows the combination to your front door."

"That is odd, isn't it?" Eteye said. She smiled in a way that Solo had not seen before. She handed him his wallet and his cell phone. "Goodbye, Solomon Goldman. You have always been my one true love."

She stepped back inside the door, which closed behind her automatically.

Solo's driver did not speak English, and the two-hour ride to the Zurich airport passed in silence. The darkness of the countryside completely disoriented Solo's sense of where they were and where they had been. He did not see a single street sign or town marking until the lights of Zurich appeared on the horizon. Inside, he was torn up over Eteye and returning to what now felt like his former life. He stared out the window in silence.

The flight back to New York was even longer and quieter.

46

November 24th
New York City, New York

The taxi ride from John F. Kennedy International Airport to Ella's apartment was emotionally difficult. Solo wasn't sure if Ella would throw a drink in his face or scream *thank god you're safe!* In the end, she did neither.

Ella opened the door to her apartment at nine o'clock that morning. She was still talking on her cell phone as she swung it open, and she didn't move when she saw Solo on the other side of her threshold. She simply stared at him as if he were a ghost.

"Ella, it's me," Solo said softly. They stood there for a moment, frozen.

She looked at him closely as she hung up her phone. Then, in an instant, she grabbed him by the shoulders and pulled him through her front door. She hugged him hard, pressing her body against his.

"You better have amnesia or just gotten out of a hospital after waking up from a coma!" She said smiling, and then she kissed him hard and passionately on the mouth.

Solo let her kiss him, but he did not return the kiss.

"It's so good to see you, Ella," Solo said calmly as he pulled back slightly from her embrace.

Solo had wrestled the entire overseas flight with what to tell her. If he told her some—but not all—of what had happened to him, he knew she would see through his half-truth right away. But Ella had always understood him, as he had always understood her. They had been close friends, on the verge of becoming something more, for quite some time. He knew she would quickly figure out that he was telling her a partial truth, and he knew that would not be good enough for her.

However, in the end, that is exactly what he did. He did not mention the Ark, his trip to Egypt with Ike, or his final meeting in Rome. Instead, he told her about the trouble his brother was in and how his father was wrapped up in the growing nuclear crisis in the Middle East.

He sensed that she knew there was more to his story and his unexplained absence, but she did not press him. Solo had felt her hurt as soon as she'd opened the front door, and he knew she could tell that something had changed between them.

They had always been more than just two people who'd worked together closely every day, and he knew that Ella had been waiting for him to make the first move for a long time. Their relationship had teetered on intimacy for years, and they'd both hoped that eventually something would happen between the two of them. It never had, though, and now, sitting in her apartment, the two of them needed to come to terms with that fact.

Ella brought him up to speed on the law firm.

"So now what, Boss?" Ella asked as she leaned back on the couch next to him.

"I'm glad you asked," Solo smiled. "How about some of your amazing black coffee? "I could use some caffeine. Do you still have your Turkish coffee maker?"

They both paused, remembering the antique coffee maker Solo had given her several Christmases ago over dinner. They'd just won a large case, and it was one of two presents he'd given her that year: the coffee maker, and a hand-crafted sterling silver necklace. Solo remembered it well, and he purposely didn't ask if she still had the latter.

Ella stood and went into the kitchen. He could hear her shuffling around and the *clang* of her putting the teapot on the stove to boil the water.

"I'm going to give you a promotion at work," Solo said to her from the living room.

"And a raise, too?" she asked, rejoining him on the couch.

"A handsome raise, indeed, *and* a new title."

"You mean I'm not going to be called *That Lawyer Who Kisses the Boss's Ass* anymore?"

"Who calls you that?" Solo laughed. "You can fire them all next week."

"Never mind," Ella laughed. "What are you thinking?"

"I'm going to put you in charge of the entire law firm. You're going to run the show."

Ella sat back in her chair and considered his proposition.

"People are not going to like that," she said after a moment. "*You* have run things ever since your father went to the State Department. I'm not sure they will—"

"—I'm taking some time off," Solo interrupted.

Ella stopped talking for a second. She looked into his eyes, and he could tell she was searching for what lay behind them.

"You met someone, didn't you?"

Her statement did not surprise him. She had always been incredibly intuitive, and she knew him extremely well. Even before he told her about Eteye, he could sense that she'd already known. *Woman's intuition*, he thought.

"I did, and I didn't."

"That's a great lawyer's answer," Ella said, getting up and walking back to the kitchen. She returned with their two cups of coffee.

"I could see it in your eyes after I kissed you," she said. "You've been looking for the love of your life for as long as I've known you."

They sat on the sofa in silence for a moment as Ella contemplated the drastic change in their situation. In the background, a fire truck's siren roared down the street outside the apartment.

"I think I secretly hoped it was me," Ella at last said with sad resolve. "I sure hope you finally found her."

Solo sipped his hot coffee.

"I didn't find her. She found me," he said with a hint of a smile.

"Where is she, then?" Ella asked.

He could see the hurt on Ella's face, and he saw her posture become erect and formal—signs of her emotional withdrawal. Ella was nothing if not in control and professional, and, even now, as she sat in her own apartment, next to the man she cared more deeply for than any other, she kept her emotions in check.

"I have no idea how to even find her again."

"What did you mean, she found you?" Ella asked dispassionately, sipping her coffee.

"Do you believe in past lives?" Solo asked.

"I guess I've never really thought about it much," Ella said.

"Me neither, until I met her."

"You think you knew this woman in a past life or something?" Ella said with disbelief on her face. "I guess you do need some time away to clear your head."

"It *is* very strange, but I think I've always known her and been with her. It's like we're meant to be together."

"Wandering around the earth, looking for each other?"

Solo drank his coffee.

"Something like that, I guess."

Ella returned to the kitchen and made them each a second cup of coffee.

"So you really want me to run your law firm?" she said, returning to the couch and changing the subject to something less painful.

"From this afternoon forward, it will all be yours. I have to go straighten things out with my brother and my father."

"About damn time," she said. She finished her drink. "You know, some tough-looking government agents came looking for the two of you. They scared the shit out of me. Came to the office and tried to interrogate me. They really had me worried about you."

"I'm really sorry that happened. I didn't know," Solo said.

"What really happened to Levi?"

"You wouldn't believe me if I told you."

"Try me," Ella said.

"The short version is the military thinks he stole some of their secrets, and they're going to keep him locked up until he tells them what he did with them. My father is trying to use his State Department contacts to locate him."

"You don't even know where he is?" Ella asked.

"My father doesn't, but I do. I have to try and broker a deal for him."

"What do you have to trade?"

"The military secrets."

Ella just stared at him.

"I really shouldn't tell you any more than I already have," Solo said, putting his coffee cup down on the table in front of them. "It could place you in danger."

"I think I understand."

"How long will you be gone, helping your brother?"

Solo stared as his lap and didn't reply. She continued to look at him for a moment before his thoughts became her own.

"Wow," she finally said. "I really missed that one. I didn't know my new job was *permanent*."

Solo could feel the sadness in her voice, and he knew that she was incredibly hurt that he was leaving her and their life together in New York. He knew she was heartbroken that he had found someone else whom he wanted to be with more than her. He watched as she accepted his news as best as she could.

Solo shifted uncomfortably acknowledging her pain and put his hand on her knee. "I think you should make some more coffee."

47

November 25th
New York City, New York

Solo waited for his mother to arrive at her favorite Jewish deli. He had spent the previous night on Ella's couch. It was routine for him to be gone for lengthy periods of time and to be out of touch during trial, so his mother conveniently hadn't noticed he'd been out of the country for the last several weeks. He had spoken to his father last night and learned of his return to New York and the numerous inquiries that he had endured by the government. Since he had no knowledge of Solomon's whereabouts or activities, the interrogations had been fruitless.

He picked up *The New York Times*. The headline said it all: *War looms in Egypt!* The entire front half of the newspaper was dedicated to the dire situation in Egypt. The Israeli navy had placed a full blockade over the Suez Canal, and all the northern Egyptian ports were desperately attempting to block any nuclear contraband from entering the country. The American navy had placed itself between the Turkish navy approaching from the north and the Israeli blockade. It was only a matter of time before hostilities overflowed in the Middle East.

Solo read what he already knew to be true. A French deep-sea recovery ship had vanished, and an unnamed source in the

Department of the Navy had confirmed that an undisclosed submarine graveyard had been looted. The story made clear that someone had figured out how to recover lost American nuclear torpedoes, and Israel believed the nuclear material was heading their way.

"It's just horrible, isn't it?" Solo's mother said as she approached and saw the large headline on the front page of his paper. She gave him a big hug before removing her coat and setting it beside her on the red-vinyl booth seat. She was a petite and serious woman with casual blonde hair and a wrinkled face. She ordered her favorite—chai with soymilk—and Solo ordered his usual black coffee. He wanted to know how things were going between her and his father.

His father had recently moved back into the family apartment that Mother had kept since the divorce. He still could not believe that they were living together. However, his mother seemed sincerely pleased that she and his father were a couple again. Maybe she laughed just a little less and had a slightly more solemn look to her than what Solo had remembered as a boy, but he could tell they were genuinely happy to be back together, even though she insisted on remaining pragmatic about the entire situation.

Sitting across from each other, Solo asked her why she'd let his father back into her life after all he had done to her in the past. He wanted to know how she could ever trust him again. He loved his mother dearly, and he didn't want to see her hurt a second time by the same man. Her decision to allow his father back into her life—intimately, nonetheless—confounded him.

She never really answered as to why, though. All she said, simply, was that it was *her business*.

"There has been some trouble with Levi," Solo suddenly blurted out over his coffee cup.

"Has he been wounded?" his mother asked, alarmed. "I've been trying to get a hold of him for some time, and he hasn't returned my emails."

Solo paused and thought for a moment. In his mind, he could still see the remnants of the compound in which Levi was being held, and he knew what they were doing to him there.

"He's okay, but he has gotten into some trouble with the Marine Corps. I need to go meet with some governmental officials to see if I can get him out of the pickle he is in."

Solo wanted to tell his mother everything. Of all people, she would fully understand the magnitude of what he had just gone through over the last few weeks. She would marvel at the discoveries under the great Giza Pyramid. She would comfort him over Minkoff's sacrifice and the death of Ike, and she would tell him how proud she was that the Ark had chosen the Pope to be its new keeper. But he could not tell her any of it. If the Ark were to remain safe from the lunacies of the modern day, no one could know where it had been hidden. Solo knew he had to be as secretive and as skilled as the Prophet Jeremiah had been, and he knew the Ark had to stay out of the modern-day pages of history. It must vanish again, just as it had from the pages of the Bible.

"Is he still in Iraq?" his mother asked, still concerned.

"No, he's not. It's complicated, Mother," Solo said. However, he knew he had to tell his mother about her son. She deserved that much. "He is being held in a prison in Turkey by our government. He is in real trouble, and I'm not sure I'll be able to get him out."

"Turkey?" she asked. "Solo, what's going on?"

"Levi did what he knew was right, even though it was against his beloved Marine Corps' orders."

"What orders?"

"He found religious documents in Iraq that were right out of the pages of the Bible, and he knew that if he turned them over to our government they'd use them for their own political agenda, turning Jews, Muslims, and Christians against each other in the process. He knew their discovery would spark a religious world war, and he decided that he couldn't let that happen, even if it meant that he'd be considered a traitor by his government."

Solo's mother had put her hands to her mouth as he spoke. However, when he finished, she went straight for the bullseye.

"He sent you the documents, didn't he?"

Solo was surprised at how fast his mother had connected the dots.

"Mother, it's better that you know less than more right now. It's for all our good. It's a massive political mess, but I think Father and I have figured out a plan."

"Your father? How is he mixed up in all of this?"

"You should talk to him about that, but it's going to take both of our skills to get Levi out of this."

"Are you going somewhere?"

"We leave this afternoon for Tel Aviv," Solo answered. He reached across the table and held his mother's hand while they finished their morning beverages. "I'm sorry none of us will be here for Thanksgiving."

"You just take care of your father. He's an old man these days, and life has taken its toll on him."

"I will," Solo answered.

"And you tell Levi he better come see his mother."

Solo smiled and kissed her on the cheek and then gave her a large hug.

"I will make sure we both do."

He wondered if he would ever see her again.

48

November 26th
Transatlantic flight to Tel Aviv, Israel

Solo sat next to his father on the overseas flight from New York to Tel Aviv and watched him doze in and out of sleep. He was covered with two first-class blankets, and shortly after dinner service he'd fallen asleep, snoring loudly.

Solo never slept on international flights. In the past, he had always worked on a trial or the client matter for which he was jetting across the world to handle. This flight, however, he had no trial to prepare for, no client's business to handle. His father had arranged for a meeting with the National Security Administration through his contacts with Israeli Intelligence and the infamous Rabbi Geller. They would meet with the U.S. government officials who were unofficially holding his brother to offer them a deal: the source scrolls, in return for his brother's release.

The terms of the exchange had already been generally discussed between the interested parties, with Defense Minister Koslov brokering the deal on behalf of his good friend, Ambassador Goldman.

First, Levi would be released and honorably discharged from the United States Marine Corps, and his United States citizenship would be permanently revoked, with no reinstatement options.

Levi would never be considered an American afterward, and he would never again see his beloved country. He would be forever exiled in Israel.

The second part of the agreement was Israel's end of the deal: they would immediately grant Levi Israeli citizenship, with no passport privileges.

Solo's role in the exchange was delivering all the source documents that had been uncovered in the Babylonian library to Rabbi Geller. Solo knew that Geller would be anxious to begin his divine quest for the lost Ark and recover the ultimate weapon of mass destruction, which he would use for his God's glory.

The Americans would give up a single Marine, whom they had tortured with prejudice. The only recorded statement they had obtained from him was some sort of boot camp song about someone named *Jody*. The Marine colonel had sung it over and over again.

In exchange for the stubborn Marine, the Americans would receive the exact location of the stolen nuclear material from Ambassador Goldman. Solo had informed his father of precisely where the terrorists intended to detonate their bomb, and his father had sold that information to the Americans in the exchange. It was far easier for everyone to believe that Ambassador's Goldman's former Muslim contacts in Egypt had turned over the bomb's final location than it would be to believe that Solo had mysteriously *seen* the location and the plans for the Muslim bomb during one of his interactions with the Ark of War. The Americans were desperate to both recover their nuclear material and diffuse the situation between Turkey and Israel, two of its strongest Middle East allies.

Solo's plan ensured that everyone received something more valuable than what they'd given up in the highly classified intelligence exchange. The only item he kept back was the ancient Book of the Dead.

He watched his father sleep and was amazed at how old he had become. He thought about how long it had been since the two of them had shared anything meaningful. Whenever Solo had been in New York City during the High Holy Days, his mother had always made sure they'd spent the religious season together, but it was never like it'd been when he was a kid—when they had all been one family.

And then he'd simply left. His father was just *gone* one day. He'd chosen another woman over all of them, and everything had changed overnight. Anger and bitterness had set in, and Solo had mistrusted people after that, refusing to let anyone inside his heart, including Abay. And now his father lay sleeping in the seat next to him. Long since divorced from his second wife, he had found his way back into his mother's life. Life certainly was ironic.

He marveled at how his Catholic mother had been such a good Jewish influence growing up. She'd been a far better parent and friend than his holocaust-surviving father had ever been, and she'd turned out to be a classic *baleboste*, as the Yiddish would say.

The two Goldmans had departed New York City at 2:11 p.m. the day before, and they walked through Israeli customs at 8:45 the next morning. They were scheduled to meet with the I.D.F. before their meeting with the Americans. Solo knew that the meeting with Rabbi Geller and Defense Minister Armand Koslov would have no pretense of friendship and cooperation this time.

Solo proceeded with the assumption that neither the Israelis nor the Americans knew that Ike and his team had been involved in last week's operation. Solo had no idea whom Ike had ultimately been working for, or who the mysterious *Fat Man* was, but he knew that by now they must be looking for their missing men and aircraft. At some point they would follow Ike's trail to Cairo and then to the pyramid.

Solo knew the exchange had to take place before anyone connected the dots regarding the recent archeological discoveries in Egypt, Ike's missing black ops team, and the relationship between Ike and Levi. If Geller thought for a second that he was being double-crossed, the deal would unwind on the spot.

The key to safekeeping the Ark at Vatican City was ensuring that no one could ever follow its path to Rome. Geller must never connect the Ark's existence to its current whereabouts. That meant that Solo had to be extremely convincing over the next two days. He had to keep the Ark's trail far away from Vatican City, and he had to stand up to the scrutiny and interrogations that were coming his way. Above all, he had to protect the Ark's hiding place, and he had to protect John Paul, even if it cost him his own life and his brother's.

Ambassador Goldman had made it unabashedly clear that he wanted to know nothing of Solo's search for the Ark after they'd parted company at the French Embassy in Tel Aviv. He said that even a pathetic interrogator could get answers out of him at his old age. It was at that moment that Solo realized the significance of just how few people in the world knew what he had found in the tombs of the great Pyramid or where the greatest treasure of all time had been relocated and hidden away.

Being back on another international flight so soon after his return from Zurich made his heart ache. It seemed Eteye did not want him to know where she lived—that she didn't want him showing up on her doorstep unannounced. She had artfully said goodbye to him over the their two days in Zurich. Solo hadn't even known she was saying good-bye.

If only he hadn't slept through their trip from the airport to the little unknown town in the mountains where she lived. The more Solo thought about it and tried to remember, the more he realized how unremarkable Eteye had made it. He had no idea what train they got on at the main rail station in Zurich. For that matter, he had no idea which direction they had even gone.

Remembering the small train station they got off *somewhere* in the mountains of Switzerland made him smile. No name—no signs—no remarkable features of any sort. He could just imagine asking some Swiss information officer at the train station how to get to the old, run down, white depot about an hour or maybe two hours up the mountain. *Somewhere maybe towards the north, maybe south, maybe east, or was it west?*

He knew he had always been in love with Eteye Azeb, and now he realized he would likely never see her again. He loved the positive energy she exuded, and he seemed to soak her up like a starving sponge in a buffet of puddles. Now that she was gone, he realized how much life she had added to his own. *And who would have ever thought that they would one day save the world?*

"Egyptian parents," Solo said.

"Excuse me?" his father said as they cleared customs and were approached by four armed Israeli soldiers.

What had she said when they first met? An Egyptian father who was a politician, or something. A "royal politician" is what she had said. She had been married before to someone . . .

"'He was my king, and I was his queen,'" Solo said under his breath. "Was King Solomon's wife an Egyptian princess?"

"King Solomon from the Bible?" his father asked.

"Yes."

"It's said that his soul mate was his bride from Egypt. She was the one that he wrote all of his romantic poems about in the Song of Solomon in the Bible," his father, answered showing his passport to the senior military officer standing in front of them.

"'He was my king and I was his queen,'" Solo whispered to himself again. *How could it be true?*

"I heard that sometimes the Ark was called the *Fountain of Youth*," Solo said. "Have you ever heard that?"

"Oh, there've been many wild and fanciful stories about it. I think the best legends are those contained right in our holy books—parting the Jordan River and making dry land for everyone to walk across, killing an innocent man who just touched it—"

"Yes, but what about the Ark prolonging life or making people immortal?"

"I've heard of those legends too," his father answered. "Just as the Bible says that the Ark could kill a man for just touching it. Other stories from our long ago past speak of it prolonging life."

They followed the several uniformed Israeli soldiers who had been awaiting their arrival under strict orders to escort them directly to I.D.F. headquarters. They exited the airport through a section reserved for the military. Solo climbed into the military's white, suburban-looking vehicle, and then it all hit him at once. *She was there!* She had been watching over the Ark ever since *her husband* had placed it in the royal Temple and had entrusted it to her.

It made no sense to Solo, but he knew it to be true. She had let him believe all along that *he* was solving the mystery to the Ark's location, but she had been shepherding him all along. She saw the upheaval in the Middle East, the coming war in Egypt, and she knew the Ark had to be moved to a new, safe location. It was too fantastic to believe. *No one would believe him*, he thought. But then he realized he had no one to tell.

He realized there was far more to Eteye Azeb than he was currently aware of, but he was starting to . . . Solo paused for a second as he watched his father and the four military members climb into the vehicle with him. *What was it his consciousness was about to tell him, from deep inside his soul?* He looked out the window as the military transport left the airport and headed toward downtown Tel Aviv—then he *stared to remember!*

"You talk to yourself a lot," Solo's father said, interrupting his stream of consciousness.

"I know," Solo replied. "I always have."

"I guess your mother told you that I moved in with her."

Solo focused on his father and away from Eteye and her fantastic past.

"Yes, she did."

"How do you feel about that?" his father asked.

"Mother seems genuinely happy to have you back. It's like she always knew you'd be coming back."

"I think you're right."

The two of them sat in silence for a moment.

"I know I have to let it all go," Solo said quietly.

His father said nothing. The pain of what he had done to his family and to his son was as tangible as the numerous rifles around them.

"I've been angry with you for far too long. I've also buried my heart for far too long. It has to end," Solo said, turning to look at his father.

His father had wet eyes, but he still did not speak and continued looking straight ahead.

"I realize now that it wasn't you at all that I was angry with. It was *me* that I had an impossible time accepting. You leaving, Abay's death . . . they were the distraction of my pain, but I was the source. I was running from myself."

Solo's father slowly slid his hand over to Solo's and held it. The two men looked out their respective windows as the olive trees passed by. They sat there, holding hands. That was enough for them.

49

November 27th
Israeli Defense Force Headquarters, Tel Aviv, Israel

Solo walked out of I.D.F. headquarters alone. It seemed like just yesterday that he had been there with Eteye. The bright Mediterranean sun flooded his face with warmth. He closed his eyes and tilted his head up towards it. He felt the light waves emanating from the burning, nuclear hydrogen ball in the sky. He remembered how good the sunlight had felt when he'd gotten out of the submarine in Haifa a couple of weeks ago. He smiled at the sun as he reflected on all that had happened since that first day.

The military attaché to the U.S. Ambassador had just thoroughly interrogated Solo during the half-day meeting inside the I.D.F. headquarters. The attaché was a gray-haired Army colonel, who had joined the Army as a private before being commissioned an officer, and he'd served his country for over thirty-two years before his path crossed Solomon Goldman's. The Colonel was a middle-aged, average-looking American, but he'd immediately challenged Solo's attempt to trade the release and discharge of his brother for the military intelligence surrounding the location of the stolen U.S. nuclear material.

Solo had challenged the Colonel right back, like a witness under cross-examination, every time the Colonel had used the word *stolen*. Solo reminded everyone in the room that the Americans had been littering nuclear material all over the world for the past fifty years, and it was only a matter of time before someone figured out how to retrieve the carelessly discarded American nuclear trash and turn it into a weapon.

Solo had rehearsed his story well, as though he were giving the most important opening statement in a trial on the world's stage. He had thought through every detail; he knew every question he could answer, and every question he would refuse to answer. He had rehearsed his story of truth and misdirection to perfection.

He'd started his presentation with the truth. A made-up story was always more believable if it started with the truth. He had learned that fact from his clients over the years. Solo had provided the exact location where the Iranian atomic bomb was being manufactured from the decades-old Scorpion nuclear material: *a Palestinian hospital located on the eastern border between Israel and the Hamas-controlled Gaza strip.* And he'd told the rapt Americans that in two days' time, Hamas planned to smuggle the dirty bomb from the Gaza strip to the Sea of Galilee, then to the source of the Israeli national water carrier distribution pipeline. They would then detonate the nuclear bomb. The biggest fresh water lake and eighty percent of Israel's water supply would become permanently toxic and lethal in one bright flash of explosion. Solo had been hypnotically convincing, since everything he'd told his captivated audience up to that point was absolutely true. The Ark had shown him the Iranians' plans with great clarity.

He'd continued further with the truth and told the crowd of military advisors and politicians from both the Israeli and U.S. governments that he'd been covertly contacted by Ike Duggan after his previous meeting at the I.D.F. Headquarters several weeks ago. As he'd paced around the conference room, he'd told them that he'd discovered that Levi had used Ike's organization to smuggle all of the scrolls out of Iraq, and Ike had delivered them all to him.

Then Solo had begun his misdirection. He'd said that Ike's employers had been aware of and had been tracking the Iranian nuclear recovery operation, all the way from the hijacked French ship to the unloading of the torpedoes at the Egyptian port.

He'd hinted at the meeting that Ike's corporate employers stood to benefit enormously from the economic investment they'd made recently into Israel's seawater desalination plants along the Mediterranean coast. When almost all the natural fresh water in the region became undrinkable from the Hamas detonated bomb, Ike's employers would be the sole providers of the life-giving water supply. Their desalinated water's value would exponentially increase on an unheard-of scale, and their seawater-made-into-fresh-water supply would become the new currency of the region.

He'd told how Ike had refused to go along with his employer's plan to assist Hamas and the Iranians, and Ike had divulged the location of the nuclear bomb-making station at the Gaza hospital before departing for Cairo. The last that he'd heard from Ike Duggan, Solo had lied, was when Ike was departing for Egypt to ascertain how the Iranians planned to get the nukes across the Egypt-Israeli border and into Gaza. No one had heard from Ike since then. Solo had told the American and Israeli audience that he'd assumed Ike had failed, and the bomb had made its way to the Hamas hospital in Gaza for final preparations.

Solo had lied with perfect, contrived sincerity, saying that the last contact he'd received from Ike before he disappeared, somewhere inside Cairo, was a garbled phone call that indicated his team had confirmed the route of the Iranian nuclear material through Egypt. Solo had sold Ike's memory as a true national hero, and his opening statement had been brilliant. More importantly, though, it had been convincing.

The U.S. Ambassador and his military attaché had challenged Solo in front of their Israeli audience as to why he hadn't immediately turned over the destination or the route of the nuclear materials.

Solo had responded calmly and dryly.

"We all know that you keep Israel on a short leash by parsing out intelligence to her and withholding intelligence when it suits America's needs. I knew that you would use the intelligence that Ike had uncovered to your political advantage."

Everyone had turned and looked at the U.S. Ambassador—they all knew it was true. The U.S. routinely withheld strategic military intelligence from its ally in order to *manage the Middle East situation.*

The second part to the negotiated settlement that Solo had secured was regarding Levi being allowed to relocate and start a new life in Israel. In exchange for those concessions, Solo had arranged for the delivery to the Israeli authorities of the original Bible source documents that Levi had uncovered south of Baghdad.

The Americans had left the conference unsure of the deal they'd just made. *If* the U.S.-Israeli joint strike force mission on the Hamas hospital in Gaza was a success in the next three hours, then they would recover their own U.S. nuclear fuel and would avert the cataclysmic international crisis they had helped create by leaving eight unprotected nuclear weapons at the bottom of the ocean floor. That was certainly worth far more than one stubborn, traitorous Marine Colonel.

The Israelis had left with everything they could have hoped for. For the first time in a long time, they were running the show and setting the agenda between the two countries. Rabbi Geller would be able to spend years analyzing and deciphering the ancient biblical scrolls that Solo would return to them.

He had told Geller that King Solomon's *Book of the Dead* never made it out of Iraq and never showed up when Ike had delivered the documents to him. He had no intention of turning the book of magic over to Geller, and he hoped that the other source documents would consume his attention. Solo wondered how the Orthodox world and the biblical historians would handle the discovery of the newest versions of holy scriptures and all the theological changes those original versions would create. *Maybe the world would never hear of the discovery after all,* he thought.

If the military operation *was* a success, Israel's standing in the international community would spiral upward overnight. Averting a nuclear crisis with minimal collateral damage, exposing the Iranian plans for nuclear fallout on its Arab neighbors, and *returning*, instead of keeping, the lost nuclear fuel would demonstrate to the world that this six decades-old Jewish democracy was ready to join the upper echelons of the civilized world.

Solo was surprised that no one had questioned him about the treasure map contained in Jeremiah's instructions inside the book. The impending doom of an imminent nuclear explosion had seemed to laser-focus the conversations elsewhere.

"That was a hell of a deal you struck," Minister Koslov said as he walked up to Solo facing the sun overhead and lit up a Noblesse cigarette. "That's what I love about you Americans."

Solo turned and looked at the aging general, who had a small patch of melted skin on his forehead.

"Yeah, what's that?"

"Can't live with 'em. Can't live without 'em," the General said as he took a long drag on his white cigarette. He let the smoke sit in his lungs for a few seconds before blowing it out, enjoying all its effects on his body. "I'm sorry your brother will never be able to see his homeland again."

"Don't be," Solo said. "Knowing my brother, my guess is he will soon take over your job. Besides, he'll protect this country as well as or better than he did his former."

The General finished his cigarette and nodded.

Solo was likely correct. Levi would most certainly find his way into the Israeli Defense Forces and would excel there, just as he had everywhere else in life. *His zeal would be put to good use here*, Solo thought.

"I hope your target intelligence is correct," Koslov said, flicking his cigarette butt to the sidewalk in front of the building's entrance. With the toe of his shoe, he ground the cigarette into the ground, extinguishing the smoldering tobacco.

"It's correct, but you have little time," Solo answered.

"The Americans are already poised to go in with our forces. They'll be operationally ready in an hour."

"I never thought the Americans would be part of the invasion force into Hamas controlled Gaza territory," Solo remarked.

The Defense Minister smirked.

"You Americans have been part of many of our questionable "preemptive" operations. We just don't go around talking about it. Besides, this one is different. Your country won't be content to just sit by and hope that their stolen nuclear material is recovered. They must be a part of the recovery force."

"If they detonate that bomb before you get there, the world will break in half in reaction to it," Ambassador Goldman said. Neither Solo nor Koslov had heard him walk up behind them. "Minister, do you mind if I share one of your smokes?"

Solo looked at his father in small surprise.

"I do a lot of things these days that I haven't done in a long time," his father said to him.

The Minister dug out a cigarette and handed it to Solo's father.

"I have never been more afraid for my country and for all men in this part of the world than I am right now. If that bomb detonates inside Israel, there will be no turning back. It will quickly turn into Armageddon."

They all stood quietly for a moment. Solo's father smoked his Israeli cigarette and the general lit a fresh one.

"It won't detonate," Solo said. "They'll find it in time."

"Wishful thinking, but I hope you're right," Koslov said.

Solo's father looked at his son and sized up his words.

"You know more than you let on, don't you?"

"It won't detonate," Solo answered. "Trust me. They'll get there in time."

Defense Minister Koslov reflected on the mission as he smoked. Solo had provided the exact location of where Hamas and its Iranian ally were manufacturing the atomic bomb. In forty-eight hours, the bomb would be smuggled to the Israeli national water supply and detonated. It was an ingeniously simple and effective military plan.

"I was impressed with your manipulation of the U.S. Ambassador and his military backing in there," Koslov said matter-of-factly.

Solo raised an eyebrow as he looked at the minister.

"For all our sakes', I hope your intelligence is accurate, regardless of its mysterious source," he continued.

"It's more accurate than you can imagine."

"Yes, somehow I believe it is."

Koslov turned to head back inside the I.D.F. building.

"What will Rabbi Geller do with all the scrolls when he gets them?" Solo asked him.

"He will use them to pursue his political ambitions," Koslov answered. He breathed in his cigarette deeply.

"What are those?"

"To create a theocracy under his ideas of what God is and is not, of course." Koslov turned and looked at Solomon to study his next reaction. "If his religious cronies find that Ark through those scrolls somehow, it will be very bad for all of us."

He returned his stare to the pure sunshine above their heads.

"He won't," Solo said, keeping his gaze straight ahead of him.

Solo and his father left I.D.F. headquarters and returned to the French Embassy that was once again providing them sanctuary. Shortly after their arrival, Solo's father received word that Levi would be landing at Ben Gurion International airport in Tel Aviv tomorrow morning—*if* the impending military operation was a success, and the nuclear fuel was recovered. He would be in possession of his Marine Corps discharge papers and his U.S.

citizenship would be forever revoked upon his entrance into the State of Israel.

Solo's father began working on his part of the bargain as soon as he'd received the update from the Americans. By tomorrow morning, Levi would have his citizenship papers and would be a fully documented Israeli citizen.

"I guess we'll all have to attend High Holy Day services in Israel now, instead of New York City," his father smiled. He put his arm around Solo. The two of them walked through the secured lobby and toward the French ambassador's office, where Solo's father would start making all the necessary citizenship arrangements at lightning speed over the next twelve hours.

"I am very proud of you, son," he continued. "Levi owes you his life, and I owe you so much more. I would ask for your forgiveness, but that just seems too cheap to say, in light of everything that's happening."

Solo hugged his father hard, right in the middle of the busy embassy lobby. It was their first embrace in over three decades. He whispered in his father's ear.

"Sometime over the last few weeks I realized that yesterday no longer exists, and tomorrow may never come. Right now, standing here with you, is all that I have. I can't just let the present moment slip away anymore. I love you. I always have, and I always will."

Solo's father hugged him.

"It will be good for the three of us to be together tomorrow when Levi arrives," he said. "It has been so long since I've had my two sons at my side."

Solo released his father.

"I won't be there," he said.

"What do you mean?"

"I'm catching a late-night flight this evening."

"Where are on earth do you need to be?"

"I have to go find a little village in Switzerland."

"What village?" his father asked.

"I'm not really sure."

"Where is it?"

"I don't really know for sure," Solo smiled as he thought about it.

For perhaps the first time in their relationship, his father understood what his son was telling him. True love was best explained without words, and the ambassador realized that his son planned to go find Eteye.

"A few years back, I was sitting under my prayer shawl during the morning service on Yom Kippur, and I realized that there was only one person who ever gave me total freedom to be myself," he said. "There was only one person who didn't judge me and never took me for granted."

Solo grinned at his attempt to share some fatherly wisdom. His father took a deep breath and slowly exhaled before continuing.

"From the very beginning, she listened to me. She never answered a sentence for me, and she never interrupted me. She was so confident in who she was, and she was one of those rare people who had no problem opening up and just letting me in."

"I can tell you're glad to be back home."

"Your mother is still the same lady I fell in love with years ago, but at the same time, she's different," Ambassador Goldman said.

Solo looked at his wristwatch.

"You're going to go search for Ms. Azeb, aren't you?"

"I have to find her. No matter how impossible it is."

"Yes, I think I understand." The former ambassador could see what Solo was feeling by the look in his eyes. He knew the look of a man who had lost his soul mate. "I wished I had died before I ever loved anyone but her."

"What?" Solo asked.

"It's a quote from Hemingway about his first wife. It hit home for me when I read McLain's book, *The Paris Wife*. I found out the hard way, just like Hemingway did, that a man can never replace his first true love."

They looked at each other softly.

"I think I have this situation covered. Get out of here and go find her. Don't let her go, no matter what. Don't follow the mistakes of your father."

"And Ernest Hemingway," Solo said as he hugged his father one last time. He turned and walked out of the embassy.

"To the airport," he said to the taxi cab driver as he climbed into the back seat.

50

November 28th
Ben Gurion International Airport, Tel Aviv, Israel

Levi stepped off the private government Learjet with his two armed escorts. The N.S.A. agents and Levi had flown directly from Turkey to Tel Aviv early that morning. He was greeted by four uniformed Israeli soldiers and led away from the crowds that were lined up to go through customs and immigration. Levi wore casual civilian clothes, and he was taken through several security doors that led into to the first public lobby that all visitors to Israel went through after passing through customs.

The senior Israeli soldier handed Levi a thick, brown folder. Then all four soldiers and the American agents turned and walked away, leaving Levi standing in front of the large sign that said *Welcome to Israel.*

He looked around. He had no idea what had just happened to him. He had received no information since being removed from his simple prison cell in Turkey and transported to the airport, where he'd boarded an unmarked jetliner. He opened the folder and found a certificate with large markings in red and blue:

Honorable Discharge
from the Armed Forces of the United States

This is to certify that Colonel Levi Goldman was Honorably
Discharged from the United States Marine Corps . . .

Next he saw a letter from the U.S. State Department, which informed him that, based on his previous written request, his United States Citizenship had been terminated, and he had successfully been registered as an Israeli citizen.

He looked up, completely confused, and realized his father was standing in front of him with a huge grin on his face.

"Welcome home," he said to his son. They hugged as the multitudes of tourists and citizens entering the country flowed by, paying no attention to any of them.

The local crowds passing by frenzied with cheer. Everyone had read the morning's headlines—the successful recovery of stolen American nuclear fuel, the thwarted Iranian plans to detonate a bomb in the region's fresh water supply. Turkey and Egypt's leadership praised yesterday's surgical military strike, and there was talk of a joint military proposal to the United Nations to address Iran's act of war.

51

November 28th
Zurich, Switzerland

Ella was the one who had figured out how to find Eteye. She reminded Solo of the obvious clues that Eteye had left him. *Bread crumbs along the trail*, Ella called them.

Solo was not amazed to find out that the pharaohs had used rare Arabian horses as far back as 1580 B.C., and Pharaoh Thotmose III had used them in wide-scale military operations. Even Solomon, King of Israel, had built 40,000 stalls for his Arabian animals. Ella's research also found that it was Solomon's Egyptian wife who had loved the exquisite animals, and she'd brought them from Egypt to Solomon's kingdom. The Egyptian Arabians were indisputably the most beautiful, courageous, and exquisite horses in the world.

There was only one registered owner of an actual Egyptian Arabian horse in all of Switzerland. The quarantine records for when the animal had been transported into the country were quite detailed, and the horse's location matched perfectly with Solo's limited recollection of where they had traveled.

His train arrived at its final stop just before noon on a Sunday. As he stepped off the train he recognized the white, run-down depot. He smiled at the lack of any name or station description on the building. *What a great place to hide*, he thought.

His walk into town was brisk and focused. He passed by Herr Zugler's porch, but there was no one around.

After only twenty minutes of misdirected searching, he found Eteye's dark, barn-like second-story apartment. Standing on the river bank and looking up at the residence made Solo's heart beat faster. He had hoped Eteye would be watering and tending to her trees on the porch that overlooked the river, where he had watched her previously from her bedroom window. Solomon had imagined this moment over the dozens of hours of recent travel. The dark apartment stood out to him like a beacon, but Eteye Azeb was nowhere in sight.

For some unknown reason, the sophisticated, molded-handprint lock still recognized his hand's signature, and it released the front door for him, which opened the same way it had previously—slowly and precisely.

"Eteye!" he called out as he peeked in the doorway and then stepped inside. He stood there, listening for footsteps or her voice, but silence greeted him like a cold graveyard would a new tenant. He waited for several minutes just inside the entryway after the front door closed itself behind him. No one came to greet him.

As he began to walk through the house, he realized its owner did not intend to return any time soon. The water had been turned off, sheets covered the furniture, and the blinds were drawn. It smelled of emptiness.

Solo began to walk up the staircase to the master bedroom, and his thoughts lingered back to the wondrous sleep he'd found in Eteye's bed upstairs. He hoped to find her here and make love to her.

However, he found himself pausing to look at the pictures that hung on the staircase wall. Every inch of it was covered in various-sized frames, and the photos inside them appeared to be very old. Some of the photos were stone carvings of ancient Egyptian pharaohs. One in particular stood out from all the rest: it was a photograph of a long-faced pharaoh with an ornate head dress and a crook and flail in his hands. The carved image of the long-dead pharaoh with the large nose seemed familiar to Solo, but his blurry memory struggled to place it.

Without pomp or circumstance, Solo understood that he was looking at Eteye's family history, all crammed together on the small staircase wall—photos and carvings, handwritten notes, and pictures of stone statues from many different centuries were all displayed in a scrapbook manner.

We will always have Paris. Eteye's words jumped into his mind like a locomotive's loud air horn at a railroad crossing. *Paris!* He remembered Paris, and he remembered being there with Eteye. *But they had never been there together. Or had they?*

Solo ran up the stairs to the master bedroom and looked at the hand-painted outdoor scene above Eteye's bed. He studied it. The canvas, thick with oil paint, told the story of a marketplace somewhere in Paris, he realized. A painted picture of a muted couple standing on the street together, looking up at a large, white dome off in the distance. Coffee shops and fall-colored trees surrounded the quaint marketplace. Solo recognized the muffled couple in the picture. The silhouetted view of them from the back showed a man and a woman walking together side-by-side. The lady was holding onto the man's upper arm, and her head rested on his shoulder.

In a sudden flood of unexplained memories, Solo realized that the woman in the picture was Eteye. And he realized just as quickly that he was the man walking next to her. The wave of unconscious events and memories was overwhelming, but Solo knew with absolute certainty that he had been to Paris with Eteye—that they'd been lovers there in the past. He could not comprehend what he now understood. He had lived in Paris, and yet he knew that he had never been to Paris. *How could both be true?*

Solo spent the next hour sitting on Eteye's couch, remembering the past several weeks he had spent with her, thinking of every comment she had made. *The best weeks of his short life*, he thought. And then suddenly, in a random flash of mental clarity, he knew exactly where Eteye was. It was the same type of vision he'd had of his brother's prison cell in Turkey; the same as the Iranian nuclear bomb being built in the Hamas hospital. Eteye was at the marketplace in the picture above her bed. He knew how to get there, and he knew he'd been there many times before.

We will always have Paris.

52

November 29th
New York City, New York

The black-ops tactical team arrived at New York City's Wall Street commercial heliport, located at Pier 6 and F.D.R. in New York City's Financial District. The four men resembled chiseled Swiss models in their dark-navy custom-made suits and blonde, slicked-back hair. Each carried a duffle bag containing the weaponry of his trade. Although they'd missed Solomon Goldman's departure from the city, they would quickly locate Ella Frank's apartment.

It took them less than an hour of torture to obtain the last-known whereabouts of Ella's former boss, and then her lifeless body was dumped in the anonymous garbage dumpster behind her apartment building.

The *Fat Man* was back on their trail.

53

The Near Future
Vatican City, Italy

The Holy See's announcement drew in large crowds at Vatican City. Never had the Pope and the Chief Rabbi of Israel attended a ceremony together. Today, they announced the opening of a new Jewish-Catholic history exhibit, built inside one of the grand museum wings inside Vatican City.

The entrance to the museum was filled with Jewish artifacts from the Vatican archives—pieces of antiquity that had been saved by the Vatican from destruction over the centuries.

The most anticipated event, though, was the ceremony later in the day, when the Pope would return the golden menorah, which had for centuries been preserved in the basement archives of the Holy City, to the Chief Rabbi. Missing since the Roman destruction of the second Jewish Temple in 70 A.D., the menorah had long been rumored to be part of the Vatican's treasuries, and John Paul would finally return it to its rightful owners—a symbolic gesture of the new relationship between the two religions.

In addition to this momentous event, the Pope would unveil a replica of the ancient Ark of the Covenant that he'd had commissioned, which sat at the entrance of the new museum as a memorial to the two previous Temples and served as a reminder of the religions' shared history.

The Pope's replica was a beautiful golden chest that sparkled when the sunlight struck it. Although the model was twice the size of the Holy Scripture's biblical description, its handcrafted details were profuse and inviting. There would be no fences or guards to keep people from touching it, and since it was only an imitation of the still-lost original, there were no religious prohibitions against touching it. In fact, everyone at the Vatican would encourage the masses to freely place their hands on the sculpture of the magical object. Each person who poured into the new museum passed right by the Ark, and they all rubbed their hands on the spectacular icon, as if drawn to it by some invisible force. A sense of peace and awareness filled each one of the pilgrims and visitors as they walked by and interacted with the golden replica of the Ark of Covenant.

The Pope smiled as he saw the people streaming by the gargantuan chest of Moses. Some stopped and prayed in front of it, while others enthusiastically rubbed their hands all over the glowing box, *communing with it.*

John Paul was pleased with his final destination for the Ark of War. Instead of wasting its power and purpose by hiding it deep in the dark basement of the exclusive, restricted Vatican archives, he had hidden it in plain view of everyone; it rested peacefully inside its golden replica, which was now on display for all to see. Somehow he knew that the Ark was happy to be intermingling with creation again.

Maybe the world can be changed, one person at a time, he thought.

54

The man looked out from his penthouse at the top of the city's tallest skyscraper and gazed upon the city's landscape. His organization owned the entire building and several others like it. In fact he owned most of the city.

He was closer than he had ever been before.

The unexpected news of the woman with the serpent necklace had pleased him more than anything else had in a long, long time. *The Ark, the serpent, and the two trees! They were finally within his grasp. He was close. He was very close!*

The Fat Holy Man smiled.

Epilogue

The present
Base of La Butte Montmartre, Paris, France

Solo sat in the same wooden chair that he'd been sitting in for the last two days. He ordered his Americano coffee from a young, attractive French waitress who was working her way through culinary school. Solo's ability to speak fluent French had returned to him from a place he'd never known existed. It was just a few minutes past ten in the morning, and the sun had cleared the rooftops of the marketplace, bathing the round courtyard in its warm, life-giving rays.

Artists of every kind camped out in the courtyard's tree-covered hilltop park. Painters, sculptors, and artists, drawing with every conceivable type of chalk and pencil, had set up their easels and canvases early that morning. They were busy painting and drawing the large, white church that towered over the marketplace in front of them. The basilica's travertine stone constantly exuded calcite, which ensured that it had remained white, even after a hundred years' worth of weathering and pollution.

The Sacré-Cœur Basilica's construction had begun in 1875, but the church that had been dedicated to the sacred heart of Jesus was not consecrated until after the end of World War I in 1919. Its white stone contrasted with the yellow sunlight and fall colors of the market trees, making it resemble a Claude Monet painting.

Solo wondered how many days he would sit in the marketplace and wait for Eteye. *Days? Or lifetimes?* He watched an elderly couple approach one of the local artists who had several of his paintings on display. The tourists admired his work, quickly selected a painting, and began to negotiate for its purchase. Solo could remember doing the same thing a long time ago, when he'd negotiated for the painting that now hung in Eteye's apartment in Switzerland.

In his memory he could see carts and horse-drawn carriages, and people had been pushing large, wooden wagons. He'd purchased Eteye's painting a long time ago, when the park had been a real marketplace and not the bevy of modern coffee shops and artists peddling products.

Solo knew she had arrived before he saw her. He stood up slowly and turned around, looking back across his left shoulder at the rear of the marketplace. A large, leather duffle bag hung across her shoulder. She had stopped walking, and she stood perfectly still, looking up into the sunlight's reflection on the whitish basilica. She wore a brown, tailored trench coat with black trim, and her thick, straight hair was pulled back in a long, single ponytail. Her normally dark-skinned face looked a warm brown in the direct sunlight. She appeared to be departing on a trip.

Solo slowly began to walk towards her. He thought he would have called out to her or yelled her name to attract her attention immediately, but instead he calmly and elegantly began to walk towards her. His heart was slow this time, and he realized his feelings for her were no longer that of a lovesick teenager. As he saw her face again, he understood that they had been together as partners, friends, lovers, and king and queen for a very long time. How long, he could not yet be certain.

He approached Eteye from the side, among all the busy townspeople moving in and out of the square, and she never noticed him. She continued to absorb the warm morning scene, like it was her last time to see it.

Solo spoke, breaking her trance.

"We always did have Paris, didn't we?"

She spun around, realizing she hadn't been aware that someone was standing so closely to her. Her face sprung from demur to a radiant glow almost as quickly as the bag fell off her shoulder. She jumped into Solo's arms.

"You remember!?"

Solo kissed her on her neck just below her ear and then held her face with both of his hands.

"I've been sitting here for two days, remembering."

Eteye squeezed him and started sobbing in the crook of his neck. She spoke rapidly in between sobs, trying to get everything out all at once.

"It took me so long to find you this time," she said. "It's getting harder and harder each time. I'm sorry I let you leave in Zurich, but you didn't remember me—you didn't remember *us*, and I couldn't keep you for myself . . . if you didn't remember."

Solo let her cry on his shoulder.

"I remember enough to know that I don't want to be apart from you for the rest of this lifetime," he said softly.

"Oh, Solomon. It's so good to have you back. I've missed you terribly. It's just not the same without my best friend."

"When did you know it was me?" Solo asked.

"When I worked with Levi in Iraq he often mentioned his brother, back in New York. When I finally saw a picture of you and found out your name was Solomon, I knew it was you. I have always been able to tell by your eyes and your name."

"Unbelievable," Solo said.

He motioned towards a coffee shop that had outdoor seating with heaters and hot espressos to keep the local clientele warm on the crisp fall day.

"Can we sit down for a moment?"

They moved to the nearest table and sat next to each other. The waitress did not disturb them, as it was obvious they wanted to talk more than they wanted to sip hot beverages.

Eteye wiped away her tears and continued.

"When I finally saw you at your naval trial, I knew that the God of Fate had brought us back together again. How far back can you remember?" she asked, excitement entering her inflection.

"I remember being in Paris with you a long time ago, before any of this was even here. How can that be possible? I think I remember being with you on an ocean liner, and making love to you on a sandy beach somewhere. I think I also remember your huge smile around thousands of horses?"

Eteye smiled largely.

"It will all come back much quicker now," she said. "Once the door is cracked open, memories begin to spill out."

"I'm glad you'll be with me when they do," Solo said.

"Me too. When did you remember us?" Eteye asked.

"I think I've always known," he replied, looking at her intently. "It was the picture of Paris above your bed that finally triggered the memories to our past. Even before that, though, your serpent necklace would always draw me back, every time I saw it. It made me feel like we have always been together, like past lives or something."

"I have missed you so much, my dear. It was so hard not to grab your face and kiss you all over when we spent all that time together on the submarine to Israel," Eteye said. "I have worn this necklace . . ."

She paused and pulled the necklace out from beneath her jacket, moving it so that Solo could hold it in his hands. He could feel its peculiar metal resting on his fingers.

". . . ever since you gave it to me."

"*I* gave you this necklace?"

"Yes, you did."

"But you told me it was thousands of years old."

Eteye said nothing. She watched as Solo pondered her statement.

"Tell me who I am," Solo said.

"You have shared many lives with me, Solomon Goldman. Who are you? You are my soul mate, and I am yours. It seems like we've been together since the beginning of time."

Eteye leaned in and put both her arms around Solo's shoulders. Her eyes were big and moist.

"I just don't understand how that can be possible," Solo said. His mind hurt trying to wade through the fog of his consciousness. "After being with the Ark, though, I now know that anything is possible."

"It has special powers, indeed. It does not exist to destroy mankind or to be used as a weapon. Its purpose is to heal and bring mankind together as one."

"You don't age, do you?" Solo asked.

"Let's not talk about all that right now. Let's just enjoy the fact that we're finally together again. It has been a long time since we were a couple without interruptions."

"I'm not the same as you," Solo insisted, refusing to put off the topic. "Somehow I know that. You were some sort of *keeper* of the Ark, weren't you? Dav'd and Ashki—you were all its keepers."

Eteye nodded.

"In time, you'll remember what you need to remember. We were destined to be together, though. That much has not changed. Look at us," Eteye said, gesturing to the marketplace, "finding each other among a million people, right here in Paris. That should be enough amazement for one day."

"You said I've shared many lives with you, but you didn't say the same about yourself," Solo said. He paused briefly to look into her eyes. "You don't live and die, like I do—the Ark changed you, didn't it?"

"Much is coming back to you already," Eteye said with a deflecting smile.

"Dav'd told me about the legend of the Ark being some sort of fountain of youth, but I never connected the dots. That is why you have to keep finding me. You never die, but I do. Every new life of mine you have to find me again, and you have to help me remember . . . us."

"I miss you terribly when we're apart. It gets so lonely without you."

"I'm starting to remember what it's like for you—watching me fade away each time, while you live on," Solo said, holding both her hands as he continued to stare deep into her eyes. He could see the profound sadness behind her happy smile, and he saw what a toll their on-again, off-again love affair had taken on her.

Suddenly another memory hit him, and he saw Eteye as his young Egyptian bride. *He was in Egypt, meeting the pharaoh and marrying the pharaoh's daughter. He was falling in love with her beautiful face and wide smile. He was attempting a treaty between his country and Egypt. He was looking at the three beautiful, large, white pyramids on the horizon. Then, he was back in Jerusalem with his new bride. There were arguments with his political advisors. He was standing in a huge, barn-like structure, watching his beautiful Egyptian wife ride the most stunning horse he had ever seen. He remembered placing the snake-like gold necklace around her neck and freeing her from captivity. He was madly in love with her.*

"You said you knew it was me because of my name . . ."

Eteye smiled deeply.

"In every life, you've always had the name 'Solomon.' Somehow fate ensured that your name remained as it was in the beginning. I like to think it's so I can always find you."

Solomon understood.

"My very first name was Solomon?"

Eteye didn't respond. She'd been through this moment many times before. All she could do was comfort her lover. As much as it pained her, she could not help him through this process.

"Not *the* Solomon?"

"You were a *magnificent* king!" Eteye said.

"And you were my Egyptian princess? My queen!" Solo answered his own question. "Oh, my God. We're the story in the Bible—that's *us*!" Solo laughed.

"We were quite the talk of the town," Eteye said with a giggle. "The greatest Hebrew king, falling madly in love with an Egyptian princess. I'm really named after the famous Egyptian Queen Tiye. In Egyptian, the first vowel in every name is silent," Eteye said.

"Eteye without the 'E'—I remember now. *Tiye*. And *Azeb* means *Zeba*."

"Yes. As it's pronounced today, *Sheba*," Eteye said, grinning from ear to ear. "Eteye Azeb is the ancient name for Queen Tiye of Sheba."

"The Queen of Sheba! I remember it all now. Solo said with a look of wonder on his face. "Then I put you in charge of the Ark of War. You were its guardian."

"It changed me into what I am today," Eteye answered. "I'm not sure I really understand what I am anymore, but you are right—I never age."

"The Ark needed you to be that way," Solomon said. "It wanted you to take care of it through the ages. It knew you were ready for that enormous responsibility."

"And I did watch over it, but I failed when Babylon marched on Jerusalem."

"What happened?"

"It doesn't matter anymore, but Jeremiah was also a keeper of the Ark, and he saved us all by getting the Ark out of Jerusalem before the city fell."

"You lost the Ark after that?"

"I never saw it again. It was a terrible time, and I felt like I had let you down."

"Let *me* down?"

"When you were my king, you made me vow to protect the Ark, no matter what. I failed when Nebuchadnezzar overran Jerusalem. He captured me and so many others, and he forced us back to Babylon, where we were slaves."

"It's not your fault," Solo said, comforting his long-ago wife and queen.

"But . . . now I think *you* are the same as me. I think the Ark changed you, like it did to me a long time ago," Eteye said. She cupped Solo's face with her palm. "I believe that I'll never have to find you again, and we will never be apart anymore!"

Solo kissed her. He wanted her, and their love of a thousand lifetimes overtook him.

"I know you're right. Somehow, I can tell I'm different," he said. He looked down at the bag at her feet. "You're going somewhere, aren't you? When I first saw you, you were saying goodbye to this place? I realize that now."

"I'm so glad you found me. And yes—*we* are leaving this place, right now!" Eteye said, taking his hand and then his arm. "I need your help."

"My schedule is suddenly wide open," Solo answered.

"The ancient Temple of Isis has been discovered, and we have little time to get there before the entire world plunders the secrets it protects."

"The Temple of Isis? Back to Egypt?"

Eteye grabbed his arm and pulled him up from his chair.

"Not Egypt," she said. "The Temple of Isis is hidden below the cliffs of the Grand Canyon."

Eteye started explaining as she grabbed her leather bag and began to guide Solo out of the marketplace.

"The story almost leaked out in 1909, when the *Arizona Gazette* and the Smithsonian Institute ran a story about an archeological expedition in the heart of the Grand Canyon, where a labyrinth of man-made tunnel systems high above the Colorado River were found. The stories said the tunnels were filled with artifacts, hieroglyphs, armor, and mummies."

"The Grand Canyon has a hidden Egyptian temple with mummies?" Solo asked. They reached the main street surrounding the marketplace, and Eteye began looking for a taxi.

"We had enough people inside the Smithsonian back in 1909 to bury the official version, but the local newspaper ran their story anyway. Luckily, nothing ever came of it, and the story just died there."

"What did the Egyptians build in the Arizona desert?" Solo asked as a taxicab pulled up in front of them. Her story had piqued his curiosity.

Eteye smiled and leaned in towards Solo, so she could speak privately with him.

"Not the Egyptians. The Hebrews. It used to be the frontier of your empire, and it is where we all fled when civil war broke out in ancient Israel. There is an exact replica of the Giza Pyramid above the Colorado River, *and* they built the Temple of Isis below it. Any visitor today looking from the South Rim of the Grand Canyon can see the obviously man-made pyramid hewn from the solid rock on the cliff top. That rocky hilltop is called *The Isis Temple* to this day."

"Hidden in plain view?"

"That's the best way to hide something. The real entrance to the Temple is some fifteen hundred feet down the sheer face of the canyon wall, underneath the pyramid marker on top, and the entire ancient sacred site is located on government land. No visitors are allowed in the area anymore."

"Another Giza Pyramid?" he asked.

Solo smiled and kissed Eteye as they climbed into the back seat of the taxicab. He knew that somehow Eteye was part of this Isis Temple. Somehow, she had been there.

"I love you," he said, holding both of Eteye's hands in his lap. "I remember that I have always loved you."

Eteye answered him with a deep kiss. The cab pulled away from the corner.

"Aéroport," she instructed the cab driver. He nodded his head.

"I wish I could just remember it all at once," Solo said.

"It will all come back to you. It just takes time," Eteye responded as she snuggled up to his shoulder.

Solo squeezed her hard.

"I can't believe you sent me away after you had finally found me."

"You had unfinished business in your life that I was keeping you from, and you needed to figure who *we* were on your own."

"I no longer have unfinished business. I'm all yours, from here on out."

"Please, don't ever leave me again," Eteye said. "My heart can't take it anymore."

"Agreed. Now, what ancient treasure are we off to protect this time?" Solo asked as the taxicab began to wind its way through the streets of Paris.

"You should know. It's your temple. You told me to hide all of your treasure there," Eteye said. She grinned and kissed Solo. "I am so glad you found me here in Paris."

"Me, too," Solomon said as a large, happy smile spread across his face.

The brazen serpent necklace sparkled in the warm Paris sunlight as the two modern-antiquity soul mates clung to each other in the back seat of their taxicab. They had lifetimes to catch up on and they wasted no time.

The God known as fate found brief contentment, watching its most favorite king and queen reunite and continue their endless journey together.

Thus they set out from the mount of the LORD three days' journey, with the Ark of the Covenant journeying in front of them for the three days, to seek out a resting place for them. The cloud of the LORD was over them by day when they set out from the camp. Then it came about when the Ark set out that Moses said, "Rise up, O LORD! And let Your enemies be scattered, And let those who hate You flee before You."

Numbers 10:33-36

————————————————

When they came to the threshing floor of Chidon, Uzza put out his hand to hold the ark, because the oxen nearly upset it. The anger of the LORD burned against Uzza, so He struck him down because he put out his hand to the Ark; and he died there before God.

I Chronicles 13:9-10

————————————————

"It shall be in those days when you are multiplied and increased in the land," declares the LORD, "they will no longer say, 'The Ark of the Covenant.' And it will not come to mind, nor will they remember it, nor will they miss it, nor will it be made again."

Jeremiah 3:16

————————————————

He struck down some of the men of Beth-shemesh because they had looked into the Ark of the LORD. He struck down of all the people, 50,070 men, and the people mourned because the LORD had struck the people with a great slaughter.

I Samuel 6:19

———————————————

Solomon made an alliance with Pharaoh, King of Egypt, and married his daughter. He brought her to the City of David until he finished building his palace and the temple of the LORD, and the wall around Jerusalem . . .

. . . King Solomon summoned into his presence at Jerusalem the elders of Israel, all the heads of the tribes and the chiefs of the Israelite families, to bring up the Ark of the Covenant from Zion, the City of David.

The priests then brought the Ark of the Covenant to its place in the inner sanctuary of the temple, the Most Holy Place, and put it beneath the wings of the cherubim. The cherubim spread their wings over the place of the Ark and overshadowed the Ark . . .

When the priests withdrew from the Holy Place, the cloud filled the temple of the LORD. And the priests could not perform their service because of the cloud, for the glory of the LORD filled his temple. Then Solomon said, ". . . I have indeed built a magnificent temple for you, a place for you to dwell forever."

Then the king made a huge throne, decorated with ivory and overlaid with fine gold . . . All of King Solomon's drinking cups were solid gold, as were all the utensils in the Palace of the Forest of Lebanon. They were not made of silver, for silver was considered worthless in Solomon's day!

The king had a fleet of trading ships that sailed with Hiram's fleet. Once every three years the ships returned, loaded with gold, silver, ivory, apes, and peacocks. They sailed to Ophir and brought back to Solomon some sixteen tons of gold.

So King Solomon became richer and wiser than any other king on earth.

I Kings 3:1 – 10:23

Acknowledgements

This book has been a long journey for me, one on which many have accompanied me. The idea for this story came from a paper I wrote in a graduate Hebrew class many years back. I was fascinated by both Egyptian and Jewish history and their common roots. Over the years, my fascination with Hebrew pharaohs would not leave me. I found myself captivated by the concept and searched for more of their stories.

I must acknowledge my guide throughout the early years, Rabbi Joe, who is the most genuine and caring soul I have ever met to this very day. You are missed. Also, my Hebrew teacher extraordinaire, Irv – an amazingly talented man whose passion for life is excelled by none.

My dear friend Lu has been with this story the longest. She fell in love with Eteye and Solo from the beginning and encouraged their love affair in my imagination. She spent over a year of her life helping me mold and refine my storylines. There are not enough *thank-yous* out there for her efforts and support.

I owe my final, edited creation to Ms. Lisle, who has been a wonderful addition to this project.

My amazing artist was my younger brother. His drawings cover the front of this novel, and he also created the artwork for my very first novel. His love-hate relationship with his work is exactly what makes it so fantastic.

My friend, Ms. Petrove, did a fantastic job in taking all of my brother's wizardry, putting it together, and telling my story on the cover of this book.

To my new writing companion Taylor Hart-Bowlan who has massacred this third edition with the skill of a surgeon's scalpel. I eagerly await your band *Timeless Bacon's* newest album.

My personal library was a dedicated educational friend to me throughout the writing of this book. I have listed some of my source materials, and they were a constant source of inspiration as I wrestled through the history of the Jewish and Egyptian people over the last six thousand years. These books are a treasure trove of pirate booty to me.

I also want to thank all the Biblical historians, scholars, theologians, and dreamers out there who opened my eyes and my heart to the wondrous world of antiquity. Thank you for unmasking the myths and legends of my beliefs, and for challenging me to have the courage to look behind the Wizard of Oz's curtain. The world would still be flat without you.

Finally, I want to acknowledge that Source of Divine Being that is in all of us, who allowed me to experience a world of great imagination. Your creation is a remarkable place.

About the Author

Charles Feldmann has previously written *Pharaoh's Daughter* the prequel to Ark of War, *Murder3Gun*, and *The Sons of Sheriff Henry*, along with publishing numerous professional works, most recently *Navigating the Military Justice System: What Service Members Need to Know*.

He attended law school in Colorado, served in the United States Marine Corps, worked with a D.E.A. drug task force, and now litigates courts-martial all over the world as part of his own law firm. Very recently, he found atonement in helping veterans navigate their way through the end of cannabis prohibition.

When not working on Book III to the *Ark of War*, you will find him traveling to exotic ports of call, enjoying cigars and ancient scotch with friends and colleagues at his favorite cigar bar in Denver, consuming too much wine, and indulging in his own love affair. Those closest to him know him as more tumultuous than delicious, and he tries his best to live by Benjamin Franklin's sage advice: *Either write something worth reading or do something worth writing.*

Source Materials

Bauval, Robert, *The Egypt Code*, Disinformation 2008.

Bloom, Harold, *Jesus and Yahweh*, Riverhead Books, 2005.

Bokenkotter, Thomas, *A Concise History of the Catholic Church*, Image Books 2004.

Brettler, Marc, *The Creation of History in Ancient Israel*, Routledge 1995.

Campbell, Joseph, *The Hero with a Thousand Faces*, Princeton and Oxford 2004.

Carroll, James, *Constantine's Sword, The Church and the Jews*, Mariner Book 2001.

Close, Frank, *Antimatter*, Oxford University Press 2009.

Coogan, Michael, *The Oxford History of the Biblical World*, Oxford University Press 1998.

Corteggiani, Jean-Pierre, *The Great Pyramids*, Abrams 1987.

Crossan, John Dominic, *The Birth of Christianity*, Harper San Francisco 1998.

Dennis, *The Encyclopedia of Jewish Myth, Magic and Mysticism*, 2007.

Drosnin, Michael, *The Bible Code*, Simon and Schuster 1997.

Dorlin Kindersley, *Eyewitness Travel Tokyo* 2008.

Ehrman, *The Orthodox Corruption of Scripture*, 1993.

Finkelstein, Israel, *David and Solomon*, Fress Press 2006.

Freke, *The Jesus Mysteries*, 1999.

Friedman, Richard, *Who Wrote the Bible*, HarperCollins 1987.

Friedman, Richard, *The Bible with Sources Revealed*, HarperSanFrancisco 2003.

Gadalla, Moustafa, *Historical Deception, The Untold Story of Ancient Egypt*, Tehuti 1999.

Gardiner, Philip, *The Ark, the Shroud, and Mary*, New Page Books 2007.

Gardiner, Philip, *Gnosis, The Secret of Solomon's Temple Revealed*, Career Press 2006.

Ginzberg, Louis, *The Legends of the Jews*, John Hopkins Press 1998.

Grabbe, Lester, *Judaic Religion in the Second Temple Period*, Routledge 2000.

Halpern, Paul, *Collider, The Search for the World's Smallest Particles*, Wiley 2009.

Hawass, Zahi, *Tutankhamun, The Golden King and the Great Pharaohs*, National Geographic Society, 2008.

Hemenway, Priya, *Divine Proportion, Phi in Art, Nature and Science*, Sterling 2005.

Humphreys, Andrew, *Egypt*, "National Geographic Traveler," 2009.

Johnson, Marshall, *The Evolution of Christianity, Twelve Crises that Shaped the Church*, Continuum 1989.

Joseph, Frank, *Opening the Ark of the Covenant*, New Page Books 2007.

Konstam, Angus, *Historical Atlas of The Crusades*, Mercury Book 2004.

Lederman, Leon, *The God Particle*, Delta 1993.

Lehner, Mark, *The Complete Pyramids, Solving the Ancient Mysteries*, Thames and Hudson 1997.

Leiman, Sid, *The Canonization of Hebrew Scripture*, The Connecticut Academy of Arts and Sciences, 1991.

Ludermann, *The Unholy in Holy Scripture*, 1997.

McManners, John, *The Oxford History of Christianity*, Oxford University Press 2002.

Mesorah, *The Wisdom in the Hebrew Alphabet*, 1983.

Metzger, *The Canon of the New Testament*, 1997.

Miller, Kenneth, *Finding Darwin's God*, Harper Perennial 2007.

Neusner, *Early Rabbinic Judaism*, 1975.

Osman, Ahmed, *The Hebrew Pharaohs of Egypt*, Bear and Company 1987.

Podhoretz, Norman, *The Prophets*, The Free Press 2002.

Rivkin, *The Shaping of Jewish History*, 1979.

Roffman, Barry, *Ark Code*, Green Shoelace Books 2004.

Rubenstein, Richard, *When Jesus Became God, The Epic Fight over Christ's Divinity in the Last Days of Rome*, Harcourt Brace 1999.

Sabbah, Messod, *Secrets of the Exodus, The Egyptian Origins of the Hebrew People*, Helios Press 2004.

Sandmel, Samuel, *A Jewish Understanding of the New Testament*, Jewish Lights Publishing 2005.

Schiffman, *From Text to Tradition, A History of Second Temple Rabbinic Judaism*, 1991.

Rivkin, Ellis, *The Shaping of Jewish History*, Scribner 1971.

Washburn, Del, *The Original Code in the Bible, Using Science and Mathematics to Reveal God's Fingerprints*, Madison Books 1998.

Young, Brad, *Jesus the Jewish Theologian*, Hendrickson 2004.

Made in the USA
San Bernardino, CA
02 December 2019